"Lessing wields a formidable analytic intelligence that makes this work provocative and often astonishingly beautiful."
—*Publishers Weekly* (starred review)

"Lessing strips away the romantic surfaces, ultimately tracing the roots of love and longing all the way down and back to the primary emotional attachments formed (or deformed) with the earliest parent-child bond."
—*Chicago Tribune*

"Reading *Love, Again*, we find ourselves watching in awe, enjoying and admiring, as Lessing bravely and unselfconsciously chops away with her axe until at last she has revealed that brilliant kernel at the heart of it all that we recognize as the truth."
—Francine Prose, *Washington Post Book World*

"Compassionately insightful . . . Lessing handily ties the surprises of inappropriate love to the sharp iss of ageism, emotional instability, the roles of women at the end of   Century, the shaky states of marriage and parent-child rela   orary English culture and the ongoing general quir   condition."
—*Miami Herald*

"An exhilarating and   on on old age and romantic love. Lessing leads   deep into the irrational zones her characters in   to settle in and make ourselves uneasily at home."
—*The Nation*

"Beautifully written and psychologically penetrating. . . . Lessing has discovered an aspect of love that few have written about before."
—*Newark Star-Ledger*

Photo © 1992
by Ingrid Von Kruse

DORIS LESSING was born of British parents in Persia in 1919 and moved with her family to Southern Rhodesia when she was five years old. She is the author of more than thirty books—novels, stories, reportage, poems, and plays. Her most recent works include *African Laughter* and the autobiography *Under My Skin*. Doris Lessing lives in London.

love, again

Also by Doris Lessing

Novels

The Grass Is Singing
The Golden Notebook
Briefing for a Descent into Hell
The Summer Before the Dark
The Memoirs of a Survivor
The Diaries of Jane Somers:
    The Diary of a Good Neighbor
    If the Old Could . . .
The Good Terrorist
The Fifth Child

"Canopus in Argos: Archives" series

Re: Colonized Planet 5, Shikasta
The Marriages Between Zones
    Three, Four and Five
The Sirian Experiments
The Making of the Representative
    for Planet 8
Documents Relating to the
    Sentimental Agents in the
    Volyen Empire

"Children of Violence" series

Martha Quest
A Proper Marriage
A Ripple from the Storm
Landlocked
The Four-Gated City

Short Stories

This Was the Old Chief's Country
The Habit of Loving
A Man and Two Women
The Temptation of Jack Orkney and
    Other Stories
Stories
African Stories
The Real Thing: Stories and
    Sketches

Opera

The Making of the Representative
    for Planet 8 (Music by Philip
    Glass)

Poetry

Fourteen Poems

Nonfiction

In Pursuit of the English
Particularly Cats
Going Home
A Small Personal Voice
Prisons We Choose to Live Inside
The Wind Blows Away Our Words
Particularly Cats . . . and Rufus
African Laughter
Under My Skin
The Doris Lessing Reader

love, again

a novel

DORIS LESSING

HarperPerennial

A Division of HarperCollins*Publishers*

Grateful acknowledgement is made for permission to reprint from:

"Memory" by W. B. Yeats: Reprinted with permission of Simon & Schuster, Inc., from *The Poems of W. B. Yeats: A New Edition*, edited by Richard J. Finneran (New York: Macmillan, 1983).

"Falling in Love Again (Can't Help It)" by Frederick Hollander & Sammy Lerner: Copyright © 1930 by Ufa Verlag (renewed 1957). Copyright © 1930 by Famous Music (renewed 1957). Copyright © U.S. Copyright 1991 Samuel M. Lerner Publications. International Copyright secured. All Rights Reserved. Used by Permission.

"Just Like a Woman" by Bob Dylan: Copyright © 1966 by Dwarf Music. All rights reserved. International Copyright secured. Reprinted by permission.

Two poems from *Cautionary Verses* by Hilaire Belloc, published 1941 by Alfred A. Knopf, Inc. Copyright © 1941 by Hilaire Belloc.

A hardcover edition of this book was published in 1996 by HarperCollins Publishers.

First HarperPerennial edition published 1997.

Designed by Nancy Singer

The Library of Congress has catalogued the hardcover edition as follows:

Lessing, Doris May
    Love, again : a novel / Doris Lessing. — 1st ed.
      p. cm.
    ISBN 0-06-017687-3
    1. Theater—England—London—Production and direction—Fiction.
  2. Middle-aged women—England—London—Psychology—Fiction.
  3. Man-woman relationships—England—London—Fiction.   I. Title.
PR6023.E833L47   1996
823'.914—dc20   95-53317

ISBN 0-06-092796-8 (pbk.)

97 98 99 00 01 ❖/RRD 10 9 8

With respectful salaams to the great cartographers of this region, particularly Stendhal, in Love, and Marcel Proust. And with friendly but perhaps abashed waves at some of the famous travellers in it: Goethe, Richardson in Clarissa, Henry Handel Richardson (a woman) in Maurice Guest, Christina Stead in For Love Alone, and the incomparable Colette in Chéri.

acknowledgements

D. H. Lawrence, Gerard Manley Hopkins, Shakespeare, Elizabeth Barrett Browning, Edward Thomas, Publilius Syrus, Byron, Browning, Alfred Lord Tennyson, Louis MacNeice, Plautus, George Eliot, Charles Dickens, Ecclesiastes, T. S. Eliot, Sappho, Bob Dylan, François Villon, John Vanbrugh, Aphra Behn, John Dryden, Andrew Marvell, Cecil Spring Rice, Archbishop Whately of Dublin, Harry Graham.

Memory

One had a lovely face
And two or three had charm,
But charm and face were in vain
Because the mountain grass
Cannot but keep the form
Where the mountain hare has lain.

W. B. Yeats

love, again

I'm falling in love again,
Never wanted to . . .

*E*asy to think this was a junkroom, silent and airless in a warm dusk, but then a shadow moved, someone emerged from it to pull back curtains and throw open windows. It was a woman, who now stepped quickly to a door and went out, leaving it open. The room thus revealed was certainly over-full. Along one wall were all the evidences of technical evolution—a fax machine, a copy machine, a word processor, telephones—but as for the rest, the place could easily be some kind of theatrical storeroom, with a gold bust of some Roman female, much larger than life, masks, a crimson velvet curtain, posters, and piles of sheet music, or rather photocopies that had faithfully reproduced yellowing and crumbling originals.

On the wall over the word processor was a large reproduction of Cézanne's *Mardi Gras*, also the worse for wear: it had been torn across and put together with cellotape.

The woman next door was energetically attending to something: objects were being moved about. Then she reappeared and stood looking in at the room.

Not a young woman, as it had been easy to imagine from the

vigour of her movements when still half seen in the shadows. A woman of a certain age, as the French put it, or even a bit older, and not dressed to present herself, but wearing old trousers and shirt.

This woman was alert, full of energy, yet she did not seem pleased with what she looked at. However, she shook all that off and went to her processor, sat down, put out a hand to switch on a tape. At once the room was filled with the voice of the Countess Dié, from eight centuries ago (or a voice able to persuade the listener she was the Countess), singing her timeless plaints:

I must sing, whether I will or not:
I feel so much pain over him whose friend I hold myself,
For I love him more than anything that is . . .

The modern woman, sitting with her hands ready to attack the keys, was conscious she felt superior to this long-ago sister, not to say condemning. She did not like this in herself. Was she getting intolerant?

Yesterday Mary had rung from the theatre to say that Patrick was in emotional disarray because he had fallen in love again, and she had responded with a sharp comment.

'Now, come on, Sarah,' Mary had rebuked her.

Then Sarah had agreed, and laughed at herself.

Feeling disquiet, however. There seems to be a rule that what you condemn will turn up sooner or later, to be lived through. Forced to eat your vomit—yes, Sarah knew this well enough. Somewhere in her past she had made a note: Beware of condemning other people, or watch out for yourself.

The Countess Dié was too disturbing, and Sarah switched the plaint off.

Silence. She sat breathing it in. She was altogether too much affected by this old troubadour and trouvère music. She had been listening to little else for days, to set the tone of what she had to write. Not only the Countess, but Bernard de Ventadour, Pierre Vidal, Giraut de Bornelh, and other old singers, had put her into a state of . . . she was restless, and she was feverish. When had music affected her like this before? She did not think it had. Wait, though. Once she had listened to jazz, particularly the blues, it seemed day and night, for months. But that was when her husband died, and the music had fed her melancholy. But she did not remember . . . yes, first she had been grief-ridden, and then she had chosen music to fit her state. But this was a different matter altogether.

Her task this evening was not a difficult one. The programme notes were too stiff in tone: this was because, writing them, she had been afraid of being over-charmed by the subject. And she was being charmed by the sensuous voice of the Countess—or the young woman Alicia de la Haye.

She did not have to do the programme notes now. In fact she had made a rule for herself not to work in the evenings at home: a rule she had not been keeping recently. To spell it out, she had not been keeping her own prescriptions for balance and good mental health.

She sat listening to silence. A sparrow chirped.

She thought, I'll look up that Provençal poem by Pound; that's hardly work after all.

The desk was stacked with reference books, files of cuttings, and on one side of it bookshelves rose to the ceiling. A book lay open on one side of the word processor.

Growing old gracefully . . . the way has been signposted. One might say the instructions are in an invisible script which becomes slowly legible as life exposes it. Then the appropriate words only have to be spoken. On the whole the old don't do badly. Pride is a great thing, and the necessary stances and stoicisms are made easy because the young do not know—it is hidden from them—that the flesh withers around an unchanged core. The old share with each other ironies appropriate to ghosts at a feast, seen by each other but not by the guests whose antics and posturings they watch, smiling, remembering.

To this set of placid sentences full of self-respect most people getting old would subscribe, feeling well presented and even defended by them.

Yes, I'll go along with that, thought Sarah. Sarah Durham. A good sensible name for a sensible woman.

The book where she had found these sentences had been on a trestle in a street market, the memoirs of a society woman once known for her beauty, written in old age and published when she was nearly a hundred, twenty years ago. A strange thing, Sarah thought, that she had picked the book up. Once, she would never have even opened a book by an old person: nothing to do with her, she would have felt. But what could be odder than the way that books which chime with one's condition or stage in life insinuate themselves into one's hand?

She pushed away that book, thought Pound's verses could wait, and decided to enjoy an evening when nothing at all would be expected of her. An evening in April, and it was still light. This room was calm, usually calming, and like the other three rooms in this flat held thirty years of memories. Rooms a long time lived in can be like littered sea shores; hard to know where this or that bit of debris has come from.

She knew exactly where the bits of theatrical junk had originated: which play, or what actor. But on the window sill was a bowl of coloured pebbles she had picked up outside a village in Provence where she had gone walking with her two children, then aged twelve and thirteen. What was the name of that village? She had been several times to that region, and she had always picked up stones to take home. Strings of beads in all shades of red were pinned in a fan shape on a board that filled a good part of a wall. Why had she kept the thing? Piles of books on the theatre climbed the walls: she had not opened some of them for years. And there was the poster of *Mardi Gras*. He had been eye to eye with her for decades, that arrogantly sexy youth in the red and black diamond pattern costume with his touch-me-not look. He was like her own son—well, yes, that had been a long time ago, and George was now an almost middle-aged scientist. These days, when she did look at it (after all, one doesn't much look at what is on one's walls), her eyes went to the uncertain youth with his dark thoughtful eyes in the ill-fitting Pierrot dress. Her daughter, aged fifteen, had demanded a Pierrot costume, and she, Cathie's mother, had known it was a statement. *I am like him. I need a disguise. I wish I were not unsure but like the Harlequin, who knows how beautiful he is.* There was nothing unsure about Cathie these days, a successful matron, with children, a job, a satisfactory husband.

Sarah knew she saw the picture as portraits of her own children. Why did she keep it there? Parents often secretly cherish photographs of their offspring that have nothing to do with their present ages, and these are not always appealingly helpless infants.

She should get rid of all this rubbish . . . and now, suddenly, she sat up straight in her chair and then stood and began a prowl around the room. This was not the first time she had had the thought. Years ago, she had looked around this room, full of things that had come to rest there for some reason or another and thought, I must get rid of it all.

The poster was there because her daughter Cathie had brought it home. *It had nothing to do with her, Sarah.* What could she say was hers? The books, the reference books: her working necessities. And the rest of her home? An extended prowl then, repeated now, took her past dishes of shells collected by the children decades ago, a cupboard that still had their old clothes in it, postcards, stuck on a cork board, from people on holiday. Her clothes? Could she say that these were here because she had chosen them? Well, yes, but fashion had dictated them.

On that evening years ago, she had come to the unsettling conclusion that very little in these four large rooms was here because of
some considered choice of hers. A choice from that part of her she
thought of as *herself.* No, and she had decided to go through the
rooms and throw everything out ... well, almost everything: here
was something that would stay if everything else found itself bagged
up for the dustbins. It was a real photograph, which took itself seriously. A pleasant man, a bit worried perhaps, or tired?—a net of fine
lines around frank and comradely blue eyes, and with grey in his
fair hair (whose soft silkiness she could feel in her fingers), which
was probably the first sign of a heart attack that was to strike him
down so young, at forty. He sat with his arms around two children,
boy and girl, aged eight and nine. The three of them were smiling at
Sarah. The photograph was in a silver frame, art deco, not Sarah's
taste, but it had been given to her by her husband who had had it
from his mother. Should she throw out the frame because she had
never liked it?

Why hadn't she made a clean sweep? It was because she had been
too busy. Some new play, probably. She had always worked so hard.

Sarah came to a stop in front of a mirror. She looked at a handsome apparently middle-aged woman with a trim body. Her hair,
always in tight smooth bands for convenience—she could not be
bothered with hairdressers—was described as fair on her passport,
but it was more a dull yellow, like neglected brass. Surely by now she
ought to have at least the odd grey hair? But that shade often does
not go grey or white, at least not until real old age. Young, its posses-
sors yearn for lively colour and might dye it, and when older gratefully leave it alone and are accused of dyeing it. She did not often
look in the mirror: she was not anxious about her looks. Why
should she be? She was often thought twenty years younger than her
real age. In another mirror, through the open door to her bedroom,
she seemed even less her age. She could see the reflection by twisting
herself about. Her back was erect and full of vitality. Her osteopath,

when treating her for back trouble (it did seem to be making itself felt these days), enquired if she had been a dancer. The two mirrors were there because decades ago her husband had said, 'Sarah, these rooms are too dark. Can't we get some light into them?' The walls were painted bright white, but they had dimmed, and the curtains had been white, were now dark cream. When the sun shone in, the room filled with light, shadow, and moving reflections, a place of suggestion and possibilities. Without sun, the mirrors showed furniture that stood about in a still light like water. A pearly light. Restful. She liked these rooms, could not think of anything worse than having to leave them. They could be criticized for being shabby. Her brother said they were, but she thought his house smart and awful. Nothing had been changed here for years. The rooms gently dimmed into acceptance: of her being so busy always, and of her being, at heart, not much interested, and of the way the years accumulated, leaving deposits, books and photographs, postcards and things from the theatre.

All this junk should go out. . . . Here on the wall of her bedroom was a group of photographs. Some were of her grandmother and grandfather in India, posed and formal, doing their duty, but she had added one cut out of a magazine, of a girl dressed in the fashions of the year Sarah Anstruther went out to marry her fiancé, doing well in the Indian Civil Service. This girl was not Sarah Durham's grandmother, but all the photographs Sarah had of this woman she had never met were of a young matron competently facing the world, and the shy, frightened unknown was—Sarah Durham was pretty sure—rather more to the point. A girl of eighteen, travelling to a country she knew nothing about, where she would marry a young man she hardly knew, to become a memsahib . . . common, in those days, but what courage.

Sarah Durham's life had held no such dramatic choices. In a potted biography, of the kind seen on book jackets or theatre notes, it would look like this:

Sarah Durham was born in 1924 in Colchester. Two children. Her brother studied medicine. She went to a couple of reputable girls' schools. At university she studied French and Italian, and then spent a year at the University of Montpellier doing music, living with an aunt who had married a Frenchman. During the war she was a chauffeur for the Free French in London. In 1946 she married Alan Durham, and there were two children. He died, leaving her a widow in her mid-thirties. She had lived in London, with the children.

A calm and reasonable woman . . . true that Alan's death had thrown her into unhappiness for a time, but it wore off. That was how she put it now, knowing she was choosing not to remember the misery of that time. Hypocrite memory . . . *kind* memory that allowed her to claim a tranquil life.

She went back to her workroom and read the exemplary passage in the book again, the one beginning, 'Growing old gracefully . . .' It ended a chapter, and the next one began, 'What I liked best about my trip to India was the early mornings, before the heat got bad and we had to stay inside. When I decided not to marry Rupert after all I am sure now it was the heat rather than him I was refusing. I was not in love with him, but I did not know that then. I had not learned what being in love was.'

For the third time she read 'Growing old gracefully . . .' to the end of the chapter. Yes, that would do. She found herself at sixty-five telling younger friends that there was nothing to getting old, quite pleasurable really, for if this or that good took itself off, then all kinds of pleasures unsuspected by the young presented themselves, and one often found oneself wondering what the next surprise would be. She said this sort of thing in good faith, and while observing the emotional tumults of those even a decade younger than herself even indulged private shudders at the thought of going through all that again—a formula which included love. As for being in love, it had occurred to her it was twenty years since she had been in love,

she who had once fallen in love easily and—she had to admit it—
even eagerly. She could not believe she would be in love again. She
said this too with complacency, forgetting the hard law that says you
must suffer what you despise.

She was not going to sit down and work . . . it occurred to her
that one reason for this exaggerated *no* to another evening spent
doing what she did all day was her—well, yes, the word had to be—
fear of that music. Those plaints from long ago were a drug. Had
jazz really taken her over as the Countess Dié and Bernard, Pierre
and Giraut, had done? And what about the woman who was, these
days, her occupation—Julie Vairon, whose music stood in yellowing
stacks on a table? No, she distrusted music. She was in good company after all; many of the great and the wise had thought music a
dubious friend. She had always listened in the spirit of: You're not
going to take me over, don't you think it!

No: no work, and no music. She was restless enough to . . .
climb a mountain, to walk twenty miles. Sarah found she was tidy-
ing this room, which certainly needed it. She might as well vacuum
the floor . . . why not all four rooms? The kitchen. The bathroom. By
twelve her flat was a paragon. You would think this woman took
pride in her housewifely skills. Instead she had a cleaner in once a
week, and that was it.

Surely she wasn't nervous of meeting—as she had to do tomorrow—Stephen Ellington-Smith, known jokingly in the company as
Our Angel. She could not remember being nervous ever before
about this kind of encounter. After all, it was her job to meet and
soothe patrons, benefactors, and angels, she did it all the time.

Sarah's memories divided her life into two eras, or different
landscapes, one sunny and unproblematical, and then all effort and
difficulty. (Yet the war with its anxieties was somehow accommodated in the first sunlit stretch. How could that be? And all those

family money difficulties? Nonsense, mere trifles, compared to what followed.) Her husband's death, that was when this Sarah Durham had begun, poor and desperate. Her parents did not have much money. There had been no insurance. She could not really afford to stay in this flat but decided she would, preserving continuity for the already traumatized children. She earned her living and theirs by all kinds of badly paid freelance work for newspapers and magazines, publishers and the theatre, one theatre in particular, The Green Bird, then not more than a group putting on plays with small casts where they could, sometimes in pubs. In the seventies there were many brave small companies, chancing their luck. A certain Italian play which she had translated for them, and which they thought they had the rights to, became unavailable, and to fill the gap she adapted from a novel some sketches of contemporary life. These were a success, and she found herself one of the people running the theatre: first there was the fact that she was there all day, casting and then directing; then a regular salary. A regular theatre too. She was one of the four who decided to risk a long lease. These three were her closest friends, for surely the people you spend all day and most evenings with must be that. For ten years they had precariously survived, and then five years ago a play transferred to the West End, did well, and seemed likely to run forever. The Green Bird was now established as one of the best of the fringe theatres, and critics came to their first nights. From being an almost amateur, badly-paid hanger-on to the edges of real theatre, she was now known in the theatre world as the influential manager of The Green Bird and, sometimes, as the director of a play. The fact is, the four all did everything, and had from the beginning. Their success had brought them concomitant envy, and they were known—inevitably—as The Gang of Four. These changes had taken years, and at no point had she made claims for herself. She sometimes privately marvelled that hard work and—of course—good luck had added up to so much: it will be seen that she was not a self-admiring woman, nor even an ambitious one.

Who were these colleagues with whom she had shared so much? Mary Ford had been a pretty wisp of a thing with vast hazy blue eyes and a tremulous stubborn little face, but the years had made of the waif a solid calm competent woman of about forty, whose main job in the theatre was publicity and promotion. Roy Strether, another paradigm of competence, was formally stage manager. He was a solid, apparently slow man, who never allowed himself excitement, no matter what the crisis. He joked of himself that he looked like a footballer gone to seed. He was large, untidy, even clumsy. They remembered him as young, a sixties drop-out, who had earned his living as so many future successes did, painting houses. The fourth member of the permanent staff was Patrick Steele. They would joke, in front of him or not, that it was as well they three were so boringly stolid and reliable, for he was volatile, shrill, and moody; a slight, bird-like boy (he remained a boy while the years changed them) with soft black hair like plumage and black excitable eyes. He was homosexual and, these days, pretty scared. He would not go and be tested, saying that if he was HIV positive he did not want to know, but meanwhile he was being responsible and no danger to anyone. He often wept, for his emotional life gave him frequent cause for tears. He was brilliant, a magician: he could create moonlight, a lake, a mountain, with light and silver paper and shadows. Other theatres tried to lure him away but failed, for these four shared a belief that their talents together were larger than they could ever be apart. Patrick was as versatile as them all. He had written a libretto for a musical that had been so near a success they jested that next time he would soar off away into fame and be forever lost to them.

These were their public personas, their 'images'—how people from outside saw them, perhaps while they sat in their daily get-together for discussion, in a small office they might liken to a cockpit or an engine room. It was the usual mix of elegant technology, each machine already obsolete almost before it was installed, and old chairs and tables they felt disinclined to get rid of.

Four people, energized by their competence and success. Behind each there was that hinterland called personal life, which here was very far from being separated from working hours.

Mary was unmarried—without a man—because she had to look after her mother, who had multiple sclerosis and was pretty helpless. When she had been unable to organize other help, sometimes an old woman with shaking hands sat in a wheelchair in an aisle and watched the rehearsals.

Roy Strether was married, with a child. The marriage was unsuccessful. Sometimes the little boy would be inserted into a seat near his father's at a rehearsal and was commended by everybody for behaving well. Tired or demanding attention, he might sit on the old woman's lap, she delighted that at least she had some limited usefulness.

Sarah's responsibilities were self-imposed. For ten years now her vital energies—emotional—had been engaged, not by her own children and grandchildren, established successfully in other continents (India and America), but by her brother's youngest girl, Joyce. Hal and Anne had three daughters, the older two ordinary and just like everybody else's children. Joyce had been a problem since birth. Why? Who knows? She was a screaming baby, a grizzling toddler, a disagreeable child. Sent to school, she at once fell ill and had to come home. She simply could not manage school and other children. Her parents both being doctors, her condition never lacked diagnoses. Her records were voluminous and in several hospitals. A psychiatrist recommended that she be allowed to stay at home. Sarah was appealed to, and Joyce spent her days with her, in the room that had been the children's room. In those days Sarah often worked at home, and when she did go out for appointments Joyce stayed happily by herself. What did she do? Nothing at all. She made herself cups of tea, watched television, and sometimes rang telephone numbers at random until someone was willing to talk to her, when she would chat away sometimes for an hour or two hours. The telephone bills were enormous, and Hal and Anne did not offer to pay for them.

Joyce became anorexic and was again in hospital. She was 'stabilized' and despatched back to Sarah, who protested it was not fair, she could not deal any longer with Joyce. Hal had said in his kindly judicious way that it must be nice for Sarah to have Joyce around when her own children were so far away. But when the unsure and suffering Pierrot, now the efficient mother of two children in California, or the arrogantly beautiful boy, now a marine biologist with two sons, came bringing grandchildren to visit their grandmother, Joyce went home and there was no argument about it. As Joyce became fifteen, sixteen, seventeen, things went from bad to very bad. Suicide attempts, crises, cries for help. It was Sarah who took her to hospital and talked with the doctors, who had been briefed, of course, by the parents. It was always Aunt Sarah who was summoned. Back home, Joyce went to bed. Sarah fought with her and often succumbed to the low painful state threatening those who take on the psychic burden of those—as we put it—who cannot cope with ordinary life. There were times when she felt that she too would take to her bed and stay there, but her colleagues sustained her. And then all at once everything changed. One of the people, a girl, who chatted with Joyce on the telephone suggested they should meet. Sarah rang her brother, saying she had not seen Joyce for days, and now it was for him, for Joyce's parents, to make decisions. When Hal said he was afraid Joyce looked on her—Sarah—as her effective parent ('You are her effective parent, Sarah, surely you must know that'), Sarah said she was sorry, she had done her bit. Of course that was not the end of it. She worried quite dreadfully about Joyce: it had always been a waste of time worrying about Joyce. As the result of a television programme about people living rough, she went to the police, who suggested a certain café in King's Cross. Joyce's name was known to these addicts, pushers, and prostitutes. Sarah again rang her brother, who said, 'She's old enough now to take responsibility for herself,' and then added with cheerful spite, in his way that said since he took pleasure in malice then his interlocutor must too, 'We've been meaning to tell you. You should do something about yourself. You could do with a lick of paint.'

Postponing the lick, she went to the psychiatrist most often consulted about Joyce, where she heard that Joyce's flight into the great world could be seen as a step into maturity. An interesting notion, that a loony girl's development might be better furthered by joining drug users, pushers, and prostitutes than by taking refuge in her family. But there was nothing she, Sarah, could do. She would at last lead her own life. No, she did not expect to feel immediately better without the interminable drag and drudge of Joyce. Then she did take herself in hand, at last. She examined herself in the dim mirrors, switching on all the lights. Not bad, she supposed. She looked a handsome middle-aged matron. A hairdresser had improved her hair-do: a small smooth head went well with clothes more expensive than anything she had bought for years. At the theatre, her colleagues commended her. They also allowed her to know she had let herself be put upon and she should stand up for herself.

Besides, they all needed undivided energies. They were all working on a production more ambitious than anything they had done. Only a year ago, *Julie Vairon* had been on a list of possibilities, and now it was a big co-production, with American, French, and English money. They knew they would have to engage more people, expand, but they put off doing this. They confessed there was something disturbing about *Julie Vairon*'s irresistible sweep, and Mary Ford wondered aloud if they would have taken on *Julie* if they had known what an upheaval would result, but Patrick said it was not *Julie*

Vairon but Julie Vairon who was the trouble; and he spoke with the whimsical self-satisfaction which is, because of a secret identification, felt as flattering.

In the eighties of the last century, in Martinique, a beautiful girl—a quadroon, like Napoleon's Josephine—fascinated a young French officer. This is where *Julie Vairon*, the play—or, as it was later billed, An Entertainment—began. She was the daughter of a mulatto woman who had been the mistress of a white plantation owner's son. When he inherited the plantation he married suitably, a poor but aristocratic girl from France, but remained Sylvie Vairon's protector, while gossip claimed he was much more. He agreed the girl should be educated, at least to the level of the daughters of the neighbouring rich family, also landowners. Perhaps his conscience troubled him, but it was said, too, that he had enlightened ideas and these were expressed only here, in Julie's education. She had music lessons and drawing lessons and read quantities of books recommended by tutors who fitted in her lessons between the more formal lessons they gave the rich girls in their big house five miles away. The tutors were fiery young men who regretted they had not been born in time for the Revolution, or at least to fight in Napoleon's armies, just as in our time young men or women mourn because they were not in Paris in '68. 'But '68 was a failure,' a practical elder may protest, only to be demolished by passionately scornful eyes. 'What of it! Think how *exciting* it must have been!'

One of the young ladies, more enterprising than her sisters, decided to satisfy her curiosity about the mysterious Julie and contrived to visit her secretly in the house in the forest where Julie lived with her mother. She boasted about her exploit, which was evidence of her brave indifference to convention, and added to the already noisy rumours. The visit was invaluable to Julie, for she had had nothing to measure herself against. She learned from it that she was more intelligent than these respectable girls—her visitor was supposed to be the cleverest of them—but learned too how socially disadvantaged she herself was, for she was educated above her prospects and even her possibilities. Also, she knew why the tutors were all so ready to teach her. They might all be in love with her, but they could also talk to her.

Of herself at that time she wrote less than ten years later, *Inside that pretty little head what an olla podrida of incompatible ideas. But I envy that girl her innocence.* She had read the Encyclopedists, was devoted to Voltaire, while Rousseau, so appealing to anyone dependent on natural justice, had to hold sway. She could debate (and did, endlessly, with her tutors) about the acts and speeches of every personage on the great stage of the Revolution as if she had lived through it. She knew as much about the heroes of the American War of Independence. She adored Tom Paine, worshipped Benjamin Franklin, was convinced she and Jefferson were made for each other. She knew that had she been old enough she would have got on a ship to America to nurse the victims of the Civil War. But in fact she was living on her father's banana estate, the illegitimate part-black (she was a light brown colour, like a southern French or Italian) daughter of a black lady whose house in the sultry forest was where successive waves of young officers, all bored out of their minds in this beautiful but dull island, went for entertainment, dancing, drinking, food, and the delightful singing of beautiful Julie. A very young officer, Paul Imbert, fell in love with her. He adored her, but did he adore her enough to marry her or even take her with him to France? Probably not, if she had not refused to see difficulties and insisted they should run away together. His parents were respectable people living not far from Marseilles, his father a magistrate. They refused to receive Julie. Paul found for her a little stone house in hilly and romantic country, and there he visited his love daily for a year, riding through aromatic pines, poplars, and olive trees. Then his parents pulled strings, the army forgave his young man's lapse, and he was sent on duty to French Indo-China. And now Julie was alone in the woods, with no means of support. The magistrate sent her money. He had glimpsed the girl walking with his son in the hills. He envied Paul. This was not why he sent money. Paul had confessed with all suitable remorse that Julie was pregnant. For a time she had believed she was. With only a few francs between her and starvation, she returned the money to Paul's father, saying that it was true she had been pregnant, but nature had quickly come to her aid—to the aid of all of them. Thus she made a claim on him, on his feelings of responsibility. She thanked him for his interest and asked him to help her get employment in the middle-class homes of the small town near to her, Belles Rivières. She could draw well, and she painted in water colours—unfortunately oils were too expensive for her. She played the piano. She could sing. 'I believe that in these accomplishments I shall prove in no way inferior to the tutors currently employed in this district.' She was asking for far more than the generous sum of money he had offered. By now everyone knew of the pretty but dubious girl who had tried to ensnare the son of one of their most respected families and lived all by herself like a savage in the woods. Her lover's father thought for a long time. Probably he would not have responded had he not caught that glimpse of her with Paul. He went to see her and found an accomplished, witty, and delightful young woman, with the most charming manners in the world. In short, he fell in love with her, as everyone did. He could not bring himself to refuse her, said he would speak to selected families on her behalf, but kept himself in face by asking for an undertaking that she would never contact any member of his family again. She replied with a quick and impatient scorn he had to see was genuine: 'I had assumed, monsieur, that you would have already understood that.'

For four years she taught the daughters of a doctor, two lawyers, three chemists, and a prosperous shopkeeper. All of them begged her to move into the little town, 'where you will be more comfortable.' Meaning that they were uncomfortable because this girl, no matter how well-bred and clever, was living by herself a good three miles from Belles Rivières. She refused, delightfully but firmly, telling them about the great forests of Martinique, the flowers and the butterflies and the brilliant birds, where she had wandered, absolutely by herself. She could not be happy living in streets, she said, though the truth was she dreamed of the streets of Paris and how she could reach them without worsening her already bad position. If she was going to try her chances in the big city it should be now, while she was still young and pretty, but she still dreamed of Paul. That she had been bound to lose him she had very soon learned, and knew that if he came back from the army she could not have him. Living, as she insisted on doing, free but alone told everyone she was waiting for him, and everyone—father, mother, sisters, would be writing to tell him so. Far from enticing him to her, this would put him off, as all her instincts, and the worldly wisdom imparted by her mother, told her. But she could not leave the place. Freedom! Liberty! she often cried to herself, roaming about her forests.

What did she look like at this time? How did she see her prospects? How did she strike the good people whose daughters she taught? How did they strike her? We know. We know it all. She drew self-portraits all her life, not because she had no other model, but because she was engaged in discovering her real, her hidden nature: we have a phrase for this search. She kept journals from the time she reached France. And there was her music, that would have told us everything even without her journals. The picture that emerges is not merely of an intelligent and attractive woman, but one who disturbed and challenged even when she did not intend to, who all her life fed malicious tongues, who always had men in love with her though she did not expect them to be or try to attract them. When she was accepted as tutor into these good houses, she behaved like a paragon of propriety, but she knew it would take only a small mistake to have the doors shut on her. She walked on a knife-edge, for above all, she had charm, that double-edged gift, arousing more expectations than it can ever fulfil. She certainly disappointed the young ladies she taught, who called her best friend and championed her to doubtful mothers and fathers, yet secretly hoped for more than her prudent advice: 'Do you really want to be like me?' she might sweetly enquire, when some over-protected daughter asked her aid in some minor rebellion. 'Do what your parents say, and when you are married you can do as you like.' She had learned this from Stendhal's letters to his sister.

In her journals she wrote she would rather be herself, 'an outcast,' than any one of these privileged girls.

When she was twenty-five she took a big step up the social ladder. She taught the two daughters of a Comte Rostand. The Rostands were the leading family in the area. They lived in a large and ancient château and sent a carriage for her twice a week. That was when she gave lessons in the dark hours as well as in the light, for before the carriage she had insisted that since she had to walk miles back and forth from her little house, she would teach in the town only in the day. This caused sarcastic comments. Everyone knew she wandered about all by herself at night in her forests. Yet she was too delicate to walk back in the dark from the town? And how about dancing by herself among the rocks, banging a tambourine, or something that looked like one—a primitive looking thing, probably from that primitive country she came from. Dancing naked—some claimed to have seen her.

Did she? There is no mention of it in her journals—though when she began to keep a record, there were only notes and jottings, and only later did it develop into a running commentary on her life. There is, however, a drawing of a woman dancing in a setting of trees and rocks. A full moon. Naked. This drawing is so unlike anything else she did of herself it shocks. Interesting to watch when some fan of Julie's was handed a pile of her drawings. The face froze, there was an indrawn breath and—then—a laugh. The laugh was from shock. But how often is shock no more than a moment of half-expected revelation? A door opens (perhaps literally) onto a scene that is beautiful, or ugly, something ferocious or shocking—at any rate, the other side of the well-lit and ordered world we know: there it is, the truth. But why was there never mention of dancing in her journals? Perhaps it only happened once, and she got some kind of a scare. A pretty risky thing, to dance like that. She knew people spied on her. The gendarmes certainly did, but if one of them took a look through her uncurtained and unshuttered window—she hated feeling shut in, she said—he would see the proper young woman of the drawing rooms standing before her easel or playing her harp or writing at a small table under an oil lamp that showed the open book, her neatly ringed hand with the pen, her face, her bands of black hair, her bust smooth in a dress that went high to her throat, where there was a small white collar.

The gendarmes would also report that there were many books. If they took a good look when she was out, down in the town, they would not now be able to report anything consistently seditious or troubling. For while she still loved Revolutions as a matter of principle—she would not have been able to think of herself as a serious person if she did not—her shelves now provided a more balanced diet. Montaigne sat by Madame Roland, Madame de Sévigné with *Émile. Clarissa*—that novel whose influence on European literature had been and still was so strong—was in a pile with Rousseau's *Confessions*, while Victor Hugo and Maupassant, Balzac and Zola, saw no reason why they should not share space with Voltaire. Beside her bed—small and narrow, with a single pillow—was evidence that she was taking possession of the part of France she found herself in, because she was reading whatever she could find of regional literature, had fallen in love with the old Provençal poets, and they and the newest Provençal poet, Mistral, were by the little blue enamel candlestick with its modest white candle on her night table.

A learned young woman, even a bluestocking, so the talk went, side by side with the other, more appetizing rumours, and when the château sent the carriage for Julie—it had to wait a good mile from her house, and even then there was only a cart road—this meant that the Rostands did not know about her nocturnal activities, or perhaps they did not care, were at the very least respecting her insistence on being considered, at least for form's sake, as one of them.

The youngest son, Rémy, soon fell fatally in love with her. If Paul had been the essence of the romantic hero, dark, handsome, impetuous, full of temperament, then Rémy was the mature love, sober, patient, observant, with that small dry humour women love as a sign of seriousness, of experience.

When she began to love him it was against her good sense, and then she abandoned caution, just as she had in Martinique with Paul, and loved him absolutely. The carriage no longer waited for her where the cart track ended, for she ceased to give lessons at the château, but he visited her in her forest house and sometimes stayed with her for days at a time. The family knew he would get over it, and waited. He begged them to allow him to marry her. She dreamed of marrying him, while common sense told her to stop. All this went on for months—three years in fact—of bliss, of anguish, or despair, heights and depths of all kinds. She continued to give lessons in the town, while he begged her to rely on him. The citizens were able to ignore the hideous rumours, because their aristocratic family were being so cool, and because the pair was so discreet. They were never seen together. Besides, the young woman was such an excellent teacher. And above all her fees were so moderate.

This time Julie did get pregnant, and the lovers were happy and dreamed of the life they would have with their child. The baby was born, was a healthy child, but died of a minor ailment, the way children did so easily then. The two were ill with grief, but soon learned that the rumours in the town were more than ugly—they were dangerous. Criticism of Julie, so long repressed because of her confidence, and her skills, and because she always seemed to have power-ful protectors, now expressèd itself in the gossip that she had killed the child. It was known where and how. Half a mile from her house, a river ran fast downhill over rocks into a deep cold pool. The child's death ended the family's patience. Rémy was told to remove himself into the army. He was twenty-three. Julie was then twenty-eight. The two parted in an agony of grief, hardly able to move, as if they had been slowed by a deadly cold, an invisible ice. They told each other they would never get over it, and somewhere or other, they did not.

She had not been able to teach in the town since her pregnancy showed. With what she had saved, and what Rémy could give her when he left, she had enough to live on for a year. While she was slowly putting herself together again, and her journals tell us how painful a process this was, she repeated former behaviour. In a letter beginning, 'There is no more helpless and unfortunate being than a young woman without a family, without a protector . . . ,' she asked Count Rostand to get her work as a copier of music. This he did. He knew she was more than adequately equipped for anything in this line. The family was a musical one. Musicians both well known and amateur played in their salons on feast days, and Julie's own music had been played at these evenings, and sometimes by herself. It was a strange music—but then, she did come from an exotic island. The family knew she was a real musician, wrote serious music.

For years she lived quietly by herself, earning her living in a variety of ways. She copied music and even, on request, composed pieces for special occasions. She sang at the more respectable pub-lic feasts or festivals, always careful to refuse an invitation that might lower her status as a respectable woman. She drew and painted, in pastels and water colours, the picturesque scenes she lived among, and made studies of birds and animals. These pic-tures were sold from a printer's shop in the town. She was never well off, but she was not poor either. Several times her journals recorded timely gifts of money from the Rostands, presumably at Rémy's request.

She was alone? Yes, always. She was not able to forget Rémy, and he did not forget her. Occasionally they wrote long letters. Three years after he was banished into the army in French Equatorial Africa, he came on leave, and visited her, but they were both so affected they decided never to meet again. He was already engaged to marry a girl from a suitable family.

This romantic story, the reader has probably long ago decided, is hardly unusual. Beautiful young women without family support, and disadvantaged—in this case doubly, being both illegitimate and coloured—have this kind of history. In the rich parts of the world. In the poor countries of the Third World most particularly. Even in the Second World (but where is that?), poor and pretty girls match dreams to expectations, but with their hearts, not their heads.

Julie's head was far from weaker than her heart. As her journals show. And her self-portraits. And, not least, her music. While her unfortunately not unusual story unfolded itself, her mind remained—bad luck for her—above it all, as if Jane Austen were rewriting *Jane Eyre*, or Stendhal a novel by George Sand. An uncomfortable business, reading her journals, because one has to feel that it is bad enough she had to suffer all that pain and loneliness, without having to endure her own severe view of herself. She might have adored her lover Paul, and more than adored Rémy, but she often described these passions as if a busy physician were making notes about calamitous illnesses. Not that she dismissed these calamities as worthless or meaningless: on the contrary, she gave them all the weight and meaning they did have in her life.

Five years after the loss of her lover Rémy, she was asked in marriage by a man of fifty, Philippe Angers, the master of the printing works where she sold her pictures. He was well-off, a widower with grown-up children. She liked him. She wrote that talking with him was the best thing in her life, after her music. He visited her in her own house, openly, his horse and sometimes his carriage left standing under the pines and turkey oaks where the cart track ended. She walked with him in a public garden at Belles Rivières. They spent the day together at a fête in Nice. This was his way of telling the world that he approved of Julie and her way of life, and proposed to take her on regardless of public opinion. But by now people were pleased that this vagabond and disturber of minds should be made harmless at last.

She was writing, *I like him so much, and everything about this proposition is sensible. Why then does it lack conviction?* She mused that the word *conviction* was an interesting one in this context. Paul had been convincing, and Rémy most certainly was. What did she mean by it, though?

For a long sober year Julie and the master printer planned their marriage. His children met her and presumably approved. One of them was a farmer, Robert. She describes how Robert joined the printer and herself for a meal. *I could love that one*, she remarks. *And he certainly could love me. When we looked at each other we knew it. That would have conviction, all right! But it doesn't matter. He lives with his wife and his four children near Béziers. We shall probably never see each other.*

Remarks about her future husband continue, and they are calm, sensible, one could say respectful. There is, however, an entry describing a day in her married life. *I shall wake up in that comfortable bed beside him, when the maid comes in to do the fire. Just as his wife did. Then I will kiss him and I will get up to make the coffee, since he likes my coffee. Then I shall kiss him when he goes downstairs to the shop. Then I shall give the girl orders. At last I will go to the room he says I can have for myself and I shall paint. Oils if I like. I will be able to afford anything I like in that line. He usually doesn't come to the midday meal, so I shall ignore it and walk in the gardens and make conversation with the citizens, who are longing to forgive me. Then I shall play the piano a little, or my flute. He has not heard the music I am writing these days. I don't think he would like it. Dear Philippe, he is so warmhearted. He had tears in his eyes when the dog was sick. He will come in for supper and we will eat soup. He likes my soup, he likes how I cook. Then we will talk about his day. It is interesting, the work he does. Then we will talk about the newspapers. We shall often disagree. He certainly does not admire Napoleon! He goes to bed early. That will be the hardest, to be shut up in a house all night.*

Not once is there a suggestion of a financial calculation. Yet she was quite alone in the world. Her mother had been killed in the Mount Pelée earthquake, having gone to visit a sister living at St Pierre, which was destroyed. It is not recorded whether Julie ever asked her father for help.

A week before the mayor, who was an old friend of Philippe's, was to marry them at the town hall, she drowned herself in the pool where gossips said she had killed her baby. They did not believe she had killed herself. Why should she, now that all her problems were solved? Nor had she slipped and fallen, which was what the police decided. Absurd!—when she had been jumping around those woods for years, like a goat. No, she was murdered, and probably by a disappointed lover no one knew about. Living all by herself miles from any decent people, she had been asking for something of the sort.

There were suitable condolences for the citizen who had lost his love, for no one could doubt he adored her, but people said he was well out of it. The gendarmes collected up her papers, her sketches, her pictures, a good deal of sheet music, and for lack of a better idea put it all into a big packing case that went to stand in the cellar of the provincial museum. Then, in the 1970s, Rémy's descendants found some of her music among their papers, were pleased with it, remembered there was a packing case in the museum, found more music there, and got it played at a local summer festival. That is where the Englishman Stephen Ellington-Smith heard it. As music lovers will know, Julie Vairon quickly became recognized as a composer unique in her time, an original, and people are already using the word *great*.

But she was not only a musician. The artistic world admires her. 'A small but secure niche . . .' is how she is currently evaluated. Some people think she will be remembered for her journals. Excerpts appeared in both France and England, and were at once praised: very much to the taste of this time. Three volumes of her journals were published in France, and one volume (the three abridged) in Britain, where no one disagreed with the French claim that she deserves to stand on the same shelf as Madame de Sévigné. But some people have too many talents for their own good. Perhaps better if she had been an artist with that modest sensitive unpretentious talent so becoming in women. Which brings us to the feminists for whom she is a contentious sister. For some she is the archetypal female victim, while others identify with her independence. And as a musician, so one critic complained, 'the trouble is one doesn't know how to categorize her.' All very well to say now how modern she is, but her music was not of her time. She came from the West Indies, people remind each other, where there is all that loud and disturbing music and it was 'in her blood'. No one forgets that 'blood', an asset now, if not then. No wonder her rhythms are not of Europe. But then, they aren't African either. To add to the problem, her music had two distinct phases. The first kind is not hard to understand, though where it could have come from certainly is: nearest to it is the trouvère and troubadour music of the twelfth, thirteenth, and fourteenth centuries. But that music was not available in Julie's time, as it is now, in recordings of arrangements made using the instruments of then and re-created from difficult-to-decipher manuscripts. There are ways of bringing that old music back to life. One tradition of Arab music has changed little in all those centuries from what was taken to Spain, whence it came to southern France and inspired the singers and musicians who wandered from castle to castle, court to court, with instruments that were the ancestors of the ones we know. Yet when music has to be inferred, re-created, 'heard', the interpretation of an individual has to be at least in part an original inspiration. The words of the Countess Dié are as she sang them, but exactly how did she sing them? Did Julie see old manuscripts somewhere? We all know the most unlikely things do happen. Where? Did the Rostand family have ancient manuscripts in their possession? The trouble with this interesting theory—which postulates that this ancestor-loving, music-loving clan were so careless with a treasure from the past that they did not recognize its influences on Julie—is that Julie wrote that kind of music before knowing the family, for her songs of that time were fed by her grief over losing Paul. One may speculate harmlessly that among those solid middle-class families whose daughters she taught was one with an ancient chest full of . . . it is possible. Very well, then, how did this kind of singing come into her mind, living in her hilly solitude? What was she hearing, listening to? It was certain there were the sounds of running and splashing water, the noise of cicadas and crickets, owls and nightjars, and the high thin scream of a hawk on its rocky heights, and the winds of that region, which whine drily through hills where the troubadours went, making their singular music. There are those who say fancifully that she was visited by their essences during those long evenings alone, composing her songs. A music lover actually played them at a concert of trouvère and troubadour music, and everyone marvelled, for she could have been one of them. So that was her 'first phase', hard to explain but easy to listen to. Her 'second phase' was different, though there was a short period when the two kinds of music were in an uneasy alliance. Oil and water. Nothing African about the new phase. Long flowing rhythms go on, and very occasionally a primitive theme appears, if by that is meant sounds that remind of dancing, of physical movement. But then it becomes only one of several themes weaving in and out, rather as the voices in late medieval music make patterns where no one voice is more important than another.

Impersonal. Perhaps it is that which disturbs. The music of her 'troubadour' period complains right enough, but formally, within the limits of a form (like the fado or, for that matter, like the blues) which always sets bounds to the plaint of a little individual calling out for compassion, for surcease—for love. Her late music, cool and crystalline, could have been written by an angel, as a French critic said, but another riposted, No, by a devil.

It is hard, listening to her late music, to match it with what she said of herself in her journal, and with her self-portraits. Just before she threw herself into the pool, because that sensible marriage 'lacked conviction', she drew in pastels a wreath of portraits of herself, a satirical echo of those garlands of little cherubs or angels to be found on greeting cards. The sequence begins at top left with a pretty, wispy baby who is staring with intelligent black eyes straight back at the viewer—at, it must be remembered, Julie, as she worked. Next, the delightful little girl, her white muslin dress, the pink ribbons, vigorous black curls, and a smile that both seduces and mocks the viewer. Then an adolescent girl, and she is the only one who does not look directly back out of the picture. She is half turned away, with a proud poised profile, like an eaglet. Nothing comfortable about this girl, and one is glad to be spared her eyes, bound to demand strong reactions and sympathies. At the bottom, a spray of conventionalized leaves to match a bow of white ribbon at the top. At bottom right, opposite the eaglet, a young woman, seen as the apogee of this life, its achievement: she is not unlike Goya's Duchess of Alba, but prettier, with black curls, a fresh vigorous figure, and black bold amused eyes, forcing you to stare back into them. On the opposing side to the adolescent girl, in her way matching or commenting on her, is a coolly smiling woman in her early thirties, handsome and composed, nothing remarkable about her except for the thoughtful gaze, which holds you until: *Very well, then, what is it you want to say?* There is a black line drawn between this portrait and the next two: two stages of her life she chose not to live. A plump middle-aged woman sits with folded hands, eyes lowered. All the energy of the picture is in a yellow scarf over her grey hair: she could be any woman of fifty-five. The old woman is only an old woman. There is no individuality there, as if Julie could not imagine herself old or did not care enough to think herself into being old. And having drawn that emphatic black line, she had walked out of her house through the trees and stood—for how long?—on the edge of the river, and then jumped into a pool full of sharp rocks.

This was just before the First World War, which so rapidly and drastically changed the lives of women. Supposing she had not jumped, decided to live?

Before jumping she put her pictures, her music, her journals, into tidy heaps. She did not seem to have destroyed anything, probably thought: Take it or leave it. She did write a helpful note for the police, telling them where to look for her body.

Oblivion, for three-quarters of the century. Then the summer recital in Belles Rivières where her music was played for the first time. Shortly after that, her work was included in an exhibition of women artists in Paris, which came successfully to London. A television documentary was made. A romantic biography was written by someone who had either not read the journals or decided to take no notice of them.

This was where Sarah Durham had entered the story. She read the English version of the journals, thought it unsatisfactory, sent to Paris for the French edition, and found herself captivated by Julie to the extent that she was actually making a draft of a play before discussing it with the other three. They were as intrigued as she was. Afterwards no one could remember who had suggested using Julie's music; this kind of creative talk among people who work together is very much more than the sum of its parts. They could not stop talking about Julie. She had taken over The Green Bird. Sarah did another draft, with music. This was shown to potential backers, and at once *Julie Vairon* began to escalate. Then another play arrived, written by Stephen Ellington-Smith, who had done so much to 'discover' and then 'promote' Julie Vairon: 'Julie's Angel'.

They all read this new play, which was romantic, not to say sentimental, and no one would have given it another thought had Patrick not demanded a special meeting. Present were Sarah, Mary Ford, Roy Strether, Patrick Steele—the Founding Four. And, too, Sonia Rogers, an energetic redhead who was being 'tried out'. They were still saying that she was being tried out when it was evident she was a fixture, because no one wanted to admit an era was over. Why Sonia? Why none of the other hopefuls who worked in and around the theatre, sometimes without payment or for very little? Well, it was because she was there. She was everywhere, in fact. 'Turn the stone and there you find her,' jested Patrick. She had come in as a 'temp' and had at once become indispensable. Simple. She was at this meeting because she had come into the office for something and was invited to stay. She perched on the top of a filing cabinet as if ready to fly away at one cross word.

Patrick opened fire with 'What's the matter with Stephen Whatsit's play? It just needs a bit of tightening, that's all.'

Mary sang, '"She was poor but she was honest, victim of a rich man's whim".'

Roy said, 'Two rich men, to be accurate.'

Sarah said, 'Patrick, these days you simply can't have a play with a woman as a victim—and that's all.'

Patrick said, sounding, as he did so often, trapped, betrayed, isolated, 'Why not? That's what she was. Like poor Judy. Like poor Marilyn.'

'I agree with Sarah,' said Sonia. 'We couldn't have a play about Judy. We couldn't do Marilyn—not just victims and nothing else. It's not on.'

There was a considerable pause, of the kind when invisible currents and balances shift. Sonia had spoken with authority. She had said *We*. She wasn't thinking of herself as temporary, on trial. Right, the Founding Four were thinking. And now that's it. We have to accept it.

They all knew what each of the others was thinking. How could they not? They did not need even to exchange glances, or grimaces. They were feeling, were being made to feel, faded, shabby—past it. There sat this Sonia, as bright and glossy as a lion cub, and they were seeing themselves through her eyes.

'I agree absolutely,' said Mary, finally, assuming responsibility for the moment. And her smile at Sonia was such that the young woman showed her pleasure with a short triumphant laugh, tossing her fiery head. 'They wouldn't do an opera about Madame Butterfly now,' Mary went on.

'Everyone goes to see *Madame Butterfly*,' said Patrick.

'Everyone?' said Sonia, making a point they were meant to see was a political one.

'How about *Miss Saigon*?' said Patrick. 'I've read the script.'

'What's it about?' asked Sonia.

'The same plot as *Madame Butterfly*,' said Patrick. 'You talk your way out of that one, Sarah Durham.'

'It's a musical,' said Sarah. 'Not our audience.'

'Disgraceful,' said Sonia. 'Are you sure, Patrick?'

'Absolutely.'

Patrick pressed his attack. 'Then how about the Zimbabwe play? I don't remember anyone saying it should be a musical.'

The Zimbabwe play, by black feminists, was about a village girl who longed to live in town, just like everyone else in Zimbabwe, but there is unemployment. Her aunt in Harare says no, her house is already over-full. This precipitates a moral storm in the village, because the aunt's refusal is a break with the old ways, when the more fortunate members of a family had to keep any poor relation who asked. But the aunt says, I have already got twenty people in my house, with my children and my parents and I'm feeding everyone. She is a nurse. The village girl catches the eye of a local rich man, the owner of a lorry service. She gets pregnant. She kills the child. Everyone knows, but she is not prosecuted. She becomes an amateur prostitute. She never thinks of herself as one: 'This time the man will love me and marry me.' Another baby is left on the doorstep of the Catholic mission. She gets AIDS. She dies.

'I saw it,' said Sonia. 'It was good.'

'But that was all right, because she was black?' said Patrick, and laughed aloud at the political minefield he had invited them into.

'Let's not start,' said Mary. 'We'll be here all night.'

'Right,' said Patrick, having made his point.

'It's too late anyway,' said Roy, summing up, as he generally did. Calm, large, unflappable, one of the world's natural arbiters. 'We've already agreed on Sarah's play.'

'But,' Sonia directed them, 'I do think we should at least remember that it is the story of girls all over the world. As we sit here. Hundreds of thousands. Millions.'

'But it's too late,' said Roy.

Mary remarked, 'I don't think the French are in on it because they like the idea of a good cry. They don't see it as a weepy. When I talked to Jean-Pierre on the phone yesterday about the publicity, he said Julie was born out of her time.'

'Well, of course,' said Sarah.

'Jean-Pierre says they see her as an intellectual, in their tradition of female bluestockings.'

'In other words,' said Roy, ending the meeting by standing up, 'we shouldn't be having this conversation at all.'

'What about the American sponsors?' demanded Patrick. 'What have they agreed to? I bet not a French bluestocking.'

'They bought the package,' said Sarah.

'I can tell you this,' said Patrick. 'If you did Stephen Whatsit's play there wouldn't be a dry eye in the house.'

As Mary and Roy went banging off down the wooden stairs, they sang, '"She Was Poor but She Was Honest"', and Patrick actually had tears in his eyes. 'For goodness sake!' said Sarah, and put her arms around him. As people did so often: There there! He complained they patronized him, and they said, But you need it, with your wounded heart always on view. All this had been going on for years. But things had changed . . . Sonia wasn't going to spoil him. Now, at the foot of the stairs, she looked critically at Patrick who—always ornamental, and even bizarre—was today like a beetle, in a shiny green jacket, his black hair in spikes. But Sonia, in the height of fashion, wore black full Dutch-boy trousers, a camouflage T-shirt from army surplus and over it a black lace bolero from some flea market, desert boots, a jet Victorian choker necklace, many rings and earrings. Her hair, in a variation of a 1920s shingle, was in a tight point at the back, and in front in deeply curving lobes, like a spaniel's ears. But her hair was seldom the same for more than a day or two. Her get-up did not please Patrick. He had already been heard shrilly criticizing her for lack of chic. 'Being a freak isn't smart, love,' he had said. To which she had replied, 'And who's talking?'

Sarah did not go to bed on the night before she was due to meet Stephen Ellington-Smith. For one thing, she had not finished cleaning until three in the morning. Then she decided to do the programme notes after all. Then she reread Julie's journals, preparing herself for what she believed would be a fight with Julie's Angel.

'Look,' she imagined herself saying, 'Julie never saw herself as a victim. She saw herself as having choice. Until 1902 and her mother's death, she could have gone home to Martinique. Her mother actually wrote saying she was welcome any time. There's even a rather silly letter from her half-brother, who took over the estate when the father died, making jokes about their relationship; it was insulting in a sort of schoolboy way. He said the father had told him to "look after" Julie. But she didn't reply. She wondered whether she should be a prostitute—don't forget this was the time of *les grandes horizontales*.

But she said she had no taste for luxury, and that did seem to be essential for a high-class tart. She was offered a job as a *chanteuse* in a nightclub in Marseilles, but she said it would be too emotionally demanding, she would have no time for her music and her painting. Anyway, she hated provincial towns. She did actually have the chance of going to Paris in a touring company as a singer. But this was nothing like her dreams of Paris. She said in her journal, *If Rémy asked me to go to Paris and live with him there . . . we could live quietly, we could have* real *friends . . .* The underline there says everything, I think. She goes on. *Of course it is out of the question, though I saw him with his wife at the fête. It is clear they do not love each other.* She was invited to go as governess in a lawyer's household in Avignon: he was a widower. Several men wanted to set her up in Nice or Marseilles as a mistress. These offers were merely recorded, as she might have written, It was hot today, or, It was cold.

'We could easily present Julie in terms of what she refused. And what did she actually choose? A little stone house in the forest. "The cow-byre," as the citizens contemptuously called it. She chose to live alone, paint and draw and compose her music and, every night of her life, write a commentary on it.

'Yes, I agree it is not easy to make of this a riveting drama. Not easy even if we keep the form you have chosen. Act One: Paul. Act Two: Rémy. Act Three: Philippe. Yes, you could argue that she did write, *I don't think I could bear to move away from my little house where everything speaks to me of love.* As George Sand might have written. But don't forget she went on, *I live here exactly as my mother did in her house. The difference is that she has been kept all her life. By one man—my father. She always loved him and never had choice. She could not leave his estate because if she did she could have earned her living only as a brothel-keeper (like her mother and her grandmother, or so she hinted). Or as an ordinary prostitute, or perhaps as a housekeeper. What were her accomplishments? She could cook. She could dress. She knew about plants and herbs. Presumably she knew about love but we never discussed love, that is, the making of it, because she destined me to be a young lady and she didn't want to raise thoughts in my mind about her, about what she is really like (and that is in itself so touching it could almost break my heart, because how else could I have defined myself, what I am, if not by understanding her?). But I am very much afraid, if we sat alone and talked like women, I would hear her say, I live here in this house because everything in it and near it reminds me of love. And included in this love would be memories of the shadows of great trees on her walls, and in the mirror of her sitting room and on the ceilings of her bedroom, and the damp, the everlasting humidity, and the heavy smell of flowers and of wet vegetation, and a smell something like the wet fur of animals that filled the house when it rained. But the fact is, my mother could not have left her house and her life even if she wanted to, but I can leave here at any time.*

'Where in all this do we see the victim?'

It was not that she was afraid of any financial consequences of refusing his play, because he had written, 'I am sure it goes without saying that my support for the play will not be in any way affected if you all decide my little attempt is not good enough.'

He was already at a table in a restaurant she was relieved to find was not one of the currently fashionable ones. A large, rather dark, old-fashioned room, and quiet. He was at first glance a country gentleman. As she advanced towards him she reflected that it was surely remarkable that when she returned to the office and answered Mary Ford's query, 'What's he like?' with 'He's a country gentleman, old style'—then Mary would at once know what she meant. Her parents, or Mary Ford's, her grandparents or Mary's, would not at once be able to 'place' many people in today's Britain, but they would know Stephen Ellington-Smith at a glance. He was a man of about fifty, large but not fat. He was big-framed and, authoritatively but casually, seemed to take up a lot of space. His face was blond and open: green-eyed, sandy-lashed; and his hair, once fair, was greying. His clothes were as you'd expect: but Sarah found herself automatically making notes for the next time they needed to fit out such a character in a play. Their essence, she decided, was that they would be unnoticeable if he was stalking a deer. His mildly checked brownish-yellow jacket was like a zebra's coat in that it was designed to merge.

He watched her come towards him, rose, pulled out a chair. His inspection, she knew, was acute, but not defensive. She felt he liked her, but then, people on the whole tended to.

'There you are,' said he. 'I must say you are a relief. I don't know quite what I expected, though.' Then, before they had even settled themselves, he said, 'I really do have to make it clear that I'm not going to mind if you people have decided against my play. I'm not a playwright. It was a labour of love.'

He was saying this as one does to clear the ground before another—the real problem is faced. And she was thinking of a conversation in the office. Mary had remarked, 'All the same, it's a funny business. He's been involved with Julie Vairon for a good ten years one way or another. What's in it for him?' Quite so. Why should this man, 'A regular amateur of the arts, old style, you know'—so he had been described by the Arts Council official who had suggested approaching him as a patron—have been involved with that problematical Frenchwoman for a decade or more? The reason was almost certainly the irrational and quirky thing that is so often the real force behind people and events, and often not mentioned, or even noticed. This was what Mary Ford had been hinting at. More than hinting. She had said, 'If we're going to have problems with him, let's have them out in the open right from the beginning.' 'What sort of problems do you expect?' Sarah had asked, for she respected Mary's intuition. 'I don't know.' Then she sang, to the tune of 'Who Is Sylvia', 'Who is Julie, what is she . . .'

They began by talking practicalities. There was the difficulty that began *Julie Vairon*'s career. The play was to have gone on in

London at The Green Bird, one of three planned for the summer season. By chance, Jean-Pierre le Brun, an official from Belles Rivières, heard from the Rostand family, which had been very co-operative, that a play was imminent, and he flew to London to protest. How was it that Belles Rivières had not been consulted? The truth was, the Founding Four had not thought of it, but that was because they had not seen the piece as ambitious enough to involve the French. Besides, Belles Rivières did not have a theatre. And, as well, *Julie Vairon* was in English. Jean-Pierre had accepted that the English had been quicker to see the possibilities of Julie, and no one wanted to deny them that honour. There was no question of taking Julie Vairon away from The Green Bird. That was hardly possible, at this stage. But he was genuinely and bitterly hurt that Belles Rivières had been excluded. What was to be done? Very well, the English version could be used for a run in France. Yes, unfortunately it had to be admitted that if tourists were attracted, then they would be more likely to speak English than French. And besides, so many of the English themselves were settled in the area . . . he shrugged, leaving them to decide what he thought of this state of affairs.

So it was decided. And what about the money? For The Green Bird could not finance the French run. No problem, cried Jean-Pierre; the town would provide the site, using Julie's own little house in the woods—or what was left of it. But Belles Rivières did not have the resources to pay for the whole company for a run of two weeks. It was at this point that an American patron came in, to add his support. How had he heard of this, after all, pretty dicey proposition? Someone in the Arts Council had recommended it and this was because of Stephen's reputation.

At this point, mutual support and helpfulness was being expressed mostly in photographs back and forth, London to Belles Rivières, London to California, Belles Rivières to California. It turned out that there was already a Musée Julie Vairon in Belles Rivières. Her house was visited by pilgrims.

Stephen was disturbed. 'I wonder what she'd think of so many people in *her* forest. *Her* house.'

'Didn't we tell you we were going to use her house for the French run? Didn't you see the promotional material?'

'I suppose I hadn't really taken it in.' He seemed to be debating whether to trust her. 'I even felt bad about writing that play—invading her privacy, you know.' Then, as she found herself unable to reply to this, for it was a new note, and unexpected, he added abruptly, thrusting out his chin small-boy style, 'You have understood, I am sure, that I am hopelessly in love with Julie?' Then gave a helpless, painful grimace, flung himself back in his chair, pushed away his plate, and looked at her, awaiting a verdict.

She attempted a quizzical look, but his gesture was impatient. 'Yes, I am besotted with her. I have been since I first heard her music at that festival. In Belles Rivières, you know. She's the woman for me. I knew that at once.'

He was trying to sound whimsical but was failing.

'I see,' she said.

'I hope you do. Because that's the whole point.'

'You aren't expecting me to say anything boring, like, She's been dead for over eighty years?'

'You can say it if you like.'

The silence that followed had to accommodate a good deal. It was not that his passion was 'crazy'—that portmanteau word, but that he was sitting there four-square and formidable, determined that she should not find it so. He waited, apparently at his ease because he had made his ultimatum, and he even glanced about at this familiar scene of other eaters, waiters, and so on, but she knew that here, at this very point, was what he was demanding in return for his very sizeable investment. She had to accept him, his need.

After a time she heard herself remark, 'You don't like her journals very much, do you?'

At this he let out a breath. It would have been a sigh if he had

not been measuring it, checking it, even, for too much self-revela-
tion. He shifted his legs abruptly. He looked away, as if he might
very well get up and escape—and then made himself face her
again. She liked him very much then. She liked him more and
more. It was because she felt at ease with him, absolutely able to say
anything.

'You've put your finger on . . . no, I don't. No, when I read her
journals I feel—shut out. She slams a door in my face. It's not
what I . . .'

'What you are in love with?'

'I don't think I'd like that cold intelligence of hers directed at
me.'

'But when one is in love one's intelligence does go on, doesn't it?
Commenting on—'

'On *what*?' he cut in. 'No, if she'd been happy she'd never have
written all that. All that was just . . . self-defence.'

At this she had to laugh, because of the enormity of his dis-
missal of—as far as she was concerned—the most interesting aspect
of Julie.

'Oh all right, laugh,' he said grumpily, but with a smile. She
could see he did not mind her laughing. Perhaps he even liked it.
There was something about him of a spreading, a relaxation, as if he
had held a breath for too long and was at last able to let it go. 'But
you don't understand, Sarah—I may call you Sarah? Those journals
are such an accusation.'

'But not of you.'

'I wonder. Yes, I do, often. What would I have done? Perhaps she
would have written of me as she did about Rémy. *I represented to
him everything he had ever dreamed about when he hoped to be larger
than his family, but in the end he was not more than the sum of his
family.*'

'And is that what she represents to you? An escape from your
background?'

'Oh no,' he said at once. 'To me she represents—well, every-thing.'

She could feel her whole self rejecting this mad exaggeration. Her body, even her face, was composing itself into critical lines, without any directing intention from her intelligence. She lowered her eyes. But he was watching her—yes, she already knew that close, intelligent look—and he knew what she was feeling, for he said, 'Please don't tell me you don't know what I mean.'

'Perhaps,' she said cautiously, 'I have decided to forget it.'

'Why?' he enquired, not intending flattery. 'You are a good-look-ing woman.'

'I am a good-looking woman *still*,' said she. 'I am *still* a good-looking woman. Quite so. That's it. I haven't been in love for twenty years. Recently I've been thinking about that—twenty years.' As she spoke she was amazed that she was saying to this stranger (but she knew he was not that) things she had never said to dear and good friends, her *family*—that is what they were—at the theatre. She put on the humour and maternal style that seemed more and more her style: 'And what was it all about, I wonder now, all that . . . absur-dity?'

'Absurdity?' And he let out that grunt of laughter that means isolation in the face of wilful misunderstanding.

'All that anguish and lying awake at night,' she insisted, forcing herself to remember that indeed she had done *all that*. (It occurred to her she had not even acknowledged, for years, that she had done *all that*.) 'Thank God it can never happen to me again. I tell you, getting old has its compensations.' Here she stopped. It was because of his acute examination of her. She felt at once that her voice had rung false. She was blushing—she felt hot, at any rate. He was, there was no doubt, a handsome man, or had been. He was a pretty good proposition even now. Twenty years ago perhaps . . . and here she smiled ironically at him, for she knew her hot cheeks were making confessions. She went on, however, actually thinking that if he could be so brave, then so could she. 'What I think now is, I was in love too often.'

'I'm not talking about the little inflammations.'

Again she had to laugh. 'Well, perhaps you are right.' Right about what?—and she could see he was finding the phrase, as she did the moment it was out, a bromide, dishonest. 'But why do we assume it always means the same thing to everyone—being in love? Perhaps "little inflammations" is accurate enough, for a lot of people. Sometimes when I see someone in love I think that a good screw would settle it.' Here she took from him, as she had expected to, a surprised and even hard look at the ugly term, which she had used deliberately. Women who are 'getting on' often have to do this. One minute (so it feels) they are using the language of our time (ugly, crude, honest), and in the next, they have become, or feel they soon will if they don't do something about it, 'little old ladies', because the younger generation have begun to censor their speech, as if to children. But, she thought, critical of herself, there is no need to take up stances with this man.

He said, after a long pause, while he examined her, 'You've simply decided to forget, that's all it is.'

She conceded, 'Very well, then, I have. Perhaps I don't want to remember. If a man had ever been everything to me—that's what you said, *everything* . . . but I did have a very good marriage. But *everything* . . . let's talk about your play, Stephen.' And she deliberately (dishonestly) let this look as if she didn't want to talk about her dead husband.

'All right,' he agreed, after a pause. 'But it's not important. I don't really mind about it. Scrap it.'

'Wait. I'm going to keep a good bit of it. The dialogue is good.' This was not tact. His dialogue in parts was better than hers. Now she knew why. 'Do you realize you have made Rémy the focus of everything? The real love? What about Paul? After all, she did run away to France with him.'

'Rémy was the love of her life. She said so herself. It's in her journals.'

'But she didn't get into her stride with the journals until after Paul ditched her. Suppose we had a day-by-day record of her feelings for Paul, as we have for Rémy?' He definitely did not like this. 'You identify with Rémy—and it is your own background. Minor aristocracy?'

'Well, perhaps.'

'And you've hardly mentioned the son of her worthy printer. Julie and Robert took one look at each other and, quote, *If you have a talent for the impossible, then at least recognize it.* After that, she killed herself. It seems to me the printer's son could easily have been as important as Rémy.'

'It seems to *me* you want to make her a kind of tart, falling in love with one man after another.'

She couldn't believe her ears. 'How many women have you been in love with?'

Obviously he couldn't believe his. 'I don't really see the point of discussing the double standard.'

They were looking at each other with dislike. There was nothing for it but to laugh.

Then he insisted, 'I have been in love, seriously, with one woman.'

She waited for him to say 'my wife'—he was married—or someone else, but he meant Julie. She said, 'It's my turn to say that you have decided to forget. But that isn't the point. At the risk of being boring, art *is* one thing and life another. You don't seem to see the problem. In your version, her main occupation was being in love.'

'Wasn't being in love her main occupation?'

'She was in love a lot of her time. It wasn't her main occupation. But these days we cannot have a play about a woman ditched by two lovers who then commits suicide. We can't have a romantic heroine.'

Clearly she could not avoid this conversation: she reflected it was probably the tenth time in a month.

'I don't see why not. Girls are going through this kind of thing all the time. They always have.'

'Look. Couldn't we leave it to people who write theses? It's an aesthetic question. I am simply telling you what I know. Out of theatre experience. After all, even the Victorians made a comic song out of "She Was Poor but She Was Honest". But I think I know how to solve it.' Her duplicity with him would be limited to not telling him she had solved it already. 'We can leave the story exactly as you have it. But what will put the edge on it . . . there is something; I hope you are going to ask what.'

'Very well,' he said, and she could see that this was the moment when he finally gave up *his* play. With good grace. As one would expect from someone like him.

'We will use what she thought about it all . . .'

'Her journals!'

'Partly. Her journals. But even more, her music. There are her songs, and a lot of her music lends itself—we can use words from the journals and fit them to the music. Her story will have a commentary—her own.'

He thought about this an uncomfortably long time. 'It is astonishing—it is really extraordinary—the way Julie is always being taken away from me.' Here he looked embarrassed and said, 'All right, I know that sounds mad.'

She said, 'Oh well, we are all mad,' but, hearing her comfortable maternal voice, knew at once she was not going to be allowed to get away with it. Again she was finding his acute look hard to bear. 'I do wonder what it is you are mad about,' he remarked, with more than a flick of malice.

'Ah, but I've reached those heights of common sense. You know, the evenly lit unproblematical uplands where there are no surprises.'

'I don't believe you.'

You could say their smiles at each other, companionable but satiric, marked a stage.

The restaurant was emptying. They had come to the end of what they had to say to each other, at least for now. Both were making the small movements that indicate a need to separate.

'You don't want to hear any more of my ideas for the play?'

'No, I shall leave it to you.'

'But your name will be on it, with mine, as co-authors.'

'That would be more than generous.'

They left the restaurant, slowly. At this very last moment, it seemed they did not want to part. They said goodbye and walked away from each other. Only then did they remember they had been together for nearly three hours, talking like intimates, had told each other things seldom said even to intimates. This idea stopped them both, and turned them around at the same moment on the pavement of St Martin's Lane. They stood examining each other's faces with curiosity, just as if they had not been sitting a few feet apart, for so long, talking. Their smiles confessed surprise, pleasure, and a certain disbelief, which latter emotion—or refusal of it—was confirmed when he shrugged and she made a spreading gesture with her hands which said, Well, it's all too much for me! At which they actually laughed, at the way they echoed, or mirrored, each other. Then they turned and walked energetically away, he to his life, she to hers.

In the office, Sarah found Mary Ford making a collage of photographs for publicity, while Sonia stood over her, hands on her hips, in fact learning, but making it look as if she was casually interested.

Sarah told Mary that Stephen Ellington-Smith was a country gentleman, old style. That he was too magnanimous to be petty about his play. That he was, in fact, a poppet. Mary said, 'Well, that's a good thing, isn't it?' Sonia took in this exchange with her little air of detachment.

Sarah sat with her back to the two young women, pretending to work, listening . . . no, one young woman and a middle-aged one: she had to accept that about Mary, even if it did hurt. They had all become so used to each other. . . . Sonia was there in that office—not strictly her territory—not only to learn but to stake a claim. She wanted to be made responsible for the next production, *Hedda Gabler.* 'You people will be busy with your Julie,' she said. There was no need for the two senior officials to confer: they knew what each other thought. And why not? They were not likely to find anyone sharper, cleverer—and more ambitious—than Sonia. 'Why not?' said Mary, and without turning around, Sarah said, 'Why not?' In this way confirming Sonia's position, and a much larger salary. Sonia left. 'Why not?' said Mary again, quietly, and Sarah turned herself about and smiled confirmation of Mary's real message, which was that there really was no doubt of it—an epoch was indeed over.

Sarah did not need a week to use Stephen's dialogue where it fitted, but decided to pretend she had needed that time, so he would not feel his contribution was inconsiderable. But when she was actually seated there, in her room, the mess of papers she was already calling the script spread about, a week did not seem too much. For one thing, she was unhappy with the existing translation of the journals. She had made her own of some of the passages, those that would accompany the music. She had had to get permission from the Rostands. 'After all,' she had written, 'it is only a question of a few pages. It is not as if I were proposing to make a new translation of all Julie's writings.' In fact she wished she could. She privately believed that people loving literature who chanced to read her translations would at once see how much better, more vivacious, her language was, how much closer to Julie's self. Perhaps one day she would make a new translation, choosing different passages: she did not necessarily agree with the English translator's choices. She understood Julie much better than . . . Sitting there, the word processor pushed to one side, for she was still at the stage of words scribbled on loose sheets with a Biro—yes, pretty old-fashioned, she knew—she thought, That's something of a claim I'm making . . . conceited? Perhaps. But I think it's true. This young woman hasn't understood the first thing about Julie . . . I care very much that her translation is flat, no effervescence. *I care too much.* I am altogether too much involved in this business. Yes, of course you have to be totally submerged in what you are working on, even if a week after it's finished you've forgotten it. . . . What is it about that bloody Julie: she gets under people's skin; she's under mine. Look how this thing takes off, spreads itself about—she's blowing us all apart, and we know it. I really am intoxicated—probably all these months of listening to the music. Well, I have to listen to it this week . . . I'm making everything too complicated: I've spent years and years weighted with Duty, working like a madwoman, and if I don't watch out I'll go sailing off into the sky like a hydrogen balloon.

She sat, hour after hour, choosing words, hearing them: seductive. Like music, particularly when choosing words that will be congruous with music. The words, which she was already hearing sung, were running in her head. This is an affliction of words' users and makers. Words appear in your mind and dance there to rhythms you consciously know nothing about. Tags and rags of words: they can be an indication of a hidden state of mind. They can jiggle or sing for days, driving you mad. They can be like invisible film, like cling film, between you and reality. She was hardly the first person to have noted this. D. H. Lawrence, for instance: 'She was angry with him, turning everything into words. Violets were Juno's eyelids, and windflowers were unravished brides. How she hated words, always coming between her and life: they did the ravishing, if anything did: ready-made words and phrases, sucking all the life out of living things.' Yes, this was an illustration of exactly what she complained of: there was the quotation, pat and patented, colonizing her mind. Well, when she had finished this task, Julie's words, not to mention the Countess Dié's, would linger and then sink back into that vast invisible Book of Great Quotations, leaving her in peace . . . she had long ago created a saving mental image, to be used at moments when her brain was so abuzz with words she seemed to prickle all over with their energy.

She imagined a shepherd boy from a long time ago—hundreds of years, for it was more restful if this scene lived in an antique air, as if it had come off a wall or the side of a vase. This young creature was illiterate, had never seen words on a page, or on a parchment. There were tales in his head, for there has never been a country or a culture without them. But when he sat on his dry hillside, under his tree, watching—what? sheep, probably—his mind was empty, and memories or thoughts came to him in the shape of pictures. Sarah did not allow this poor youth even the traditional shepherd's pipe. Silence it had to be. Only a breeze moving through the tree he sat under. A cricket. The sheep cropping the grass. This figure had to be a boy. A girl—no. She would almost certainly be wondering whom she would be married off to. Girls were seldom allowed to be alone, but it did not matter, a girl or a boy—and silence. Sarah tried to imagine what it would be like not to have a brain set by the printed word. Not easy.

When the week was up, Sarah telephoned Stephen to say she believed the script—the libretto? how was this hybrid to be described?—was ready. No doubt that he was pleased to hear her voice, and she was disproportionately pleased that his voice warmed and lifted. Then he said, 'But you know, you really don't have to . . . ,' in the way of someone not expecting much consideration. Which was surely remarkable?

'But of course,' said Sarah. 'We are co-authors after all.'

'I'm not going to complain. Tomorrow?'

And now began a time which, when she looked back on it, seemed like a country where she had gone by chance, one she had not known existed, a place of charm, a landscape like a dream landscape, with its own strong atmosphere, that speaks in a language one half knows or has forgotten. Before meeting Stephen some-where—a restaurant, a garden, a park, she would say to herself, Oh come on, you're imagining it. When it was time to part, she was reluctant, and made excuses to put off the moment. She knew he was doing the same. He too probably thought before meeting her or after they separated, 'Nonsense, I'm imagining it.' But they could not doubt that when they were together they were in a pleasantness, an ease, an air different from quotidian life. A charmed place where anything could be said. And yet this was not a case of two people finding each other's lives a reason for being intrigued. If she was not much interested in his, it was because she had not experienced any-thing like it: he was rich, he owned a large and historic house. When he asked about her life, she gave him the facts: she had been married young, widowed young, she had successfully brought up two chil-dren by herself. She had almost by accident—so it seemed now—become well known in the theatre. Oh yes, she had for a time been responsible for her brother's child. He listened, thought, and remarked, 'When people tell you about their lives—well, the plot—they don't tell you much about themselves. Not really.' As if he thought she was about to disagree, he went on, 'That is, not if they are people with anything to them. What's interesting about people is not what life hands out to them. We can't help that, can we?'

He was making some kind of plea for himself, or an explana-tion, so she believed. But why did he need to? He often seemed to feel the need to apologize. What for?

Meanwhile they went on—well, yes, they were enjoying them-selves.

'I do enjoy being with you,' he said, and not only did this have the frankness—the generosity—she expected from him, but he sounded surprised. Was enjoyment not something he expected? Well, this kind of delightfulness was not anything she was used to either. She really had had to work so hard, had been so weighed down with responsibility . . . but surely a man with so many advantages did not lack opportunities for . . . but it was the two of them, their being together, as if they both owned a key to this place whose air was happiness.

And they might shake their heads, offering each other ironic smiles because of the improbability of this affinity. Charm. Like opening a wonderfully wrapped package and finding in it a gift secretly hankered after for years but never really expected. Her life had become charmed because of this Stephen What's-his-name, who was in love with a dead woman. Which passion they discussed a good deal, he with perfect good humour because, as he informed her, he had carried away *his* Julie into some fastness where she, Sarah, could not come. 'I simply have to save her from you,' he said. They had fallen into the habit of talking whimsically about his craziness—she could use the word because he did. 'You're crazy, Stephen.' 'Yes, I'll freely admit it, Sarah.' But to say someone is crazy is almost to make it all harmless. It is a joky little word.

Yet she believed he was doing himself real harm. Sometimes, when a silence had fallen between them she saw his face sombre, abstracted: yes, indeed 'his' Julie was in some deep place inside him where he visited her. But this was not doing him good, to judge from the dark hurt look he wore then. Sometimes, when she saw that look, she decided not to think about what it meant, for fear she too would succumb. She had learned this habit of self-protection with Joyce: there was a point when she decided not to enter imaginatively into the poor girl's state of mind, for fear of being taken over. Surely there was something here that contradicted the outward life of this man, which was everything it should be, public-spirited, sane, generous, open for anyone to look at and judge. To joke about his 'crush' on Julie, choosing to avert her mind from what it might mean, saved their friendship from Julie. For Sarah—and she was ashamed of the irrationality of it—wondered more and more what witchery that woman must have had to influence people so strongly after she was dead. One might even fancifully see her as Orpheus, charming victims into dark places, by the power of her music and her words.

As for Sarah's play—or script—Stephen said, 'You've got her pretty well. I do realize I was being partial—I mean, in the play I did. And I'm glad you've made me see her . . . rounded out. It's odd, what a block I had about reading her thoughts. But it hasn't changed what I feel about her. You see, we were made for each other, Julie and I. Well, Sarah, your face isn't exactly designed to hide what you think . . . is that because you don't believe there can be someone made for you? I remember I thought that once. But the truth is, there can be just the one person. It's funny, isn't it, how few people there are who . . . but you can have this feeling about the most unlikely people. I remember once—I was in Kenya, on active service. Everyone's forgotten Kenya. Too many wars, I suppose. I met this woman. She was an Indian woman. Older than I was. And it was there . . . we knew each other at once. You have to trust in this kind of thing. If you don't, you are denying the best part of life. You and I have something of the kind—well, we know that. It has nothing to do with age, or sex, or colour, or anything of that sort.'

Sarah was saying to herself, about 'this thing I have with Stephen', that if she had had a brother—a real one, not a clown like Hal—then this is what it might have been like. Extraordinary it had not ever occurred to her that to have a brother might be a pleasant thing.

Sarah and Mary flew together to Nice. When high in the air over Europe, Sarah observed that Mary's mouth was moving as she sat with closed eyes. No, Mary was not praying. She made a point of repeating her mantra as a public relations woman several times a day: 'This summer dozens of festivals will compete for attention. The Julie Vairon Festival will be only one of them. I shall make sure it will be the best, the most visible, and that everyone will want to come.'

They were met at the airport by Jean-Pierre le Brun, whom they felt they already knew, after so many consultations by telephone. He was dark, good-looking, well-dressed, combining in that uniquely French way correctness, politeness, and a practised scepticism, as if at university he had taken Anarchy and Law as his main subjects, and these had merged and become subdued to a style. Meeting the Englishwomen, also officials of a kind, he managed to express an extreme of respectful politeness, with a readiness to be affronted. He was not aware that he radiated resentment as well, but in no time he had forgotten about it, for he decided he liked them. They enjoyed an amiable lunch at Les Collines Rouges, Belles Rivières' main café-restaurant. It then being late for business in the town hall, he drove them off into the wooded hills behind the town, first speeding along a tarmacked road and then driving not much slower when it became a rough track. This was the road Julie had followed when she walked to and from Belles Rivières. 'She walked in all weathers, la pauvre,' said Jean-Pierre. Here two unsentimental Englishwomen smiled at the Frenchman who was being so formally sentimental, exactly as expected. And in fact he had tears in his eyes.

At the track's end they walked up a rocky path till they stood in a wide space between trees and rocks. The soil was a vibrant red in the late afternoon sun. The green of the trees was intense. The air was full of a murmur like bees, but this was the river and the water-fall: apparently there had been heavy rain. There was not much left of the 'cow-byre' the citizens had complained about. To quote from Mary Ford's publicity brochure: *A little stone house, cold, uncomfortable, was where Julie Vairon lived in the south of France, from the day of her landing penniless off the ship until she died. It had been a charcoal burner's house.* 'Well, why not?' Mary demanded. 'Someone must have lived there before she did.' *After Julie's death it stood empty for many years. Then the farmer Leyvecque, whose grandsons*

still farm in the area, used it as a stable. A storm took off the tile roof.
If the town of Belles Rivières had not rescued it, there would be left
only a heap of rubble, but instead the site is now a charming theatre,
where this summer . . .

There wasn't much left of the house. The long back wall stood,
and parts of the side wall, now capped with cement to stop them
collapsing further. Behind the house red earth sloped to the trees.
Umbrella pines. Oaks. Olives and chestnuts. Some of these trees had
known Julie. The air was full of healthy aromatic smells. The three
people walked back and forth over the site where Julie's life would
shortly be re-enacted. Well, her life as edited by the necessities of the
production. The acting would be on the space on a side of the
house. The musicians would be on a low stone platform—at once
Sarah and Mary began explaining that this platform must be larger,
and nearer the acting area, because of the importance of the music.
Jean-Pierre argued for form's sake and then said he had not understood the music would carry so much of the meaning. He gracefully
gave in, as he had been going to from the start. These negotiations
were going on in a mixture of French and English—the English for
Mary's benefit. She had explained over lunch that she could not
learn languages, in the way the English have, as if afflicted by a
defective gene as yet unknown to science. Because it was Mary who
was going to have to work with Jean-Pierre on publicity, Sarah listened to what turned out to be a pretty fundamental clash of views.
He said he expected an audience of about two hundred for each
night of the two weeks. Mary protested that many more must be
planned for. Jean-Pierre said that one could not expect large audiences for a new play, and one with only local significance. Still
gracefully disagreeing, the three arrived back in the town. Jean-
Pierre left them at their hotel to return to his family, and it was with
regret. Mary and he were making a game out of her inability to
speak French and were communicating in Franglais. Clearly he
enjoyed the surprise of this large, calm, apparently stolid young

woman, with her equable blue eyes, taking off into ever surrealer flights of language.

There were three hotels. Among them the whole company would be distributed. All this was arranged by Sarah next morning, before the visit to the town hall, which was a formality, since everything had been already agreed on. Then Mary went off to interview descendants of the Imberts and the Rostands, Paul's family and Rémy's. Jean-Pierre went with her. Both clans had announced themselves only too willing to aid the Julie Vairon Festival, which would add such lustre to the little town. She also intended to visit the Julie Vairon Museum, and the archives, and the house—still as it was—where Julie would have lived had she decided to marry Philippe the master printer. And how about Philippe's son Robert's family? Perhaps they would agree—but they were a good way off. All this was going to take at least three days. Sarah flew back to London by herself.

She telephoned Stephen. On hearing each other's voices they at once entered a region of privileged complicity, like children with secrets. This new note had been struck from the moment the script was judged finished by the Founding Four. When adults do this, it often means they are over-burdened, or even threatened in some way. Well, Stephen's Julie was certainly threatened. 'Now Julie's gone public . . . ,' as he put it.

She told him what she had seen of Julie's house. Stephen had visited it ten years earlier when bushes were growing up through the floors and dislodging stones from the walls. She told him of the three hotels, two new, all named after Julie. She described Jean-Pierre. Because of her tone, he enquired, 'And how does he see her?' and she was enabled to murmur, 'La pauvre . . . la pauvre . . . ,' so that Stephen was able to exclaim, 'Sentimental bloody . . .' and she laughed. In short, they behaved as they had to in this ancient business of the French and the English finding each other impossible, to the satisfaction of both. But perhaps each nation's need always to find the same traits in the other imposes a style, and so it is all per-petuated.

And now she and anyone else from The Green Bird who was interested were invited to the house in Oxfordshire, because there would be an evening of music and dancing, a miniature festival, and Julie's music would be sung. Sarah had been invited for the whole weekend. She did not really want to see him in his house, his other life—his real life? Their friendship was threatened, so she felt. Surely it was a tenuous thing, based on imaginings, on phantoms? She knew very well what she was afraid of: that the 'magic', the charm, would simply evaporate. But of course she had to go, and she even wanted to. During the week before that weekend, they met for din-ner, on his suggestion. She could see that he too was uneasy. He was giving her information, facts, one after another, fielding them to her, she thought, and even said it to him, earning a smile—like an elder brother practising bowling on a sister, watching to make sure she accepted what was sent in the right way. 'No, no,' she parodied, 'don't step back, you'll knock the stumps off! Elbow *up*, as you bring the bat forward.'

The house was his wife Elizabeth's. His was the money. No, it certainly was not for mutual convenience they had married, but the house was central to their lives: they both loved it.

There were three children, boys, at boarding school. They like boarding school, he insisted, in a way that said he often had to insist. She was interested that people like him felt they had to defend the sacred institution. Boarding school suited them, said Stephen. Yes, it was a pity they hadn't a daughter. 'Particularly for me,' he said. 'Perhaps if we'd had a daughter, Julie wouldn't have got to me the way she did.' But there would not be another child. Poor Elizabeth had more than done her bit.

They were good friends, he and Elizabeth, he said, choosing his words, but not looking into her face, rather down at his plate. Not because he was evading something, but because—she felt—there was more he might be saying, which he expected her to see for herself.

He liked to think he managed the estate productively. Elizabeth certainly ran the house well. Every summer they had festivals. 'Half the county come to them, and we do them proud. Elizabeth had the idea first, but it was because she knows it's the kind of thing I like. Now we both put everything we've got into it.' This was said with satisfaction, even pride. They were going to expand, become something like Glyndebourne, only on a much smaller scale. And only in the summers. Sarah would see it all for herself, when she came.

Again she felt that another meaning was carried by these words: and wondered if he was aware that everything he said seemed to be signalling: Listen to this carefully.

'I want you to see it all,' he insisted, this time looking at her. 'I like the idea of your being there. I'm not really the kind of man who likes his life in compartments—yes, I know there are plenty who do, but I . . .' His smile had energy in it, the mild elation that seemed to expand him when he talked of his house and his life in it. 'You mustn't think I don't know how extraordinarily lucky I am,' he said, as they strolled to the tube. 'Well, you'll see for yourself. I don't take anything for granted, I assure you.'

She was to take the train to Oxford in the mid-afternoon on Friday. At two the doorbell rang, and there was Joyce. Having not seen her for some time, Sarah saw her with new eyes, if only for a moment. At once her heart began to feel an only too familiar oppression. As Joyce walked in she seemed to be straying, or wandering in some private dream. She was a tall girl, now very thin. When her sisters put make-up on her she could be lovely. Her hair—and this is what struck to the heart—was marvellous, a fine light gold, and full of vitality, loose around her pasty spotty little face. 'Make yourself some tea,' said Sarah, but Joyce fell into a chair. She really did seem ill. Her great blue eyes were inflamed. Her characteristic smile—she had faced the world with it since she stopped being a child, was bright, scared, anxious. Yes, she was ill. Sarah took her temperature and it was 101.

'I want to stay here,' Joyce said. 'I want to live here with you.'

Her dilemma was being put to Sarah in as dramatic a form as it could be. She had been afraid of something like this. All kinds of pressure, though none that could be visible, or even probable, to anyone but herself, were urging her to give in at once. But she was remembering something Stephen had said: 'You've been looking after her for—how long? Did you say ten years? Why don't her parents look after her?' And when Sarah could not reply, 'Well, Sarah, it looks a funny business to me.'

'At the time it seemed quite natural.'

But his silence was because he had decided not to say what he thought. Yet usually they did say what they thought. Would he have said, 'You're crazy, Sarah' and admitted her to the company of those who behave as they do because they cannot help themselves? And another time he had remarked, 'If you hadn't taken her in, what do you think would have happened?' This was not the hot and indignant voice she was used to hearing from people who feel threatened, because they are thinking, If you take on such a burden, then perhaps I shall be expected to sacrifice myself too. No, he had been thinking it all out. She had never wondered what would have happened to Joyce if she had not looked after her. But would Joyce have been worse off if her aunt had left her to her parents? She couldn't be much worse off, could she?

Now she made herself say, the effort putting severity into her voice, 'Joyce, I'm just leaving. I'm off for the weekend. I'll take you home and put you to bed there.'

'But I've lost the door key,' said Joyce, her eyes filling with tears.

Sarah knew the key had not been lost, but to prove that meant she would have to search Joyce's pathetic grubby bag, which once had been a brightly striped Mexican affair.

She told herself that on this ground she would have to fight, though it was poor ground. If she did not . . . She telephoned the hospital where her brother was a consultant, was told it was his afternoon in Harley Street, rang Harley Street, was told he was with a patient. Sarah said to the receptionist that this was Dr Millgreen's sister, and the call concerned his daughter, who was ill. She would hold on. She held on for a good ten minutes, while Joyce cried quietly in her chair.

At one point she said in a little voice, 'But I want to stay here with you, Auntie.'

'You can't stay here with me now. You're ill, you need treatment.'

'But he'll make me go to hospital. I don't want to.'

'No, but he'd make you stay in bed, and so would I.'

'Why are you all so horrible to me? I want to live with you always.'

'Joyce, none of us has heard one word from you—good God, it must be five months. I was running all over London looking for you.'

At this point the receptionist said Dr Millgreen could not come to the telephone, Mrs Durham must manage. 'Tell my brother that his daughter is in my flat. She is ill. I shall be away until Monday.'

She was angry. That she was full of guilt goes without saying. It was no use telling herself she had no reason to feel guilt.

She said to Joyce, 'I suppose someone will come and fetch you. If not, I should simply get into a taxi and go home.' Here she put some money into the Mexican bag.

Joyce whimpered, 'Oh Auntie, I don't understand.'

Because this was a child talking, not even Joyce the unpredictable adolescent, who did manage to cope with life on some sort of level, Sarah did not reply to her. Instead she said to an adult, reminding herself that Joyce was twenty, 'Look, Joyce, you understand perfectly well. Something or other has happened out there, but of course you'll never tell us what . . .'

Joyce interrupted angrily, 'If I did tell you, you'd take advantage of me and punish me.'

Sarah said, 'I don't remember my punishing you for anything, ever.'

'But my father does. He's always horrible.'

'He is your father. And you have a mother; she stands up for you.' Joyce turned away her face. She was trembling, in spasms. 'You are a grown-up woman, Joyce. You're not a little girl.'

At this a little girl looked vaguely in her aunt's direction with enormous drowned eyes. A small pink mouth stood pathetically half open.

'I'm not going to spend my life looking after you. I don't mind if you come and stay here when I'm here. But I'm not going to wait on you. If you like I'll take you for a holiday somewhere. You certainly look as if you could do with one. Well, we'll talk about it, but not now. I've got a train to catch. I'll ring up from Oxfordshire and find out if you've gone home.'

Joyce would not go home. Late that night Hal might mention to his wife, if he remembered, that the girl was ill and alone in Sarah's flat. Rather, 'Joyce has turned up at Sarah's, and Sarah seems to think she's not well.' Anne, exhausted and irritable, would instruct the two girls, Briony and Nell, to go over to Sarah's. They would be angry with Joyce for disappearing for so long. They would be angry with Sarah for not coping. Everyone would be angry with Sarah. As usual. It crossed Sarah's mind now to think that was indeed a bit odd.

When Sarah got off the train, it was Elizabeth who came to introduce herself. The two women frankly inspected each other, Elizabeth in a way that made Sarah wonder exactly what Stephen had said about her, for Elizabeth had the look of someone checking to make sure information had been correct: apparently, yes, it had. Elizabeth was a smallish woman, with shiny yellow hair held by a black velvet ribbon, and this made her look both efficient and spirited. Her face was round and healthy and her cheeks were country pink. She had unequivocal bright blue eyes. Her body was firm and rounded: if one touched it, one's finger would bounce off, thought Sarah. Everything about this woman told the world, but in a take-it-or-leave it voice, You can rely on me for anything reasonable. She seemed pleased with Sarah and was certainly thinking, Good, I don't have to bother with her, she can look after herself. For Elizabeth—like Sarah—was one of the people who wake every morning with a mind's eye list of items to be dealt with. Sarah had already been crossed off the list.

Now Elizabeth strode off to a station wagon, but slowed so as to adjust to Sarah's pace. The back of the car seemed crammed with large healthy dogs. Elizabeth drove fast and well—what else? She commanded the car with every muscle of her body, as if it were a horse she could not trust not to get out of hand. Meanwhile she gave Sarah information about what they saw as they drove through the jolly countryside. At the top of a rise she stopped the car and said, 'There it is, there's Queen's Gift.' Although she had lived in the house all her life and could hardly be unused to this view, she sounded like a child trying not to be too pleased with itself, and Sarah liked her from that moment.

The house stood four-square on its slight rise, dignified but sprightly, as if a country dance had been magicked into brick, but not without suggestions (the eight barred windows at the top?) that in its long centuries there must have been plenty of drama. It was a hot still afternoon in that summer of 1989, when one perfect day followed another. The house seemed determined to soak in sunlight and store it against the English weather that was bound to set in again soon. There it sat glowing redly amid its English lawns and

shrubs and judiciously disposed trees, take me or leave me, not a
house one could live in without submitting to it, and, clearly,
Elizabeth felt that in presenting the house she was defining herself.
Now she told Sarah she had been born there. Her father had been
born there. Queen's Gift had been in her family one way or another
since it had been built.

They drove slowly through appropriately impressive gates, the
dogs barking and whining at being home, then through a wood of
beeches and oaks, and turned a corner abruptly to approach a side
view of the house, where, on a tall board that pointed the way to a
beech walk, was Julie's face—an impetuous smiling girl—styled in
black and white on a poster. At once Sarah was returned to her own
world, or rather the two worlds slid together. There are times when
everything seems like a film set or a stage set, and the old house had
become a background for *Julie Vairon*, incongruous though that
certainly was.

Stephen emerged from tall doors at the top of a flight of stone
steps that were an invitation (only conditional, for above them was
a notice that said, discreetly, *Cloakrooms*) to the public to ascend
them. Stephen seem worried. He descended the steps, smiling at her,
but on the last one he stopped, and his large hand was curving
around a gently eroded stone ball that crowned a pillar, as if,
because of the habits necessary to a busy man, he was assessing the
condition of this sphere since it might be time for him to do something about it.

He took her suitcase, set it on the bottom step, and said he
would show her around. At this Elizabeth laughed and said, 'But
poor Sarah, can't she have a cup of tea first?' as she relinquished
their guest, her own duty done, to her husband. Sarah waited for a
signal or glance that recognizes a situation, and it came: Elizabeth
shone that smile on them both that says—in this case with good-
humoured irony—'I know what is going on and I don't mind,'
before going off on her own affairs. In fact she had so little interest

in this obligatory little act that the smile had faded before she turned away. There are not many spouses, or partners, strong-minded enough to forgo that look, that smile, or laugh, for it makes a claim, and an even stronger one than jealousy or anger. Stephen glanced at Sarah to see if she had noticed, and then a small grimace signalled, *A pity*, and he said aloud, 'Don't mind. She's got it wrong. If she had ever asked, I would have . . .'

'Oh, but it's a compliment,' she said.

He put his hand inside her elbow. This hand both took posses-sion of Sarah and said it was prepared to relinquish her at the small-est sign that it was taking too much for granted. Sarah, from the world of the theatre, laughed, put her arms around him, and kissed him on both cheeks, one, two. He at once went bright red. He was pleased, though.

'Sarah, I really am so glad to see you here. Don't ever think I'm not.'

Why should she think such a thing?

Apparently he still felt she needed essential instruction. Again he took her arm, this time with confident masculine proprietorship, which she enjoyed (she was prepared to concede) more than per-haps she ought. They walked slowly through gardens and shrub-beries, and past long warm reddish brick walls where roses sent out waves of scent. Late May: the roses were early.

Stephen said he hoped that she, Sarah, and the whole company would give Elizabeth credit for all the work she had done. It was she who had persuaded artistic friends in Paris to get Julie Vairon's pic-tures exhibited. It was she who had approached the television peo-ple to make a documentary. Elizabeth was a generous woman, he insisted.

They walked on grass between two hedges of beech, whose attribute is to remind you, when in full healthy green, that it will hold its own through long winters, withstanding gales, frost, any-thing at all nature chooses to throw at it, never losing so much as a russet leaf. A beech hedge, whether it likes it or not, makes statements of confidence. It refuses pathos.

'She is always generous,' he said again, and, feeling she was being prompted, she asked, 'What does she make of—well, of you and Julie?' But it was the wrong question, for his face said he had already answered her. Disappointment in her made him relinquish her arm, and she, disappointed in her turn, insisted, 'She would admit that one may be jealous of a . . .' She could not bring herself to say, 'a dead woman,' for it was too brutal. Instead she said, '. . . of a ghost?' A foolish, harmless word.

'I don't think she would admit to anything so irrational.'

They had strolled on a good few yards through air that was a mix of warm dry scents all making claims on her memory, when she remarked, 'For one thing, you can't compete with a . . . dead woman.' It was not easy to use that word.

He stopped and turned to look close into her face. 'You say that as if you knew all about jealousy.'

'Did I? I suppose I did.' And hearing in retrospect how she had spoken, she was discomfited. She was off balance. Meanwhile his eyes, green but—seen so close—as full of variegations as the surface of a cut olivine, green specked with black and grey, were full on her face. Trying to laugh, she said, 'I remember saying to myself, That's it, never again, I'll never feel jealousy again.' She knew her voice was full of resentment.

'So you were generous too?'

'If you want to make it generosity . . . I thought of it as self-preservation. I know one thing—funny that I haven't thought of it for ages: but you can kill yourself with jealousy.' She was trying to make her voice light and humorous. She failed.

'You said to whoever it was, Bless you, my child, run off to your little amusements, what we have is so strong it can't affect our marriage?'

'It wasn't my marriage. It was later than that. And I certainly never said, Run along! On the contrary, that was it—finished!' She was surprising herself by the cold anger in her voice. 'I could never say it couldn't affect a marriage or anything else. It was a question of . . .'

'Well?' he demanded, and gripped her elbows in large and confident hands. The strength of those hands spoke direct to her, reminding her . . . His eyes, those interesting pebbles so close to her own, seemed to her now to be tinged with—was that anxiety?

Violent needs conflicted in her. One was to comfort and heal, for she always felt he emanated an appeal, a need: she had never been more aware than now that he guarded a hurt place. But it seemed her own need was stronger, for what burst out of her was: 'Pride. It was pride.' And she was surprised—if she could be more surprised than she had already become, seeing what was revealed of a forgotten past—at the violence in the word. What's the matter with me? she was asking herself, while she withstood the pressure of those uncompromising eyes. 'Of course it was pride. Do you imagine I'd keep a man who wanted someone else?'

She, Sarah—that is, the Sarah of today—had not spoken these words. Some long ago Sarah had said them. It was getting harder every second to stand there between Stephen's hands and sustain that long close examination. She felt ashamed, and her face burned.

'You are talking like the kind of woman you seem determined not to be—to seem to be.'

'What kind of woman?'

'A love woman,' he said. 'A woman who takes her stand on love.'

'Well,' said she, attempting humour again, but with no success, 'I do seem to remember something of the kind.' And was about to walk away from the situation, when he tightened his grip on her elbows.

'Wait, you always run away.'

'But it was all a long time ago. . . . All right, then, I'll try. Do you remember Julie's journals—yes I know you don't like them. When she was writing about her master printer, she said, *And there will inevitably come that night when I know it is not me, Julie, he is hold-ing in his arms, but the wife of the chemist or the farmer's daughter who brought the eggs that afternoon. I'd rather die.* And of course, she did.' Her voice was full of defiance. 'Immature—that's what our Julie was. A mature woman knows that if her husband chooses to fancy the chemist's wife or the girl who is driving the Express delivery cart, and fucks them in her stead, well, it's just one of those things.'

'And vice versa, I think.' He smiled. 'The husband knows he is holding in his arms the stable boy, because his wife is?'

'That's your—his affair.'

'Well, well, well,' he said, full of sardonic relish. He let her go. And as they walked on, while the essences of flower and leaf mean-dered past their faces, 'And that marriage of yours? I really am curi-ous. That little way of yours, all passion spent, amuse yourself, my children, while I benevolently look on.' This was not spiteful, or even resentful: he laughed, a bark of sceptical laughter, but gave her the look of a friend.

Sarah fought to become that Sarah who was able benevolently to look on.

'It lasted ten years. Then he died.' Now she believed that the younger Sarah had taken herself off, back into some dark corner. 'I don't look back on my pursuit of love after that with much admira-tion for myself. I was so immature, you see. I was never prepared to settle for the sensible—you know, a widow with two young children should look for a father for her children.'

He snorted a kind of amusement. Then, 'A real romantic. Who would have thought it? Well, actually, yes, I did, I really did.'

'And I am walking on a lovely afternoon with a man who is besotted—may I use that word?—with a phantom.'

'She is no phantom,' he said gravely.

In front of them the shrubs were thinning: an open space was imminent, showing through the branches.

She heard herself sigh, and he sighed too.

'Sarah! Do you imagine I don't know how all this sounds? I am not so mad that . . . give me some credit.' They stood on the edge of a vast lawn, glimmering a strong green in yellow light. 'For a time I believed I was possessed. I even considered going off to be exorcised—but for that kind of thing to work, surely you have to believe in it? But I'm afraid I don't believe that some Tom, Dick, or Harry of a priest can deal with . . . Someone no better than I am? Nonsense. And then I began to do a lot of reading, and I found that Julie is that side of myself that was never allowed to live. The Jungians have a word for it. My *anima.* What's in a word? It seems to me all that kind of thing amounts—well, not much more than the pleasures of definition. Why is a word like that useful when you are experiencing . . . ? All I know is that if she walked towards me now I wouldn't be in the least surprised.'

The great lawn, as flat as a lake, was backed by beeches, chestnuts, and oaks; and some shrubs that were all in flower, pink, white, and yellow, although well grown themselves, were made so small by the trees they seemed like flowers in a border. In the middle of the green expanse was a wooden stage, about three feet in height. There the musicians and singers would be tomorrow. A few wooden chairs idled on the grass: apparently this was an audience that liked to stroll about while it listened. Slowly the two approached the little stage, which was like a flat rock in still water. This place, this stage, this lawn, was a vast O framed by trees, green heights around flat green. Now the two were circling the stage. On the far side of it was a poster of Julie, or rather of Julie's drawing of herself as an Arab girl, a transparent veil across the lower part of her face, her eyes black and—yes, the word *haunting* would do. Stephen came to a standstill. He made a small sound—a protest. 'Elizabeth didn't say she was using this one,' he said. It was not the picture on the other posters. 'What's wrong with it?' she asked. He did not reply. He was staring helplessly, as at an accident, or a catastrophe. He was pale. Sarah put her hand into his arm and moved him away. He walked stiffly, even stumbled. He turned his face to her, and Sarah almost let out that laugh which says, 'You *are* doing it well, congratulations.' Nothing that he had said, nothing she had thought about him—and she believed she had been prepared to dive deep into his wells of fantasy—had prepared her for what she saw. His face was pulled into that mask that illustrates Tragedy—the other side of Comedy; the theatrical stereotypes. She was standing still, staring at him. Her heart beat. Foreboding. Fear—yes, it was that. Yes, she had seen his face wretched; she had said to herself the sanitized sets of words we use in this time of ours, which has banished this kind of thing, has decided it is all an affair of horoscopes, or 'ghosts', and that if they squeak and gibber, then they are comic rather than not. She had never even begun to imagine what she was seeing now, the haunted tragic face with the dragged-down mouth that seemed as if an invisible hand held it, a mouth all suffering. She was shocked as if she had opened a door by mistake and seen something like a murder or an act of torture, or a woman in an extreme of grief, sitting rocking, clutching at her hair with both hands, then raking her nails across her breasts, where the blood runs down.

He's ill, she thought. She thought, That's grief. What I am looking at—that's grief. She felt ashamed to be a witness of it and turned her face away, thinking, I've never, ever, felt anything like that.

Now he remembered she was there, and he turned his own face away and said, his voice rough, 'You see, you have no idea at all, Sarah. You simply don't understand . . . well, why should you? I hope you never will.'

At supper that night there were seven people. The informal meal was taken in a room that had a hatch through into the kitchen, and it had been cooked and served by a pleasant motherly sort of woman not unlike an auburn-haired blue-eyed sheepdog. This was Norah Daniels, a housekeeper, or something of that sort, and she sat at the table with Stephen and Elizabeth and Sarah and the three boys, James, about twelve, George, ten or so, and Edward, seven. These children were beautifully behaved, in a style imposed on them by their parents: a light impersonal affection, and it was joky, for there was a lot of banter of the kind Sarah remembered from her school days. It was mostly Norah who played this game. Stephen was silent. He claimed he had a headache and they must forgive him. *Not ask too much of him* was what he meant and what they all heard. It was evident that this was a message heard often in this family, from him, and from Elizabeth, because she was so very busy. She kept saying she was, and that was why she had not done a variety of things she had promised—ring up a friend's mother, write a letter about a visit, buy new cricket balls. But she would do all these things tomorrow. The three boys, fair, slight, blue-eyed, angelic-looking children, watched the adults' faces carefully for signals. This was their habit. This was their necessity. They had been taught never to ask too much. Only Norah was outside this pattern, for she smiled special smiles at each of them, helped them to food in an indulgent way, remembered personal tastes, gave Edward, the smallest one, an extra helping of pudding, kissed him warmly, with a hug, and then excused herself, her own meal finished, saying she had things to do. At once the boys asked permission to leave the table, and they slid away into a warm dusk. For a time their high clear voices could be heard from the garden. Soon music sounded from the top of the house—some pop group. Elizabeth remarked that it was time the boys were asleep, and departed, but only briefly, to make sure they were in bed.

Then Stephen and Elizabeth apologized to Sarah, saying they needed a couple of hours to discuss arrangements for tomorrow, for more people were coming than they had expected. 'This Julie of yours is obviously a great draw,' said Elizabeth, but it did not seem she meant anything special by it.

Sarah walked about in the dusk for a while, until the birds

stopped commenting on the affairs of the day and the moon made itself brilliantly felt. She telephoned her brother's house. Anne answered. Yes, she had sent the girls to collect Joyce, who, on arriving home, had at once disappeared again. Anne did not suggest this was Sarah's fault, as Hal would have done. He had said they should all have a serious talk about Joyce, and suggested Monday night. Sarah agreed, but knew her voice communicated to Anne, as Anne's did to her, that nothing would come of this.

Sarah's room was full of moonlight and overlooked the great lawn and the trees beyond, the scene full of glamour and mystery, like a theatre set.

She lay in bed and was determined she would not think about Joyce, for she did not feel strong enough to accommodate the anxiety thoughts of Joyce always brought with them, when she was already anxious enough. She had expected to be disturbed by this visit, and she was. Not in the way she had been afraid of. Whatever it was that Stephen and she shared, they shared it still. No, now she felt she had been selfish, for she could not get out of her mind the look on his face that afternoon—such grief, such pain, such a degree of suffering. It was crazy. He might be sane in nine-tenths of his life, this intelligent hard-working many-sided life of his, but in one part of it he was, quite simply, not normal. Well, what of it? It did not seem to be doing much harm, and certainly not to Elizabeth. But there was something bothering Sarah, and she couldn't put a finger on it. She went off to sleep, glad to forget it all, and woke completely and as suddenly as if there had been a clap of thunder. The moon had left her room. She was remembering a scene at the table of Norah handing Elizabeth a glass of wine, and Elizabeth's smile at Norah. Well, yes, that was it. And she shut her eyes and replayed the scene. Stephen was at one end of the table, Elizabeth at the other, Norah beside Elizabeth. The women's bodies had carried on a comfortable conversation with each other, as well-married bodies often do. And Stephen? Now it seemed to Sarah that he was an outsider in his own house—no, for this house had, for all those centuries, accommodated any number of eccentricities and deviations. It was certainly not the house that excluded Stephen. Was he excluded at all? He had said he and his wife were good friends, and evidently they were. But her picture of Stephen— at least tonight, as she lay half asleep—seemed to be merging with that of Joyce, the girl, or child, who was always on the fringes of life, unaccepted by it, unacceptable. And that had to be ridiculous, for Stephen was firmly set in this life of his, born to it, could not be imagined outside it.

Sarah briskly got up, had a long bath, and watched early light come streaming through great trees. Five in the morning. She went quietly down the great central staircase, found a side door where bolts slid easily back, and went out. Two red setters came rushing around the corner of the house, silently, thank goodness, their fringed ears streaming. They put wet noses into her palm and their bodies wriggled with pleasure. She had not gone far into the woods when Stephen came through the trees. He had seen her from his bedroom window. Nothing now could seem more absurd than her earlier thoughts about Stephen. Nor could anything be more pleasant than this strolling about in the trees with cheerful dogs, listening to the raucous exchanges of the crows and the chattering of the small birds as they got their affairs together. At one point Stephen even casually mentioned Elizabeth and Norah, like this: 'You must have noticed, I'm sure . . .' He did not seem disturbed, and there was no sign of the tragic mask she had stared at yesterday. He seemed in good spirits and entertained her with a comic view of himself as a Maecenas. As a young man, he said, he had been a bit of a red, 'but not too inappropriately extreme for my station in life,' and had had nothing but contempt for rich patrons. '"We know what we are, but know not what we may be,"' he quoted, and added—and this was the only moment that morning when there was a suggestion of something darker, 'But the truth is, if we did know what we are, then we would know what we could be. And I wonder how many people would be able to stand that?'

Later, after breakfast, the boys made friends with her in their easy well-mannered way and took her off on a tour around the estate. She could see they had been told to do this. 'Not Angles, but angels' inevitably popped into her mind.

After lunch the theatre contingent arrived. Mary Ford, to take photographs of everything and to interview Elizabeth; Roy Strether, and, unexpectedly, Henry Bisley, the American chosen to direct because of the American money in the production. Besides, he seemed by far the best available. He was in Munich directing *Die Fledermaus* and had come for the weekend to hear this music. Henry was at first all defensive. There are men who carry with them, as some half-grown fishes are attached to yolk sacs, the shadow of their mothers, at once visible in an over-defensiveness and readiness for suspicion. It happened that on his arrival he walked into a room that had in it four women, Elizabeth, Norah, Mary Ford, and Sarah, and he was on the point of fleeing, when Sarah rescued him and took him out to the gardens. They had become acquainted during the casting session a month before. He was bound to be wary of her on two counts: first that she was co-author of this play, and then that as one of the four who ran The Green Bird, she had engaged him. Soon he was reassured. For one thing, he was not by tempera-ment ever likely to remain in one place, physically or emotionally. A man of about thirty-five: his restlessness seemed appropriate for someone younger: he danced rather than walked, as if to stay still might make him vulnerable to attack, and black eyes darted enquiries into a place, a person, and moved on to the next thing, which was also bound to be a challenge. She talked soothingly about this and that, noting that she was employing the murmuring mater-nal persona identified and rejected by Stephen. She showed him the gardens. She showed him the big lawn—the theatre area. She took him to see a half-built new block of rehearsal rooms. He was subdued by the beauty of the place, and flattered by it, being absorbed, as they all were, into a munificence like a general blessing. As they went back into the house he stopped to look up at its façade and ask why those top windows were barred. She did not know. Encountering Norah, who was pushing through the hall a trolley laden with cleaning equipment, like those used in hotels, Sarah asked about the barred windows, and Norah said they were probably for the first Mrs Rochester. 'Well, they must have had plenty of loonies here, in all that time.'

The afternoon went enjoyably past, while Mary Ford photographed them all. A buffet supper was served, in a much larger and grander room, Elizabeth and Norah supervising Alison and Shirley, two girls from the near town, whose healthy and wholesome prettiness reminded everyone that so recently there had indeed been country girls. Guests arrived, it seemed far too many, but these grounds could accommodate large numbers without seeming overpopulated. People went wandering about, stood on the lawn talking, sat on the grass. A company from London did Elizabethan dances. A local group sang songs composed by Tudor monarchs. Then came the main event, Julie's music, with the words Sarah had put to it. This was the late music, and there were singers only, without accompaniment, for it had been agreed that her 'troubador music' needed the old instruments to do it justice, and not all had yet been found. The singers stood on the little stage in a strong yellow evening light, four girls in white dresses with their hair loose, a style appropriate, they had decided, for this music that filled the great grassy space between the trees with shimmering uncomfortable patterns of sound continually repeating, but not exactly, for they changed by a note, or a tone, so that when you thought you were listening to the same sequence of notes, they had subtly changed, gone into a different mode, while the ear followed a little behind. The words were half heard, were cries, or even laments, but from another time, the future perhaps, or another place, for if these sounds mourned, it was not for any small personal cause. The music floated in the dusk, and the dark filled the trees and the moon lifted over them, and the singers too seemed to float in their pale dresses. Lights came on in the big house, but not here. The girls were chanting to a silent crowd.

Sarah stood in anxiety with her colleagues. None had heard this music sung with words. Solid and sensible Mary, solid and reliable Roy, stood on either side of Sarah, reserving judgement, and then, unable to contain themselves, exclaimed that it was marvellous, it was wonderful, and Sarah herself could hardly believe it was she who had done this—though it was not her at all, it was rather Julie Vairon. The three stood close, part of their attention charmed into passivity, listening, while the other part was energetically at work on this material, imagining it in various settings and modes. Stephen came up and said, 'Sarah, I'm hearing something I simply didn't expect. I had no idea . . . ,' and he strode off into the dusk. Mary Ford summed up professionally: 'Sarah, it's all going to work.' And Henry Bisley materialized in front of her, his dark eyes shining in the light from the high windows of the house, and said in a voice full of surprise and gratitude, 'Sarah, that's so beautiful, it's so beautiful, Sarah.'

They all had to get back to London, and Henry to Munich. Sarah went with them. She said she had to work, but the truth was she did not want to spoil by daytime ordinariness the other-worldly charm of that evening. Charm . . . what is it, what can account for it? One says, charm, enchantment, and nothing has been said. But this place, and this group of people who were going to work together to make *Julie Vairon*, were charged with some subtle fascination, like the light that fades from a dream as you wake.

That night at home, Sarah thought she could not remember another time in her life that had this quality of . . . whatever the word should be. She found herself smiling, as at a child or a lover, without meaning to, without knowing she was going to. But what was making her smile, or even laugh, she had no idea at all.

> *If you find a ghost in your arms, better not look at its face.*
> —Julie Vairon's Journals,
> English edition, page 43

But Sarah was choosing not to remember Stephen's tragic mask.

And now it was Monday night. It occurred to Sarah, as she waited for the doorbell, that her exhilaration could only be because she actually believed some sort of sensible solution would end this talk. You're living in a dream world, she told herself, and hummed 'Living in a dream world with me.' All the same, she strolled about her rooms arranging sentences in her mind which would be persuasive enough to make Hal—well, make him what?

The bell rang. Peremptory. Hal stood there, stood dramatically, apparently waiting for a formal invitation, while Anne, with glances and smiles that managed to be both apologetic and exasperated, simply came in and stood with her back to both of them, at the window.

'Oh, do come in, Hal,' said Sarah, annoyed with him already. She left him standing and went to sit down. Hal did not at once enter. He was giving her living-room a good once-over: he had not been in it for some time. The room had been variously used in this family flat's long history. It had once been her children's bedroom, but it had been a living room now for years. She was seldom in it. She would not have invited her brother into her study or her bedroom, where he would see photographs, piles of books, all kinds of objects that would emanate the intensely personal look of continuous use, which he would find irritating, even shameless, like underclothes left lying about. As he stood there, he sent suspicious glances to a drawing of Julie pinned on the door. Anne at the window could not be saying more clearly that she did not consider herself part of this scene. She was a tall woman, thin—too thin, a rack of bones—and her pale dry hair was tied back roughly behind her head. As usual she was surrounded by a fug of tobacco smoke, which seemed the very essence of dry exhaustion. She had lit a cigarette already, but furtively: she always smoked with guilt, as if still in her hospital, knowing she was giving a bad example to her patients. At the sight of her, Sarah's compunctious heart reminded her that Anne's perennial exhaustion was why she, Sarah, could never bring herself to 'put her foot down' over Joyce. She had never not pitied her sister-in-law.

And now Hal did come in, letting it be understood by means of compressed lips and raised brows—useful perhaps for indicating to patients that their lifestyle did not meet with his approval?—that it was time his sister took her room in hand. He looked judiciously at a cheerful if faded chair opposite Sarah's—would he allow himself to sit in it? He did.

Hal was not the elder brother, as his air of command might suggest, but three years younger than Sarah. A large comfortable man, with an affable manner; everything about him must give his patients confidence. He was a success in his professional life, and his family life wasn't so bad either, though he had always been unfaithful to Anne. She forgave him. Rather, one deduced that she must, since she did not go in for confidences. Probably she did not care, or perhaps it was that one could not imagine him unforgiven. Now Hal was sitting on the stiff chair, his arms folded high on his chest, legs apart and braced, as if he might otherwise bounce as he sat. He looked like a great delightful baby, with his little wisps of black hair, his fat little tummy, his little chins. He had small black eyes like large raisins.

Sarah offered them drinks, tea, coffee, and so forth, and her brother's impatient shake of the head made it clear he was pressed for time.

'Now look here,' he said. 'We do realize you have always been amazingly good with Joyce.'

There are occasions, when it becomes evident they are bound to develop in a certain way, that have a quite intoxicating momentum.

'Yes, I think I have too.'

'Oh, really, Sarah,' he exclaimed hotly, his wells of patience already overdrawn.

And now he began on the rhetorical statements (the counterpart of her prepared reasonings to him) rehearsed and polished on the way here. They had the theatrical ring which goes with a thoroughly false position. 'You must see that Joyce looks on you as a mother,' he said. 'You have been a mother to her, we both know that.' Here he looked at Joyce's mother, wanting her agreement, but she was smoking furiously, her back turned. 'It really isn't *on* for you to drop her like this.'

'But I haven't dropped her, any more than you have.'

He registered this shaft with a hostile look and a quiver of his lips which said he felt he was unfairly treated. 'You know very well what I am saying.'

'What you are saying is that I should give up my job and sit here for when she does turn up, even if it is only once in six months for an evening. Because that is what it amounts to.'

'Exactly,' said Anne angrily.

Hal sat puffing his lips out, hugging himself with both arms: he was a threatened man; he had two women against him. 'Why can't you take her with you to rehearsals, that kind of thing?'

'Why don't you take her to your hospital and to Harley Street? Why doesn't Anne give up her work and sit at home waiting for Joyce?'

At this Anne let out a loud theatrical titter. 'Exactly,' she said again, through swirls of smoke. She swatted her hand at the smoke, to show how she deplored her weakness.

'Look, Hal,' said Sarah, keeping her voice down. 'You're talking as if nothing has changed. Well, they have. Joyce is a young woman. She's not a little girl any longer.'

'No,' said Anne, 'he can't see it. Or won't.'

'Oh really,' exploded Hal, and then he collapsed. He let his arms fall, and stared, his face all disconsolate lines.

This man who had all his life been lucky and successful had met something intractable. But the point was, this had happened not this week but years ago. It was as if he had never taken the truth in. 'It is really quite appalling,' he said. 'What are we going to do about it? She runs around with drop-outs and layabouts and all sorts of people.'

'Alcoholics and drug pushers and prostitutes,' said Anne, and at last turned herself around. Her face was flushed, and brave with the determination to have her say. 'Hal, at some point you have to face up to it. There's nothing we can do about Joyce. Short of chaining her down and locking her up. All we can do is to take her in when she does turn up and not lecture her. Why do you always shout at her? No wonder she comes here to Sarah.'

Some people are the moral equivalent of those who have never, ever, been ill in their lives and, when they are at last ill, might even die from the shock. Hal could not face up to it: if he admitted one defeat, what might then follow? He sat silent, breathing heavily, arms hanging, not looking at them. His little pink mouth stood slightly open—like Joyce's, in fact. 'It's awful, awful,' he sighed at last, and got up. He had inwardly shelved the problem, and that was that.

'Yes, dear, it is awful,' said his wife firmly. 'It has always been awful and it will probably go on being awful.'

'Something has to be done about it,' he said, just as if beginning the conversation, and Sarah breathed, 'Good God!' while Anne said, with a tight and derisive smile, 'You two are so funny.'

Sarah felt all the indignation due when one is in the right but being classed with someone in the wrong.

Anne explained apologetically, 'You both seem to think that if

you just come up with something, then Joyce will become normal.'
She shrugged, gave Sarah an apologetic grimace. Husband and wife
went to the door, the big man drifting along beside Anne, his eyes
abstracted. He had inwardly removed himself. Sarah was able to
visualize furious scenes between these two, when Anne tackled Hal,
and Hal simply repeated, 'Yes, we must do something.' For years.
Meanwhile good old Sarah looked after Joyce. Nothing at all would
change as a result of this talk. Well, something had. Sarah had not
before seen that somewhere or other she did believe that Joyce
would suddenly become normal, if only they could come up with
the right recipe.

The door was shut, and she listened to their feet on the stairs,
their voices raised in connubial disagreement.

Sarah sat at her desk and stared into the watery depths of the
mirror. She had to do more work on the songs, fitting Julie's words
to music and even making some words up. *I don't know why it is*,
Julie had written, and this was when she had just agreed to marry
Philippe the master printer, *but every scene I am part of, when there
are people in it, rejects me. If someone were to reach out a hand to me
and I stretched out my hand to him, I know my hand would go into a
cloud or a mist, like the spray that lies over my pool when there has
been heavy rain in the hills. But suppose in spite of everything my fingers closed over warm fingers?* She called the music she wrote that
spring 'Songs from a Shore of Ice.'

Sarah began, 'If I reached my hand into cloud or river spray . . .'
She, Sarah, had found a hand in a cloud or mist—for Stephen had
certainly been an unknown—a warm hand, kindly by habit, a
strong one, but holding it, she had felt its grasp become desperate.
Help me, help me, said that hand.

The rehearsals were to be in London, in a church hall, a utilitar-
ian place that managed to be dim enough to need some lights on, in

spite of the sunlight outside. Fewer than the full company arrived for the first rehearsal. The musicians and singers would come later. Henry Bisley was in New Orleans for the opening of his production of *La Dame aux Camélias*, set in the brothels of that town at the turn of the century. Roy Strether, Patrick Steele, and Sandy Grears, the lighting and effects man, were all busy on the final rehearsals for the opening in The Green Bird of *Abélard and Héloïse*, which would precede *Hedda Gabler*. Patrick had announced that he was glad *Julie Vairon* would need so little in the way of scenery. He was so disappointed: Sarah had turned his Julie into a bluestocking, he explained, and he did not think he could ever forgive her.

Julie had arrived, a strong healthy girl with the misty blue eyes that can only be Irish. She was Molly McGuire, from Boston. Philippe the master printer was Richard Service, from Reading, a quiet middle-aged man of the observing non-commenting kind: probably similar to Philippe Angers. Paul, or Bill Collins, was a handsome, in fact beautiful, young man, who at once claimed he was all cockney, and proved it by singing 'She Was Poor but She Was Honest'—a song which by now they had all understood would be the theme song of the rehearsals. Actually he was from a prosperous London suburb, or at least partly, for he had lived half his life in the States, because of the complicated marriages of his parents. In impeccable English, he said, 'I'm all things to all men, that's it, mate, that's me, Bill, the all-purpose all-weather dancing and singing cockney actor from Brixton.' The Noël Coward drawl that went with this vanished, as he said in an American accent, and this had the effect of changing him completely: face, smile, set of body, 'Don't you believe it. I'm a pretty limited sort of guy. "I won't dance, please don't make me, I won't sing, please don't make me . . . ,"' singing this not badly at all. 'Limitations I do have—' He hesitated and might have stopped there, but added, compelled to it, with a sudden cold ruthlessness, 'But I know how to sell myself.' Now he gave a swift look around to judge the effect of all this, saw them disconcerted, realized the reason was what he had said last, heard it as they had, and sent a nervous small boy's smile all around. Then, with the grimace that goes with *I don't know why I do this sort of thing*, he walked quickly to a chair in a corner and sat there alone. So unhappy did he look that Julie's mother, Madame Sylvie Vairon (Sally Soames from Brixton—really from Brixton; she had been born there), went over to sit with him, apparently casually. She was a large stately beautiful black woman, who, it was already clear, was going to dominate any scene by her looks, just as Bill did.

Rémy Rostand, or Andrew Stead, was a Texan, with sandy hair, freckles, and pale blue eyes which had too many wrinkles around them for his age, probably forty. He had just come from making a film about the old gauchos, shot on the high plateaux of north-west Argentina. He walked like a horseman, stood like a film gunman, and had shortly to become Rémy, with all the diffidence and hard-to-achieve self-respect of a youngest son. Had Henry known what he was doing when he cast this bandit for the role? In the early days of every production, this unvoiced query is in the air. An unemphatically good-looking, ordinary young man, George White, was going to be Paul's comrade-in-arms in Martinique, then Rémy's older brother, not to mention Philippe's assistant in the printing shop.

On the first day, Sarah and Stephen were more prominent than they had planned, because of the absence of Henry, but luckily Mary Ford had ordered a photo session, and the six actors and two authors were photographed, separately and in couples and in groups, endlessly photographed, the actors at least posing with practised good nature, obedient to the god Publicity. And Mary's face was solemn, concentrated, for she was utterly given up to her devotions as she took the pictures. Photographers are always in search of that perfect, that paradigmatic, but just out of reach summit of revelation. The next one—yes!—that will be it . . . do you mind turning your head just half an inch . . . that's it, but no, don't smile . . . yes, this time smile. . . this one will be . . . just one more . . .

one more . . . and now . . . yes, I think I got it that time . . . but I'll just use up this roll . . . All over the world these pictures are stacked up in piles, in files and folders, in drawers, on shelves, on walls, the visible record of that race of transcendence-seekers, the photographers' compulsive quest.

And while Mary sat chatting with them all, her camera was held between alert fingers, ready to swoop it up into place to catch that unique and utterly unrepeatable pose or look which would transform a summary biography—twenty lines on the programme—into irresistible truth.

During that first day a good deal was said about how wonderful a thing *Julie Vairon* was, how altogether unique. This was because the actors were all taking a chance, much more than is usual with that hazard the theatre. The piece was a sport: not a play, not an opera. They had not heard the music that would fit the words. All of them confessed to having been attracted to *Julie Vairon,* but they did not know why, for all they had been sent—all they could have been sent—was an assemblage of scenes so lightly sketched that sometimes only a phrase or a sentence indicated passionate love, or renunciation. They were reassuring themselves.

First Molly came to Sarah, who invited her to sit down between her and Stephen, to say she had been told by those who had been at Queen's Gift how wonderful the music was, and the songs, and she simply couldn't wait to hear it all. Stephen only allowed himself a glance at this dangerous girl and then stared off at the others, while Sarah talked for him. Molly went, and then Bill, who had been watching for an opportunity, appeared by them, murmuring congratulations on the script and the lyrics. It was a shock to hear the word lyric used to describe those bitterly sad, some said abrasive, songs of the 'first period', and the broken lines of the 'second period', when there might be no more than a phrase repeated many times, or a word chosen for its sound.

'I seem to hear it all already,' claimed Bill, sliding into the seat between Sarah and Stephen, but smiling at Sarah. Then, having established his right to intimacy with Sarah—she could see this was his style, or his need—he glanced at Stephen. But Stephen was not going to succumb, for there was a sharp, not to say critical, look to him, as he examined the young man. Bill quietly got up and walked away, not, however, without the quick flash of a smile at her.

Walking to the tube with Sarah, Stephen remarked, 'Molly doesn't look remotely like Julie.'

'She'll convince you when the time comes.'

'And Andrew might as well be a cowboy.'

'Rémy must surely have spent a lot of time on horseback?'

'And as for that young . . . Julie would never fall for that pretty face.'

'But Julie did fall for a pretty face. Paul has to be a romantic young lieutenant, and not much more, don't you see? For the sake of dramatic contrast.'

'Good God.'

'Nothing she wrote indicated he was more than a good-looking boy.'

They stood together on the pavement. She was thinking that this querulous note in him was new. More, that in the first weeks of their friendship she would have thought him incapable of it. She was relieved to see that now he seemed to be fighting to preserve an obstinate self-respect, while his eyes were full of misery.

Unexpectedly he said, 'Sarah . . . I'm out of my depth. . . .' He grimaced, then made this a smile, walked away to the Underground entrance, turned to give her a small apologetic wave—and vanished.

It was the first read-through of the first act. They were nearly all present now, but there did not seem many people scattered about in the large hall. Henry had announced that he would be putting them all into position right from the start, because how people stood, or were, in relation to each other changed their voices, their movements—everything about them. The actors exchanged those smiles—*what else?*—meaning that from him they expected no less. Their smiles were already affectionate, as they stood about like dancers waiting for lift-off, and for him to command them. He had arrived that morning by plane from New Orleans, but he was already almost dancing his instructions, falling for seconds at a time into the characters they were going to play. He had been an actor, surely? Yes, and a dancer too, but that was before he had become an old man, and he had worked in a circus too: and here he became a clown, staggering over his own inept feet, miraculously recovering himself, and jumping back into his own self with a clap of the hands that summoned them into their positions. He must be of Italian descent, with those dark and dramatic eyes. Often, in southern Europe, you see a man, a woman, leaning against a wall, standing behind a market stall, all loud exclamatory sound and gesticulation, in the moment before they suddenly go quiet, black eyes staring in sombre fatalism: too much sun, too much bloody history, too much bloody everything, and a bred-in expectation of more of the same. And here was Henry Bisley, from the northern United States, standing limp, switched off, his eyes sombre and abstracted, southern eyes, eyes from the Mediterranean, but even as he leaned briefly against a wall, he seemed already on his way somewhere else. And the idea of movement was emphasized by his shoes, for they would have been useful for a marathon. For that matter, all their shoes seemed designed for a hundred-yard sprint.

Stephen and Sarah sat side by side at a table which was a continuation of Henry's—the director's. At the table beyond that was Roy Strether, watching everything and making notes. Mary Ford was photographing at the theatre.

The read-through began with the scenes in Julie's mother's house in Martinique, and the evening party where the handsome lieutenant Paul, brought by his comrade Jean, was introduced to Julie.

Since the musicians were not there, it was a question of going through the scenes while the words of the songs were spoken, so that everyone would get an idea of what would happen. Roy read, in a voice as flat as the recorded telephone announcement 'Your number has not been recognized'.

This first scene had Julie standing attractively by her harp, shoulder outlined in white muslin (in fact Molly wore jeans and a purple T-shirt), a dress bought by papa on his last visit to distant Paris, on mother Sylvie's insistence. Julie was singing (today she only spoke) a conventional ballad from sheet music (a piece of typing paper) brought by the father from Paris with the dress. For while the reputation of this house and the two beautiful women was exactly what might be expected among the young officers who were unwillingly on service in this attractive but boring island, Julie and her mother disappointed expectations by behaving with the propriety used by the mothers and sisters of these young men, and even more so. Nor had they expected to find Parisian fashions.

It was only when the officers had gone that the women became themselves and spoke their minds, in words recorded by Julie.

To start with, beauty was not so much in the eye of this beholder, for that first evening all I thought was, That's a pretty hero! No, it was Maman who was dissolved by Paul. I said to her, He's too much, he's like a present in pretty paper, and you don't want to unwrap it because it would spoil the parcel. Maman said, 'My God, if I were even ten years younger.' Maman was forty then. She said, 'I swear, if he kissed me, it would be my first time ever.'

The two women were to sing a duet, 'If he kissed me it would be my first time ever,' using the first-period music, like a blues.

This was hardly likely to be the first time for Julie, not with all those young officers about. Sarah passed a note to Henry that unless they were careful, this song would get the wrong kind of laughter. He tilted a page towards her to show he had already marked the danger point with an underlined *Laughs!*

'But I wouldn't mind a smile,' he said, and smiled at her to show the kind of smile.

This cast did laugh a lot. Laughter kept breaking out during the duet, which of course was being spoken, not sung. Henry asked them to cool it, and at once they sobered, the impassioned words being exchanged without emotion, producing an effect of hopeless despair. So sudden was the change that there was a sigh, the long slowly released breath that means surprise, even shock.

'Right,' said Henry. 'That's it. We'll have to wait for the music.'

They were already a group, a family, partly because of their real interest in this piece, partly because of the infectious energies of Henry. Already they were inside the feeling of conspiracy, faint but unmistakable, the we-against-the-world born out of the vulnerability of actors in the face of criticism so often arbitrary, or lazy, or ignorant, or spiteful—against the world outside, which was *them* and not *we*, the world which they would conquer. They already believed they would conquer. It was because of *Julie Vairon*'s special atmosphere.

How easily, how recklessly we join this group or that, religious, political, theatrical, intellectual—any kind of group: that most potent of witches' brews, charged with the possibilities for harm and for good, but most often for illusion. Sarah was not exactly a stranger to the fumy atmospheres the theatre creates, but usually she was in and out of rehearsals, doing this job and that, and she had not before written a whole play, based on journals and music she had soaked herself in for months, then been in on the casting, then committed herself to what would be two months, more, of day-by-day involvement with rehearsals. She would not this time be flitting off to other productions, other rehearsals. She would be part of *Julie Vairon*, day and night, indefinitely.

Meanwhile minor annoyances were being absorbed into a general effervescence, which was surely pretty unusual so early in a production. Having to wait for the music was testing them all. This was not the most comfortable of rehearsal places. It was too big, and their voices echoed in it: there was no way of judging how they should be pitched and used. Even with the sun blazing down outside, the old hall was dismal, and a shaft of light striking down from a high window showed up the dust in the air, like a column of water full of algae, or like bits of mica.

'Solid enough to climb up,' said Henry, actually making a pantomime of climbing up, defusing possible complaints with a laugh. And they all laughed again at the unexpected effect when the column of light, moving as the earth turned, reached the actors at exactly that moment when Paul and Julie stole away from Maman's house on a dark night, though she was not deceived, and knew they were going, while the bright column pointed at them like the finger of God.

After the read-through Sarah and Stephen were going off to lunch with Henry Bisley, for they had to know one another better, but as they stood at the exit into the outside world, Paul the handsome lieutenant, or rather Bill Collins, was there with them, though he had not been invited. They climbed the stairs together, and when they went to the little local restaurant, Bill was the fourth. In the restaurant, the rest of the cast sat at one table, but Bill was at theirs. Sarah did not take much notice of him, because of getting to know Henry. This was going to be a satisfactory director, she was thinking, and could feel Stephen thinking too. He was sharp, competent, knew the material inside out, and, as a bonus, was very funny. Anywhere near him, people laughed. Sarah was laughing, and Stephen too, though when he did, it sounded as if he was surprised at himself for doing it. Halfway through the meal, Stephen left them. Elizabeth was preparing another recital of Tudor music, but this time with dancing, modern dancing, athletic and vigorous. Apparently it 'worked', though one could tell he did not much care for the combination. He said to Sarah, 'You see, it's my part of the bargain. She would never say anything if I was not there, but if I didn't turn up, she'd feel let down. And rightly.' He did not want to go. She did not want him to go. She was surprised at the strength of the pang she felt. Henry was called over to the other table: Andrew Stead wanted advice. That left her and Bill. He was eating heartily—Henry had eaten a little salad; Stephen had left most of his food. She thought that this is how a very young man ate, even a schoolboy—or a young wolf. Well, he was very young. Twenty-six, and she guessed much younger than that in himself. All those winning smiles and sympathetic glances—he kept them up although, clearly, he was famished and that was his first consideration. Behind her she heard laughter at the other table, and turned her head to listen. Bill at once saw this and said, 'I simply have to tell you, Sarah, what it means to me, getting this part—I mean, a real part. I'm afraid I've had to take quite a few parts that—well, we have to eat, don't we?'

Laughter again. Mary was telling a tale which concerned Sonia, and it ended: 'Two knives, on his seat.' 'Knives?' said Richard. 'Surgical knives,' said Mary. The laughter was now loud, and nervous, and Richard said, 'You can't expect a man to laugh at that,' and laughed. 'All the same . . . serves the little creep right.'

'Sarah,' said Bill, leaning forward to claim her, his beautiful eyes on her eyes. 'I do feel so at home with you. I felt that so much, at the casting session, but now . . .' She smiled at him and said, 'But I have to go.' He was genuinely disconcerted, rejected. Like a small boy. Sarah went past the other table, smiling generally and said to Mary, who was about to return to the theatre, 'Ring me tonight?'

Bill was already settling himself beside Mary. Sarah paid her bill and looked back. Bill sat straight up, head slightly back. He looked like an arrogantly sulky adolescent, *touch me not* at war with *oh yes, please.* Henry was reaching out with a pencil in his hand to mark a passage in Richard's script. He was looking over it at her, eyes sombre.

That evening she sat thinking about brother Hal, because of her feelings about Stephen. There were no new thoughts in her head. Hal had been her mother's favourite, she had always known and accepted that. Or at least she could not remember ever having not accepted it. He was the much wanted and loved boy, and she had taken second place from the moment he was born. Well, unfair preferences are hardly unusual in families. She had never liked Hal, let alone loved him. And now, for the first time, she was understanding how much she had missed in her life. Instead of something like a black hole—all right, then, a grey hole—there would have been all her life . . . what? A warmth, a sweetness. Instead of always having to brace herself when she had to meet Hal, she could have smiled, as she did when thinking of Stephen. She knew she did, for she had caught the smile on her face.

Late that night Mary rang. First she said her mother was in a bad patch, with a leg that was paralysed, perhaps temporarily. One had to expect this kind of thing with multiple sclerosis. She was going to have to pay someone to come in twice a day when she, Mary, was working so intensively. She did not say this was going to be financially difficult. Sarah did not say that extra money would be found. All their salaries were due to go up: the four had always accepted less than they could have claimed. But now, with *Julie Vairon*, there was suddenly much more money . . . if none of this was said, it was understood.

Then Mary told Sarah about Sonia and the knives.

From time to time, in London, some young man desiring to attract attention announces that Shakespeare had no talent. This guarantees a few weeks of indignation. (Usually it is the perpetrator who has no talent—but Bernard Shaw, who had, made this particular way of shocking the bourgeoisie permissible.) Shakespeare had been announced as having no talent quite recently, and a new ploy was needed. What better than to say, in a country with a genius for the theatre, that theatre itself is stupid and unnecessary? A certain young man who had created for himself and his cronies a style of sneering attack on nearly everything not themselves, had become editor of a well-known periodical. A school friend, Roger Stent, meeting his suddenly well-known chum, asked if there was a job for him on *New Talents*. 'Do you like theatre?' 'I don't know anything about it.' 'Perfect,' cried this editor. 'Just what I want. I want some-one who is not part of that old gang.' (Newcomers to a literary scene always imagine cabals, gangs, and cliques.) Roger Stent went on his first visit to the theatre, the National, and in fact rather enjoyed himself. His review would have been favourable, but he put in some criticisms. The editor said he was disappointed. 'Really my ideal the-atre critic would be someone who loathed the theatre.' 'Let me have another try,' said Roger Stent. His reviews became notorious for their vindictiveness—but this was the style of this new addition, the Young Turks, to the literary scene in the early eighties. He perfected a sneering, almost lazy contempt for everything he reviewed.

Abélard and Héloïse had opened, and his review began, 'This is a turgid piece about a sex-crazed nun and her life-long pursuit of a Paris savant. Not content with being the cause of his castration, she felt no shame about boring him with wittering letters about her emotions. . . .'

The policy of The Green Bird was to rise above unpleasant or even malicious reviews, but Sonia said, 'Why? I'm not going to let him get away with it.' She wrote a letter to him, with a copy to the editor, beginning, 'You ignorant and illiterate little shit, if you ever come anywhere near The Green Bird again, you'd better watch it.'

He wrote her a graceful, almost languid letter, saying that per-haps he had been mistaken and he was ready to see the piece again and he 'trusted there would be a ticket for him at the box office' on such and such a night. This last bit of impertinence was very much in the style of this latent incarnation of Young Turks.

She left a message that there would be a ticket for him, as requested. When he reached his seat, he found two surgical knives lying crossed on it. They were so sharp that he cut his fingers pick-ing them up and had to leave the theatre, bleeding profusely. Sonia supplied full details to a gossip columnist.

Sarah laughed and said she hoped this was not how Sonia was going to react to every unfavourable review.

Mary, laughing, said that Sonia had explained that bullies only understand the boot. 'The new brutalism, that's what she says it is. She says we lot are all living in a dream world.'

'She said, "you lot"?'

'Well, she did say "we" the other day.'

'So she did. We must hope.'

At rehearsals that week she missed Stephen, but she rang him or he rang her to find out how they were going. Meanwhile she sat by Henry, or rather by his chair while he was working with the actors. If Henry did actually arrive back to sit down for a moment, he was off again after whispering a word or two, usually a joke. This was becoming their style: they jested. Yet he felt threatened. For he must: she could see herself, that watchful (that maternal) presence, making notes. And she was still at work on the lyrics, if that was the word for them, for often the actors said something, improvised, suggested changes. She was needed here: she had to reassure herself because she knew how very much she did not want to leave. Julie had her in thrall. A sweet insidious deceptiveness seemed now to be the air she breathed, and if it was a poison, she did not care.

The actors all came to sit by her, in Henry's empty chair, or in Stephen's, but she soon saw that Bill was there oftener than any of them. This gift of his for establishing instant intimacy—she felt she had known the young man for years. But she was not the only one being offered his charm. He seemed to be making a gift of himself to everyone. During this first week, which was devoted to the first act, the handsome lieutenant Paul had to dominate: he was in nearly every scene. And his part was so sympathetic, for he was so innocently as well as so madly in love with Julie. From the moment he first saw Julie standing by her harp, he was in a fever, not only of love, but the intoxication of the discovery of his own tenderness. The apprentice loves of young men tend to be brutal. He was truly convinced of their happiness once they reached France, and did not know it was an idyll possible only in Martinique, in this artificial and romantic setting, with its outsize butterflies, its brilliant birds, its languorous flowers and insinuating breezes. He forgot that it had been not his but Julie's idea to run away, taking their idyll with them. The young man simply shone with the confidence of love, its triumphs, its discoveries, and this was not only during Paul's scenes with Molly, where the two were entirely professional, making the jokes about their passion necessary to defuse those stormy love scenes. And yet, more than once, Sarah had caught him glancing at herself while he was making love to Molly, a quick hard calculating look from a world far from the simplicities of sympathy they enjoyed when he sat chatting in a chair beside her. He wanted to know if she was affected by him. Well, she was. But so was everybody else. Sally, that handsome black lady, who always wore an air of sceptical worldly wisdom and a sweet derisive worldly smile, a woman who commanded attention even when she sat knitting in a chair offstage (not one to waste time, she knitted not only for her family but for sale to a certain very expensive shop)—Sally watched Bill Collins with exactly the same fatalistic short laugh and shrug that, as Julie's mother, she allowed herself when first observing her daughter's passion for Paul. She and Sarah exchanged glances of female appreciation for the young man, but they were critical too, because he was so conscious of his looks and so skilled at using them. Well, good luck to him, those looks said. The other females present were the same. Mary Ford and Molly (as Molly) caught each other's eyes and grimaced: no, he is really altogether too much.

He continued to pay Sarah a much more than professional attention. Several times, Henry, returning to his station to check notes or even to rest for a moment, had smilingly to ask him to vacate his chair. Then Bill gracefully and modestly got up, and brought Stephen's chair closer to Sarah and sat in it.

There was no doubt he genuinely liked her. Perhaps a little

more? He looked at her, when she was not looking at him, in ways she remembered (had to make herself remember, for she had so thoroughly put all that behind her). He made excuses to touch her. She was flattered, amused, and curious. If she wanted to be cynical, then her possibilities for doing him good professionally were not large. The Green Bird was not such a big deal for an actor who—he allowed them to know, but without boasting—was in demand. Though not always for parts he respected.

At the end of the first week this incident occurred: Bill had been sitting by Sarah, and they had been chatting in their way of easy intimacy, when he was summoned by Henry to go through a certain scene again. Sarah watched how he positioned himself by Molly in order to rehearse the moment when they finally decided to run away. They had—naturally—to embrace. First they looked long into each other's eyes, braving the future. Then Paul ran his hand from Julie's shoulders to her buttocks. Rather, Bill ran his hand from Molly's shoulder to her buttocks. For this quick movement was absolutely not impersonal and professional, but intimate and sexual, with something brutal about it. This slithering insinuating caress was calculated. Sarah saw how he sent her, Sarah, a swift diagnostic glance to see if she had been watching, had seen, had been affected. She had, and so had Molly, who went stiff under that skilled caress, took a step backwards, and then, as Julie, moved forward into an embrace that had again become professional. But Molly's look at Bill had been everything that was not professional. She had fallen in love, or in lust, instantly, because of that infinitely skilled and promising caress. Her body had burst into flames, had filled with need, and as she stepped back out of the embrace, her face, turned up to the triumphant (he could not hide it) young man, confessed to him, Yes, here I am.

Sarah did not like what she herself had felt.

She did not waste time saying it was absurd, for that went without saying. That weekend she was forced to acknowledge she had fallen a little in love with the young man. He had certainly taken enough

trouble to make sure that she did. This was probably his way of deal-
ing with life. By now she knew his story well. His mother was the centre of his life, they were close. The father was . . . 'Well, he's a coper,'
Bill had said, laughing. "'E's a coper, aren't we all, just a coper, after all,'
sang Bill, to the tune of 'I'm a Dreamer', inside his cockney persona,
which apparently went with moments when he felt threatened. And
then, seeing she had comprehended more than he had wanted, he
said, sardonic, intimate, reckless, 'Yes, tha's i', inni, tha's 'ow i' is, awlri'.'
And he danced a few steps, his long legs, in pale blue jeans, and his
whole body as satirical as his face. But for one flash of a moment he
had a crumpled look, and she could see where, in thirty or forty years'
time (but probably sooner if the signs were there already), that beautiful face would crease and wrinkle. American Molly, American
Henry, intrigued with this little cockney act, had clapped and
demanded more, and Bill obliged with a repertoire of cockney songs,
first—of course—'She Was Poor but She Was Honest', making Molly
sing it with him, so that the two clowned together.

It seemed to Sarah certain that this young man had had to survive
a childhood—but then, who does not?—and had found very young
that he had this lucky gift of good looks and—even more potent—
instant sympathy. Self-doubt, weakness, discouragements, could be
silenced because he could make people fall in love with him.

Perhaps the pleasure of any new company of people, particularly in the theatre, is simply this, that the families, the mothers and
fathers, the wives and husbands and girlfriends and boyfriends, the
siblings and the children, are somewhere else, are in another life.
Each individual is sharply herself, himself, is simply there. That
leech, that web, that box of distorting mirrors, is out of sight. The
strings we dance to are invisible. But already—and it had only been
a few days—two of the men here were no longer magnificently
themselves. She could see the puppet strings only too clearly, though
she did not want to. And Stephen? It occurred to her that she had
known Stephen for weeks, could call him friend, could say they were

intimates, yet while she observed how he was pulled and tugged by something deadly, she could not see the strings.

Joyce arrived on the Saturday night, and Sarah was pleased to see her, because it would take her mind off being in love and the outrage she felt about it. Joyce offered Sarah her sweet, weak smile but did not ask for anything. She said she had been with Betty. Who was Betty? 'Oh, just someone.' The girl was clearly in need of food, sleep, and probably medicine. She did not eat the food Sarah put in front of her, though she was pleased to have a bath and to put her filthy clothes in the washing machine. Sarah was happy that Joyce was connected with ordinary life enough to want to keep herself clean. She lay in bed knowing that Joyce sat up watching television and probably would not go to bed at all. She was thinking that in Joyce's case it was not easy to say, Here are the puppet strings. Her father was hardly ideal, but one could think of many worse. She had an adequate home and family, proved by the fact that her two sisters were, as it is put, 'viable'. Joyce was not viable. Perhaps one day soon 'they' (meaning, this time, the scientists) would come up with an explanation. Joyce had an 'I cannot cope' gene, or lacked an 'I can cope' gene, or had one in the wrong place, and her life had been governed by this. The puppet strings do not have to be psychological, though it is our inclination to think they are.

What Sarah was thinking of mostly, though, was Stephen. She was beginning to have for him an entirely unwelcome fellow feeling. She attempted humour, with 'At least I am not in love with somebody dead.' She tried comfort, with 'And anyway it isn't serious, just a crush.' She also reflected that in her attitude towards Stephen and his affliction had been a condescension she was now ashamed of, though until she could make the comparison she had not been aware of this.

Joyce stayed until Sunday night. At some point she took a dose of something. Injected, probably, for she was a good while in the bathroom, which afterwards had a chemical smell. Her eyes stared dolefully, the pupils were enormous, she tittered inconsequentially and then wept. When Sarah was in the bathroom, she again walked out of the flat.

When one's heart aches, this is seldom for a single reason, particularly when one is getting on a bit, for any sorrow can call up reserves from the past. Again Sarah decided she would refuse heartache. Yet she had only to think of Joyce, let alone sit in the same room with her, for her heart to feel it had slipped on a leaden glove.

The second week of rehearsals would be spent on Act Two. This meant that Bill Collins relinquished first place to Andrew Stead, or Rémy. Hardly possible for Bill to become invisible, though it seemed he was modestly trying to be, sitting by himself out of the way in a corner, or by Sarah. For a day or so it seemed that Bill's looks and sexiness were going to make the second, the great love improbable. But then, slowly, it became clear that Andrew knew what he was doing.

Sarah telephoned Stephen and said, 'You should come and take a look at the gaucho; he's wonderful.'

She could hear him breathing, an intimate sound, as if they had their arms around each other. 'Really, he's got it all. To begin with I thought he was going to be too hard and macho, but he was using that deliberately. He's the youngest son, remember. Now he's got that slightly over-the-top cockiness—oh, sorry!' But he did not laugh, only gave a sort of grunt. 'You know, a young man over-compensating. An easy sexual assurance—that's Paul. But Rémy has something deeper than that. Being in love with Julie proves to himself and his family that he's grown up. He has a marvellous masculinity, quite unlike the beautiful lieutenant, but he hasn't come by it easily. He sees Julie walking through the trees in the Rostand park, and you can positively see him becoming a grown-up man at that moment. Do you realize you haven't said a word? Are you all right, Stephen?'

'Well, Sarah, apart from being crazy, yes, I'm all right. And thank you for not saying, But aren't we all.'

'But I was thinking it.' It was at this moment that she knew it would be hard to tell Stephen she had fallen in love. No matter how briefly or lightly.

'I've discovered what my trouble is—why I find rehearsals so difficult. It's this business of mixing reality and illusion, it undermines me.'

And now she was astonished and could not say anything.

'Are you there, Sarah?'

'Yes, I'm here.'

'I'm sure you don't know what I mean, because you are so sensible.'

'You are saying that your being in love with Julie is real, while a play about her is illusion?'

Silence. Then, 'Is that so hard to understand?' As she did not speak, 'It's the music as well. It really turns me inside out, I don't know why. I'm quite terrified of when they start rehearsing with the singers.'

'Aren't you coming to any more rehearsals? Because I miss you.'

'Do you, Sarah? Thank you for that. Of course I shall come; one shouldn't simply give up.'

Stephen's chair remained empty. Bill was in it most of that week. This intimacy of theirs, how pleasant it was. Instant intimacy, and she had the gift too. You could say it is the great modern talent. Watching the people of a hundred years ago working out their lives, it was like a little dance of fowl. Ornamental fowl, of course. Formality. But formality makes us uneasy; we see it as an insult to sincerity.

It was not going to be easy to make the casually moving, easy-mannered people of now hold themselves, walk, sit down, stand up, in the right way. Henry called a special rehearsal. 'You all look as if you were wearing jeans,' he said. 'But we are wearing jeans,' they

said, making the point that not until they put on the old clothes
could they be expected to conduct themselves properly. But Henry
wasn't having that. 'You—Molly—you've had your mother nagging
at you all your life to keep a straight back, hold yourself properly,
comme il faut. Now do it.' And Molly, wearing jeans and a T-shirt
that left shoulders and neck bare, her hair tied in a knot to get it off
her skin because of the heat, tried to move as if she wore corsets and
a long skirt. For two hours Henry kept them at it: they stood, they
sat, they walked, and again and again got up from chairs—this company in their jeans, their singlets, their sports shoes, with their natural instinct to slouch. 'By the time we get to the dress rehearsal it
will be too late,' said Henry. 'We've got to get it right now.' Some did
better than others. The gaucho apologized, said he would practise at
home, and retired to watch the others. Bill Collins soon was showing them all how. He explained modestly that he had been a dancer,
and the first thing he had learned was not to walk slumping into his
hips. Sarah watched him—but they all did—walk across those bare
and dusty boards as if he were held upright in a tight uniform.
Every line of him was conscious of itself, and when he turned his
head with a smile, or bent over an empty chair to kiss an invisible
hand, he made a gift of himself to them all. The marvellous arrogance of it, protested Sarah to herself, as her heart beat, and did not
doubt the other women felt the same. To be as handsome as that—it
was not a joke, it should surely impose obligations, the first of them
being not to use himself as he did. Well, thought Sarah, and who is
talking? Had she the right? She hadn't been too bad herself . . . oh
yes, indeed she remembered walking across a room knowing that
everyone watched her, holding herself as if filled to the brim with a
precious and dangerous fluid. Young girls do this, when they first
discover their power: luckily most do not know how much they
have. What can be more entertaining than to watch some grub of a
girl, thirteen years old or so, astonished when a man (old as far as
she is concerned) starts to stammer and go red, shows the nervous

aggression that goes with an unwelcome attraction. What's all this? she thinks, and then is seized with illumination. Her wings burst forth, and she walks smiling across a room, reckless with power. And this condition can last until middle age deflates her. Sarah did not want to think about all that. She had closed the doors on it long ago. Why had she? She could sum it all up with Stephen's 'You're a romantic, Sarah!' . . . And then there had been Joyce, as good as a chastity belt. But the loss of 'all that' she had come to terms with long ago. She had been attractive and, like Julie, always had people in love with her. *Basta.* She could not afford this new feeling of loss, of anguish. She glanced at her forearm, bare because of the heat, shapely still but drying out, seeing it simultaneously as it was now and as it had been then. This body of hers, in which she was living comfortably enough, seemed accompanied by another, her young body, shaped in a kind of ectoplasm. She was *not* going to remember or think about it, and that was the end of it.

But she did think about Bill. When he sat beside her they chatted nicely about any number of things, but particularly about him. Often, his childhood, mostly in a good school in England: as she had thought, he had come from a solid middle-class family. Often, too, he was in that or this school in the States: good schools, for he had been privileged financially if not emotionally. Sometimes there were holidays with both parents, undergone for his sake, since they were divorced. These had not been a success. And he talked a lot about his mother.

Sarah reflected that this easy understanding was the same as the one you enjoy with a child, until, let's say, the age of eleven. Children you have known all their lives—like her brother's girls. (Not Joyce, who had always been on a different wavelength: you did not have a relationship with her as much as with her anxious and timid smile.) It is the pleasantest of relationships, a simple friendship, a sweetness. With early adolescence it may disappear, it seems overnight, and while the adult mourns, the child forgets, for she, he, is fighting for self-definition, cannot afford this absolute trust and openness. And who was she enjoying it with again? Bill Collins, a man of twenty-six or so, who so much loved his mother.

But the special understanding was being submerged in a group elation that was like a Jacuzzi, currents of feeling swirling around, stinging, slapping, bubbling. The group temperature was rising fast, as it was bound to do, to culminate in the euphoria of *the first night*, after all not such a long way ahead.

Henry, when he dropped into his chair by Sarah's, or rather flung himself into it, was all jokes. He liked this play—if it could be called a play. He liked the cast—well, he had chosen it. He adored the music and the words Sarah had chosen to accord with it. And he was glad Julie herself was not around, because he was very much afraid he would adore her too. And here he rolled up his eyes and for a moment was a clown in love.

Richard Service, or Philippe, often sat by Sarah. He was a modest man, serious, full of surprises, for since he was unable to make a living entirely in the theatre, he worked as well as a lecturer in an agricultural college: his father, a farmer, had insisted he must not rely on the theatre. Sarah joked that he saw Julie as a farm girl, for he had said Julie had been brought up in one forest and lived to the end of her life in another. Why had she committed suicide? As much that she did not want to live in a town as that she was afraid of domesticity. He argued about this too with Sally, for these two often sat together, talking. Sally said in those days everyone was still close to the land one way or another, and what ailed Julie was that she was a woman. At least, Sally said, the girl had the sense not to become an actress. 'Look at me. There aren't so many parts for a fat black woman,' she announced, laughing and sighing. 'No, not so many.' What Richard and Sally talked about most was their children. Both had three. Sally's eldest daughter looked after the two smaller ones when her mother was working. Sally never mentioned a husband. She had wanted this girl to stick it out at school and then go to college, but she was threatening to leave school and take her chances. 'She's a fool,' said Sally. 'I tell her, You're a real fool, girl. In ten years' time you'll think it was the worst thing you ever did. But you can't talk to them at that age. Any more than Julie's mother could make her listen.' Richard's fifteen-year-old had 'dropped out' but been persuaded to try again. His 'dropping out', on that level of income, was hardly the same as Sally's daughter's. It was infinitely touching, the friendship of these two, with their differences. They had for each other a humorous gentleness—a respect? was it curiosity too?—precisely because of these differences.

In that second week, 'Rémy's week', Andrew Stead did not have much time for sitting about. He was busy making himself over from a man you could barely imagine without his horse to Rémy, in one of the heartbreaking transformations one may watch when an actor subdues one personality, using something that looks like a ferocious discipline (though perhaps it is more like a submission, all sensitive patience, a kind of listening?), to another that might very well be the opposite of his own. Andrew remarked that he liked being Rémy, for he was always typecast, and in one film after another he was gangster, crook, cowboy, cop, rancher. And that was because in the very first film he had done he was an outlaw, stealing horses. And so what was he doing here? Ten years ago, he had been at Cannes for the film festival, where a film he was in had won a prize, and he had spent a day in the seductive country behind the coast, visiting the ancient hill towns, and by chance had found himself in a town, Belle-Rivières, where there was a music festival. He had heard Julie Vairon's music and did not think much about it, until later, when he could not get it out of his head. It was the 'troubadour' music that had got to him. His agent had sent him *Julie Vairon*, and he had turned down a film to do it. No, it was very far from his usual line, and perhaps he wasn't up to it . . . but there was a side benefit—could he call it a benefit, though? He was being thoroughly unsettled. He was wondering now how much he had become 'typecast' in his life as well. Hard to remember now much about what he had been like before the age of nineteen and his first film: he had positively fallen into it, only chance he had become an actor. Yes, he was a Texan, but that didn't mean he necessarily had to spend his life as a cowboy. ""Orses and dogs is *not* vittles and drink to me", he quoted, and was pleased that though she guessed Dickens, she did not know it was *David Copperfield* and he had to tell her. 'Despite appearances, it ain't necessarily so.'

He was not a man one could easily imagine needing reassurance, and when he did arrive in the chair beside Sarah, she did not offer it. How differently people did sit in that chair. Bill sat back, balanced, alert, hands palm down on his thighs, chatting to her while that handsome face of his was always ready to offer to anyone looking his way the smiles he was so good at.

Henry could hardly be said ever to sit, if by that word is meant a submission to relaxation.

Sally sat with her large body filling the space allotted to it, calm as a monument.

Molly was not much there, because she was seldom offstage. If she did arrive beside Sarah for a moment, it was to express vigorous disapprobation of Julie, who needed her head examined. 'She screwed up her whole life for love'—and the violence here made Sarah follow Molly's gaze to Bill, a usually limpid, candid, and even innocent gaze, now clouded by self-doubt. Thank God, said Molly McGuire, that she was living now and not then.

As for Andrew, he sat loosely, his muscular hands relaxed on the chair's arms, exactly as that lean hard body of his was relaxed, on principle and by training. He watched her calmly, with those pale blue eyes of his that were no longer inflamed by the altitudes of north-west Argentina. He seemed to be waiting for something from her. What? He made her uncomfortable, forced her to examine her role here, in her chair, always ready to provision anyone who needed it with praise and reassurance. Was she being insincere? She believed not. She did think the company very good, and Henry admirable. Her own work was not bad at all. But sometimes Andrew reminded her of Stephen, who had the same way of sitting in judgement. It was a masculine judgement: they were both men who would never dispense themselves in charm or an appeal to be liked. She was also remembering that both of these, by chance, had been at a ten-years-ago festival in the south of France, and both had 'fallen for' Julie's music.

But the music was not here, and its lack was being felt more every hour. Sarah observed how Andrew, in the middle of a scene with Molly, suddenly broke off, asking Henry if he could do the scene again, then doing it again, and finally coming to a stop with a shrug and a shake of the head. Henry and Andrew went to one side to confer. While they talked, the scene was arrested, like a film still, emphasizing the animation of these two men. Henry came to Sarah and explained that Andrew could not get the 'feel' of the piece, could not find his pace. And he was not the only one who complained. 'But no one's going to get it until we have the music.' 'I know, but never mind, just do it, Sarah. Come out and demonstrate.'

Sarah complied. After all, she had been rehearsing plays and 'entertainments' for years. As she walked forward to take her place, she caught herself thinking she was pleased she had taken trouble with her appearance that morning. She was wearing a dark blue working outfit, but in a silky-looking material, and had for some reason put on big silver earrings and elegant shoes.

In this scene, words and phrases spoken by the two lovers were taken up by the musicians and sung, almost like a part-song, words said and words sung in counterpoint.

As my lover you must leave me,
All the world applauds your choice.

But you're my friend and you should stay.
A friend does not his friend betray,

Giving pain is for the lover,
A friend does not a friend betray.

The words had come from Julie's journals. *This man loves me and so it is in order for him to stab me to the heart, and if he actually did stab or shoot me, French law could easily acquit him; it would be a* crime passionnel. *But he is my friend. My only friend. I have no other friend. Friends are not applauded when they betray each other.*

The song would be sung by the three girls, with the countertenor holding the words *lover* and *friend* in long notes not unlike the groaning shawm, underlining the young high fresh voices in their conventional reproach.

What Julie was saying to Rémy was, 'You love me, you are my lover, but not a soul in the world will condemn you for obeying your father and abandoning me. But if I were your friend and you betrayed me, you would be condemned by everyone.'

Rémy was saying, 'But I am your friend. You'll see that I am your friend. I'll prove it. You think that I am abandoning you, but I never will.'

Julie says, 'Ah, but you're my lover, and that cancels the friend.'

Sarah's voice was a small one, but it was sweet and true. Long ago when she was a student in Montpellier, there had been talk of training it, but instead she studied music for a year. She was confident she would not disgrace herself. When she began, 'As my lover you must leave me . . . ,' she felt as if she had stepped out from a shadow into the light, and from her passive role, sitting there, always observing, into performer. Hardly new for her, taking command, showing how parts should be played or songs sung, but she had not done anything of the kind here, with this company. She was conscious of the silence in the hall, and how they all watched her and were surprised at this revelation, Sarah so assured and so accomplished. She felt herself full of strength and of pleasure. Oh yes, she did like it, she was liking it too much, being admired by this particular assembly of people.

When she had finished there was light applause, and Bill called out 'Bravo' and stood up to clap, so that he would be noticed. She made a mock curtsey to him, and a general one to everybody. Then she called them to order by lightly clapping her hands.

Henry came forward, because he had understood there was a need.

Now, when she sang the verses again, Henry supplied the counter-tenor's *friend* and *lover*. He could not resist slightly exaggerating, so that his voice was a low yell, like an unknown instrument from an exotic shore, and it was very funny. They had to laugh. The four, Sarah, Henry, Andrew, and Molly laughed staggering into each other's arms, where they embraced. They sobered as Henry clapped his hands.

This time it 'worked'. The counterpoint of *friend* and *lover* was not funny but added a depth and darkness to the verses.

And now Molly began her speech. 'You love me, you're my lover, but not a soul in the world . . . ,' and Henry came in with *lover*. Sarah followed, singing, 'As my lover you must leave me,' and when Molly reached, 'But if I were your friend . . . ,' Henry sang, or perhaps groaned, *friend*, and Sarah sang the last couplet against Molly's, 'Giving pain is for the lover . . . ,' and repeated it while Andrew began, 'But I am your friend . . .' and so on.

Timing. It all fitted. Now Andrew was convinced, but what they all saw coming out in him was a stubbornness they had not seen before, a quite deadly persistence. He needed not only to be convinced but to be sure it could be done again. And again. The four of them took the scene through several times, until Andrew said, 'Right. And thanks. I'm sorry, but I had to have that.'

And Henry said, 'Right. Break for lunch.'

On the Friday of Rémy's week, Stephen came to sit in his chair by Sarah, to watch a run-through of Act Two. Molly had put on a long skirt to help her, and she seemed as if by magic to have become thinner, lithe, wild, vulnerable. It broke the heart to watch her, the brave one, battling with such a destiny. The young aristocrat, son of the Rostand château, was touching in his love for the girl he would never be allowed to marry.

Meanwhile there was still no music, and Molly was speaking the words of her song, which would be sung later by the counter-tenor.

If this song of mine is a sad one,
Love, who I hold in my arms,
Our joy as wild as a hawk circling,
Think that when summer comes
They will send you far from me,
Then you will remember these days
And my sad song tonight.
With you gone I am forever exiled from myself.

Stephen said, 'I don't remember that. I suppose you made it up?'

'I thought it was in the style of a troubadour song.' She put in front of him what Julie had actually written, in her translation.

It's all very well! Love, love, love, we say, weeping for joy all night. Next summer we'll be singing a different tune. I saw how your father looked at me today. Time's up, that look said.

'Fair enough,' he said. He was sitting with his head bowed, not looking at the players. Far from laughing, or even smiling—for she did believe the transmutation of one mode into another merited at least a mild smile—he seemed like a miserable old man. Yet once (once! it was a few weeks ago) the humour they shared had been the best part of their friendship. She was telling herself that she must accept it—*must*—that a phase of their friendship was over. This was not the man with whom she had those weeks of companionship.

And as she thought this, the leaden glove she associated with Joyce threatened to enclose her heart, and she snapped at herself, No, stop it, stop it *at once*. And she went off and away from the chair by Stephen, to stand with her back to the players, pretending to examine some props, as it happened, brilliant flowers and fruit from Martinique, there to give the 'feel' of the place. She was muttering, "'No, I'll not, carrion comfort Despair, not feast on thee; not untwist, slack they may be . . .'" And was furious with herself. Melodramatic bloody rubbish! she shouted silently to that part of her memory that had so patly come up with these words, feeding them to her tongue, while her mind refused them. Feeling someone behind her, she composed her face to turn, smiling, at Henry, but she had not composed it sufficiently, for he was thrown back at the sight of her. 'What's wrong, Sarah, don't you like it?' he half stammered, and she had to remind herself that the most confident of directors needed reassurance, and this was a far from confident one. Over his shoulder she saw Sonia (her successor at The Green Bird— she could not remember seeing this so clearly before) go up to Bill with some letter, or telegram that had come for him. He took it, making a joke, and they stood laughing, the attractive redhead, the handsome boy—no, no, *not* a boy, he was a man. . . . She said to Henry, 'Yes, I do like it, very much,' and saw how his body relaxed out of the tension of anxiety. The traitor memory was offering to her tongue, as she watched Sonia and Bill stroll down the hall, in perfect step, "'. . . keep back beauty, beauty, beauty, from vanishing away . . . O no, there's none, there's none, O no, there's none . . .'" and she put her hand in Henry's elbow and turned him about with a laugh, out of his posture as a suppliant, for she did not want to feel maternal, and together they stood to watch as Rémy and Julie held each other in an embrace that had in it all the sorrows and disciplines of valediction.

'I thought, when you went off like that . . . And Stephen doesn't like it, does he?'

'Yes, he does. He likes it very much.'

'He really does?'

'Yes, really.' And she discarded various sets of words, all to the effect that the play touched Stephen too nearly.

When the time came to go for lunch, she went with Stephen to a restaurant not the same as the company's usual choice. It was obvious he did not want to be with them. There he said he was not hungry. He sat, all dejection, while she trifled with her own food. His breathing wasn't right: he sighed and then sat as if he had forgotten to breathe. He kept shifting his position, leaned forward, leaned back, even unconsciously putting his hand to his forehead in a gesture that was pure theatre: I am suffering. His look at her, when he did at last become conscious of her being there, was a close inspection, apparently hoping to find something in her face, but failing. And there was shame in it, as if he wanted to observe her, though without being observed.

As he parted he said to her, 'All right, but if I'm mad I'm not the only one. I overheard that young jay tell Andrew Stead he was in love with a woman old enough to be his grandmother. Well, you, obviously.' And he gave an angry laugh, the first that day. And it was not an accusation of her, but rather on behalf of the lunacy of the world. He went off to catch his train and she went home, dissolved in love. Well, yes, she had known Bill was in love with her. 'In love'—a phrase as you take it, all things to all men. And women. There are as many shades of being in love as there are graduations of colour on cards in the paint shops. All right, then, he had a crush on her. Why not? People had been having crushes on her all her life—or so she seemed to remember. (She added the rider hastily, defensively.) But the interesting thing was her bursting into flame because of hearing it said. Bill had said it knowing it would get back to her. Her body had filled at once with a most horrible desire. A reckless desire. All through that weekend she sat down and jumped up, flung herself on her bed and out of it again, because she would not, would *not*, succumb, walked around her room for hours, in such a daze and a dream she would not have been able to say at any moment what she had just been dreaming, yet no matter how far gone she was in dreaming, she was stopped again and again by that word *impossible*. Meaning just that. She was thinking of Aschenbach's passion as an elderly man for the boy in Venice. Is it that we all have to suffer the fate of falling in love, when old, with someone young and beautiful, and if so, why? What was it all about? One falls in love with one's own young self— yes, that was likely: narcissists, all of us, mirror people—but certainly it can have nothing to do with any biological function or need. Then what need? What renewal, what exercise in remembering, is Nature demanding of us? . . . And so she exclaimed and protested, and quite soon found herself murmuring—tranced, or hypnotized—speaking words she did not take responsibility for, since she did not know what they meant. '*Who? Who is it?*' Accepting that she had in fact said or muttered these words, she commented on them that it was not possible she was in love with a handsome youth she had nothing at all in common with except the instant sympathy she owed to his love for his mother. Perhaps when he was seventy, well pickled by life, they might mean the same thing when they used words—yes, possibly then, but she would be dead. He was as innocent as a kitten. What could she possibly mean when she said that? He was horribly calculating. Yes, innocent, for only a man unsure of himself, like an adolescent or someone inexperienced, would need the kind of tricks and seductions he used. (That long, slithering, seductive, calculated caress, innocent?)

Memories she had refused to admit for years now stood around her in beguiling or accusing postures, forcing her to attend to them. She was being forced to remember past loves. And she was remembering her husband. But her memories of him had been put into a series of frames, like photographs, or scenes in a novel—a short novel, since he had died so young, at forty. (Once, and not long ago, to live to be forty in Europe was a great thing, an achievement.) Not a sad novel, not sad photographs. No, for she could scarcely remember the pitiful ending, young widow left with two small children, and those tears—surely she must have shed plenty?—might have been wept by someone else, for all she felt now. And had she ever loved him, her great love, with this burning, craving love? No, that had been a gradual love, leading to the satisfactory marriage that followed. And as a girl, before her husband? More pictures in an album? No, this love was forcing her to feel old loves, making her remember, bringing her face to face with loves she had got into the habit of dismissing with: Oh, adolescent crushes, that's all. But in fact that love, or that, or that, had been intense and terrible, with exactly the same quality of impossibility as this one. And before that? What nonsense that children did not love, did not suffer: it was as bad for them as for their elders. No, she would not think about that, she refused to. She would force herself to recover from this illness. For that is what it was.

She sent Stephen a fax:

'Love is merely a madness and, I tell you, deserves as well
the dark house and whip as madmen do, and the reason
why they are not so punished and cured is that the lunacy is
so ordinary that the whippers are in love too.'

He sent her one:

'Who so loves believes in the impossible.' Faxes are all very
well, but I'd rather hear your voice.

Early on Sunday evening a card was pushed through her door. It was the most charming and guileless card, of a frieze of pink deer, Bambis, rather, nose to nose—kissing. It could not have been in worse taste—for anyone but a small child. The person who sent this card (had asked someone to drop it in?) was a child. (What had he in common with the brutal youth who had slithered that insinuating caress down Molly's back and buttocks?) The card made the statement, I am a little boy. A shock of cold water, but only to her mind. Her emotions were not affected. Her body burned more fiercely, if this were possible. ('I have to tell you how much it means to me, getting to know you. All my love, Bill.') Burn, the word we use, shorthand for such shameful, such agonizing physical symptoms. Quite poetic, really, the word *burn*.

She had his telephone number, in her capacity as administrator of the theatre. His hotel was not far away. She waited half an hour and telephoned. Exactly as she would have done when 'sexually viable'—a phrase she had found in a sociological article, making her laugh, a dry safe phrase, putting everything in its proper place. (Like *burn*.) She thanked him for his card and suggested he should come over. It seemed impossible that he would not come over at once, and into her bed. Such are the side products of the physical swellings, wettings, and aches shorthanded in the word *burn*. She could hear how his voice put guards on itself. She was not too far gone to judge the voice (hearing it like this, without the benefit of his presence) as a trifle vulgar, because of its self-satisfaction, its complacency. She was furious: she had not persuaded him! She had never once gone to sit by him, gone to talk to him, initiated anything. And what did he mean by saying *All my love*? (Her mind did inform her that she had done this a thousand years ago, finding everything *she* felt in a phrase or a word: one did this, when in love.) He would drop in, in about an hour. Her body rioted, but her mind, as much under threat as a candle flame in a strong draught, made derisive comments.

She remembered an incident from her childhood, one she had put into a frame long ago, with an appropriate smile. She was six years old. A small boy—he seemed to her a small boy, for he was a year younger than she was—stood with her under a great tree that had in it a tree house and told her that he loved Mary Templeton.

He had just embraced her, fat little arms around her neck, a fat wet kiss on her cheek, and an impulsive 'I love you'. Because of the kiss and the arms and the 'I love you' she told him—outraged, self-righteous, dissolved in love for him—that he couldn't love Mary, for she was too old; he must love her. And when he said stubbornly that he really loved Mary, she was full of a conviction of his unfairness. He had kissed her, he had said he loved her, and she could still feel the warm little arms around her. Mary Templeton was the most glamorous of the small girls, because she went every week to ballet school and was nine years old. (Surely as a female creature she—Sarah—should have known that it was inevitable he must love Mary, because she was out of reach.) Sarah told him that he and she together should set up life in the tree house just above their heads, an arboreal paradise, for she had already in imagination planned the cheese and tinned ham she would take from the pantry, and the old eiderdown from the understairs cupboard. The small boy hesitated, for he did like the tree house, but repeated that he loved Mary.

This incident frozen all those years ago, a baby mammoth in ice, was filling her with the emotions of then. She had adored the plump little boy with his soft dark locks and his wide blue eyes. His wet kiss on her cheek and his 'I love you' had utterly melted her. It was inconceivable he did not adore her. But he had decided to dream of Mary Templeton instead. Long ago, under that tree in a garden since bulldozed to make a housing estate, a desolation of grief had swallowed her. A little child's love. So she had filed it away: a childish love, not to be taken seriously.

When Bill arrived he had with him Molly, Mary Ford, and Sandy Grears, the lighting man. Sarah thought, while hot knives sliced her back, Of course, Bill and Molly are in the same hotel. And Sandy? He was a strong young man, capable, with the good looks of health, a recent addition because of the demands of *Julie Vairon*, and she had not had time to notice him much. It seemed he had invited the actors to his flat for lunch, and they had all accepted, and some had afterwards gone to Bill's room, and then Sarah had so kindly rung Bill to ask him over. Sarah looked quietly (she hoped) at Bill while he came out with this, but he was only smiling, not looking at her. The four young people were smiling as they came in. In this context Mary Ford was one of them. They were a group she was excluded from as absolutely as if she were dreaming them, and they would vanish when she woke. Meanwhile, in a moment that was short for them but frozen for her in the intensity of observation, she saw them in a frame: Bill standing there in her living room, laughing, his hand on his hip, and the two young women's bodies turned towards him and passive with desire. Their faces were all a hopeful waiting. (Mary Ford too? Interesting.) Sandy broke it, by flinging himself into a chair, saying as he saw Julie's picture pinned there, 'A home from home.'

And now they were all in the camaraderie of the theatre. But only in appearance, for Sarah was on that other shore, excluded, watching. She saw how Bill was dispensing himself in looks and smiles, and how the women suffered. They could not take their eyes off him, any more than she could. He was like a young glossy animal, a deer perhaps? She thought of the biblical scene where all the women, entranced by Joseph, cut their hands with their fruit knives, not knowing what they did, a scene reinterpreted by Thomas Mann—bound to be reset, always, in a thousand contexts, by life. The scene had the same slowed-down underwater quality as an erotic fantasy or an erotic dream.

A lot of chat went on, badinage. Messages were being sent out in that other language that so often accompanies the ostensible exchange. Bill was telling a long humorous tale of how in New York there had been a goodish interval between one engagement and another. 'I was weeks out of work. The telephone didn't ring for me once. Then, suddenly, it didn't stop. I was offered four parts in a week. I didn't know myself.' He was looking not at the women but at Sandy as he spoke. Switching into cockney: 'Reely I di'n't, oo'd'v thort it, me, Bill Collins.' And then in BBC standard, 'The cynosure of all eyes.' Mary Ford murmured, 'Oh dear, I do wonder why.' At once he despatched her a genuinely wounded glance, went red, laughed with pleasure, and at once recovered himself with 'Four! All at once! Too much!' And who was the fourth, Sonia? He tilted back his head and laughed, exposing his strong and perhaps too full throat, and from that position—arrogant, touch-me-not—defended himself with a diagnostic inspection of them all. 'I chose this one, of course. I chose Julie. I couldn't resist her. Besides, I've never been in France, let alone worked there. From dearth to plenty,' he drawled, an American, malicious, and very far from the dear little boy. Molly listened to the real message here, and smiled. It was a small, tight smile. Mary Ford even nodded as she smiled. Sarah could feel that same smile on her own face. Then Bill smiled at Sandy and understanding sliced into Sarah and at the same time—surely?—into the other two women. Of course. This excessively beautiful young man . . . the theatre . . . New York. And yes, he had a girlfriend, he had said so. All young men have girlfriends and even wives, if feeling sufficiently threatened. These thoughts careered through Sarah's head while she shouted silently at herself, For God's sake, stop it!

The telephone rang. It was Stephen. He had been crying. He probably still was, for his voice was unsteady. 'I want you to talk to me. Don't say anything sensible, just talk. I'm going mad, Sarah.'

This was not an occasion when one might say, I'll call you back. She told the young people (nearly middle-aged Mary still included with them?) that it was a call from New York about *Abélard and Héloïse.* She knew that Mary Ford knew this was untrue. Mary at once got up, and the others followed suit—Bill, she saw, and felt a quite excessive pleasure, with obvious reluctance. 'We'll leave you,' said Mary. 'I hope it's not bad news. Not our American sponsor?'

'No, it's not our American sponsor.'

Mary Ford went off down the stairs, that solid young woman like a milkmaid in jeans—her joke. Sandy asked to use the bathroom.

Molly went to the door, with Bill just behind her. Sarah, returning from showing Sandy to the bathroom, saw that Bill, unable to resist the waves of longing from Molly, had bestowed himself in an embrace. Molly was dissolved in it, eyes closed. Over Molly's head Bill saw Sarah. He put Molly away from him; she went blindly off. Bill came to Sarah, slid his hand down her back, and kissed her. On the mouth. Nothing at all brotherly about this kiss. He breathed in her ear, 'See you, Sarah,' and slid a hot cheek against hers. Sandy could be heard coming from the bathroom, and before he appeared, Bill had quickly stepped back from the embrace and was going out. Sarah watched the two young men depart down the stairs.

She returned to her bedroom and sat on the edge of her bed and listened to Stephen. He was talking in broken sentences. 'What is this all about, Sarah? What is it? I don't understand. If only I could understand it . . .' He was on the other end of that line for perhaps half an hour. Silences. She could hear him breathe, long, sighing, almost sobbing breaths. Once she thought he had put down the telephone, but when she said, 'Stephen?' he said, 'Don't go, Sarah.'

Later he said, 'I suppose I must go and help Elizabeth. I said I would. She does need me, you know. Sometimes I think I'm just an irrelevance, but then I see she relies on me. That's something, I suppose.' Then, '*Sarah?*'

'Yes, I'm here.'

'And I rely on you. I can't imagine what you're thinking. I feel as if something has come up from the depths and grabbed me by the ankle.'

'I understand, absolutely.'

'You do?' He was disquieted: solid and equable Sarah, that was her role.

Act Two ended with Julie's miscarriage of Rémy's baby, theatrically so much easier than the death of a small child, which, they knew, would have taken the play over, have had the audience awash with tears. Besides, a child was always a nuisance at rehearsals, and if they took her to France she would need minders and nannies. Interesting, how much discussion went on about this. Some found the decision cynical. Henry particularly did. He said, 'It's much easier to believe that this child didn't mean all that much to her, oh no, it was just one of those things, she was pregnant and then she had a miscarriage, too bad.' Henry had a small son, carried photographs of his family, American-style, showed them to everybody and rang his wife every night. Andrew Stead certainly didn't like it. He protested that his child had been callously disposed of. In life, he pointed out, Rémy had gone to the house in the forest to play with the child, had begged the family to see that the child was a reason for marriage. Then Bill reminded them that Julie had had a real miscarriage, of his child. Everyone forgot that, he complained. He was sure Paul minded about that miscarriage. Julie had said he did. The journals were consulted. Everyone was reading them. Sarah took her stand on what would 'work'. The point was the effect on the townspeople. They said that Julie had killed her child. But in the play they say Julie induced a miscarriage by swimming in the forest pool's icy water. The essential thing was that she must be blamed for the loss of the child. 'And we can't have two miscarriages—two deaths.' Attempting an echo, from Oscar Wilde, she said, 'To lose one child is sad, to lose two simply careless.' She noted that the Americans did not laugh but the English did. The English in this context included Bill Collins. Sandy and Bill broke, on a single inspiration, into a recital of 'Ruthless Rhymes', an exuberant performance.

> *When baby's cries grew hard to bear*
> *I popped him in the Frigidaire.*
> *I never would have done so if*
> *I'd known that he'd be frozen stiff.*

My wife said: 'George, I'm so unhappé!
Our darling's now completely frappé!'

sang Bill.

Billy, in one of his nice new sashes,
Fell in the fire and was burnt to ashes;
Now, although the room grows chilly,
I haven't the heart to poke poor Billy.

sang and danced Sandy, Bill joining in. The Americans seemed mildly shocked. Henry was even reproachful. Andrew's face indicated that he was well accustomed to adjusting himself to different degrees of culture clash. Sarah, Mary Ford, Sonia, Roy Strether, George White, all, as one says—accurately in this case—fell about. They needed to clown and laugh because of Julie's infant, disposed of heartlessly for theatrical reasons.

Who laughs at what is a far from simple business. All the younger people were in an uproar of laughter, both at the theatre and at rehearsals, because Roger Stent had sent a letter to Sonia: 'I hope you are proud of yourself. Those witty little knives of yours cut my fingers and I had to have two stitches.' Sonia had sent him two red roses with a card saying merely 'Diddums'. Sarah found herself a bit shocked. Mary confessed she was too. 'I am beginning to wonder,' remarked Mary, 'if I'm really in tune with the times.'

Act Three began with Julie alone in her little house, seeing nobody except when she went to the printing firm where she took her drawings and pictures to be sold, or returned the music she had finished copying. This was the trickiest part of the play, for nothing much happened for several minutes, and it was where the music came in most usefully.

Julie believed she was visited by inspiration: the music was 'given' to her: but from a very different source than the 'first period' music.

This gift . . . whose hand brings it, whose mouth sings it? I wake at night and hear voices in the trees, but they are not angels of God, I am sure of that. God's angels would never come to me, because they do not condone despair. According to the old ideas what I feel is a sin. This forest is full of presences from the past. Once the troubadours walked here on their way from one castle or defended hill town to another. They sang of love, and of God, for no matter how sad they were, they never forgot God. The music I am hearing now surely cannot be theirs. But perhaps it is, for where God is, the devil is too. The ideas I am writing now are not mine, not Julie Vairon's, for I am a newcomer in the forest, we are all brand new these days, with ideas that have dispensed with God and the devil. If I went back to Martinique I would find in the forest what I felt as a girl—the devil Vaval. But the devil there is different, he's primitive and full of tricks. I was never afraid of those presences, because my mother knew how to keep them quiet. Besides, in my mind I was already in Europe, I did not belong to them. I knew I would come here one day. I don't think the music I used to write would be strange to anyone in the world—everyone's heart breaks for love at some time in their lives. No, this new music that comes into my mind now is like draughts of sweet poison, but I have to drink it. I feel it running in my veins like a cold fever. At such times I cannot lift my head from my pillow and my hands and feet are lead. Perhaps it is my little girl who sings these songs to me? She was not allowed to live. She has taken her unlived life with her somewhere. Where? But we do not believe in hell, or purgatory or heaven. Why is it so easy for us not to believe in all the things people so recently believed—that they believed for thousands of years? All those books in my father's library . . . no, I shall not call him my father, for he did not acknowledge me, or say I was his daughter in front of the world. He gave me presents and paid for tutors. I had a mother and no father.

My mother said to me, I come from a long line of unmarried mothers, and I don't want you to be the same. (It was her idea of a joke. I refused to laugh then but I do now.) But I am the same, and my little girl too, if she hadn't died. But perhaps in her lifetime things would have changed and the choice would not be between a safe husband and being an outcast or eccentric. (Stendhal's advice to his sister Pauline.) In Paris or any big city I'd be thought a bit eccentric, a sort of vagabond, and find a place in the theatre and with artists. Why am I writing like this? I don't want anything else. I am happy with my little house among the trees and the rocks, with the waterfall and the wind singing my music to me. But this excerpt was from after she had regained an equilibrium.

For months—no, more, years, at least two years, for it is hard to mark the point where the tone of her journals changed, Julie raved. She was rather mad. This was when they sent her Rémy off to the Ivory Coast as a soldier and her child had died. She was knocked clean off balance: *All our balances are so precarious, a touch can do it, send us spinning, and down we go, into the whirlpool.* Sometimes her pages are so scrambled and scratched only odd phrases are readable. *The devil . . . the devil . . . who is the devil, if he has such sweet music?* She scrawled variations of this phrase over many pages: these were clearly verbal equivalents of the music itself.

The name Rémy filled pages. *Rémy, Rémy, Rémy,* she wrote, blotching pages with tears. The pages she wrote about Paul are dry and her tone ironical. But she wrote retrospectively about Paul: thus do we make safe stories about the raw pain of the past. Not all the comments are self-mocking. *When I think of Paul,* she wrote, and this was before she loved Rémy and was still full of pain because Paul had gone, *I feel a smile on my face. I hold the smile and go to the little mirror. I see an angry and even vicious curl to my lips. I don't know myself in that smile. I remember Maman gave me a doll. It came from the 'big house'—that is, my so-called father brought it from Paris. She was beautiful. She had long fair ringlets and blue eyes. She wore a dress like those after the Revolution when the rich people returned to*

Paris and fashions mocked the guillotine. She had a bright red ribbon around her neck. It was an expensive doll. I broke the doll and buried it. Maman said, What are you doing? I said, I have killed Marie. Maman gave me one of her looks. I can sometimes feel that look on my face. She was not angry. She wanted to understand. She watched me put a little cross on the grave. Then I put a gift of bananas and wine by the cross for the forest spirits and Vaval. I did not know then how in parts of the world the old spirits, and even devils, have become part of Christianity. I said to Maman, 'I didn't kill Marie, Vaval killed her.' Maman didn't say anything. She was smiling. That is the smile I have on my face when I think of Paul. But it was he who killed me. I believed I would die when they sent him away. I looked at him in his uniform when he came to say goodbye to me. He was crying and so was I. But I thought, When you are killed there will be blood on that beautiful tunic of yours. But he hasn't been killed. He is having a dis- tinguished career in the army in Indo-China. His father told me when he came to find out how I was getting on. He is a fine man, Paul's father. He told me he himself had to give up the girl he loved, because his parents made him. I asked if he thought parents were compelled to make sure their children suffer as they had themselves. He said, 'I am sorry; believe me, I'm sorry.' He had tears in his eyes. Such tears come cheap.

In the period when Julie was off balance, the music she wrote sounded, as the Russians put it, like cats scratching the heart. And then she recovered, and wrote about God and the Devil like a true daughter of the Enlightenment. And yet she did believe that she heard voices in the river sounds and in the wind. *No one calls people crazy who enjoy conjuring up faces in the fire.*

Theatrically there was a difficulty, condensing the 'scratching' music coming between the 'troubadour' music and the 'second- period' music so that it was merely suggested. But was it honest to compress the period of rage and despair into a few bars, when she herself said it was the worst thing that ever happened to her? But art

has to be a cheat and a sleight of hand, we all know that. Using time
as a measure, it was honest, for there were years to come before the
friendship with Philippe and his sensible proposal for her future,
the years when she wrote the music that was all pure cool sound,
and painted her charming pictures. There was another difficulty
too. After all, the Master Printer had a son Robert, met just once but
with such a potential for reviving everything she had renounced. In
the play he was not mentioned at all. There was too much of everything: too many ragged ends, false starts, possibilities rejected—too
much life, in short, so it all had to be tidied up. Julie's journal, where
she imagined her married life with Philippe, which would suffocate
her, was not in the play. Instead her rejection of him was in a song:
Good man, you are not for me, good man, you don't know who sings to
me at night among the rocks . . . These words were in her journals.

Act Three, then, was the Master Printer's Act. It will be seen that
the shape of this play had after all turned out to be Act One: Paul.
Act Two: Rémy. Act Three: Philippe.

During Act Three, Bill Collins and Andrew Stead, Julie's two former lovers, sat about on the edge of the action, watching.
Sometimes they sat on either side of Sarah, and then she was
divided. With only Bill there, she allowed herself to submerge in a
bath of warm sympathy, not to mention anything else, while
Andrew seemed cool and ungiving. But sitting with Andrew, when
Bill was not there, seeing Bill through his eyes, then the young man
was certainly too much of a good thing, and Sarah felt uneasy.
'Pretty baby'—she had found the words of the song on her tongue
when she woke, not once but several times. It never does to ignore
these messages from the depths. Nor the 'snapshots'—when people
you love and have become used to are seen as if for the first time.

Seeing one another in frames or poses was certainly a feature of
that week. Mary was taking pictures of Act Three: she had already
taken everything possible of Acts One and Two. The cast was photographed together and separately, inside the building and out of it,

in restaurants and by the canal. Hundreds, thousands of pho-tographs. Perhaps thirty or forty of them would be used. The prodi-gality, the waste, was taken for granted.

A difficulty was that neither Andrew Stead nor Richard Service photographed as well as Bill, who dominated every picture he was in. Mary took pictures where she 'phased Bill out,' as she put it. 'Go on, tone yourself down,' she said to him, and he went red and lost composure, as he so often did.

'Photogenic,' sighed Molly, and Mary echoed, 'The camera loves him.' 'The camera can't help loving him,' said Molly. And Mary, 'It can't help loving that man.'

Sarah saw the two women clowning and singing, 'Mad About the Boy'—not caring that Bill had just come into the hall and must see them: he was certainly not stupid. Watching the young women was Sandy Grears, grinning. Every line of his body shouted that he had to stop himself from joining in. Bill hesitated, then stepped lightly across to become part of 'Mad About the Boy'. This enabled Sandy to become a fourth. There was a wild flinging about of limbs and hair, most inappropriate for the drawling syllables of 'Mad About the Boy'.

Bill came fast across the hall to where Sarah was sedately in her chair, and dropped into Stephen's, with a direct laughing look that had nothing to do with the dear little boy who sent pretty Bambi cards but *was* the satirical dancing and singing he had just been involved with, was the swift slither of a brutally cynical caress.

She was raging with desire. (*Rage*: a good word, like *burn*.) But why describe it, since there is no one who has not felt the mix of anguish, incredulity, and—at the height of the illness—a sick sweet submersion in pain because it is inconceivable that anything so ter-ribly desired cannot be given, and if you relinquish the pain, then the hope of bliss is abandoned too.

Sarah could not remember suffering as she did now. Yet she knew she had, for the 'snapshots' from her childhood told her so.

She could not match this particular degree of being in love with anything in her adult life, only with childhood loves. After the little boy who had been tempted not by her but by the tree house, she had been in love a good part of the time with one boy after another. Adolescent, she fantasized kisses: she could not believe that this happiness would be hers soon, 'when she was grown up'. (This was the euphemism everyone used then for 'when you have breasts.') The point was, no matter how wonderful, apt, satisfying, kisses had been when she was grown up, none had had the magic ascribed to them in her imagination when too young for kisses. And so, now, 'If you kissed me, it would be my first time ever . . . ,' said Sarah to herself. Satirically: and told herself that if she could still laugh she must be all right. Poor Stephen could not laugh. The Green Bird was laughing its head off, and so was the company rehearsing *Julie Vairon*. Roger Stent had sent Sonia a fax: 'I take it you are not going to bar me from *Hedda Gabler*? If you do I'll make sure everyone knows your theatre bars critics on the strength of one bad review.'

Sonia to Roger Stent: 'You've never written a good review, or even a halfhearted one, in your life. You don't like the theatre. You know nothing about it. Get something into your little head: The Green Bird doesn't need you or *New Talents*. Fuck off.'

The rehearsals in the fourth week were run-throughs of the whole play, but still without musicians, who would arrive on the Friday.

In this last week something new happened. The main characters—Julie and her mother, Sylvie, the three lovers and the two fathers—were not starkly set in scene after scene showing confrontations, mostly two by two, but were absorbed into a setting of minor characters who, hardly noticed during the first weeks of rehearsals, now showed how much they determined destinies. As in life. In Madame Sylvie Vairon's house had been many young officers, suggested here by one, George White. In the programme notes—already with them in draft—it was said that the two women every evening entertained a crowd of young officers. This gave George White an importance that showed in how he carried himself and in an exaggeration of his attitude towards the two women, for the correct young officer did not approve of Paul's romantic love. Later there was not only Paul's father to contend with (George White again) but his mother, who, though never an actual presence, was always just offstage, a rock of rectitude and disapproval. When it came to Act Two, there was Rémy's mother (she spoke precisely two words, *No*—twice), Rémy's father (Oscar Friend, who, however forceful he was onstage, in life was a shy man, usually in a corner with a book), and also Rémy's brother, George White. In life there were four brothers, all older than Rémy, and very likely it was that weight of seniority crushing him down that made loving Julie essential to him. Theatre economics dictated one brother. This meant that Rémy's love seemed less determined by Destiny (the family) than in life, more of a romantic choice (the puppet strings invisible), though since George White had read the journals and knew about the four brothers, he did try to suggest forceful sibling pressure. In Philippe's establishment there had been twenty or so printers, apprentices, and sales people, and it was not possible that their various reactions did not affect Julie. The interior of the print shop was only mentioned in the programme notes. Philippe and Julie conducted their courtship in the public square (a park bench). Once only was the attitude of Philippe's employees shown, and that was when his manager (George White) came with a message from the shop, which enabled his frigid attitude to Julie, and her correct politeness to him, to suggest all the rest.

It was when it came to the townspeople that the audience would have to use their imaginations most. Julie's life had been cursed by the suspicious surveillance of the citizens. They stared at her in the streets and muttered imprecations if they came on her by chance (or design) in the forest. George White represented these invisible people. (He complained that all his parts were of disapproving people, but he adored Julie.) It would all go better in France, because Jean-Pierre had promised a crowd of extras.

On Friday the music arrived, in the shape of a counter-tenor and three girls and the musicians. The instruments were a guitar, a flute, a lute, a shawm, and a viola—the vielle of other times. The play, which without the music had been 'too much', 'over the top', 'pastiche,' and 'a weepy'—this last was Bill, when thoughtfully passing Kleenex to Molly—changed, distancing itself from tears. The story told on this stage, or rather in this dull church hall, where the thick beam of sunlight picked out a scene or a character, became an aspect of the music. In the drawing room in Martinique, the conventional ballad, whose function was to show off Julie's charms to the young officers, when accompanied by the music which had in counterpoint phrases from Julie's 'second period', now commented, and even cruelly, on the period itself and made it as remote as Elizabethan players dancing the minuet at Queen's Gift. The company was disconcerted by this shift from the personal, and even dismayed. Molly McGuire—as Molly—actually burst into tears. 'What was it all for, then?' she demanded. 'What was the point of them going through all that? What for?'

'A good question,' said Bill quietly, showing—as he often did—how far he could be from the 'young jay' of Stephen's criticism. And he put his arm around Molly to comfort her, nicely, like a brother.

As the story moved on, more and more did it seem that the sufferings and heartbreaks were a rather conventional accompaniment to her troubadour songs and, then, the late music, when angels or devils chanted of impermanence.

'A very good question,' said Henry to Sarah, at the end of the rehearsal, as if Molly had only just that moment wept and questioned. 'Well, did you know all that was going to happen?'

'Yes, but not that it would happen so well.'

'Yes,' he said. He was sitting, for once, in the chair near hers, leaning back, conditionally at rest, and he regarded her with those intelligent dark eyes that so often seemed prepared to see much worse than what in fact they were seeing. Now, however, they were wet.

'I didn't write the music,' said Sarah.

'Oh, I don't know about that,' he said lightly, jumping up and away. 'I don't know about that at all. All I know is, the old black magic's got me by the throat.'

On the Saturday there was a dress rehearsal. And now, at last, *Julie Vairon* was all there. Particularly was Julie present. Molly's long dark smooth hair, looped up and braided, spoke of unwelcome social disciplines. Her eyes behind long dark lashes seemed black, with a gleam of Africa. She had a feral air, for her formal move-ments had in them, only just controlled, the impatience which said she found propriety all but impossible. Julie had come to life, and Sarah heard Stephen, who had forced himself to come, let out a breath. 'Good God, it isn't possible.'

It was all going to be a success. It 'worked'.

'It all works, it's great, just fantastic,' said Henry, striding about. 'Bless you, Sarah,'—and they embraced, theatre fashion.

When Bill came to embrace her—an absolute dream in his uni-form—with 'Sarah, it's lovely, I had no idea,' she found herself mut-tering, Little bitch, and she moved away from the embrace. She watched the young man go from woman to woman, kiss, kiss, kiss, and then how he moved off and stood aloof, as if he drew an invisi-ble circle around himself: keep off.

They were now all parting, until they met again in France.

There was the usual reluctance to part. They had become a fam-ily, they said. 'All the good things about a family, none of the heartaches,' said Sally. She had insisted her own situation was not all that different from Sylvie's. 'No, I am not a mother hoping to marry my daughter off to a rich man, but my daughter, she could give Julie points.' She was desperate, though she laughed, and Richard Service, standing by her, put his arm around her. These two were friends—real friends, sitting together whenever they could, talking for hours. An unlikely couple, though.

Unable to bring themselves to part, they all went out to supper after the dress rehearsal. Stephen sat next to Molly, who had shed Julie with her clothes. He was trying to find in her the girl who had enchanted him for three hours that afternoon, and she knew it, and was sweet to him, while her eyes seldom left Bill. As for Sarah, she was determined not to look at Bill at all, and more or less succeeded. This had the effect of making him nervous, and he tried to get her attention by sending her winning looks.

As they stood on the pavement saying goodbye, kisses all around (but Sarah well out of reach of Bill's), Stephen said to Sarah that he wanted her to come and stay for a couple of days, before France. 'If you haven't got anything better to do.' This was so much like him she had to laugh, though he did not see why. As if it were likely that an invitation to his house (or perhaps she should say Elizabeth's) would not seem to nearly everyone in the world like drawing a lucky ticket.

That night Bill telephoned her for advice about the delivery of one of his lines. He must know he did it well, and know that she knew he did. Her heart thumped, making her even more angry than she was. She sat hugging the receiver and giving professional advice. That she was more angry with herself than with him goes without saying.

The other person who telephoned her was Henry. They now enjoyed the pleasantest relationship in the world, easy, joky, intimate. He sent himself up, saying, 'Sarah, I have a problem—yes, a *problem* . . . I can't deal with it. I'm not as happy as I might be—yes, you could put it like that . . . about what Julie writes about Rémy. You know, they'd only met a couple of days ago, for Christ's sake.'

'You mean, *Why is it when I see your face?*—and so on?'

'Particularly and so on. You'd expect her to be singing her little heart out about the guy, but what she sings is, *Why is it when I see your face, I see it sad, alone. You look back at me across the years and you are quite alone . . .* well, Sarah?'

'It's all in her journals.'

'They've just fallen in love.'

'Wait, I've got them here.' She read aloud: '*Why is it when we have only just begun to love each other and he is talking of how we will live together for the rest of our lives I pick up my pencil to draw his face and I can't draw it full of happiness, as I've seen it, but sad, so terribly sad. It is the face of a lonely man, he is alone, this man. No matter how hard I try to draw him the way he is when he looks at me, I can't do it, that other face puts itself on the page.*'

'What did happen to Rémy? No, I haven't read the journals. I decided not to. I didn't want to mix it.'

'Three years after he was sent off to the Ivory Coast as a soldier by his family, he came back to marry the daughter of a local landowner. He came secretly to see Julie. They wept together all night. Then he married and had a family.'

'Did they meet after that?'

'If so, it isn't recorded. She did see him at public occasions, though. She said he wasn't happy.'

'A sad story,' said Henry, apparently trying out the phrase.

'I thought it was agreed it is a sad story.'

'I mean, that he came back after three years and they hadn't forgotten each other.'

'You say that as if you think it is impossible.'

'It isn't really our style.'

'Isn't it?'

'I haven't experienced anything like that.'

'You sound as if you wish you could.'

'Perhaps I do.'

'Shall I read you what she wrote about that parting? *Together we poured hot salt on what was left of our love, and where it was is brack-ish sand.'*

'I'm glad you didn't make a song out of that.'

'What do you suppose that late music is saying?'

'Then I'm glad it hasn't got words.'

They discussed possible rearrangements of certain lines and in the end decided to leave them as they were. This conversation went on for over an hour.

Joyce turned up next morning. Evidently she had been sleeping rough. In the bathroom Sarah picked the grimy clothes off the floor as Joyce stepped out of them. She was as thin as an asparagus shoot, and like one she was dead white, but with bluish marks on her arms and thighs. Censoring every word of advice or criticism as it arrived on her lips, Sarah put the clothes in the washing machine, put Joyce in the bath, made tea, made toast, cut up an orange.

Joyce wore her aunt's best white silk dressing gown and sat drinking tea. She did not eat. When asked what she had been doing, she replied, 'This and that.' Then, after a silence, she seemed to remind herself that conversation was expected, and asked Sarah like a little child, 'And what are you doing, Auntie?' Heartened by this evidence of an interest in other people, Sarah described the play and told the story. Joyce sat listening, obviously with difficulty. Then, putting on a dozen years in a moment, she jeered, 'I think they were all nuts.'

'I wouldn't argue with that.'

'You said it was *recent*?'

Somewhere about middle age, it occurs to most people that a century is only their own lifetime twice. On that thought, all of history rushes together, and now they live inside the story of time, instead of looking at it from outside, as observers. Only ten or twelve of their lifetimes ago, Shakespeare was alive. The French

Revolution was just the other day. A hundred years ago, not much more, was the American Civil War. It had seemed in another epoch, almost another dimension of time or of space. But once you have said, A hundred years is my lifetime twice, you feel as if you could have been on those battlefields, or nursing those soldiers. With Walt Whitman perhaps.

'It wasn't very long ago,' said Sarah.

Joyce was about to protest but decided to behave tactfully, as her aunt so often did with her.

'You said it was going to be in France?'

'Yes. Next week.'

'And how long will you be away?'

'About three weeks.'

At once Joyce showed all the symptoms of panic. '*Three weeks.*'

'But Joyce, you disappear for months at a time.'

'But I know where you are, you see?'

'You never think that we worry about you?'

'But I'm all right, really.'

The InterCity train interrupted its impetuous progress, one felt as a favour, at the country station where she was to get off, instead of at Oxford, because Stephen wanted to show her a different road. She descended onto a deserted platform in a burst of birdsong. 'Adlestrop . . . it was late June . . . all the birds of Oxfordshire and Gloucestershire . . .' Well, what else? And did it matter that her head (like most people of her kind) was always full of rags and tags of verse, that she knew the first lines of a hundred popular songs? Her mind resembled one of those self-consciously decorative maps that have little scrolls saying, The Battle of Bannockburn, or Queen Elizabeth Hunted Here. Sometimes, though, the interventions were apt enough. This morning she had woken with 'Oh who can hold a fire in his hand by thinking on the frosty Caucasus?'

She walked out of the station while a cuckoo, inspired by several hundred years of literature, commented invisibly from a vast oak. Stephen was waiting in the station wagon. She realized that in town he shed a dimension, was less than himself, while here, in his setting, he was immediately full of authority. They were hardly inside the car when he said, 'Sarah, I cannot begin to say how sorry I am for inflicting so much nonsense on you. Let me try and make it up to you.' He began by driving her for an hour or so through countryside that was the distillation of poetry, on charming little roads. England in late June on a sunny day, two people who knew they liked each other . . . 'My soul, there is a country far beyond the stars . . .'

Stephen amused her with an account of what had happened at last week's Entertainment ('We call them Entertainments because it has an Elizabethan ring'), when, instead of the expected three hundred people, there arrived a thousand. There was not room for more than half of them. When some young people had turned up their transistors and began dancing, Elizabeth suggested that this field rather than that (too near the horses) would be best, and the dancing and singing went on until dawn. 'We couldn't help feeling that what went on in that field was even more to the point than the Entertainment itself. After all, the Tudors were a pretty savage lot.' 'And the field?' 'Oh, it was due to be resown anyway.' He didn't sound put out. 'Extraordinary! Why is it? I wonder. This is a theatrical time again. That's how we seem to have to express ourselves. There must be a reason for it. From one end of the country to the other, everyone is acting, singing, dancing, staging mock battles, what is it all about?' While they talked, she occasionally stole a look, she hoped unnoticed. He was not finding it easy. His determination did him credit, but there was a tightness about his face like headache strain. When she asked, he said he had never felt better. She wanted to believe this. It was so pleasant to be with the real Stephen again—so she felt it: 'He is himself again'—that it was easy to ignore anxiety.

At the house it was lunchtime. Elizabeth and Norah were off for the day to attend a music festival in Bath. He asked Sarah what she would like to do, and she said she would enjoy seeing something of his life.

'Then I hope you are not going to find me too much of an eccentric.'

'But it's part of your role to be an eccentric.'

A new building, which would turn these semi-amateur Entertainments into so much more, was nearly finished. It stood near the great lawn—the theatre—and was concealed by shrubs and trees. The plans had become even grander in the weeks since she had been here: they were thinking of doing operas. Until now more ambitious spectacles had been impossible, with the big house a couple of hundred yards away, too far for actors, singers, dancers, to make costume changes. Now there was going to be plenty of room for costumes, lighting equipment, and musical instruments, and ample rehearsal space. The place had been designed by an architect to take its place unnoticed among these historic buildings. It would look similar in style without making any claims for itself.

Two workmen were laying bricks on an internal wall. One straddled the wall, the other was handing bricks to him. Stephen spoke to them and came away: 'I'm not needed. Sometimes I can be useful. But these are not our people; they are a firm in town.'

They walked slowly through trees, away from the house. She was thinking, for she could not stop herself, of that young man who was with his 'mate' in France: Bill had said he would use the opportunity to be a tourist for a week. No, she certainly did not see a girlfriend. 'Perhaps my girlfriend will get over for a few days.' She wondered if Stephen was thinking of Molly, who was also there somewhere. After they had been silent for some minutes, he said unexpectedly, 'It occurred to me, thinking it all out, you know, that I must be lonely. It seems improbable, but there it is. No, no, believe me, Sarah, I'm not trying for sympathy. I'm trying to understand it all, you see.'

'Did you know Elizabeth loved women when you married her?'

'She didn't, not then.' Taking her silence for criticism, he defended himself, with a stubbornness, a determination, she could see was because he had made a decision to tell her all this. Because he needed to hear how it sounded? 'No, you see, we have known each other all our lives. We really married because . . . you see, we both of us came to grief at the same time.'

'A good phrase, that, came to grief.'

'Yes, it is. Not that I understood it until . . . you see, something I hoped for didn't happen.'

'You were in love—impossibly?'

'I didn't think it was impossible. It wasn't impossible. She was married, but I hoped she would leave her husband and marry me. But she changed her mind. And Elizabeth was hoping to marry someone . . . he's a good chap. He's a friend of mine. Well, in fact he's on the next estate. But he was engaged to be married, and it was all too difficult. And there we both were, the two of us, Elizabeth and I.'

They sat on a log in a hot dry shade. At least fifty feet above them, on the other side of the beech canopy, burned an un-English sun.

'It all fitted in. She was in trouble with money. A complicated will—that sort of thing. And if we married, her problems would be over.'

'And you were happy?'

'We were . . . content.'

'That is a very big word.'

'I suppose it is. Yes, it is. And then I began to feel . . .' He contemplated what he had felt, and for a pretty long time.

'Did you feel there was no conviction in it?'

'That's it, exactly. I began to feel like a ghost in my own house—no, well, it's not my house. Better say, in my own home. I tried to . . . earth myself. I learned to do all kinds of things. I'm a pretty good carpenter now. I can do any kind of electrical work. I can do plumbing and lay drains. I did it all deliberately—do you understand? Yes, of course you do. To make me part of the place. And to stop me . . . I felt as if I were floating away. Well, it has certainly made all the difference to the estate. We stopped losing money. We never have to call in workmen. Except for a big building job.'

'And all that didn't help?'

'Yes, it did. To a point. And then . . . I came to grief. That's it. I don't understand it. It was as if there was a hole in my life, and blood was pouring away. I know that is very melodramatic. But that's how it was.'

'So when did Julie come into it?'

'She slowly took possession. I heard her music at the festival—you know all about that. And then I went in search of everything to do with her. It was enjoyable at first, like a treasure hunt. And then . . . it was *La Belle Dame sans Merci*, all right.'

'Whatever it is, it will pass,' she quoted.

'Do you really believe that?'

'Yes. At least, I haven't experienced anything different.'

It was at this point she was tempted—and almost began on her confession—to tell him of her state. But she was in a certain role with him: someone strong, to whom he could show his weakness and not be afraid. Would their friendship survive her saying, 'I am in love to the point of insanity,' with a young man, and one he didn't have much time for? No, for him to be in love with Julie was certainly crazy, but for a woman her age to be in love with a beautiful youth . . . Even if the said youth was in love with her. He was, to a point. *In love*: there are people who keep a lock of hair or a piece of cloth in an envelope, sometimes come on it, and tenderly smile. *In love*: a glow of tender lost possibilities, like the light left behind in the sky at moonset. That would be appropriate to her position: in fact people would like it. Ah me, my sweetly fractured heart that aches gently like a rheumatic knee with the approach of bad weather. As for Bill, what he would like probably would be a kiss and a good cuddle. (At this a savage and forgotten sexual pride raised its head and remarked: Yes? I'd show him better!) Apart from anything else—cowardice was the word—it would be unkind to tell this suffering man who relied on her (who had put a desperate hand into hers), 'I am weaker than you are. Worse, I'm ridiculous,' and expect him to add this burden to his. He would have to overcome, for a start, some pretty orthodox reactions. Most men and more women—young women afraid for themselves—punish older women with derision, punish them with cruelty, when they show inappropriate signs of sexuality. If men, they are getting their own back for the years they have been subject to the sexual power of women. She consoled herself with: When this business with Bill is forgotten, I shall still be Stephen's friend.

He said, 'I suppose what I feel is, well, if I could spend one night with her, just one night, that's all, then everything marvellous would be given to me.'

'One night with *whom*?'

'Yes, all right,' he said, but he was not conceding an inch to common sense.

They sat on, for a while, in silence. Rather, in a jubilation of bird sound. Birds, disturbed by their arrival, had forgotten about them. She could actually feel the sounds, loud, shrill, sweet, soft, ringing along her nerves. Surely nothing like this had happened to her before: that sounds, even the sweetest, were dangerous, made her feel over-exposed? She got up, to escape the assault; Stephen did too, and they strolled towards the house. She was telling him, making a humorous thing of it, about the two tiny children and their tree house, about her pain, as a child. It occurred to her she was entertaining Stephen, making funny stories as one does with an acquaintance or somebody one doesn't want to come too close: the counterfeit offered to most of the people one knows. A glance showed that he was painfully listening, and he remarked, 'I think one's early experiences are mostly pretty awful. I don't like thinking about them myself.'

She had been rebuked and was glad of it: he wasn't going to put up with any second best.

Elizabeth and Norah returned very late that night, saying they had had a wonderful time: they had learned useful things about the organization of festivals. Why didn't they have a festival at Queen's Gift? They stood at the window in a drawing room, looking out into the glamorous night, which they seemed reluctant to relinquish for bed, as they chatted. Both brown with the summer, full of health and accomplishment, they were two handsome women who seemed to have dropped into that room at all only as a favour to a guest: and Sarah thought that Stephen himself looked rather like a guest. He gave his wife today's news about the Entertainment that would take place in three days' time: in French, with French music, and singers who were friends of Elizabeth's from Paris. Sarah then remarked that they could soon expect trouble from the actors' and musicians' unions if foreign performers were used. Elizabeth said that when they had expanded and the new building was in use, their Entertainments would no longer be considered amateur, she knew that. Perhaps Sarah could give them good advice? The two women went off to bed with the look of those who have done a social duty.

Stephen asked Sarah if she would enjoy a stroll, and they walked for an hour across fields, through woods, while the moon slid away and lengthened the shadows. They did not talk. It occurred to Sarah that she was enjoying the silence. More, she was submitting to it, like a cure. A bird breaking out of a tree as they came under it startled her, the noise painfully loud.

Sarah stayed three days in the house that had stood there four

centuries. She was enjoying the feeling that she was one of the hundreds—thousands?—of people who had passed through it. She did
any number of agreeable things in it, looked at its pictures and furniture, read its history. Elizabeth and Norah took her for energetic
walks, while she advised them on theatre problems. She liked them
both, and, particularly, the exuberance of their plans for the future.
It appeared that they planned to invite The Green Bird to put on
Julie Vairon here at the end of summer, after the run in France. The
facilities might not be ready, but the workmen had been given
instructions to hurry up everything. This meant Stephen felt he had
a good excuse to work with them in the task of putting up a frame-
work of rafters for the roof. On the last afternoon, observing that
Sarah was watching, he came down and took her off to walk in the
trees.

'I suppose you think it is pretty ridiculous?' he enquired, meaning his doing physical work. She was thinking that it suited him, for
he looked so much better, the cloud gone from his face. Then he
said that Elizabeth was grateful for all the advice. 'That was what
we've lacked, really. What you've got—all the experience of the business side. I know that Elizabeth can seem pretty offhand, but don't
imagine she isn't as pleased as she can be.'

Sarah had not thought of Elizabeth as offhand: she was familiar
with this kind of woman, borne along on the energy of her competence, not impatient of others' lesser efforts so much as oblivious of
them. Sonia was going to be the same.

'Do you think Elizabeth and Norah believe we are having an
affair?' she made herself ask, and he at once went red. 'Well, yes,
probably, I suppose so. But don't mind about it. I'm sure she doesn't.
Perhaps she even likes me better for it.' And then, in a switch of
mood, even of personality, for he was suddenly hard and angry: 'A
very sensible woman, Elizabeth. I don't think I've ever known anyone
as sensible. She doesn't have much time for weakness of any kind.' A
pause. A long one. It was touch and go, she could see, whether he

would go on. Then, deliberately, 'I think I find that as intolerable as
anything in my life, that I can't talk to a woman I've lived with for fifteen years as I can to you.'

'Intolerable,' she said: she was not used to excessive language
from him.

'Yes, that's the word, I think. Yes, intolerable. I find a good deal
intolerable, and that more than anything. You see, I don't think she
knows much about me. If you are thinking, But she doesn't care
about you—well, that's a different issue. But there's something
about a woman you've known since you played on a seesaw together
not knowing a damned thing about you—yes, intolerable.'

When she left, they were separating for only a couple of days,
because they would meet on Saturday at Belles Rivières.

The town's three hotels had been called Hôtel des Clercs, Hôtel
des Pins, and Hôtel Rostand. Now there were l'Hôtel Julie, Hôtel la
Belle Julie, and Hôtel Julie Vairon. Any muddles about bookings, letters, and telephone calls were considered by the proprietors unimportant put against the benefits of being associated with the town's
illustrious daughter. The hotels had been booked out a month
before the opening of *Julie Vairon.* To avoid ill-feeling, the company
had been disposed equally among the three.

Sarah's window overlooked a main square composed of houses
left to merge into a palette of pastel colours, chalky white and
cream, gentle greys, and the palest of terra-cottas, so sympatheti-
cally worked on by time (from the look of things, many decades)
that only a freshly painted wall, the end wall of Hôtel la Belle Julie,
glared white, explanation enough why the town authorities preferred this graceful fading. Sarah's room was on the corner of
l'Hôtel Julie, and from it she could see the windows of a room in
Hôtel la Belle Julie, also on the second floor, which had a balcony,
with white and pink oleanders in pots. There Bill Collins lay in

bathing trunks all Sunday, and from there he had waved to Sarah before sinking back, arms behind his head, in his chair. His eyes hid themselves behind dark glasses. Between Sarah and the young man stood an umbrella pine with a rough reddish bark, and this thick trunk absorbed into itself such a charge of erotic longing she could not bear to look at it, but directed her eyes at an ancient plane tree, with a bench under it, where children were playing. She tried not to look at all at that dangerous balcony once she saw that Bill had been joined by Molly, who lay on a parallel chair. She was not half nude, for her milky Irish skin could not be safely submitted to this sunlight. She lolled in loose blue pyjamas, her arms behind her head. Her eyes were invisible, like his. The two had the luxurious show-off charm of young cats who know they are being admired. Sarah admired them with abandon, while pain sliced through her. Knives had nothing on this: red-hot skewers were more like it, or waves of fire. She had not felt physical jealousy for so long, she had had at first to wonder, What is wrong with me? Have I got a temperature?

She was poisoned. A fierce poison ate her up, wrapped her in a garment of fire, like the robes used in antiquity to enwrap rivals, who were then unable to pull the cloth from their flesh. Not only the sight of Molly—Bill's equal, being young—and the hot rough trunk of the tree, but the grainy texture of her curtain, which held hairy light like sunlight on skin, the solid curves of cloud shot with golden evening light, the sound of a young laugh—all or any of these squeezed air from her, leaving her eyes dark and her head dizzy. Certainly she was ill; if this was not illness, then what could you call it? She felt, in fact, that she was dying, but she must put a good face on everything and pretend nothing was happening. No use to pretend to Bill himself, though. When they met that evening as the company assembled outside Les Collines Rouges, his close hold of her did not lack information that he was responding to her condition and wanted her to know it. He let his mouth brush her cheek and murmured, 'Sarah . . .'

They all sat in a crowd on the pavement, tables pushed close, while the sky lost colour and the sound of the cicadas became loud when the roar and grind of the cars and motorcycles abated because there was not one inch left anywhere to park. Thirty or so of the company, English, French, American, and combinations of these peoples, they were united by Julie, and did not want to separate. They ordered food to be served there, on the pavement, and when that was consumed, sat on drinking in the southern dusk that smelled of petrol, dust, urine, perfumed sun-oil and cosmetics, garlic, and the oil used for *frites*. A hundred years ago, the smell would have been made up of the aromatics released by sun from foliage, and dust and food being cooked in these houses. This evening there was, too, a smell of freshly watered dust: a hose-pipe had begun to spin out arcs of spray under the plane tree.

It was entertaining to see how they had all disposed themselves: she was sharing with Mary Ford glances that were the equivalent of gossip. She, Mary Ford, had next to her Jean-Pierre, not only because so much was depending on her publicity, but because he fancied her. Opposite Bill sat Patrick. There was nothing for him to do in France, and he was at work on *Hedda Gabler*, but he had insisted he wanted to see what they were all up to. He sat dramatically sulking because of Bill's popularity, and because Sandy Grears had no eye for Patrick himself. These three made a triangle drawn in invisible ink on this map of the emotions. On the edge of the crowd sat Sally and Richard, the handsome black woman, the quiet and diffident Englishman, quietly conversing. Sarah had been careful to sit not near Bill but beside Stephen, who was where he could watch Molly. That he had not sat near Molly was an acceptance of his situation that brought tears to Sarah's eyes, but she knew she was weeping for herself. Tears stood far too often in eyes that until *Julie Vairon* had seldom to accommodate them. Stephen was gazing at the solid, creamy-fleshed, lightly freckled girl with her hazy Irish eyes, no doubt trying to understand the secret that would transform her—had on occasions already transformed her—into the lithe and fiery Julie. As for Molly, she could hardly be unaware he was attracted to her, but had no idea of the dark lunacies possessing him. When for some reason his eyes were not on her, she stole thoughtful looks at him. Well, Stephen was an attractive man. Handsome. Only when sitting here among so many vivid young people did he have to suffer comparisons. In fact Molly did rather fancy Stephen, or would if she were not besotted by Bill. Probably in his ordinary life Bill was a young man no more conceited than was inevitable, with such looks. Tonight he was absorbing hot rays of desire like a solar panel and was positively shining with complacent self-consciousness, intolerable if underneath had not lived an anxious small boy who sometimes peeped out through those lovely eyes. Meanwhile the company were aware that people strolling past on the pavement looked twice to make sure the young man was as handsome as their eyes told them he was.

Sarah sat observing her anger growing like a fat and unstoppable cancer. She did not know if she was more angry or more desirous. She was thinking that if this young man did not come to her that night she would very likely die, and this did not seem an exaggeration in her feverish state. She knew he would not do this. Not because she was old enough to be his grandmother, but because of the invisible line drawn around him: *Don't touch*—that sexually haughty look that goes with a much younger state, the late teens, and says, 'I'm not for you, you shameless people, but if you knew what I *could* do to you if I chose, then . . . ,' a look that is accompanied by the (silent) raucous jeer of the adolescent, full of sexual aggression, desire and self-doubt. An impure chastity. Was this (his unavailability) why she had not put him not in her own hotel but in the one next door? She had decided this was out of pride or even a sense of honour. But she had put Molly in the same hotel as Stephen, murmuring to herself something like *Fair's fair*, meaning that Stephen should have the benefit of this sojourn in Julie's country even if she, Sarah, could not. But if she had done what Molly obviously wanted, the girl would have been put in Bill's hotel. (She, Sarah, had not allotted rooms, only handed lists of names to the hotels.) Was it out of jealousy she had done this? She believed not. For one thing, there was nothing to stop Molly (or Bill—a likely story!) walking a few yards to the other's hotel. After all, she had spent the day on his balcony. But Sarah's ruling thought had been, Stephen wants her a thousand times more than Bill ever could.

While these amorous calculations went on, Sarah chatted and laughed and generally contributed to this amiable occasion, and she watched Stephen, her heart aching for him and for herself, and she knew that she was housing separate blocks or associations of emotions that were contradictory to the point it seemed impossible they could live together inside one skin. Or head. Or heart.

First of all was the fact she was in love. There seems to be a general agreement that being in love is a condition unimportant, and even comic. Yet there are few more painful for the body, the heart, and—worse—the mind, which observes the person it (the mind) is supposed to be governing behaving in a foolish and even shameful way. The fact is, she thought, while she refused to allow her eyes to be drawn to Bill but sat talking to Stephen, who was happy to have this distraction, there is an area of life too terrible even to be acknowledged. For people are often in love, and they are usually not in love equally, or even at the same time. They fall in love with people not in love with them as if there were a law about it, and this leads to . . . if the condition she was in were not tagged with the innocuous 'in love', then her symptoms would be those of a real illness.

From this central thought or area led several paths, and one of them was to the fact that the fate of us all, to get old, or even to grow older, is one so cruel that while we spend every energy in trying to avert or postpone it, we in fact seldom allow the realization to strike home sharp and cold: from being *this*—and she looked around at the young people—one becomes *this*, a husk without colour, above all without the lustre, the shine. And I, Sarah Durham, sitting here tonight surrounded mostly by the young (or people who seem young to me), am in exactly the same situation as the innumerable people of the world who are ugly, deformed, or crippled, or who have horrible skin disorders. Or who lack that mysterious thing sex appeal. Millions spend their lives behind ugly masks, longing for the simplicities of love known to attractive people. There is now no difference between me and those people barred from love, but this is the first time it has been brought home to me that all my youth I was in a privileged class sexually but never thought about it or what it must mean not to be. Yet no matter how unfeeling or callous one is when young, everyone, but everyone, will learn what it is to be in a desert of deprivation, and it is just as well, travelling so fast towards old age, that we don't know it.

And yet, if it really is so terrible, so painful, that sitting here I feel like a miserable old ghost at a feast, why is it that for two decades, more, I lived content with a deprivation I only now feel is intolerable? Most of the time I hardly noticed that I was ageing. I did not care. I was too busy. My life is too interesting. With better luck (meaning, if I had not entered Julie's territory), I could have lived comfortably with something like a light dimming, or a fire dying down almost unnoticed, and arrived at being really old, hardly feeling the transition. And I suppose I can expect soon to be cured of this affliction, when I will look back and laugh. Though at the moment laughing is certainly something hard to imagine. I couldn't forget how I am suffering now—could I?

How could I have been so callous? When I was young—and not so young—men were always falling in love with me and I took it for granted, exactly like Mary Ford sitting smiling kindly at Jean-Pierre, exactly like Molly *being sweet* to Stephen, and like Bill, sitting there with his hands behind his head and looking up at those stars (not as bright as they might be, with so much pollution—Julie's stars were certainly much brighter), knowing that we are looking at him, our eyes dragged towards him while he is (apparently) unaware of it. When a man looked at me in that particular way, the burning accusing eyes, the aggression, the body that made the single flagrant assertion, *I want you*, did I then give him a single compassionate thought? Yet I knew what a terrible thing love is, and there is no excuse. There is a terrible arrogance that goes with physical attractiveness, and far from criticizing it, we even admire it.

It was late. The square's load of cars was dispersing. It actually seemed, as the vehicles left, that the pavements and cafés and hotels stood higher in relation to the hills, the stars, the trees. People were dispersing, if reluctantly, saying they must go to bed, they must get their beauty sleep.

From a hotel car, arriving late from the airport, there alighted on an empty pavement Henry, with Benjamin Greenfield, the American who had flown in to take a look at his, or his bank's, investment. Sarah was already on her way to her hotel (her beauty sleep) when Henry came fast up to her, saying, 'I'm starving. The plane was late. I've got to eat. Will you join me?' She was saying she had eaten, as Benjamin Greenfield came to join them. He and she had spoken often and at length over the telephone, and now felt they knew each other. He too invited her for a late supper, but she converted the supper into a possible breakfast. Henry stood by while this went on, and then she found Bill beside her. He embraced her with 'Good night Sarah. I do so want to talk over a problem with my uniform tomorrow.' She introduced him, as he had intended, to Benjamin. 'Our American sponsor, and this is one of the stars of *Julie Vairon*.' Benjamin was led back to the pavement outside the café and its spread of tables, now mostly empty. Sarah watched how Bill deferentially pulled out a chair for the older man and sat down, leaning forward. Sarah did not allow her eyes to meet Henry's: she knew that he was thinking, as she was, Well, it's a cruel profession. Henry now decided that after all he would do without supper.

Stephen came up with Molly. The four walked together to the hotel. There Sarah stood in the foyer with Henry and they watched Stephen take Molly by the arm and lead her to a display case showing photographs of the real Julie, who could now be bought not only as her own self-portraits but as scarves, lockets, and various types of T-shirt. Stephen and Molly had their backs to them. Henry smiled, ironic, at Sarah. She smiled, ironic, back. This exchange was balm and butter on open wounds. 'Show business,' said Henry briskly, and then, 'And now I'm going to telephone my wife. An exercise in relativity, this time business. She is just putting my son to bed.' With another smile at Sarah, he ran lightly up the stairs, disdaining the lift, while Sarah chose the lift, not looking back down at the foyer, where she knew Stephen made excuses to stretch his moment alone with Molly.

It was a night of truly atrocious suffering. To be in love—always bad enough, unless kisses match imagined kisses. But to hate oneself for it: she kept seeing Bill come modestly up, then embracing her, with one eye on 'our American Croesus'.

Suppose Bill did turn up at her door now. He would not. But . . . patience. Years ago, left a widow, she had gone through months, years, believing that if she could not have him, her dear and familiar husband, beside her at night, there was no point in living. This soon converted to: if she could not sleep enfolded with a man, then . . . Soon, and expectedly, she arrived at a state where to sleep alone was a gift, and a grace, and she could not believe that so recently she had wept and suffered for the sake of a man's body companioning hers. After that—years of equanimity. Sexlessness? Well, no, for she sometimes masturbated, but not because she longed for a particular partner. She had perfected the little activity so that it was briefly accomplished, a relief from tension but without pleasure, rather with irritation because of the gracelessness of it. Self-divisive too, because the narcissism which is so much part of eroticism now could not be fed by thoughts of how she was—was now: images of her own charms could not fuel eroticism as, she only now understood, they once had, when she had been almost as much intoxicated with herself as with the male body that loved hers. Nor could she dare to admit memories of how she had been, because they had latent in them a dry anguish of loss—dangerous, for did she really want to live accompanied with multiple ghosts of herself, as old people often set around their rooms photographs of themselves when young? Now, in carefully controlled fantasies, she was voyeur, because some kind of pride, expressed as an aesthetic choice, forbade her participation in scenes of young bodies, male and female—or, at any rate, female and male bodies as central figures, the main actors, even if assisted by others in supporting roles, ambiguously sexed. The figures she imagined were never people she knew: she did not care to make use of them. This sexual landscape had about it something ritual, permitted, as part of the life of some people, or tribe, from the past (or the future?), in a place set apart for love-making. But she could almost think of this sex as impersonal, partly because of her own non-participation in it. Certainly it had as much to do with real eroticism and its multifarious submissions to pleasure, its celebration of male and female, as chewing gum has to do with eating.

Where now was the cautious woman? Her erotic self had been restored as if the door had never been slammed shut. Above all, she was no longer divided. Her fantasies were as romantic now as when she was adolescent, and as erotic as when she had been a 'love woman', and were of herself, herself now, and this was because, embraced by Bill, she had felt his desire for her so strongly announce itself. She lay mouth to mouth with Bill, and his thick red penis was inside her as far up as her throbbing heart. Lust and anger beat through her in waves, and tenderness absorbed both.

She could feel him there with her so strongly she could hardly believe he was not there, would not knock at her door. This was how the myths and legends of the incubi and succubi had emerged: born of this powerful longing. A couple of hundred years ago, she would easily have been persuaded that a sensual demon was in her bed, a demon all vitality.... That animal vitality of Bill's, what did it remind her of? Of photographs of herself, young, when she had exactly this robust attractiveness, an animal and glistening physicality, arrogant and even cruel in its demands on whoever looked—and desired. If people fall in love with their own likenesses (and you can watch them doing it, every day), then she had now, at least in part, fallen in love with that girl whose calm but proud set of the head, eyes looking straight back at the photographer, had made the statement: Yes, I know, but hands off.

It goes without saying her sleep was full of erotic dreams. The alarm woke her at eight, and almost at once, his alarm having woken him, Stephen rang from the room just above hers to say he had scarcely slept but had taken a sleeping pill in the early hours and at last felt sleepy, would she wake him later, say at eleven? 'After all, I don't really have to see this American chap, do I?' 'We thought you'd like to know your fellow sponsor.' 'I am sure I would, but another time, Sarah.'

She dressed carefully. Women of a certain age (and older) have to do this. What she wore became her, certainly. In the glass she saw a handsome woman in white linen who had about her a dewy look far from the competent asperities appropriate to her real age. This was because of the elixirs romping in her blood. Her whole body ached, but this did not show. 'Amazing,' she said aloud, and descended the stairs at a brisk rate, because her condition made it impossible for her to move slowly. Henry was in the foyer. He gave her a glance, but his eyes returned to her for a slow look, all approval. They exchanged the smiles of comrades-in-arms: if thoughts of Bill were shame, anger, and poison, then Henry and the healthful complicities of being with him were their antidote. He watched her walk out: she could feel his eyes on her.

Benjamin was waiting for her at the café table. She sat, making apologies for Stephen. She was amused that everything about this agreeable man, who was good-looking in a calm and sensible way, repudiated the casual ways of the theatre, and even the holiday airs of Belle-Rivières. He wore expensive white trousers and a white linen shirt, and filled them accurately, in the way that says, This one has to watch what he eats. His hair—greying, he must be fifty—was appropriate to his sober station in life. There was not a hint about that immaculate personage of the sartorial eccentricities allowable in Europe, and particularly in Britain. He sat at his ease, aware of everything going on around them: not much yet, for there were still only a few people on the café pavement. One was Andrew, apparently contemplating the cars already creeping around the square looking for crevices to fit themselves into. His pale blue jeans and shirt were no different from what any other member of the company might wear, but on him they suggested horizons. He was a lonely and austere figure: as she thought this he was brought a great plate of ham and eggs, and he began eating with gusto. He had not seen her and Benjamin, or did not want to see them. If it is interesting, who sits next to whom in a company of people working together, then even more so are the moments when one of them chooses solitude. As she turned her attention back to Benjamin, Andrew raised his hand in greeting, without looking at her.

She was determined not to raise her eyes to the balcony where she might see Bill: even the possibility he was there was enough to exert a gravitational pull down that side of her body, while her back had become a separate sensory zone. Over Benjamin's shoulder she saw Andrew turn his chair: now he was looking straight at her. Did he want to be asked to join them? But it was unlikely that he wanted to court this rich patron. For one thing, it was not his style, which was independent to the point of bellicosity, and for another, he did not need to. Integrity is so often the fruit of success.

Benjamin was telling her that his bank, or chain of banks, was putting money into six plays or, as he put it, theatrical enterprises.

'We have undertaken to finance six theatrical enterprises. I have to confess it was our chairman's wife who suggested it. She is interested in the arts. And we did not respond at first as generously as we should. But she kept hammering away at us, and soon the idea began to take hold. At least, it did not take very much effort on my part to talk the board into it. We don't expect to make much money, but that is not the main consideration.'

'I hope you are not going to lose money on our play.'

'After all, we do sometimes lose money on a risk, so why not on a good cause? That is how we have come to see it. Anyway, I spend my time financing new enterprises, and this isn't really so very different. And it gets me to travel to pretty places and to meet pretty people.' Here he slightly but firmly nodded, in the American manner, like a conductor's baton: You come in here. In this case he was emphasizing that the compliment was for her. She acknowledged it with a smile. She was in fact enjoying the morning and able to forget her condition. She was also intrigued. This man in her own country was referred to as a 'businessman', nearly always with faint disapprobation. If he had been British, and needing to defend himself against the genteel prejudices of his nation, he would have confessed to his occupation but by now would be talking about his hobby, growing roses or collecting fine wines, insisting that was where his heart was. Having no need to feel deficient, he was talking with energy and pleasure about his work. 'I don't sit in an office, I am glad to say; I don't want you to believe that. . . .' Nine-tenths of his time he was involved in the day-by-day struggles of new businesses, some of them risky. 'I've been doing this for ten years now, so I can offer you quite a selection, and some of them I'm proud to have godfathered.'

'Tell me,' she invited, for as long as he talked, the splendours and miseries of her preoccupation were kept at bay.

'Well now, how do you like the notion of a glass factory making exact copies of the masterpieces of the past? Using some old techniques and some new ones? "Masterpieces of the Past", we call it. I tell you, when you see one of those things, you want to own it, but they are too expensive for anything but a glass case in a museum. Museums are buying them—colleges, schools. Millionaires . . . Does that strike you as too rarefied? Here's the other extreme. We have a factory making a certain component. It is about a millimetre square, but it revolutionizes a whole sequence of processes in computer technology . . . not as exciting, I must confess.' In fact she found it exciting, but this was not how he wanted to see her. Artists are not expected to be interested in technology. 'How do you like the idea of buying a house all furnished and complete? The garden too—everything from a cactus garden to a Japanese garden. Or French formality. An English cottage garden . . . you order it, and there it is. I confess you have to be pretty well-heeled for some of our gardens.' He offered her these ideas and then some more, as he sat taking quick mouthfuls of coffee from a cup held at the ready in his hand, as if getting enough caffeine into him was the most important item on his agenda. Meanwhile he watched her face and was pleased when he saw she was interested. He liked her, it was clear. Well, she liked him—banal words for mysterious processes. It became a game. He offered her descriptions of this or that idea financed by his bank, and she indicated the degree to which it appealed to her, not necessarily truthfully but to match his picture of her. If you go along with how a person sees you, then you learn a great deal about that person. Soon they were laughing much more than this factual and sober exchange warranted, partly because she was prescribing laughter for herself as a therapy, and partly because all her emotions were sloshing about like a strong tide in a small rock pool. As for him, the gaiety of the theatre, the charm, had taken him over and he was inside Julie's spell. Now all the chairs around them were filling, mostly with the company, and they were smiling at this satisfactory scene, their Croesus having such a good time with Sarah. Andrew's smile, dry, appreciative, seemed to have become stuck there, as he frankly watched the two of them.

Then just as Sarah was telling Benjamin how pleased he was going to be with what he would see tomorrow, for there was no way he could imagine the effect of the music when it fitted the action, there was a check, a snag: he had booked to fly to London that night. This meant he would not have seen *Julie Vairon*. He had thought there was a rehearsal that afternoon, but she explained it was a technical rehearsal and they would be merely walking through their parts. 'So you won't have seen it.'

His face indicated that he did not regard this as the total disaster it seemed she did. He even remarked that he trusted them all to get it right—a joke, but she did not laugh. It did occur to her that she might be getting things a little out of proportion. She saw Jean-Pierre on the other side of the square, going to his office. She excused herself and begged him to stay exactly where he was, for he certainly should meet the French side of the production. She walked quickly through the dust under the pine tree and then the plane tree, dry again although the square had been thoroughly watered the evening before. The trees seemed to be accommodating a hundred cicadas, all in full voice. She caught up with Jean-Pierre, to whom she explained it was out of the question that the American sponsor, who was providing so much of the money, should not experience a real performance. She begged him to think of something to keep Benjamin here. Then she walked fast, full of the energy she did not command when not in love, back to her hotel, for it was time to wake Stephen.

On the balcony above the crowd on the pavement outside Les Collines Rouges, a young god, knowing he was one, all sleek warm sun-browned flesh, with glistening dark hair, melting gaze, stood among the oleanders watching Sarah's progress and waiting for her to see him. As luck would have it, she saw him only at the last moment, and her wave was perfunctory. His hand, which had been held out to her, palm forward, bestowing sensual blessings, sank to his side, rejected. He was genuinely hurt.

She went to her room and telephoned Stephen's. He was just awake and suggested she should come up. Up she went. Stephen departed to the bathroom and she sat on a fat little sofa, covered with a country cretonne, to match the nostalgic flowered wallpaper, and ordered coffee. She was lighthearted, her miseries in another country—night country.

She stood at the window and looked down through naïvely pretty curtains at a table where Bill sat with Molly. Opposite them were Sally and Richard. She yearned to be with them. Group life is a drug.

Sandy the lighting man came past, paused by Bill, and handed him something that looked like a photograph. Bill took it from Sandy and laughed, a young loud laugh that heard itself and approved. Sarah would never know what the photograph was, or why Bill found it so funny, but the scene was so strongly impressed on her, because of her state, that she felt she could not forget it. Henry went past the tables, stopping briefly to greet them all before directing himself to the end of the square where in a side street was the Musée Julie Vairon. He had said last night he would visit it this morning. Sarah watched Benjamin and Jean-Pierre emerge from a shop and walk briskly after Henry. Stephen came from the bathroom and stood by her, looking down—of course—at Molly. Sarah and Stephen stood side by side and watched Molly and Bill, who were now pretending to tussle for possession of the photograph.

'Cruel,' remarked Stephen, with affectation of dispassion.

'Cruel if not so common,' she agreed.

'Cruel, anyway. And I don't care a tinker's cuss about Molly, not really.'

She quoted,

> Do you imagine it is because of you, conceited youth,
> That I lie awake weeping?
> Rather it's because how often I've said,

No, no, no, just like you now,
Thinking that all my life
There would be sweet hot dawns and kisses.

'Who? A minor Roman? But she hasn't said no. I daren't ask her. Meanwhile I go from bad to worse. Last night I actually had to stop myself writing poetry.'

Sarah decided not to say that the verse was a result of wakefulness.

The town authorities, or perhaps it was the café, chose this moment to switch on their canned music. It came from the pine tree, and must be disconcerting the cicadas. Julie's troubadour music, that is to say, love songs, filled the town and vibrated every molecule in Sarah's body.

'Extraordinary stuff,' said Stephen. 'It takes you over.'

'Music is the food of love.'

'Is that what it is the food of?' said he, with exactly the same mix of irritation and yearning she felt.

Groups of people were moving across the square to the museum. Among them went Molly and Bill, Richard and Sally. Henry was with them. He had reappeared and was talking to Jean-Pierre. And where was Benjamin? Sarah explained to Stephen it was essential to keep Benjamin here for at least one performance, and Stephen said he couldn't see why the American chap should be made to stay here against his will. 'Ah, but it won't be against his will. And you don't understand. You rich patrons must be kept sweet and happy because we will need you next year. Not to mention the year after.'

'Happy!'

'Happiness is no laughing matter,' quoted Sarah.

They went downstairs and into the hot morning, the stinks and perfume of the south, the din of traffic, and Julie's music. They strolled, laughing from bravado, across the square, both high on these compounded stimulants, and watched Henry and Benjamin approach. Under the plane tree, Bill and Molly stood together.

Stephen stopped, unable to go on. He looked this morning like a miserable old man. Worse, there was something frivolous, or fatuous, about him. She could hardly believe this was the strong and impressive man she had seen in his own setting. And probably she had something silly and pathetic about her too.

She took his arm and moved him on.

'Even a god falling in love could not be wise,' said Stephen.

'Who? I pass. But, Who loves, raves.'

'Byron,' he said at once.

'Oh lyric love, half angel and half bird and all a wonder and a wild desire,' said Sarah, watching the two men come towards them, Henry visibly slowing his pace to the measured pace of Benjamin.

'Browning,' said Stephen.

'Browning it is.'

'And most of all would I flee from the cruel madness of love, the honey of poison flowers and all the measureless ills . . . , but in my case that is far from true.'

'Who else but?' Now Bill and Molly were approaching. She began to laugh. 'He is coming, my own, my sweet,' she mocked herself, and looked at Stephen to go on.

He said, not laughing, 'Were it ever so airy a tread . . .'

'My heart would hear it and beat . . .'

While Sarah and Stephen exchanged lines, Henry and Benjamin stood in front of them, listening.

Stephen: 'Were it earth in an earthly bed . . .'

Sarah: 'My dust would hear it and beat . . .'

Bill and Molly had arrived. Now the four stood confronting Stephen and Sarah. It was Bill whose face showed a rich and irreverent appreciation. 'Tennyson,' he breathed, like a boy in class.

'Tennyson it most certainly is,' said Stephen. 'Had I lain for a century dead . . .'

Bill cut in, looking straight at Sarah: 'Would start and tremble under my feet And blossom in purple and red.'

'What glorious, marvellous nonsense,' said Sarah, laughing fit to be sick, while Bill gave her a charming and intimate smile, saying he knew why she laughed so excessively and he could not sympathize more.

Benjamin remarked judiciously, 'I suppose it is nonsense according to whether you are in love or not.'

'That, I would say, is an accurate summing up of the situation,' said Stephen. His look at Molly caused her to blush, then laugh, and turn away. He insisted, 'Time was away and somewhere else.'

'It's no go, my honey love, it's no go, my poppet,' said Sarah, too harshly.

Benjamin took Sarah's arm and said, 'Sarah, your accomplice Jean-Pierre has talked me into not going to the technical rehearsal this afternoon. He is very kindly driving me to visit the château of Julie's possible in-laws. But he threw her over, I hear? Not a very honourable young man.'

'The Rostand place,' said Sarah. 'It's charming. And that means you will be with us tomorrow.'

He hesitated. He had decided to leave but could not resist the moment, her mock-command of him, and, no doubt, the music, pleading love throughout the town. 'Yes, I'll stay for the dress rehearsal tomorrow. That's what you want, isn't it?'

'That is what I want,' said Sarah, laughing straight up at him, reckless with the excess of everything and knowing she was behaving like a girl. Inappropriately. Ridiculously. At this moment she did not care about Bill, who stood to one side, enjoying how she was being so ruthlessly charming to the banker.

Then Stephen and Sarah went slowly on, and the others stood listening as the two played their game.

'It's good to love in a moderate degree, but it is not good to love to distraction.'

'God knows. Who?'

'Plautus.'

'Plautus!'

'I had an excellent education, Sarah.'

'I have heard the mermaids singing, each to each. I do not think that they will sing to me,' said Sarah, sure that no one had said these words from such a desert of desolation.

'But they are singing to me, that's the point,' said Stephen.

They had reached the little street where the museum was. The houses were in all shades of a chalk cliff, grey, pale, bleached, their shutters, which had once been glossy dark brown, faded to a scabby and patchy beige, like stale milk chocolate. Their tiled roofs—the same pattern of tiles the Romans used, interlocking in stiff waves—were the colours of the soil of this region, rust and ox-blood and dull orange. Against this restrained background blazed the balconies, loaded with pots crammed full of pelargoniums and jasmine and oleanders, and under them, along one side of the street, was a line of pots of every size and shape, dressed with blossom. Rue Julie Vairon seemed decorated for a festival in honour of Julie.

The museum, only a year old, was a house where it was believed Julie had given lessons, though the house next to it was just as likely. Never mind. On either side of the entrance stood shiny lemon trees in newly painted green tubs. On the inside of the entrance door, a hand was reversing a notice to say open. Henry and the others had returned to the square because they had found the place closed. It was a large door, a mere slice of glass and steel in the yard-thick stone wall, and it led into the ground floor of the old house. A dozen or so glass cabinets accommodated carefully grouped objects. One held paint brushes and crayons, half-finished drawings, a metronome, sheet music. In another was a yellow silk scarf, and beside it shabby black cloth gloves. The gloves seemed that moment to have slid off Julie's small hands, and Sarah heard Stephen draw in his breath. His face had gone white. The gloves were alive; here was

Julie, her poverty, her attempts to conform, her courage. Her journals lay behind glass, together with letters mostly to clients about
copying music, or appointments for portraits. No letters to her
mother had survived: was it possible that Madame Vairon had carried them with her, and they died too in the lava from Mount Pelée?
None of Julie's letters to Paul or to Rémy, though it was unlikely
these letters had been destroyed. Letters from Paul and from Rémy
were collected into books and were there, in stacks, ready to be consulted by biographers. Paul's were long and desperate and incoher-
ent with love, and Rémy's were long, thoughtful, and passionate. It
seemed Philippe did not write her letters. But then, he saw her most
days.

The walls were covered with her drawings and her pictures,
many of herself and of her house. The self-portraits were by no
means all flattering. In some she had caricatured herself as a
respectable young lady, dressed to give lessons in houses like this
one. A few showed her glossy black, in the clothes worn by her
father's house servants, abundant colourful skirts, frilled blouses,
bandannas. She had tried herself out as an Arab girl, the transparent
veil over her lower face, with inviting eyes—the picture on the
poster at Queen's Gift which had overthrown Stephen. Older, at the
time of Rémy, her self-portraits show her as a woman capable of
taking her place at that table, bare shoulders and bosom tamed by
lace, passive folded hands—a biddable femininity. The drawing of
the nude bacchante had a place on a side wall, not at once or even
easily seen, as if the authorities had decided that it had to be somewhere, but let's not draw attention to it. But the Julie she and pos-
terity had agreed she was she had drawn and painted endlessly, in
water colours and in pastels, in charcoal and in pencil: the fiery
prickly critical girl and the independent woman not only were on
the walls but could be bought as postcards.

Her little girl was there too, a tiny creature with Julie's black
eyes, but then, just as if she had not died, Julie had pictured her at

various ages in childhood and even grown up, for there were double portraits of Julie as a young woman with her daughter, a charming girl—but they were like sisters; and of Julie, middle-aged, with a girl like her own young self.

And there, beside a drawing of a wispy baby girl, all eyes, and by itself under glass, was a doll, with a card pinned to it, and on it, in Julie's writing, *Sa poupée*. It was not much more than a doll suggested, only a stump of white kid, its head bald and stitched across the crown, as if sutured. It was eyeless. But this wretched doll had been loved to death, for the kid was worn and the rough rag of a red dress was torn.

Stephen and Sarah stood side by side and wept, not able to conceal it and not even trying to.

'I *never* cry,' said Sarah. 'It's this damned, damnable music.'

'A time to weep and a time to laugh,' said Stephen. 'I can't wait for the time to laugh. For God's sake, let's get out of here.'

They went out into the street, made loud by music and the roar of motor bikes. The company sat around the café tables, under sunshades. They were playing a game, in emulation or mockery of Sarah and Stephen.

'All you need is love,' said Bill gravely.

'All I have to do is dream,' said Sally, and Richard, beside her, sang 'Dream, dream, dream.'

'Hey, you've got a voice,' she said.

'Let the heartache begin,' said Mary Ford, delivering this line to the air, with a smile.

'This is the right time, the right place,' said Molly to Bill.

'Another day in Paradise,' sang Bill.

'You are my one temptation,' remarked Andrew to no one in particular, and added, 'I love you, love.' He raised a glass towards Sarah and then, as an afterthought, to Stephen.

'Tossing and turning,' said Molly, to Bill.

'Ob-la-di, ob-la-da,' said Bill seductively to Molly.

'I only want to be with you,' said Sally to Richard, then sang it, and he sang, 'Too late, my time has come . . . shivers down my spine.' Sally sang at him, 'Manchild, look at the state you're in . . . Manchild, will you ever win . . .' Richard took her hand and kissed it, then held it. She removed her hand and sighed. Both had tears in their eyes.

'You said you loved me, you were just feeling kind,' said Molly, and enquired of Bill, 'What do you want to make those eyes at me for?'

Bill exclaimed, 'Goodness gracious, great balls of fire!' went bright red, so that he looked like a ten-year-old, jumped up, and said, 'I am going for a swim.'

Molly sang, as the first line of a song, 'I am going for a swim because I'm so in love with him.' She laughed loudly, seeing Bill angry. Bill lingered, expecting the women to join him, but they sat tight. It was Sandy who got up, saying, 'I'll come.' The two young men went off, and the women sat in fits of laughter, sounding angry and even spiteful. Themselves hearing it, they stopped. A silence, while everyone listened to the multilayered din of the little town.

Henry had been watching and not taking part. Now he stood and said, 'Enough. Sarah, Stephen—you can see we don't come up to your level.' Clowning it, he sang, rather well, 'Escape from reality, open your eyes, look up to the skies.' They all clapped. He bowed. 'Stephen, I've been lying in wait for you, to say we think you should go with our American sponsor to lunch. Jean-Pierre is inviting you.'

'An order?'

'Yes, please.'

'Very well. And Sarah must come too.'

'I think I'll leave you to it,' said Sarah.

'Insubordination,' said Stephen. He took Sarah's arm, while Henry insisted, 'But I need Sarah, I need her at the rehearsal.' He took her arm on the other side. Stephen let Sarah go and said, 'Very well, where do I find my co-Croesus?'

'Inside the café. He said it's too hot out here.'

Stephen went into the café, where a jukebox howled and pounded. He came out again at once with Benjamin, shaking his head like a dog freeing its ears of water, smiling but actually looking rather sick.

'That's the real generation gap,' said Sally. 'Noise. They have cast-iron eardrums, the kids.'

'They'll be deaf,' said Stephen. He and Benjamin took themselves off into the quiet of an hotel.

Then, after all, most of the company went off to swim. Where Julie had walked with her master printer in the town gardens was now a car park, swimming pool, tennis courts, café. A couple of remaining acacias shaded the boules game that was usually being played under them.

Sarah sat with Henry under an umbrella and they conferred over the words that were to be spoken by the locals, supplied by Jean-Pierre. They had sent him a deputation, complaining that they did not believe their grandparents would have been so unkind as to say the things written for them by Sarah. Which were all in the journals. 'We must tone it down,' ordered Henry. 'Otherwise we'll lose them. They aren't being paid. They're doing it all for the glory of Belles Rivières.'

Then they went up by car to the theatre, having decided to forgo lunch. There the French sound technicians were at work with Sandy, fixing cables and loudspeakers to the trees and, too, the little house, which was as frail as an eggshell. Rows of wooden chairs had been set out in a space near the house. Had this space been here before? No, trees had been cut down, chestnuts and a couple of olive trees. Cicadas shrilled from everywhere in the forest.

'A stage effect we didn't foresee in London,' said Henry.

'But she must have composed, listening to cicadas.'

'Perhaps the cicadas suggested the music? That would certainly account for some of it.'

Here Sandy came to demand Henry's directions, and the two went off. Sarah sat on a bank of gritty earth under a turkey oak, that tree which is a poor relation of its magnificent northern cousins. Soon Henry came to join her. He sat leaning back on his hands and stared moodily at the scene which tomorrow would have come to life. Without adequate rehearsal, though, for the townspeople—or the mob—would assemble for an hour in the square tomorrow morning to be instructed how to watch George White and follow what he did. Henry was in an itch of anxiety. She soothed him with jokes and, 'A ton of worry does not pay even an ounce of debt.'

He returned the words of a current song hit. 'Don't worry, be happy . . . as my son told me last night on the telephone. My wife and my son, both. Don't worry, be happy.' He compressed his lips in a non-laugh.

'Now I shall say, It's going to be all right, and then you'll feel better.'

'Odd enough I do when you do.'

Soon a coach brought the whole cast up to the theatre. Sarah would have gone back with it, but Henry said, 'Are you going to leave me?'—so she remained under the dry little tree in a mottled shade, through an interminable rehearsal that began and stopped, and repeated, while the lighting and sound technicians and Henry worked. The singers were not singing, only speaking, and the actors spoke their lines with all emotion withdrawn from them. A lot of joking went on, to relieve boredom. At one point, when the sound apparatus had squawked and gone dead, so that singers and actors could be seen mouthing words, only just audible, Bill addressed the words from earlier that day to Molly:

My dust would hear her and beat
Had I lain for a century dead;
Would start and tremble under her feet
And blossom in purple and red.

He clowned and postured, bending over Molly, who stood limp, wiping off dust and perspiration and fanning herself, trying to smile. Suddenly, instead of the grave and handsome young lieutenant upright in his invisible uniform there was a hooligan, and he ended by shouting the last two lines again up at Sandy, who was standing on the broken wall of the house, but leaning out from it to loop thick black cable over a branch. The young man's body was like an acrobat's, and outlined in tight blue cotton. Knowing exactly how he looked, he let out a loud and equally anarchic laugh, in a moment that had the power to make everyone present, and all morality and decency, ridiculous. All of them, the players actually on the stage—rather the space in front of the ruined house—the actors in 'the wings' (the trees), musicians, singers, laughed nervously but they were shocked. Bill glanced quickly around. He had not meant to betray himself, though he had meant to shock. He saw that everyone stared at him and at Sandy, who was now balanced on the wall, arms extended, just about to jump off and down to the earth. Henry came forward, and called out, making a joke of it, but with authority, 'So you've decided to do another play Bill, is that it?' Bill called back prettily, 'Sorry, don't know what got into me.' And he matily hugged Molly. She stepped back, not looking at him.

Bill then directed beseeching looks at Sarah. What she felt then was unexpected, compassion that was not tenderness but as dry and as abstract as the eye of Time. His face, in full mid-afternoon sunlight, was a mask of fine lines. Anxiety. On that handsome face, if you looked at it not as a lover but with the eyes she had earned by having lived through so many years, was always imminent a faint web of suffering. Conflict. It was costing him a good deal, it was costing him too much, the poor young man, his decision to appear a lover of women, only women. A lover of women as men love women. He loved women, all right, with that instant sympathetic sexiness natural to him; but he knew nothing of the great enjoyable combats, antagonisms, and balances of sex, of the great game. She found on her tongue Julie's *You do not even know the alphabet. Only those new lines under your eyes know how to talk to me.* But that sudden, rare, heartbreaking crumpling of his face at moments when he felt threatened—they were no new lines. Compassion of a certain kind is the beginning of a cure for love. That is, love as desire. The compassion she felt was out of all proportion, like all these emotions washing around and about *Julie Vairon.* And not unmixed either, at least at moments, with cruelty: dote and antidote together. A picture of cruelty, staining pity: you are causing me all this pain, you are as careless as an inexperienced boy with explosives, allowing all the sexuality you do not admit feeling for your mother to slop about over older women—oh yes, I watched you this morning with Sally, and I watched her respond to you. You not only let it happen, but you make sure the fires are well stoked. Well then, I'm glad for the pain that put those lines on that pretty face of yours. . . . This was ugly, a million miles from the dispassionate eye of compassion. She knew it was ugly but could not help it, any more than she could hold off the compassion that balanced with it, like a need to put one's arms around a child that for some reason is fated to stand always on the edge of a playground, watching the other children play.

The coach came to take them all back to town. Then, at the tables, decisions were made about tonight's concert. Stephen said he would take Benjamin; yes, tomorrow Benjamin would see the play with its music, but Julie's music by itself was a different thing, and he shouldn't miss it. Andrew confirmed this, saying that his life had been changed by her music: everyone laughed at the incongruity of this remark from the gaucho. Henry did not have to be there, and he decided to have an early night. So did Sarah. The two sat together in the dusk outside Les Collines Rouges. He said, 'I'll tell you the story of my life, because I like making you laugh.' It was a picaresque tale of an orphan adopted by a family of gangsters. He ran away from them, determined to be poor and honest, and worked in low joints until . . . he was watching her face to make sure she was laughing. '. . . And then I was rescued by the love of a good woman, and now, hey presto, or rather *voilà*, I am a famous theatre director.'

'I suppose you aren't going to tell me the story of your life.'

'Well, I might at that—one day.'

'And where is your mother in all this?'

'Ah,' he said. 'Yes. There it is. How did you know?'

She smiled at him.

'There are mothers and mothers. I have a mother. And you are a witch. Like Julie.' He was actually on his feet, to escape.

'Then witches come easily. There isn't a woman in the world who wouldn't have diagnosed a mother.'

He leaned forward, his eyes on hers, and crooned, 'Ob-la-di, ob-la-da'. Then, full of aggression, 'Wouldn't you say most of us have them? How about Bill, wouldn't you say he had a mother?'

'More than anyone here, I would say.'

'And Stephen?'

She was really taken aback. 'Funny, I never until this moment thought about it.'

'Hmmm. Yes, *very* funny. A real laugh, that one.' And he laughed. 'It takes one to know one.'

'Why didn't I think of it? Of course. He was almost certainly sent to a boarding school when he was seven. You know, all the dormitories full of little boys calling out for mummy and crying in their sleep.'

'Strange tribal ways, a mystery to the rest of us.'

'By the time they are ten or eleven, mummy is a stranger.'

'Love with a stranger,' he sang. Then he leaped up and said, 'But I'm glad you're here. Did you know that? Yes, you did. I don't know what I'd do without you. And now I'm going to ring home.'

When the lights of the theatre coach came dazzling across the square, she went up to her room. She did not want to see Bill. Nor

Stephen with Molly, for this mirror of her situation was becoming too painful. She sat unobserved at her window, her light off, and watched the comings and goings in the square, and the company sitting at the tables below, laughing, talking . . . young voices. Stephen and Molly were not there. Nor was Bill, or Sandy. Benjamin was being dined and wined by Jean-Pierre. She went to bed.

She woke, probably because the music had at last been switched off. Silence. Not quite; the cicadas still made their noise . . . no, it was not cicadas. The spray had been left to circle its rays of water all night on the dusty grass under the pine tree, and its click, click, clicking sounded like a cicada. The moon was a small yellow slice low over the town roofs. Dusty stars, the smell of watered dust. Down on the pavement outside the now closed café, two figures stretched out side by side in chairs brought close together. Low voices, then Bill's loud young laugh. From that laugh she knew it was not a girl with him: he would not laugh like that with Molly, with Mary—with any woman.

Sarah went back to her bed and lay awake, tormented, on the top of the sheet. The breath of the night was hot, for the water being flung about down there was not doing much to cool things off. It occurred to her she was feeling more than desire: she could easily weep. What for?

Sarah dreamed. Love is hot and wet, but it does not scald and sting. She woke as a phantom body—a body occupying the same space as hers—slid away and separated, becoming small. This baby body had been soaked in a stinging hot wetness and was filled with a longing so violent the pain of it fed back into her own body. She turned and bit the pillow. The taste of dry cotton embittered her tongue.

She lay flat on her back and saw that a street light made patterns on her ceiling. A late car's headlights plunged the ceiling into day and left it modelled with shadow. There were voices outside in the corridor. One was Stephen's, the other a girl's, very low. If that was

Molly, well then, good luck to them both: this blessing, she knew, was well over the top.

Her eyes were not, it seemed, entirely bound by this room but were still attending to the dream, or to another, for a world of dreams lay around her and she was immersed in them, and yet could observe her immersion. Very close was that region where the baby in her lived. She could feel its desperation. She could feel the presence of other entities. She saw a head, young, beautiful, Bill's (or Paul's), smiling in self-love, gazing into a mirror, but it turned with a proud and seductive slowness, and the head was not a man's but a girl's, a fresh good-looking girl whose immediately striking quality was animal vitality. This girl turned away her confident smile, and she dissolved back into a young man. Sarah put her hands up to her own face, but what her fingers lingered over was her face now. Beneath that (so temporary) mask were the faces she had had as a young woman, as a girl, and as a baby. She wanted to get up and go to the glass to make certain of what was there, but felt held to the bed by a weight of phantom bodies that did not want to be flushed out and exposed. At last she did get herself out of bed and to the window. The chairs on the pavement were empty. The square was empty. The hard little moon had gone behind black roofs. The forgotten water spray swung around, click, click, click.

There were words on her tongue. She was saying, '. . . passing the stages of her age and youth, entering the whirlpool . . . yes, that's it, the whirlpool,' said Sarah, not sure whether she was awake or asleep. Was she really sitting by the window? Yes, she was fully awake, but her tongue kept offering her, '. . . stages of my age and youth, entering the whirlpool.'

She was dissolved in longing. She could not remember ever feeling the rage of want that possessed her now. Surely never in her times of being in love had she felt this absolute, this peremptory need, an emptiness that hollowed out her body, as if life itself was being withheld from her.

Who is it that feels this degree of need, of dependence, and who has to lie helpless waiting for the warm arms and the moment of being lifted up into love?

It was four o'clock. The light would come into the square in an hour or so. She showered. She dressed, taking her time, and, ready for her day, went back to the window. The tops of the trees went pink, and light poured over the still unpeopled town. An old woman came down Rue Julie Vairon and into the square. She wore a long-sleeved cotton dress, white, with a pattern of small mauve bouquets, and black collar and cuffs. Her white hair was in a bun. She walked slowly, careful where she put her feet. She sat herself on the bench underneath the plane tree, first brushing the dust off carefully with a large white handkerchief. She sat listening to the sound of the sprayer, and to the cicadas when they started. When the birds began, she smiled. She liked being alone in the square. She did not know Sarah watched her from her window. Her mother had probably sat there on that bench, alone in the early morning. Her grandmother too, thinking cruel thoughts about Julie.

Sarah let herself out of her room, went down the stairs. No one yet at reception. She slid back the bolt on the hotel's main door and was on the pavement. As she went past, she sent a smile to the old woman, who nodded and smiled at her. 'Bonjour, Madame.' 'Bonjour, Madame.'

Julie's house in the hills was about three miles away. Sarah took her time, because it was already hot. Pink dust lay along the edges of the tarmac, reddened the tree trunks and the foliage. Leaves drooped, made soft by a long absence of rain. The sun stood up over the hills and filled the rough pine trunks with red light and laid shadow under the bushes. Julie's landscape was an ungiving one, dry and austere, nothing like the forests of her Martinique where the flowers' perfumes were heavy, narcotic. Here there were the brisk scents of thyme and oregano and pine. The tarmac had ended. Sarah walked where Julie had, thinking of all that separated her from the woman who had died over eighty years before. By the time she reached the house, hot air was dragging at her skin. Already two young men were at work setting chairs to rights and picking up the detritus of last night's concert. This empty place, surrounded by old trees, seemed the proper stage for ancient and inexorable dramas, as if onto it would walk a masked player to announce the commencement of a tale where the Fates pursued their victims, and where gods bargained with each other over favours for their protégés. Interesting to imagine Julie's little tale being discussed by Aphrodite and Athene. Sarah walked past Julie's house, now burdened with cables and loudspeakers, thinking about why one could only imagine these two goddesses like bossy headmistresses discussing a girl with a propensity for disorder. ('She could do much better if she tried.') Yet if Julie was not a 'love woman', then what was she? She had embodied that quality, recognizable by every woman at first glance, and at once felt by men, of the seductive and ruthless femininity that at once makes arguments about morality irrelevant— surely that should be Aphrodite's argument? But the woman who had written the journals, whose daughter was she?

I tell you, Julie, had said Julie to herself, something like ninety years before Sarah walked slowly in the hot morning away from her house towards the river, *if you let yourself love this man then it will be worse for you than it was with Paul. For this one is not a handsome boy who could only see himself when he was reflected in your eyes. Rémy is a man, even if he is younger than I am. With him it will be all my possibilities as a woman, for a woman's life, brought to life. And then, Julie? A broken heart is one thing, and you have lived through that. But a broken life is another, and you can choose to say no.* She did not say no. And who was it, which Julie, who said to the other, *Well, my dear, you must not imagine if you choose love you won't have to pay for it?* But it was not Athene's daughter who said, *Write your music. Paint your pictures. But if that is what you choose, you will not be living as women live. I can't endure this non-life. I can't endure this desert.*

Now just ahead was the river, with its pools and its shallow falls, and the bench the town authorities had thoughtfully provided for people who wanted to contemplate Julie's sad end. Someone was already on the bench. It was Henry. The curve of his body suggested discouragement. He stared ahead of him, and it was not because he was deaf that he did not hear her approach. His ears were plugged with sound. He had a Walkman in his pocket. The music he was listening to was sure to be as far as it could be from Julie's. Sarah could hear a frantic tiny niggling, then a small savage howling, as she sat down and smiled at him. He tore off the headphones, and as the music, no longer directed into his brain, swirled about them, he switched the machine off, looking embarrassed. He sang at her, '*Tell me what love means to you before you ask me to love you*'—Julie's words, but it was a tune she did not know, since she was not an inhabitant of the world he entered when he clamped his headphones on.

Then he put back his head and howled like a wolf.

She suggested, 'I am baying at the moon, for 'tis a night in June, and I'm thinking of you . . . of who? Of you—hoo.'

'Not bad. Not far off.'

'Have you been here all night?'

'Just about.'

'But you know it's going to be all right.'

He sang, 'Have you been here all night, but you know it's going to be all right.' He said, 'Yes, I know, but do I believe it?' He abruptly flung his legs apart, and his arms, then, finding this position intolerable, he threw the left leg over the right, then the right over the left, and folded his arms tight. A bright blowing spray set a bloom of cool damp on their faces. The river ran fast through the forest trees, past reddish and orange rocks, making baby whirlpools and eddies, leaving stains of pinkish foam on the weeds that oscillated at the river's edge. Above the fall was a wide pool where the water was dark and still, except where the main stream ran through it, betraying itself in a swift turbulence that gathered the whole body of water into itself at the rocky edge, flinging up spray as it fell into another pool, where it seethed like boiling sugar syrup among black rocks. This was not a deep pool, though it was the famous whirlpool that had drowned Julie and—so some of the townspeople said—had drowned Julie's child. (How could they have said it? Had there not been a doctor and the doctor's certificate? But if people want to believe something, they will.) Below this treacherous pool, past a mild descent among rocks, was another, large, dark, and quiet except where the water poured deeply into it. It was this pool where Julie came to swim, but only at night, when, she said, she could cheat the Peeping Toms.

'To drown herself there must have needed a real strength of mind,' said Sarah.

'She was probably stoned.'

'She never mentioned drinking or drugs in her journals.'

'Did she say everything in her journals?'

'I think so.'

'Then I'll go back to my first interpretation. When I read the script I didn't believe in the suicide.'

'You mean, you agree with the townspeople? They thought she was murdered.'

'Perhaps they murdered her.'

'But she was just about to become a respectable woman.'

'That's just the point. Suppose they didn't like the idea of this witch becoming Madame Master Printer.'

'A witch, you keep saying.'

'Do you know what, Sarah? I dream about her. If I dreamed of some sugarplum all tits and bum, then that would be something, but I don't. I dream of her when she's—well, getting over the hill. Well over.'

She turned her head to see his smile, sour, a bit angry, and close to her face.

'Sex appeal isn't all bum and tits,' said she, returning his vulgarity to him.

He sat back, gave her an appreciative but still angry smile, and said, 'Well, yes, I'd say there was some truth in that. Of course, as a good American boy, I should only be admitting to nymphets, but yes, you're right.' He sprang to his feet, grabbed up her hand, kissed it. Her hand was wet with spray. 'Sarah . . . what can I say? I'm off to get some sleep. If I can. I've got a technical rehearsal at eleven. Roy is rehearsing the townspeople. And I've got the singers this afternoon. Will you be there? But why should you be?'

'If you want me to be.'

'Lazing on a sunny afternoon,' he sang to her. Then he pushed the plugs back into his ears and walked or, rather, ran off back towards Julie's house.

She went to the edge of the pool below the falls. The whirlpool, in fact. Here Julie must have stood, looking down at the dangerous waters, and then she jumped. Not much of a jump, perhaps six feet. The stony bottom of the pool could be glimpsed through eddies. She could easily have landed on her feet, then fallen forward, perhaps onto that rock, a smooth round one, and allowed herself to be sucked past the rock to the deeper pool. Allowed herself? She could swim, she said, like an otter.

Sarah felt she should turn her head, and did so. There was Stephen, staring at her from where he stood by the bench a few feet away. She went to the bench and sat down. He sat beside her.

'We are all up early,' she remarked.

'I haven't been to bed. I suppose I look it.' His clothes were crumpled, he smelled stale, and he wore his tragic mask. Again Sarah thought, I've never, never in my life felt anything like this—this is the grief you see on the faces of survivors of catastrophes, staring back at you from the television screens. 'I went walking with Molly last night,' he said. 'She very kindly agreed to come walking with me. We walked along some road or other. It was pretty dark under the trees.'

She could imagine it. A dark road. He could hardly see the girl who walked beside him under the trees. There had been that niggardly little moon. They had walked from one patch of dim light to another. Molly had been wearing a white cotton skirt and a tight white T-shirt. Patterns in black and white.

Sarah watched the racing water, for she could not bear to look at his face.

'Extraordinary, isn't it? I mean, what happens to one's pride. She kissed me. Well, I kissed her.' He waited. Then, 'Thanks for not saying it, Sarah.' Now she did cautiously turn her head. Tears ran down cheeks dragging with grief. 'I don't understand any of it. What can you say about a man of fifty who knows that nothing more magical ever happened to him than a kiss in the dark with . . . ?'

Sarah suppressed, At least you had a kiss. At that moment anything she felt seemed a selfish impertinence.

'I've missed out on all that,' she heard, but faintly. A breeze off the water was blowing his words away. 'I've had a dry life. I didn't know it until . . . Of course I've been in love. I don't mean that.' The wind, changing again, flung his words at her: 'What does it mean, saying that to hold one girl in your arms makes everything that ever happened to you dust and ashes?'

'Julie said something of the sort. About Rémy.' A silence, filled with the sound of water. For the second time that morning, she said, 'To drown herself must have taken some strength of mind.'

'Yes. If I'd been there . . .'

'You, or Rémy?'

'You don't understand. I am Rémy. I understand everything about him.'

'Were you a younger brother? I mean you, Stephen.'

'I have two older brothers. Not four, like Rémy. I don't know how important that is. What's important is . . . well, what could I have said to her to stop her killing herself?'

'Will you marry me?' suggested Sarah.

'Ah, you *don't* understand. That is the impossibility. He couldn't marry her. Not with all that pressure. Don't forget, he was French. It is a thousand times worse for the French than for us. The French have this family thing. We have it, but nothing like as bad. We can marry chorus girls and models—and a jolly good thing too. Good for the gene pool. But have you ever seen an aristocratic French family close ranks? And it was a hundred years ago. No, it was all inevitable. It was impossible for Rémy not to fall in love with her. And until death. Because he would have loved her all his life.'

'Yes,' she shouted, since the wind had changed again.

'But impossible to marry her.'

'Funny how we don't mention the glamorous lieutenant,' said Sarah, thinking of Bill and of how ashamed she was.

'But that was just . . . falling in love,' he shouted. A silence. He said, 'But with Rémy, it was life and death.'

He sat with his eyes shut. Tears seeped out under his lids. Depressed. But the word means a hundred different shades of sadness. There are different qualities of 'depression', as there are of love. A really depressed person, she knew, having seen the condition in a friend, was nothing like Stephen now. The depressed one could sit in the same position in a chair, or on the floor in a corner of a room, curled like a foetus for hours at a time. Depression was not tears. It was deadness, immobility. A black hole. At least, so it seemed to an onlooker. But Stephen was alive and suffering. He was grief-stricken. She cautiously examined him, now that she could, because he had his eyes shut, and thought suddenly that she ought to be afraid for herself. She, Sarah, had most unexpectedly stopped a bolt from the blue, an arrow from an invisible world: she had fallen in love when she thought she never could again. And so what was to stop her from being afflicted, as Stephen was—from coming to grief?

She took his hand, that sensible, useful, practical hand, and felt it tighten around hers. 'Bless you, Sarah. I don't know why you put up with me. I know I must seem . . .' He got up, and so did she. 'I think I ought to get some sleep.'

They walked to the edge of the dangerous pool and stood looking down. The water that spattered Sarah's cheek was partly tears blown off Stephen's.

'She must have taken a pretty strong dose of something.'

'That's what Henry said.'

'Did he? A good chap, Henry. Perhaps he's in love with her too. The way I feel now, I can't imagine why the whole world isn't. That's a sign of insanity in itself.'

The sun was burning down, though it was still early. Hot, quiet, and still. No wind. Sarah's dress, so recently put on, needed changing, for it was soaked with spray and clung to her thighs. She shut her eyes as she was absorbed into a memory of a small hot damp body filled with craving.

'Just as well we don't remember our childhoods,' she said.

'What? Why did you say that?'

'Let alone being a baby. My God, it's as well we forget it all.' Stephen was looking at her in a way he never had before. It was because he had not heard that voice from her—angry, and rough with emotion. He did not like it: if she was not careful he would stop liking her. Yet she felt on a slippery slope and did not know how to save herself. She was clenched up like a fist to stop herself crying. 'I *never* cry,' she announced, and jumped to her feet, and stood wiping tears off her cheeks with the backs of her hands. He slowly handed her a handkerchief, a real one, large, white, and well laundered— slowly because of his shock. 'It's all right,' she said, 'but I do find Julie a bit of a strain. Not to anything like the extent you do, thank God.' But she could hardly get these words out, and he slowly stood up and was examining her. She found it hard to sustain that look, the one that means a man has stepped back to examine a woman in the light of remembered other women, other situations. For the first time there was embarrassment between them, and it was deepening.

And now he said, in a voice she had never heard, 'Don't tell me you are in love with . . .'

She said, attempting lightness, 'You mean the young jay? The pretty hero?' On the verge of confessing, of saying, Yes, I am afraid so, his face stopped her. He was so disappointed in her—as well as being shocked, and he was certainly that. She could not bear it and decided to lie, even while she was crying out to herself, But you've never lied to him, this is awful, it'll never be the same again, this friendship of ours. 'No, no,' she said, laughing and she hoped with conviction. 'Come on, it's not as bad as that.'

'After all my confessions to you, the least you can do . . .' But this was a far from friendly invitation.

'Ah,' she said, 'but I'm not going to tell you.' Lightly, almost flirtatiously, and as she spoke she could have burst out weeping again instead. Never had she used this false flirtatious voice to him. He hated it, she could see.

At the same moment, they set off along the path to the house and the theatre space, now empty and waiting for the day's rehearsals. Down they went, through the trees. He was covertly examining her, and she was miserable because of what she saw on his face. She began to make conversation, saying it was interesting that while Julie was doing her drawings and paintings here, not thirty miles away Cézanne was painting. Her work would have surprised no one in the last four hundred years, but Cézanne's was so revolutionary that many of the critics of the time could see nothing in it.

She hoped he would join in, save them both from this quite terrible embarrassment, and he did, but his voice was harsh when he said, 'I hope you aren't suggesting it is a criticism of Julie's work that Dürer wouldn't have been surprised at it.'

This conversation, like so many, was only apparently about what its surface suggested.

'Unless he would have been surprised at a woman doing it.'

He gave a snort—and it was contemptuous. 'Now you're changing ground.'

'I suppose so'—and her voice was a plea. 'But I wasn't thinking of it as a criticism, actually.' He did not speak. 'But if Julie had seen Cézanne's work, do you think she'd have liked it?'

A much too long pause. He said grudgingly, 'How do we know she didn't? They were always out and about, both of them.'

'Thirty miles is nothing now. Then it was enough to make sure they'd never meet.'

They walked, much too fast for that warm morning, down the dusty track, the cicadas already at full shrill. She could not remember ever wanting a time of being with Stephen to end, but now she did. She was thinking, critically of herself, It's all right when I watch Stephen, to see how he is feeling, but I don't like it when he watches me as he is doing now.

'Do you suppose Cézanne would have liked her music?' she asked quickly.

'He would have loathed it,' he said, and his voice was like a judge delivering a sentence.

'Does that mean you loathe it, in your heart of hearts?'

'Sometimes I do.'

'*I can't endure this non-life. I can't endure this desert,*' she quoted, clumsy, for she had not meant to say anything of the sort.

And now there was a pretty long silence. Stephen was asking himself if he could forgive her. He did so, with 'Now I think I've never not lived in a desert.'

She was unable to prevent herself from blurting out, spoiling everything again, 'Recently I've been thinking I was living in a desert for years.'

And, again, he was uncomfortable, and did not want to have to be with this emotional and (so he felt it) demanding Sarah. 'So you aren't in a desert now,' he enquired, wanting a real answer.

Sarah walked faster. She knew that the conversation had slipped finally into the wrong gear, but tried to sound humorous. 'I think a lot of people live in a desert. At least, what they call in the atlases "Other Desert". You know, there is sand desert, the real desert, the real thing, like the Empty Quarter, and "Other Desert". One is an absolute. But "other desert"—there are degrees of that.'

And now he did not say anything. They were walking as fast as they could, but there was a good twenty minutes of this discomfort before they reached the town square. There Stephen left her, without more than a nod and a strained smile, and he almost ran towards the hotel, where he disappeared, with a look of relief and, too, an almost furtive little movement of his buttocks, which suddenly announced to Sarah: Oh *no*, he thinks I am in love with *him*. For there is no woman in the world who has not seen, at some moment or other, a man escaping with precisely that secret little look of relief. This struck her as a complete calamity, the worst. What could she do? She was thinking, This friendship is a thousand times more precious to me than being in love, or the pretty hero. I can't bear it. And now it's all spoiled. Until this morning everything between us had been open, simple, honest. And now . . .

In the midst of this distress a thought that made it worse attacked her: A few weeks ago—but it seemed months, even years ago—she could have said anything to Stephen, and did. In those truly halcyon days before her first visit to his house, she might have remarked, laughing, 'I've fallen in love with a pretty boy— now, what do you have to say about that!' 'Oh, come off it, Stephen, I'm not in love with you, don't be silly.' But now . . . they had both of them made a long step down and away from their best.

The pavement outside the café was crowded. Sarah did not want to talk to anyone. But Bill was sitting with a sleek, brown, plump man, obviously American, and he was smiling and waving. She was about to smile and walk past, but he called to her in a casually proprietary way, as he would have done to his mother, 'Sarah, where did you get to?' And he said to his companion, 'She's one of my greatest friends. She's a really fun person.'

Sarah kept a smile on her face and allowed herself to rest on the very edge of a chair. She directed this smile at a man whose every surface glistened with satisfaction. He was Jack, who, Bill said, had directed the last play Bill had been in. Bill offered the morsel to Sarah as he might have done a box of chocolates. But he was uneasy too, for he knew he had struck a wrong note. Because of this, Sarah felt sorry for him: an extraordinary mix of emotions, extravagant, ridiculous emotions; and she was passionately disliking this Jack. As if it mattered whether she liked him or not.

'I'm on a trip around the south of France. I saw Bill last night in Marseilles. He talked me into it, and—*voilà!*' said Jack, taking possession of France with a word.

Then it must have been very late—as the thought invaded her like a tidal wave, jealousy carved her spine. Bill was still here last night after midnight, so if he drove to Marseilles—he and who?— that must mean . . . *now, stop it, Sarah.*

Bill knew she was jealous: his eyes told her so, and, too, that he was relieved because, having lost her because of his over-familiarity, he was taking possession of her again. He was back on balance but she was not. She was thinking: Stephen, what am I to do? I cannot lose Stephen.

She got off the edge of her chair and said, 'I'm sorry, I have to meet someone.' And with a smile at Jack she hoped was adequate, and ignoring Bill (at which she saw his face fall), she walked briskly into the hotel. She was having to peer through tears. What she saw was Henry, on his way out. Luckily the light was behind her.

'You'll be there after lunch?' A question, yes, but it was more of a command.

'This is a very strange role, mine,' said Sarah.

'True. Not in the contract, I know. But essential. *Please?*'

Determined not to sleep but to think of some way of putting

things right with Stephen, she was walking around her room, or rather barging and banging around it, not seeing what she was doing. She was thinking, I couldn't have told him, 'Yes, I am in love with the pretty hero.' It's unforgivable. And yet old women by the thousand—probably by the million—are in love and keep quiet about it. They have to. Good Lord, just imagine it: for instance, an old people's home full of senior citizens, or, as they charmingly put it, wrinklies, and half of them are secretly crazy for the young jay who drives the ambulance or the pretty girl cook. A secret hell, populated with the ghosts of lost loves, former personalities . . . meanwhile the other half are making sniffy jokes and exchanging snide looks. Unless they succumb too.

It was no good. She crashed into sleep, and woke in tears.

A taxi took her to the sane atmosphere of people working, for she did not want to walk in that heat.

She sat under a tree. Henry came over, and Julie's late music, high and cool, shot arrows straight into their hearts.

'God,' he muttered, his eyes full of tears, 'that's so beautiful.'

She said, her eyes wet, 'Funny how we subject ourselves to music. We never ask what effect it might be having.'

He was in that position a runner uses before a race, half squatting, the knuckles of his left hand resting among fallen leaves, to steady him. His eyes were on her face. One might call them speaking eyes.

'You're talking to a man who has been listening to pop music most hours of the day since he was twelve.'

'And you're going to say, It hasn't done me any harm?'

'How do we know if it is doing us harm or not?'

'I think it might be making us over-emotional.'

'Well, you could say that. Yes.' With that, up he sprang, and said, 'Thank you for coming. Never think I don't appreciate it.' And off he went.

Then they rehearsed the early music which was far from cool

and detached, and went back to the late music, both accompanied by the steady drilling of cicadas. Hearing Julie's music like this, disjointed, not in its development, with the reassurance of a progression, it unsettled, it even wounded, as if the singers had decided to be deliberately cynical. At the end they rehearsed the song

> *You did not hear me when I told you I will not live*
> *After you leave me,*
> *When you leave me you will take my life . . .*

The note curved up on *life*, a bent note, as in a blues. An interesting question, surely: in Indian music, Arab music—Eastern music—you could say that all notes are 'bent', a 'straight' note is the rare one. But in our music, one 'bent' note can be like a hand in your heart strings.

The rehearsal ended. The four singers stood together under their tree, while the musicians covered their instruments. For a few moments, the group kept about them the atmosphere of the music, as if they stood in the hollow bluish-gold penumbra of a candle flame, the girls in their loose summer dresses, the young men's blue jeans transformed by association and sound into the cerulean of the robes in medieval religious paintings. But when they left the trees and came through sunlight making loud remarks about showers and cold drinks, they became people in a street or at a bus stop. A limousine waited for them. The driver was a young man with whom they had achieved the agreeable intimacy of the theatre. He laid a strong brown arm along the back of the driver's seat and twisted around to smile at the girls as they piled in. 'Mademoiselle . . . mademoiselle . . . mademoiselle . . . ,' he said to each of the three singers, caressingly, as a Frenchman should, allowing tender eyes to say how much he appreciated them, and at once the gallantry-deprived Anglo-Saxon women, who are lucky to be told, by a man

who is madly in love with them, *You* are *looking fit*, radiated pleasure like stroked cats, even while they could be observed reminding
themselves and each other, with small regulated grimaces, that they
must not allow themselves to be carried away by such insincerity. He
murmured a gallant 'Madame' to Sarah, and then, feeling unable to
supply individual salutations of the same standard to everybody,
contented himself with a comradely nod to Henry and the counter-
tenor, and flashed his white teeth all around. He reversed with a
screech. 'Voilà . . . allons-y . . . il fait chaud . . . très très chaud . . . ,' he
positively crooned, reminding them he had sat waiting for at least
half an hour in all that heat, the rehearsal having run overtime, not
that he in any way begrudged them what was his duty, but. 'Faut
boire,' he announced. 'Immédiatement. Vite, vite.' And the car shot,
or waltzed, down the tricky road, hooting madly. They were in the
square in ten minutes.

An evening light was being sifted through a high thin cloud, and
the bleached colours of the buildings, flint and chalk and ash and
the crumbling white of old bone, made their case strongly, like a full
palette. The end wall of La Belle Julie was no longer a blank stare
but showed its history in modulations of plaster, creamy hollows
and slopes where a glisten of river sand lay in the folds of joins
between two areas of work separated perhaps by decades. A milky
gleam strengthened—and the sun was back and the wall again an
undifferentiated glare.

The dress rehearsal was set for seven-thirty, which was still daylight. The lighting of the piece had always been a difficulty. The first
scenes were by lamplight in the sitting room in Martinique, but the
late sun was glowing on the wires of a harp that stood on boards laid
over pink dust. The programme said: Martinique. 1882. Evening.

There was a worse difficulty. Three hundred chairs were disposed in the audience space, and these were expected to be part filled by invited guests, mostly from the French side of the production. There could not be the customary audience for a dress rehearsal, the friends of performers and management, for they were not French. Yet all the seats were occupied an hour before the play began, and crowds of onlookers had made their way up from the town and now stood among the trees, waiting. These were French and, too, many tourists, mostly English and American. No one had expected this kind of success for *Julie Vairon*, except Mary Ford, who could be observed not saying, I told you so!—and yet now that it was happening, nothing could be more plain than that it had to happen. Jean-Pierre kissed Mary's hand, and then her cheeks, many times. They went waltzing around together among the rocks, a victory dance, while Henry and Stephen and Sarah and the cast applauded them. There were no seats left for Sarah and the two Croesuses. Chairs were brought up from the town and fitted in among the trees.

There were discontented murmurs from the crowd. How could the authorities—that is to say, themselves—have been so short-sighted as not to allow for the inevitable interest? Three hundred seats—absurd! *Affreux . . . stupide . . . une absurdité . . . lamentable . . .* and so it went on. Then and there a meeting to discuss the popularity of *Julie Vairon* was arranged for breakfast time tomorrow. Meanwhile the curtain, so to speak, was due to rise. Sitting where she did, next to Henry, Sarah felt his anguish vibrate from him to her. He had confessed he had been sick all night and that was why she had found him sitting by the waterfall. He told her this in a theatrical mutter, a parody of gloom, but his eyes were darkened by the anguish of it all. He attempted a smile, failed, grabbed her hand, and kissed it. His lips left a burning place.

The musicians, who stood with the singers on their little stone platform, began a conventional introduction, for the music was a drawing-room ballad brought to Martinique with the sheet music and the pretty dresses and the fashion magazines on the insistence of Sylvie Vairon, who had made it clear from the beginning, that is to say, from Julie's conception, that if the girl was not going to be legitimate, then at least she must be equipped to get a good husband.

Molly appeared out of the trees. Her white gown left shoulders and neck bare, and her black tresses were braided, coiled, looped, and held with a white frangipani flower. She sat by the harp and played. Or pretended to: the viola made appropriate sounds. She was in fact singing: she had a pretty light voice, just right for a drawing-room young lady. Madame Vairon stepped forward to stand by her daughter, the large black woman magnificent in scarlet velvet. Then a group of young officers—George White and four young men supplied by Jean-Pierre, who did not have to say anything, had only to stand about and react—all dazzling in their uniforms, came forward one by one to bend over Madame Vairon's hand. Paul came last. He straightened, turned, saw Julie—the piece had begun.

Unable to bear it, Henry sprang up and off through the crowd and into the trees. He could be observed—Sarah observed him—striding up and down, and then he whirled about to return to his seat, but he was too late, for it was occupied by Benjamin, who had come back from a quick tour of the region accompanied by Bill's friend Jack Greene.

The sentimental ballad ended, and now the music that accompanied the love scenes between Paul and Julie was without words. Haunting . . . yes, you could call this music haunting, a word as trite as the love scenes that were being enacted, where not one movement, one phrase, one glance, was new or could be new. Everyone here—there were a good thousand people now, and more were pressing in to watch—had seen similar scenes or taken part in them. It was the music that struck straight to the heart, or the senses. The crowd was silent. They watched Julie as intently as the citizens of Belles Rivières had watched her a hundred years ago. As for the townspeople rehearsed that morning by Roy, they were unnecessary, for nothing could be more powerful than this silent staring crowd. Then, as the light slowly went, a twenty-foot-high projection of Julie the young woman appeared on a screen behind and above her house. It was at first a faint image, for the light had not gone, but it gathered substance, and changed: Julie aged on that screen, until she was the comfortable lady Philippe had wooed, and then she was a small child, her own daughter, or herself. Stephen said into Sarah's ear, 'I'm off. I'll walk. Do me good. I'm going to telephone Elizabeth and tell her what is happening here and ask her what chance there is of a decent run. We have been thinking of three or four days—but just look.' For people still approached through the trees, coming to a dead stop when the music enveloped them. As Stephen left his chair (Sarah thought that he showed all the signs of a man escaping), Henry took it. He put his lips to her ear and said, 'Sarah, Sarah, life's a bitch, Sarah . . . it's a bitch, I love you.' He said this in time with the music, so he was theatrical and absurd, they both had to laugh. But his lips were tremulous. All the appropriate thoughts clicked through her mind: But this is obviously nonsense, it's all the fault of the theatre, of show business, so don't take any notice. But at the same time she thought, This is Julie's country: anything can happen. Old women can seem like young ones, and a blue-eyed Irish girl with plump freckled shoulders can become a girl as slender and bright and tigerish as a bee, just like the fairy tales. She was shaken, oh yes, but managed to offer Henry, who was leaning as close as he could, a gently amused smile. What a hypocrite.

The scenes in Martinique were coming to an end. The sun had gone, but reflected rays arbitrarily picked out a buckle on Paul's belt, or the handkerchief Madame Vairon was sobbing into, while the golden hair of one of the singers seemed to be on fire. Julie and Paul walked away from weeping Maman into patterns of dusky forest light and shade, appropriately, since the next scene was in the forest, was in fact here. A large window frame stood up behind the actors, to show that the scene was inside the house and not—as it must appear to the literal eye—outside it. And now here was a tiny living room, where there was not only the harp but a lute, a recorder, a viola, while flutes and a clarinet lay on a rack. An easel, on which was a large self-portrait in pastels, and a table where Julie wrote her journals were carried on by the four youths who a moment ago had been officers.

The end with Paul, inevitable and perhaps not the most interesting part of the tale, came quickly, while the singers sang, most hauntingly, words that were all Julie's, if from different years and about two different men, but arranged by Sarah, who, just like Julie, half believed she heard the music of those musicians of nearly a thousand years ago and knew the words they might have sung.

Why did you not tell me what love means to you
Before begging me to love you, for so I lost
Whatever I could have had, poor girl, of hope
For a life girls of the usual sort
—Your sisters?—know they will live.
No, not for me the kindness of a simple love.
Doubly my blood denies me that. Never for me kind love,
You think it too, I can see it in your eyes,
So now I may not say, 'Tell me what love means to you.'
Never for me the kindness of a simple love,
Never for me kind love.

There was an interval, a long one, while Henry talked to the players and the singers. Words and song had been pitched for a crowd of three hundred, not for many hundreds. It must be discussed tomorrow morning whether amplifiers must be used, at the meeting which they knew must take this modest production a step up into something more ambitious. And the first night was tomorrow, with so much to be done.

During this first interval people were humming Julie's songs, and Henry made a foray into the crowd to report success, and again during Act Two, when he could return to say, with satisfaction, that there wasn't a dry eye in the house. Meanwhile on her other side Benjamin sometimes engaged her attention with this or that comment, made in the hope they would not be found inappropriate from this theatre innocent. They weren't. All were to the point, and Henry took note of them. Benjamin was pleased, and, too, that he had a golden finger in this pie.

The second interval was brief, but long enough for the company to work up a fine head of anxiety.

What were they, the audience, going to make of Julie's 'second-period' music, the impersonal music so much a contrast to the sorrowful songs that had gone before? Yet, if unemotional, why did it bring tears to the eyes? Did that mean it acted on some unnamed part of the organism, such as a disembodied heart or liver? And the third act asked so much of an audience: Julie alone, mourning for her child. Julie ostracized. The programme did say this was for the sake of dramatic simplicity, and in fact the little girl had been two years old when she died of 'brain fever'—whatever that was. And then there was the so satisfactory suitor, and the prospect of happiness—rejected, and many sound and sensible citizens must always find this a confirmation that there was something really wrong with the woman.

As the curve of a low hill finally absorbed the last rays, so they were all steeped in a hot twilight, the music ended with the chilly octaves of Julie's death, the chanting of a flute, and the long groaning under-note of the shawm. At once the evening was noisy with cicadas, their din signalling applause, at first sporadic, and then prolonged. The seated people stood up to clap wildly, and while the crowd dispersed they clapped and cheered and shouted.

Some enterprising firm, hearing of the big audience up in the hills that would need transportation, had caused three coaches to stand waiting, which was all that would fit into the space.

There were limousines for the company: Bill got in by Sarah, Benjamin on her other side.

'What a wonderful success,' said Benjamin.

'You must be so pleased,' said Bill, and kissed her cheek with suggestive lips. Furious, she turned and kissed him on the lips, a real kiss, which he took with a smile half shocked, half delighted, while he glanced, embarrassed, at Benjamin, who was staring straight ahead, apparently to listen while the engaging young driver assured them that *tout le monde* adored Julie, she must be a veritable pin-up, and he couldn't wait to see the show. The habitual bestowers of compliments and flattery slowly acquire a sated, complacent look, as if fed on honeyed larks' tongues.

When the car reached the hotel it was still not eleven. Stephen had left a note for Sarah to say he had spoken to Elizabeth. The news was good. There could be at least two weeks' run at Queen's Gift.

The company settled around the pavement tables, absorbing into itself tourists and townspeople who had been at the theatre and who were demanding autographs with that calm determination to get their rights, that is to say, a piece of the action, or the pie, or the property, which characterizes autograph hunters from one end of the world to the other. The players were restless, full of suspense. For even a successful dress rehearsal is still not a *first night*, when all the strings go snap, snap.

Molly came from the hotel, later than the others, and found an empty chair near Bill. He at once bent down to kiss her. She did not respond. The moment the kiss was over, Bill lifted his chair over to a place near Sarah's and murmured, 'You look beautiful tonight.'

Sally appeared, looking for a chair. Bill pulled one forward and Sally slid into it, while her eyes searched for Richard Service. Sally still vibrated with all the emotions of having been Julie's mother, and her black skin glistened with heat against the red of her dress. Bill smiled warmly at her and kissed her, but she turned her head so her lips were out of reach. She laughed, an all-tolerant laugh, and directed to Sarah something not far off a wink. Her smile was satirical, regretful. Then she shrewdly examined Molly, who sat suffering, but then she turned away, out of delicacy.

Then she drank off Sarah's glass of *citron pressé*, said, 'Sorry, my darling, but I had to have that,' and announced, 'And now I must ring my children and get my beauty sleep.' Up she got again. The flood of vitality subsided in her because she was becoming the mother of her real children. As she left, Richard Service arrived, and the two eye-lines made shallow arcs that intersected on an agreement. She departed like a sailing ship in full moonlight.

Roy Strether, Mary Ford, Henry, and Jean-Pierre were all so buoyant with success they could not bear to sit down but stood hovering near the seated ones, and then, as Benjamin arrived, they suggested a trip to the delights of night-time Marseilles. Benjamin's eyes enquired of Sarah's, but she said she too needed to sleep. She reminded them they were meeting at eight—very well, then, nine. She walked firmly away.

She saw Bill move into the chair near Molly. If I were Molly, she thought, I would simply go across to his hotel, open his door, and get into his bed. He would certainly say, I am expecting my girl-friend, oh dear, I am so sorry. Would I then go quietly away? I'm damned if I would.

She sat by the window. She would have liked to go up and talk with Stephen, gently unwinding, as one does with a friend. Yesterday she would have gone.

She went to look in her glass. The ichors that flooded her body created behind the face of Sarah, the face she and everyone knew, a younger face, that shone out, smiling. Her body was alive and vibrant, but also painful. Her breasts burned, and the lower part of her abdomen ached. Her mouth threatened to seek kisses—like a baby's mouth turning and turning to find the nipple.

I'm sick, she said to herself. 'You're sick.' I'm sick with love, and that is all there is to it. How could such a thing have happened? What does Nature think it is up to? (Eyeball to eyeball with Nature, elderly people often accuse it—her?—of ineptitude, of sheer incompetence.) I simply can't wait to go back to my cool elderly self, all passion spent. I suppose I'm not trapped in this hell for ever? I'm going to be really ill if I can't stop this . . . and she watched her reflection, which was that of a woman in love, and not a dry old woman.

She said, 'Enough of this,' undressed quickly, and got into bed, where she murmured, as at some point she was bound to do, 'Christ that my love were in my arms . . .'

She did sleep. She woke to ghostly kisses of such sweetness they were like Julie's music, but surprisingly, the sounds that whispered in her head were not the 'troubadour' music, like blues or like fados, but the late music, cool, transparent, a summons to somewhere else. Perhaps the paradise we dream of when in love is the one we were ejected from, where all embraces are innocent.

Again she was up early. She dressed before it was light outside, thinking, Thank God there's that meeting and I'll be working hard all day. And I won't be with Bill; I'll be with Henry.

On the pavement, Stephen sat outside the still-closed café. He looked absently at Sarah, for his eyes were clouded with his preoccupation, looked again and said, 'You have been crying.'

'Yes, I have.'

'What can I say? I'm so sorry, I'm *so* sorry.'

Now this was the moment she could put things right. 'Stephen, you are wrong. It's not like that.'

He wanted so much to believe her, but looked grumpy and cross.

'Stephen, this is an absolutely ridiculous situation. Really, I promise you . . .'

He looked away, because he was so uncomfortable. His face was red. So was hers.

Communal life was rescuing them. While the players still slept, the managerial side were all up, in spite of their having jaunted around the coast so late. Here came Mary Ford, calm and fresh in white. After her came Henry, who at once took a chair near Sarah. He appeared to have staggered from some battlefront. Then Benjamin, impeccable in pale linen. He sat opposite Sarah, studying her from under serious brows. Here was Roy Strether, yawning, and with him Sandy Grears. The proprietor of Les Collines Rouges was opening his doors, and the aromas of coffee began their insinuations.

A sparky urchin in a striped blue and white apron appeared from the other side of the square, holding aloft balanced on one hand, several tiers of cakes and croissants, the other hand poised on his hip, for style. He too wafted delicious smells everywhere. He passed them gracefully, grinning, knowing they all waited for the moment when what he carried would leave the counters of the café for their breakfasts.

'Un moment,' reproved the café proprietor, though no one had said a word. 'Un petit moment, mesdames, messieurs.' He disappeared inside, with a stern air. Because of Sartre, they knew that he was playing the role of Monsieur le Patron, just as the urchin was playing his role.

Sarah could not prevent a pretty desperate look at Stephen and caught him examining her. Appalling. How could their friendship survive such a muddle of misunderstanding?

It was occurring to them all that everyone necessary for the meeting which would decide *Julie Vairon*'s fate was here. Except for Jean-Pierre.

With the British production there was really one problem—who would be available? Elizabeth had said the last week of August and the first of September would suit her, suit Queen's Gift, because by then the new building would be finished. She had pointed out that Julie could not be expected to be as popular in England as it was in

France, but people were still talking about the evening of Julie's music, and that was a good sign. Stephen said, apologetically, that they mustn't think Elizabeth was a wet blanket. 'She has to be cautious, you see. She thinks I get carried away.'

His eyes met Sarah's—on a smile. Her heart lightened.

Roy said, 'Henry, you're the key to everything. If you're not free, we'll forget the whole thing. That means rehearsals through the first three weeks of August and then setting the production at Queen's Gift.'

'I'm doing *Salome* in Pittsburgh through July—that is, from ten A.M. three days from now. So I can make it.'

Up he jumped, took a stroll through tables beginning to fill up, kicked a carton into a refuse can—a perfect shot, and came back to fling himself down. They all watched him. 'Perpetuum mobile,' said Roy. 'How does he do it? How do you do it, Henry? I have to tell you all that this man was dancing and singing in the rain in Marseilles three hours ago in the water cart sprays. Right, Henry. You're booked for August.'

'But,' said Mary, 'the players. Bill is off to New York the day after this ends here to start rehearsal. *Carmen*. He won't be available, nor will Molly. She's working the rest of July and all August in Portland. *Pocahontas*. She's Pocahontas.'

Mary was carefully not looking at Stephen, whose face had crumpled, if only for a moment. He recovered himself and looked at Sarah. The look was not unmixed with irony, so that was something.

'We need a new Julie and a new Paul,' said Roy. He yawned. It was the loud and unabashed yawn of a man who had been up most of the night.

To the people whose hearts were cracking open like eggs, the yawn sounded derisive. Mary Ford began to laugh and could not stop. She put out her hand in apology. Roy took it in a fist and shook it up and down, oblivious but matey.

Mary stopped herself laughing. 'Sorry. Show business. It's show business . . . anyway, I asked all the cast last night, and the musicians. They are all free.'

'All free except for the two important ones. Never mind; some of the Pauls and Julies we auditioned were very good.' Henry's eyes closed.

Benjamin seemed asleep. Mary's lids dropped. Roy yawned again. When the waiter finally arrived, Sarah ordered coffee and croissants for everyone but in a low voice, as if in a room full of sleeping children.

At this juncture Jean-Pierre arrived, with the air of a man not prepared to be apologetic, just because he was later than others who had no need to be early.

'Everything's just fine,' said Henry lazily to Jean-Pierre.

'I was also up very late,' said Jean-Pierre.

'Well, it doesn't matter; we've got everything sorted out,' said Mary maternally.

'But the meeting was not arranged until nine, I think?'

The coffee arrived. Smells of sunlight, coffee, hot dust, croissants, petrol, vanilla.

'There really isn't much left to decide,' said Roy.

'And may I enquire what has been decided?' said Jean-Pierre.

At the sound of his voice, full of wounded self-esteem, Mary sat herself up, sent Sarah a glance, sent Roy another, and remarked soothingly, 'What delicious coffee.' She smiled at Jean-Pierre, who was after all in love with her. He positively winced, and then shook off unfair, not to say corrupting, pressures.

Mary outlined what had been decided. 'And there you are,' she concluded.

At this Jean-Pierre presented himself as the traditional Frenchman confronted by the ineffable, however it chooses continually to offer itself, in this case as a barbarous lack of respect for proper form. He slightly lifted his chin, let his lower jaw drop, spread his hands, and quivered with sensibility. 'And so,' he announced, having given them all time to get the benefit of his performance, 'all is decided. But without me. Without Belles Rivières.'

A crisis.

'But of course we haven't decided anything for you. How could we? But since Henry is leaving almost at once and you are losing the two main actors when your two weeks are up, it is obvious you can't prolong your run.'

Jean-Pierre began a spirited speech, in French. It could be seen from Stephen's face and from Sarah's—both of them being, as it is put at school, 'good at' French—that this was a speech to be appreciated as a performance in its own right.

'Now look here, Jean-Pierre old chap,' said Stephen reproachfully, 'any minute now I'll start to believe you actually enjoy meetings.'

At this communication from a past epoch Jean-Pierre only looked puzzled. Benjamin, a man of a thousand committees, signalled to Sarah, and then to Stephen and to Mary, leaning forward and holding them with his commanding look. 'It isn't strictly my business,' he remarked, 'but I do feel the situation would be significantly improved if there was in fact some kind of structured discussion. For instance, surely there must be a decision about finances?'

'Naturally there must be decisions,' said Jean-Pierre, already mollified. 'And if I'd been given a chance to make a statement . . . it has been decided that we shall have *Julie Vairon* in Belles Rivières next year. And very likely every year. Next year we shall have a month's run. Why not two months? It is all a question of the correct publicity.' And he bowed slightly to Mary.

A silence. They were all contemplating a yearly commitment to Julie.

Stephen's head was tilted back, and he was staring at the imperturbable blue of the Mediterranean sky with a stoic look. Sarah was thinking, Over my dead body. That's silly—you'll have forgotten it all by then. You'll probably even be thinking it was funny . . . well, if you do, it'll be dishonest.

Henry was looking at Sarah as he said, 'I'll be free, I'll guarantee it.' His terrible insecurity made him add, 'I mean, if you want me.'

Everyone laughed at him, and Jean-Pierre said, 'But naturally. I can give you that assurance.'

'And I give you notice,' said Benjamin, 'that I am coming to Oxfordshire for your first night in August. I shall be missing your first night here.'

'*Missing* the first *night*,' said Henry to him. A jest, but Benjamin actually said, quickly, 'I'm sorry,' saw it was a joke, went red, but pre-served more than ever the look of a man determined not to be undone by seductive and dangerous ways. He said to Jean-Pierre, 'I shall be here next year, I can assure you of that.'

Jean-Pierre understood that this was an important moment, in fact a guarantee of financial support. He got up, leaned across a lit-tered table, put out his hand. Benjamin took it sitting, then stood up, and the two men formally shook hands.

'We can discuss the details in Jean-Pierre's office,' said Benjamin. 'Let's say half an hour.'

'Let's *say* half an hour,' said Mary.

'I have to catch my plane,' said Benjamin.

'There's plenty of time,' said Sarah.

'There's time, but not plenty,' said Henry.

Here, on cue, the chatter around the tables was blanked out by the screaming roar of three war planes, sinister, black, like some outsize prehistoric hornets out of a science-fiction film, shooting across the sky with the speed which announces, so briefly it is easy to forget they were there at all, that they are from a world of super-technology far from our amateur little lives.

Now the players were appearing, yawning prettily. The circle was enlarged, and enlarged again to include everyone. Bill took a chair beside Sarah and enquired sulkily, 'It is true there will be a run in England?'

'Two weeks,' said Sarah.

'And I can't be there. If only I had known.'

'If only any of us had known.'

'But you will keep in touch, won't you? At least there's two weeks left of this run.' He was speaking to her like a peremptory young lover. Really, they might have spent the night together. Molly watched the two of them, puzzled. As well she might be, thought Sarah. And Stephen too. Because of Bill's closeness to his mother, he felt, as much as he saw, Sarah, but between Molly and Sarah was that gulf only to be filled by experience. Molly did not yet know that always, impalpably, invisibly, through the air rained down ashes that could be seen only when enough had settled—on her, on Stephen, on the older, on the ageing, ashes and dust dimming the colours of skin and hair. Sarah knew that this glossy young animal sitting beside her diminished her, leached colour from her, no matter how he flattered her with his eyes, his smile, enclosing her in streams of sympathy. Sarah saw Molly's serious, thoughtful, honest gaze turn from her to Stephen, the sun was not burnishing him as it did the young ones. He looked bleached, faded.

Sarah said to Bill, knowing her voice was rough, 'I shall be going home in a couple of days.'

'Oh, you can't, you can't do that,' said Bill, really upset. 'You can't leave us.' He might just as well have said 'leave *me*.'

'Everyone is leaving us,' said Molly. 'Henry . . . Sarah . . .' She hesitated, looking at Stephen. He was again looking into the sky.

'I shall be here,' said Mary. 'And so will Roy. If Sarah is going, then we must be here.'

'I have a month's leave due, remember?' said Sarah.

Here Mary's raised brows remarked direct to Sarah that she couldn't remember Sarah's ever before insisting on due leave.

'No, Sarah,' said Henry. 'Don't forget, I'll have to be over for the new auditions. I can fit it in the second week in July. And you must be there.'

'You mean, no vanishing in July?'

Henry smiled at her, and her heart tripped.

'Such a wild, marvellous, blissful success,' remarked Mary, lazing in her chair in a way that contradicted her briskly efficient linen suit. Uncharacteristically lazed, she put her arms back behind her head, exposing tender patches of damp linen. She had the look of an animal offering vulnerable parts of herself to superior strength. Jean-Pierre sighed; she heard it, blushed, and looked upwards, like Stephen. One by one, they all looked skywards. Quite low down, a single hawk circled. Lower and lower it floated, until some rogue breeze blew it ragged and tilted up a wing. The bird rocked wildly to find balance, steadied, circled once on a thermal, and swerved off to the top of a plane tree, where it sat huffing out its feathers. It looked sulky, offended, and this made them all laugh.

By now the café tables were filled with people in some way connected with *Julie Vairon*.

'We have virtually taken his café over, poor Monsieur Denivre,' said Molly.

'Il est désolé,' said Jean-Pierre. 'Guillaume,' he called to the proprietor, who was attending to customers a couple of tables away— Andrew, Sally, Richard, George White. 'Les Anglais ont peur que vous les trouviez trop encombrants.' Guillaume smiled, with exactly the shade of urbane scepticism appropriate. He said, 'Ça y est!'

'Why Anglais?' enquired Molly, exaggerating her American voice. 'I'm not Anglais. Who is Anglais here—apart from the Anglais?'

Here Bill said, in the roughest of Tennessee accents, 'I'm English, mesdames, messieurs, I am English to the last little molecule.'

They laughed, but it was one of the moments, hardly uncommon, when Europeans and Americans occupy different geographical and historical space.

The Americans were thinking, Molly—Boston. At least, that was where she lived now. Benjamin—West Coast, even if his accent could only be Harvard. Henry had been born in New York but lived, when he was at home—seldom—in Los Angeles. Andrew had been born, and lived, in Texas.

But the Europeans were thinking, Molly—Ireland. Benjamin's antecedents could only have come from that culturally fertile region, sometimes Russian, sometimes Polish, the shtetl. Henry— the Mediterranean. Andrew? Scottish, of course.

'Our American cousins,' said Mary to Sarah.

'Our cousins,' said Sarah to Mary.

Les Anglais all laughed, and the Americans laughed out of good feeling. Laughter was breaking out for no good reason, from all around the tables. The company's spirits were being lifted, borne on those currents that carry players and their minders towards the intoxications of *the first night*. The charm, the enchantment, the delightfulness of—well, of what exactly?—were slowly lifting them, seawater setting fronds of weed afloat, splashing dry rock, sending out invigorating ozone.

They sat on, while Le Patron caused the waiters to bring more coffee, and the square filled with vehicles. Not only this town was crammed; so were all the little towns round about, from where coaches would bring people—were already bringing people, at ten in the morning—to become part of the ambience of Julie, her time, her place.

Soon Henry departed to work out with the technicians the problems with sound, and Sarah, Stephen, Benjamin, Roy, and Mary went off with Jean-Pierre to his office. There finances were discussed, particularly Benjamin's—or rather the Associated and Allied Banks of North California and South Oregon's—commitment to the new plans. Stephen's as well, but as he pointed out, since he was an individual, he had only to say 'yes'. Money was talking. First things first. Money has to talk before actors can.

Then Benjamin flew off to investigate his investment in the Edinburgh Festival. Jean-Pierre insisted they must decide how to get together a much larger committee to discuss next year's production in Belles Rivières. Sarah, he trusted, would be part of it. So, he hoped, would Mr Ellington-Smith. Regular meetings throughout the year would benefit them all. All this went on until well after two. When they arrived on the pavement for lunch, it was observable that the players and musicians already preferred to be with each other, merging for their test that evening. Henry sat by Sarah. When she thought that this was the last time she would be with him in Belles Rivières—it would if she had anything to do with it—such a feeling of loss took her over that she had to admit if she were not in love with Bill, then she showed all the signs of loving Henry. It occurred to her that to be with Henry was all sweetness, while being with Bill was to be angry and ashamed. What a pity, if it was her fate to fall in love so inappropriately, that it had not been Henry from the first.

Henry returned from a reconnaissance in the late afternoon to say that crowds were already making their way up to Julie's house and that all the seats had been booked by mid-morning. He reported that several tastefully designed signs with arrows had been nailed to trees, saying in French and in English, 'One may stand in this place.' 'Please respect Nature.' 'Please respect Julie Vairon's Forest.'

By seven the woods all around the house held a couple of thousand people, most of whom could not hope to do more than hear the music. There being no 'backstage', Stephen and Sarah, as authors, Henry, as director, went together to where the players stood waiting among the trees, to wish them luck.

The three sat themselves in chairs right at the back, and this time Henry managed to stay seated through the performance. It was all wonderful! It was extraordinary! It was fantastic! These comments and a hundred others, in various languages, were to be heard all through the intervals, and the applause was unending. And then it was all over, and the company were down outside the café again, embracing, affectionate, mad with euphoria, in love and out of it, wild with relief. The brassy little moon, like a clipped coin, stood over the town, and resulting moonlight was satisfactorily moody and equivocal. Les Collines Rouges announced it would stay open as long as anyone was still up, and cars roared triumphantly around the little town. Jean-Pierre could not stop smiling. He had continually to rise and shake hands, or be embraced by prominent citizens of the area, for whom he was embodying all the success of the production. Midnight came and was past. Jean-Pierre said he had to get home to his wife and children. Henry went too, saying he must telephone his wife. He murmured to Sarah that he would be seeing her soon in London, with a look that brought tears to her eyes. Richard left, saying he was tired, looking at Sally but not saying good night to her. Soon after, Sally announced that this old woman was going to sleep. Sarah heard Andrew's low laugh, saw that he wanted to share amusement with her, Sarah, and, as she too got up, heard him say, 'Well, how about it, Sarah?' This was so improbable she decided she had not heard it. She announced that this old woman too had to sleep. Groans of protest that the party was ending. Bill leaped up to accompany her to the hotel door, there enfolding her in an embrace and murmuring that he thought of her as a second mother. She went upstairs white hot with love and with anger.

She stood at her window, looking down at the company, and knew that this loss, the desolation of being excluded from happiness, could only refer back to something she had forgotten. Had she too been that child who had stood on the edge of a playground, watching the others? She had forgotten. Fortunately.

And soon all this would have put itself into the past. *Julie Vairon* would never take shape in this way again, in this setting, with these people. Well, it was not the first time—rather perhaps the hundredth—that she had been part of some play or piece, and it had always been sad to see the end of something that could never happen again. The theatre, in short, was just like life (but in a condensed and brightly illuminated form, forcing one into the comparison), always whirling people and events into improbable associations and then— that's it. The end. *Basta!* But this event, Julie's, was not anything she had known before. For one thing, she had not been 'in love'—why the inverted commas? She was not going to make it all harmless with quote marks. No, there was something in this particular mix of people—that must be it—and of course the music . . . So Sarah talked aloud to herself, walking about her room, returning often to the window, where she could see how Stephen sat next to Molly, while Bill— but enough. She went to her mirror several times during the course of this excursion around and about her room, for an inspection that deserved to be called scientific. That a woman's interaction with her mirror is likely to go through some changes during the decades goes without saying but . . . someone should bottle this, she announced aloud to the empty room, visible over her reflection's shoulder (Woman Gazing Curiously into Her Mirror). . . . Yes, someone should bottle these substances flooding me now. They probably did bottle them. Probably potions were on sale in beauty shops and chemists: if so, they should have on the label the warning POISON—in brightest red. It is not merely that I feel twenty years younger, I look it . . .

Meanwhile she wrote:

Dear Stephen,
I simply have to write this letter, though letters being the tricky
things they are and so easily misunderstood, I am afraid. Look,
I really am not in love with you. Loving someone is one thing,
but being in love another. As I wrote that it occurs to me that
'loving' can mean anything. But I really do love you. It is
awful that I should have to spell this out. If it makes us both
easier, I can say,

> *Affectionately,*
> *Sarah*

P.S. I really cannot bear to think of our friendship being
spoiled by misunderstandings as silly as this.

This was not the letter she slid under Stephen's door on the
floor above hers, for she thought, One can't say 'I love you' to an
Englishman. Stephen would take to his heels and run. She tore up
that letter and wrote:

Dear Stephen,
I simply have to write this letter, though letters being the tricky
things they are and so easily misunderstood, I can't help feeling
nervous. Look, I really am not in love with you. I know you
think I am. I am very very fond of you—but you know that. It
is awful that I should have to spell this out. If it makes us both
easier, I can say,

> *Affectionately,*
> *Sarah*

This was the letter she took upstairs, hoping she would not run
into him.

Next morning, very early, she woke to see an envelope sliding
under her door.

Dearest Sarah,
I'm off. Unexpectedly got myself on an early flight, so won't see
you today. But see you soon in London.

> *With all love,*
> *Henry*

As she stood reading this, another envelope slid towards her
feet from under the door. She cautiously opened the door, but it
was too late: the corridor was empty, though she heard the lift
descending.

Dearest Sarah,
I am so unhappy you are going and I may never see you again.
You are a very special friend and I feel I have known you all
my life. I shall never forget our time together in Belles Rivières
and I shall always think of you with true affection. Perhaps
next year? I can't wait!!!

Gratefully,
Bill

P.S. Please feel free to let me know if other productions of Julie
are projected anywhere in Europe or the States????????? Why
shouldn't Julie *conquer New York? That is a lovely thought,*
isn't it?

While she was drinking coffee at her window, the porter
brought two letters.

Dear Sarah,
Before leaving the beguiling atmospheres and influences of
Julie Vairon, *but I am happy to say only temporarily, I feel I*
must tell you how much it has meant to me to be with you all,
but particularly with you. The financial aspects of this enter-
prise will I am sure prove more rewarding than we ever antici-
pated, but it is not this that prompts me to write to you. You
will, I am sure, find it improbable that I never even suspected
the theatre could offer such rewards, though when I think
about it, I enjoyed acting in a minor role in Death of a
Salesman *in the school theatrical group when I was a young-*
ster. When I reflect that all this has been going on ever since
and that I have had no part in it, I really can't forgive myself.
And so, my dear Sarah—I hope I may call you that—I look
forward to seeing you at Julie's first night in Oxfordshire.

Until then—
Benjamin

Sarah!
You won't know who this is, I suppose, since you are so obsti-
nately gazing in the wrong direction. I am madly in love with
you, Sarah Durham! I have not been so overthrown since I was
an adolescent. (Yes, all right.*)*
Somebody loves you
I wonder who
I wonder who it can be.

Your secret lover

P.S. I have always been crazy for older women.

At first shock, this letter actually seemed to her insulting. She
was about to tear it up, her fingers trembling, in order to deposit the
fragments in the wastepaper basket, when . . . Wait a minute. Hold
your horses, Sarah Durham. She carefully reread the letter, noting
with satirical appreciation for her inconsistency the following reactions: First, the attack of false morality. Second, irritation, because
she simply couldn't attend to it, when she was so beset with emotions. Third, the classic retort to an unwanted declaration of love,
faintly patronizing pity: Oh, poor thing: well, never mind, he'll get
over it.

Who was it? Because of what she had heard last night but had at
once said to herself was impossible—'How about it, Sarah?'—she
had to admit it must be Andrew. To whom she had never given a
thought not strictly professional.

She carefully put this letter away, to be read later when not
intoxicated. To be accurate, when no longer sick. Bill's letter she did
tear up and she dropped the pieces neatly one by one in the basket
as if finally ridding herself of something poisonous.

It was now eight in the morning. She chose a sensible dress in
dark blue cotton, partly because she thought, I will not be accused
of mutton dressed as lamb, partly because a dull dress might sober
her. The noise outside was already so loud she sat for a few minutes,

eyes closed, thinking of that long-ago youth on his hillside—absolute silence, solace, peace. But suddenly into this restoring dream the three war planes from yesterday inserted themselves, streaking across the antique sky and vibrating the air. The boy lifted his dreaming head and stared but did not believe what he saw. His ears were hurting. Sarah went quietly downstairs. She did not want to have to talk. In a side street was a little café she believed was not used by the company. The tables outside Les Collines Rouges were all empty except for Stephen, who sat with his head bent, the picture of a man struck down. He did not see her, and she walked past him to the Rue Daniel Autram. Whoever Daniel Autram was or had been, he did not merit pots of flowers all along his street, though on either side of the café door were tubs of marguerites. This café had a window on the street and, presumably, something like a window seat, for she saw two young sunburned arms, as emphatically male as those of Michelangelo's young men, lying along the back of it. The forearms rested side by side, hands grasping the elbows of the other. The arms being bare, there was a suggestion of naked bodies. This was as strong a sexual statement as Sarah could remember, out of bed. She was stopped dead there, in the Rue Daniel Autram, as noisy children raced past to a bus waiting for them in the square. I have to go back, go back, breathed Sarah, but she could not move, for the sight had struck her to the heart, as if she had been dealt lies and treachery. (Which was nonsense, because she had not.) Then one young man leaned forward to say something to the other, as the other leaned forward to hear it. Bill and Sandy. This was a Bill Sarah had never seen, nor, she was sure, had any female member of the company. Certainly his first mother had never been allowed a glimpse of this exultantly, triumphantly alive young man, full of a mocking and reckless sexuality. And the charming, winning, affectionate, sympathetic young man they all knew? Well, for one thing, *that* person had little of the energy she was now looking at: his energy was in bond to caution.

She forced herself to take two steps back, out of the danger of being seen, and walked like a mechanical toy to the table where Stephen still sat. Now he did lift his head, and stared at Sarah from some place a long way off. He reminded himself that he should smile, and did so. Then he remembered there was something else, and said, 'Thanks for your letter, I'm glad you wrote it.' And he was glad, she could see that. 'I did get it wrong, actually.'

She sat by him. There was nobody else on the pavement yet. She signalled for coffee, since Stephen had not thought of it.

'I got another letter this morning,' he said. 'A day for letters.'

'So it would seem.'

He did not hear this, and then he did and came to himself, saying, 'I'm sorry, Sarah. I do know I'm selfish. Actually I think I must be ill. I said that before, didn't I?'

'Yes, you did.'

'The thing is . . . I'm simply not this kind of person. Do you understand that?'

'Perfectly.'

He produced a letter, written on the paper of l'Hotel Julie, in a large no-nonsense hand.

Dear Stephen,
I was so flattered when I read your letter and realized you were kindly asking me to spend a weekend with you in Nice. Of course I did know you were fond of me, but this! I do not feel this could be an ongoing committed relationship where two people could grow together on a basis of shared give-and-take and spiritual growth.
I do believe I can look forward to this kind of relationship with someone I got to know in Baltimore in spring when we were both working on The Lady with a Little Dog.
So wish me luck!
I shall never forget you and the days we have all spent

*together. I can only say I profoundly regret the commitments
which make it impossible for me to be Julie in Oxfordshire.
Because there is something special about this piece. We all
feel it.*

> *With sincere good wishes,*
> *Molly McGuire*

Sarah tried not to laugh, but had to. Stephen sat with lowered head, looking across at her, sombre and even sullen. 'I suppose it is funny,' he conceded. Then he did, unexpectedly, sit up and laugh. A real laugh. 'Well, all right,' he said. 'A culture clash.'

'Don't forget they have to divorce and remarry every time they fall in love.'

'Yes, with the Yanks there is always an invisible contract somewhere.' As she shrugged: 'Am I being unfair?'

'Of course you're being unfair.'

'I don't care if I am. But they must go to bed sometimes just for love's sake. Of course, I do keep forgetting, she was writing to the old man, didn't want to hurt his feelings.'

'I believe she might easily have gone with you to Nice . . . all things being equal.'

'You mean, if she hadn't been in love with that . . . I wonder? But if she had gone to bed with Bill—or rather if Bill had kindly gone to bed with her'—here she noted an altogether disproportionate spurt of malice in herself, to match his—'then she would have been hinting about weddings by the morning. Anyway, one has really to be in love to think that kind of thing is worth it. I mean, Nice and all that. So I was a fool to ask. Otherwise it is just a dirty weekend.'

She remembered Andrew's letter and wondered if he was in love. Because to imagine him suffering from lust, that was one thing, and fair enough—but in love, oh no, she wouldn't wish it on anyone. And she didn't want to think about it. Too much of everything: she was drowning in too-muchness.

The coffee arrived. As Stephen lifted his cup, he—and she—noted that his hand shook. No joke, love, she attempted to joke, to herself. He set the cup down again, looking with critical dislike at his hand.

'Believe it or not, a good many women fall for me.'

'Why shouldn't I believe it? Anyway, you don't have to make a final assessment of your attractiveness or lack of it just because one girl turns you down.'

'Yes, and she's only a stand-in after all,' he remarked, in one of his moments of calm throw-away callousness. 'Perhaps she feels that.'

'As you said that it was as if two different Stephens slid together and one said something the other could never say. Oh, don't worry, I know the condition well.'

'Obviously people fall in love with you. I'm not exactly blind, though I'm sure you think I am.' He hesitated, and his reluctance to go on made him sound grumpy. 'I wanted to say something . . . If it's the gaucho you're . . .' He could not make himself say it. 'I should watch it, if I were you. He's a pretty tough customer.' As she did not reply, not knowing how to, he went on. 'Anyway, it's not my business. And I don't really care. That's what is intolerable. I don't care about anything but myself. Perhaps I will go to a psychiatrist after all. But what can they tell me I don't know already? I know what I'm suffering from—De Cleremont's syndrome. I found it described in an article. It means you are convinced the person is in love with you, even when she is not. The article didn't say anything about being convinced she would be in love with you if she wasn't dead.'

'Never heard of it.' She noted that he had been able to say, apparently easily, that Julie was dead.

'I would say there is a pretty narrow dividing line between sanity and lunacy.'

'A grey area perhaps?'

This exchange had cheered them both up—her disproportionately. She was wildly happy. Soon she left him to go to Jean-Pierre's office. She had not been there half an hour before Stephen rang from the hotel to say he was getting on an afternoon flight from Marseilles and he would ring her from home.

She was busy all day. The performance that night drew an even larger crowd. At the end of the first act—that is, the end of Bill being Paul for that evening, he came to sit by her, but she found herself wanting only to get away. She was missing Henry. Bill's attentive sympathy cloyed. She preferred the raw, unscrupulously sexual and vital young man she had glimpsed that morning. In fact she could truthfully say that this winning young man bored her, so things were looking up.

She left farewell notes for Bill and Molly and went to her room. She sat by the window and watched the crowd on the pavement thin. This being the second night, and the tension fast diminishing, people went off to bed early. Soon there was no one down there, and the café's doors were locked. It was very hot in her room. Airless. Sultry. A dark night, for that acid little moon was blacked out behind what everyone must be hoping was a rain cloud. She would go down and sit on the pavement, alone. She crept down through the hotel, feeling it to be empty because Stephen was gone, and Henry too. As she was about to pull a chair out from under a table, she heard voices and retreated to sit under the plane tree. She would not be seen in the deep shadow.

A group of young people. American voices. Bill's, Jack's. Some girls. They sat down, complaining that the café had shut.

'I just love it, love it . . . it's . . . you know . . .' A girl's voice.

'Er . . . er . . . you know, yah, it's right on.' Bill. This articulate young man's tongue had been struck by paralysis?

'It's just beautiful, know what I mean? It's sort of . . . mmm, yeah, I mean to say . . .'

'Sort of . . . kinda . . . actually, you know, as I saw it . . . very . . .' Jack.

Another girl. 'To me it was . . . er . . . yeah, it was just . . . it was actually . . .'

'Just wonderful, yeah.'

'It makes me feel like . . . I don't know . . .'

They all went on like this, the educated and infinitely privileged young of their great country, for some minutes. Then there was a clap of thunder, and some drops. They rose in a flock and scattered into the hotels.

Bill went last, with his pal Jack. Bill said, just as if he had not been conversing in Neanderthal, 'Yes, I do think we have the last act in balance now.'

Jack: 'I still think there should be another four or five minutes of Philippe. It's slightly underplayed there, for me.'

Rain swept across the square. She ran through it to her hotel, up the stairs, into her room, and to her window, which was blanked out by a flash flood, gravelly streams that silted up in heaps along the sill and were washed off and piled up again, showing greyish white when the lightning flickered, like the dirty heaps of snow along wintry roads. She sat approaching—cautiously—depths in herself she did not often choose to remember. Few people can reach even middle age without knowing there are doors they might have opened and could open still. Even that sensible marriage of hers had begun sensually enough, and there had been a moment when they had decided not to open these doors. What had since been christened S-M, a jaunty little name for a fashionable pastime (sado-masochism sounded, and was, real, something to be taken seriously), had appeared as a possibility. Her husband had in fact gone in for it with an earlier lover but found that love became hate . . . rather sooner, he joked, than it might otherwise have done: the two were not suited. She, Sarah, had noticed that women friends 'enjoying' S-M had come to grief. People might claim these practices were all as harmless as a game of golf, but it was not what the couple had observed separately. Together, the smallest approaches had aroused in both strong reactions, as if a door were being opened onto a pornographic hell. Enthusiastic practitioners presented a picture something like this: A couple 'respecting each other'—this was important—permitted carefully regulated cruelties, to the pleasure of both, but these were never permitted to go beyond limits. A likely story. Was it possible that the emotions of two people in any case always on the verge of exaggeration, in sex, or in love, never got out of control in S-M? (Or sado-masochism?) And surely these were not practices for parents? One could too easily imagine scenes of a rosy little bottom (mama's) and her cries of pleasure, or lethal black shiny straps and her cries of pain, while the children listened. Or papa, trussed like a roasting chicken. 'Just a minute, dear, I just want to see if Penelope is awake.' Or, 'Oh damn it, there's the baby.' Or even a childless couple. She has taken the washing out of the drier, he has parked the car, they eat a supper cooked by microwave. 'How about a little S-M darling?' No, surely these delights could only be for houses of pleasure, or for brief affairs. *Too dangerous*—even in sexual relationships of the ordinary kind (boring, so it was suggested by the proselytizers), hidden depths so easily upwelled and flooded both partners with every kind of dark emotion. It was at the time when she and her husband had actually played with the idea (not the practice) that she had found within herself, at first appearing in a dream and then presenting itself as a probable memory, the image of a small girl sitting alone in a room locked from the outside, a small girl with a doll she held between her knees and stabbed again and again with scissors while blood spurted from it . . . no, the spurting blood was the dream, but the little girl stabbing the doll, that was memory. The child went on and on stabbing the doll, her face lifted, eyes shut, mouth open in a dismal hopeless wail.

It was from this level in her that she could respond to the equivocal Bill. One knows what a man is like from the images and fantasies he evokes. This level, this 'somewhere', was to do (she thought) with babyhood. Earlier than childhood. Again and again during this sojourn in Julie's country, in sleep or in half-sleep she had seen that proud beautiful young head, its slow turn, the mocking smile that was androgynous and perverse, with a slow dissolve to the other sex, young woman to young man, young man to girl, young boy to girl-child, small girl to baby boy. Somewhere, somewhere back there, probably before the small girl sat stabbing the doll with scissors, there was something . . . So Sarah talked to herself, half aloud, sitting at the window where the streaming rain made the room dark, so that she could see only the black mass of the bed. I'm afraid. I am right to be afraid, though I don't know what I am afraid of. I know something terrible waits there . . . passing the stages of my age and youth, entering the whirlpool, yes, the whirlpool, that is what waits, and I know it.

Sarah's flat was full of sunlight and flowers sent by Benjamin, now in Scotland, and from Stephen, thanking her for putting up with him. There was also the single passionate red rose of tradition from 'Guess who?' She put this in a glass beside Stephen's flowers and Benjamin's, grateful she had not confessed her state to Stephen, because otherwise by now she would be thanking him for putting up with her. She knew that one word along the confessional path would have her weeping bitterly. Oh no, a stiff upper lip was much to be recommended. She did not feel herself appropriately surrounded by all this sunny cheerfulness.

She sat herself down to get her diary up to date, for in France she had neglected it, but after a couple of hours of restless attempts at attention, found she had written only:

> Just imagine, I was joking that I could never fall in love
> again. Now I feel I should have been making signs to
> ward off some listening little devil, or a spiteful ghost.

And trying again later rewarded her only with:

Stupid dreams. All longing and wanting.

She went to the theatre, where she found Sonia, vibrant with success and so busy she could hardly find half an hour to spend with Sarah in the office. Where was Patrick? Sonia replied that he was off on some new plan—he'd tell Sarah himself. She sounded a mite embarrassed, hardly Sonia's style. 'But he shouldn't have gone off,' said Sarah. 'Not with the three of us in France—no, no, I don't mean you haven't been coping perfectly well.'

'You do realize, don't you, that you lot are workaholics? You're truly, truly crazy,' said Sonia. 'Have you four always coped with everything?'

'Well, yes, it all seemed to work pretty well.'

'Obviously it has, but for God's sake!'

'And who's talking?' said Sarah, laughing at her.

'Yes, all right.' Sonia's mobile telephone chirped at her, and up she got and rushed out, saying, 'You haven't seen my *Hedda* yet, Sarah. I want to know what you think.'

The reviews of *Hedda* were excellent. The sets and lighting were particularly commended: Patrick's work. A couple of days in The Green Bird put Sarah sufficiently in the picture to know that Sonia's initial dislike of Patrick had evaporated: she valued him too much. They were now great friends. But what everyone was talking about was the latest instalment of the skirmish with Roger Stent.

On press night, he had arrived five minutes before the curtain went up, wearing a large curly red beard. He had bought a seat, under a false name, in the front row of the stalls and sat himself down in it, folding his arms and staring belligerently around. Clearly he expected to be evicted. No one took any notice until the first interval, when Sonia, with one of the stagehands, sauntered along to stand just in front of him.

'Auditioning, do you think?' enquired Sonia.

The well-briefed stagehand solemnly played his part: 'Looks like it, doesn't it?'

'I don't really see what we could use him for.' And she proceeded to describe his attributes as if he were being sold in a slave market, ending by pinching his thigh with a look of distaste. 'Quite meaty, though. Perhaps we could use him as a stagehand?' And she strolled on and out, followed by her accomplice. Roger Stent had not moved a muscle under this attack. People who had stayed during the interval spread the tale, and it earned a spiteful (and of course inaccurate) paragraph in the *Evening Standard*. The young man was in what he felt to be a quite tragic dilemma. He had enjoyed *Hedda Gabler*. The fact was, he had hardly ever seen a play in his life, and now he was secretly reading plays, was fascinated by this new world. Meanwhile the group of Young Turks continued to claim, as a main article of faith, that the theatre was ridiculous and, in any case, dead in Britain. What had begun as the spiteful, casual impulse of the young editor of *New Talents* had become a dogma not to be questioned. Roger was still accepted in the group only because of his willingness to despise the theatre. Like all cowardly reviewers, who for one reason or another do not want to commit themselves by saying that a play—or a book—is either good or bad, he used up his five hundred words with a description of the plot, ending 'This tedious play about a bored housewife whose symptoms would be cured by a good workout was well enough presented, but why put it on at all?'

He was secretly trying to get himself another job, but the world of newspapers and periodicals is a small one. He had booked himself in for two weeks of the Edinburgh Festival, where he could indulge this new interest, so he believed, without his cronies knowing about it.

Sarah was overwhelmed with work, and just as she had decided to telephone Mary Ford and beg her to come home, Mary rang her to say she was on her way.

'What am I doing here, Sarah? No, don't bother to answer that.'

When she got back she reported that *Julie Vairon* continued her triumphant progress, and there were already enquiries about tickets for next year.

The two women worked like demons all day, and in the evenings Mary was with her mother, who was pretty ill now, and Sarah found herself buying beauty creams, trying to find in her mirror comfort in this aspect of her face or that, and buying clothes too young for her.

I don't want to know what I was dreaming last night. I woke this morning flooded with tears. I could weep and weep. For what?

I have to come back to the same question: how is it I lived comfortably for years and years and then suddenly am made ill with longing—for what? By deprivation—of what? Who is it that lies awake in the dark body and heart and mind, sick with yearning for warmth, a kiss, comfort?

Sarah, who had not for years thought of marrying, or even of living with a man, had believed herself to be happily solitary, now watched long submerged fantasies surface. She would be on the lookout for a man with whom to share this love she was carrying about with her like a load she had to put into someone's arms. (But the fevers she suffered from had nothing to do with the affections and satisfactions of connubial living.) Forgotten selves kept appearing like bubbles in boiling liquid, exploding in words: Here I am— remember me? She told herself she was like one of those chrysalides attached to a branch, outwardly dry and dead, but inside the case the substance loses form, seethes and churns, without apparent aim, yet this formless soup will shape itself into an insect: a butterfly. She was obviously dissolving into some kind of boiling soup, but presumably would reshape at some point. Never mind about butterfly-hood: she would settle for as-you-were.

Henry flew in from Pittsburgh and *Salomé* for a weekend of auditions for a new Paul and a new Julie.

Meeting Henry again was like that deep involuntary sigh of a child finding itself lifted into longed-for arms. Henry greeted Sarah with his cry of *Sarah!* and a smile both passionate and ironical, and she fell in love there and then. An interesting moment, when you observe one man sliding out of your heart while another slides in. But did it matter? The sufferings she was going through obviously had nothing to do with Bill, or Henry. People carry around with them this weight of longing, usually, thank heavens, well out of sight and 'latent'—like an internal bruise?—and then, for no obvious reason, just like that, there he was (who?), and onto him is projected this longing, with love. If the patterns don't match, don't fit, they slide apart, and the burden finds its way to someone else. If it doesn't go underground again—become 'latent'.

It was sweet to be with Henry. There was an innocence about it, a gaiety. Innocent, when sex burned in the air, invisible flames?

Throughout all of a Saturday and a Sunday morning, Henry, herself, and Stephen, with Mary and Roy at their separate table, sat in the dusty church hall and watched Julie and Paul incarnated in a variety of young men and women, all wearing bright sporty clothes and athletes' shoes and speaking the words that Molly McGuire and Bill Collins had made their own. A girl musician, with a flute, provided enough music to suggest the rest. But while Julie's music came and went in fragments and snatches, matching the scenes chosen by Henry to try out these players, Sarah could hardly bear it, for every run of notes, or even a single note, was like that piano chord played to indicate a change of key, setting off a song, or a melody, which repeated in Sarah's head, one that had nothing at all to do with Julie. She was compelled to listen to it, had to hum it: it had taken her mind over. Had she dreamed this song? If you wake with a tune in your head or words on your tongue then you have to let tune, words, wear themselves out, you can't simply say no to them, or push them away.

'What's that you keep humming?' asked Stephen.

'I don't know,' she said. 'I simply cannot get it out of my head.'

But Henry knew, and had known all the time. He sang, not looking at her:

'She takes just like a woman, yes, she does,
She makes love just like a woman, yes, she does,
She aches just like a woman,
But she breaks just like a little girl.'

'Bob Dylan,' he said, and knowing that she must wish herself invisible, he jumped up and went over to the players.

Stephen said, 'I've got Julie's music ringing in my head all the time, and I'm surprised you've room in yours for anything else.'

His reaction to the Julie chosen by Henry surprised Sarah. The girl was typecast, unlike Molly, who did not look anything like the template. Sarah thought that for Stephen it must be as if Julie had walked into his life, but he only remarked, 'Well, let's wait and see.'

And then Henry went off, the bonds of that insidious intimacy the theatre going snap, snap, goodbye—until early August, three weeks away.

Sarah had decided to take three weeks' leave but changed her mind. She was afraid of her demons. Besides, there was so much work. *Julie Vairon* might come into the West End, if successful at Queen's Gift: there were already enquiries. There was talk of a musical based on *Tom Jones*, but this was much more ambitious even than *Julie Vairon*; would Sarah like to try her hand at the script? She thought not. She had no energy, though she wasn't going to say so to her colleagues. Did they not already have enough on their plates? *Hedda* was going to transfer to the West End, and Sonia would occupy herself with that. The rehearsals would soon begin for *Sweet Freedom's Children*, a play based on the last days in Italy of Shelley, Mary, and their circle.

Again Sonia accused them of being workaholics, and this led to a family discussion about work. Could they be classified thus if they enjoyed working and never thought of it as work? Sonia said this was just like them, sitting around in the office and chatting theoretically about something when there was a crisis. But what crisis? protested Sarah, Mary, and Roy—Patrick was still away. Sonia said she had a friend, trained in theatre management. Virginia, named after Virginia Woolf. Very well, said they, let's try her out.

'Well,' said Mary, 'it was all too good to be true, wasn't it? The four of us working for years and years without so much as a cross word?'

Sarah got herself to the theatre every day. She was able to do this, and it meant everything: meant, specifically, that she was not 'clinically' depressed. She was grading her condition according to a private scale. Although grief seemed to get worse every day, she was not anything like as bad as Stephen's face had told her he was, for instance when he saw the poster of Julie as an Arab girl in his garden, or at the waterfall in France. I've never experienced anything like that, she still thought. At least, not as far as I can remember. Of course in a long life there had been miseries . . .

She wrote:

> *Something else is going on, something I don't understand. I*
> *could not be more bereft if I had lost someone by death,*
> *been separated from someone I love absolutely.*

She wrote:

> *I think I am really ill. I am sick—with love. I know this has*
> *nothing to do with Henry or that boy.*

She thought, If I had been in an earthquake or a fire and every one of my family had been killed, if as a young woman my husband and children had been killed in a car crash, I would have felt something like this. Absolute loss. As if she had been dependent on some emotional food, like impalpable milk, and it had been withdrawn. Her heart ached: she was carrying a ton weight in her chest.

She wrote:

> *Physical longing. I have been poisoned, I swear it. In Stendhal's* Love *a young woman unexpectedly in love believes she is poisoned. But she was. I am. A doctor in the States will cure you of being in love. It is chemical, he says.*

She wrote:

> *If a doctor said to me, You have an illness, and you will have to live for the rest of your life with a pain in your chest, I would get on with it. I would say, Very well, I will have to put up with a pain in my chest. People live with withered arms or crippled from the waist down. So why am I making such a fuss about heartache?*

She wrote:

> *I could easily jump off a cliff or the top of a block of flats to end it. People killing themselves for love do it because they can't stand the pain. Physical pain. I have never understood that before. The broken heart. But why should an emotional hurt manifest itself as a physical anguish? Surely that is a very strange thing.*

But she was still not in as bad a state as Stephen's. He rang her most evenings, as the day ended. As the light went—a melancholy time. The hours before dinner were hard for him, he said. It was hard for the animals too: he could swear the horses and the dogs had a bad few minutes when it got dark. 'Our dog Flossie—you know, the red setter—she always comes to me when it gets dark so I can make a bit of a fuss over her. We forget that for millions of years every creature on earth was afraid when night came.'

'And now we don't feel frightened, we feel sad.'

'We feel both.'

He would ask her what she had done that day, and tell her what he had, in the careful, meticulous way that she recognized—though she did not want to—as a prophylactic against the absent-mindedness of grief. He asked what she had been reading, and told her what books were piled up on his night table, for he was not sleeping much.

They might talk for an hour or more, while he looked from his window over darkening fields. He could hear the horses moving about, he said. As for her, she had a plane tree outside her window, its middle regions at eye level, and through it she watched the lights of the windows opposite.

He came to town and they went to Regent's Park on a sunny afternoon, when sky, flowers, trees, and sun seemed determined to make a festival for them. They walked through scenes of pleasure, people strolling about, and children and happy dogs, but his eyes were heavy and abstracted. He kept putting his hand into a pocket where there was a book, as people touch talismans, and she asked what it was. He handed her *The Dynamics and Contexts of Grief.* She glanced into it and was about to hand it back, but he insisted, 'No, it's useful. For instance, I know now I've "internalized" Julie. That explains what happens when you hear God knows what he sees in her.'

'And therefore is Love painted blind . . . but I'm afraid I find literature more useful than the . . . psychological recipe books.'

'I didn't say I wasn't finding literature useful. But it's come down to Proust. He's the only one I can keep my attention on. At least now, when I feel like this. Funny thing is, I used to find him self-indulgent.'

'And I've been rereading Stendhal. *Love*. And he's much shorter than Proust.'

'But is it any better?'

'Both could combine being romantically in love with a very cold intelligence.'

'Like Julie.'

'You wouldn't have said that when we first met.'

'No.' And he sighed. It was almost a groan. He had come to a stop, apparently in contemplation of swans floating whitely among their reflections. A silence. It went on far too long.

'Stephen?' No reply. 'Shall I lend you *Love*?'

'Why not?' he said, but after quite an interval. He was very far away.

And now she deliberately made conversation. 'Have you read *The Sorrows of Werther* recently?' No response. 'Now, that's an interesting case. Goethe was first in love with Lotte and then with Maximiliane Von La Roche. He said himself of Lotte that she was a woman more likely to inspire contentment than violent passions, but it was Lotte he made the heroine.' Stephen was still staring at the same patch of water. Moorhens had replaced the swans. They were energetically propelling themselves about. He sighed again. Hard to tell whether he was listening. 'Obviously it was Maximiliane who inspired the violent passion, but that is not what he wrote.'

She thought he had not heard, but after a time he said, 'Are you saying he was dishonest?'

'It was a novel, after all. I would say he was circumspect. Suppose he had written a novel where young Werther was madly in love with Lotte and then passionately in love with Maximiliane. I don't think the readers would have liked it.'

She found herself counting, waiting for his response. It seemed to take him fifteen seconds to hear, or at least to frame a response.

'I dare say they wouldn't like it now.'

'But Romeo was madly in love with Rosalind and then with Juliet.'

One, two, three . . . she reached twenty. 'I suppose we've got used to that.'

She was wondering, Am I like this too? In the theatre, are they having to wait half a minute to get some kind of response from me?

'Stephen, I want to ask you something . . . no, wait.' He was beginning to walk away from her, his face clenched up. 'You said you were in love with someone before you were in love with Julie. Do you see that now as a sort of trial run for the real thing?'

She thought he was not going to answer, but at last he said, 'But that was quite different.'

'Suppose Goethe had described two passions, both strong, one after another, the first for the maternal woman, a mother figure, and the second the real thing, the grown-up passion? He didn't, so now one of the European archetypes for romantic love is an insipid Anglo-Saxon hausfrau, but the real truth was a fiery passion with Maximiliane. After all, we've all had the experience of saying, I'm in love with So-and-so, because we don't want anyone to know we are in love with someone else.'

It would be easy to believe he had not been listening, but now he said, without an interval, 'They were ready to kill themselves for Lotte. Young Germans. Dozens of them. They threw themselves over cliffs and under horses' hoofs.'

'Was that because Lotte was a mother figure?'

'I wonder if my lady was a mother figure,' he remarked, at once, looking straight at her and as if he really wanted her to say yes, or no. As she said neither, he remarked, and he sounded almost cheerful, 'Well, I suppose she was, now I come to think of it. Well, what's the matter with that? She was . . . Sarah, you'd have liked her, she was . . . If she had married me then . . .' And now he actually laughed, if gruffly, and said, 'I wouldn't have been boring you with all my nonsense all this time.' He put a hand on her arm and began directing her towards the rose garden. He was a man strolling with a friend on a path between rose beds on a sunny afternoon. He was even smiling. She realized just how worried she was about him by the way a weight had lifted off her heart, leaving her feeling positively buoyant.

'I wonder what the Goethe buffs would make of your theory?'

'But he said himself, "It's very pleasant if a new passion awakes with us before the old one has quite faded way." In this case the old faded and the new one arose in a matter of days.'

'*Pleasant*,' he said.

'He also said, "The greatest happiness is to be found in longing."'

'Good Lord.'

'And Stendhal would not have disagreed. A pleasure for superior souls, he thought.'

'Barmy,' said Stephen. He came to a stop in the middle of Queen Mary's rose garden, with people all around them admiring the roses. He took his book from his pocket and read to her: '"The self-image of the sufferer becomes identified with the image of the beloved. Previous failures in love, common in this psychological type, reinforce the present condition because each surrender to the illness adds all past hopes to the present. The sufferer values pain as a guarantee of success this time. And remember that Cupid directs arrows and not roses to his victims."' They walked on, he holding the book in his hand like a priest with a breviary or a schoolboy swotting for an exam. 'And that isn't so far from Proust,' he added.

'I think Proust's pleasure in self-analysis was stronger than his sufferings over love. As for Stendhal, I think the analysis was a way of surviving the suffering.'

'Like Julie,' he said, and at once, not after fifteen or twenty seconds' delay.

'Whereas Goethe was thoroughly enjoying the drama of it all.'

'Well, he was very young.'

'I wasn't capable of all that when I was very young. Being young was bad enough.' But Sarah was thinking of herself as a child, not as a young woman.

'I do my best never to think of being young. I have a feeling I wouldn't like what I'd remember if I did.'

'Did you know you never mention your parents?'

'Don't I? Well . . . I don't think I saw much of them. Anyway, they broke up when I was fifteen. I get along with all four of them. When we meet, that is. My father and his wife live in Italy. She's a bit of a lightweight. I've often thought he must regret swapping my mother for her. But I don't think my mother has had regrets. She and her—he's a good chap, actually. They're in Scotland. He's a farmer. He's younger than she is a good bit. By fifteen years or so. They get along all right.'

They were at the gates. When she said she would walk with him to his club, it turned out he was not in his club but at a hotel.

'Can't cope,' he said. 'Conversations, you know. No one expects anything of one at a hotel. The only person I want to talk to is you. You know, Sarah, it's a funny thing: I used to talk a lot to Julie, but now I seem to talk to you.'

A week later he was in town again. He rang from the hotel. She thought the line was bad, then understood he was fumbling with words. 'I'd like to see you,' he got out at last, making it sound as if there was something particular he wanted to say.

'All right—where?'

A long silence.

'Stephen?'

'Yes?'

'Shall I come to the hotel?'

'Oh no, *no*. There are so many people here.'

'Shall we meet in the park again?'

'Yes, yes, the park . . .'

She walked, through a brilliant afternoon, from the great formal gilded gates towards a hunched man sitting motionless on a bench. She sat beside him. He nodded, without looking at her. Then he roused himself—she watched him doing it—to make conversation. Things were going along nicely with plans for *Julie* at Queen's Gift, he said. Sarah contributed by chatting about The Green Bird. Sonia was taking the new girl, Virginia, in hand. There had been a picture of Virginia Woolf by Virginia's bed, but Sonia had made her replace it with a photograph of Rebecca West. There had been a great improvement: Virginia no longer had a wispy chignon and droopy clothes but had cut her hair and was as bright and as pretty as a parakeet, like Sonia.

After a bit Stephen smiled, so she went on. Everyone was working hard on the new play, *Sweet Freedom's Children.* She expected him to react to the title, but he did not. She suggested they walk around a bit, and he nodded. He got up to walk as if only an act of will made him, walked as if an act of will kept him in motion.

'I want to ask you something,' she said.

Because of her tone, he came out of his preoccupation enough to give her a nervous look: 'I've been waiting for you to honour me with your confidence.' Meaning, for God's sake, don't.

'No, no,' she reassured him. 'No, it's something about you, not me . . . it's important to me. You know how we go along on the surface of everything—'

'The surface! I wouldn't exactly use that word. That's why I'm so grateful to you. Don't imagine I'm not grateful.'

'No, wait . . . I've been having a dream . . . something like that anyway. Suddenly you open a door you didn't know was there, and you see something that sums it all up.'

'All?' he challenged.

They stood by the edge of the fountain, looking through rods and sprays of water to a display of massed fuchsias. Fishes and mermaids and water. And fuchsias.

'Nice fuchsias,' he remarked. 'They've never done well with us. Though we are pretty successful with azaleas.'

'All of a situation. The hidden truth of something. If you unexpectedly opened a door, what would you see there that . . . ?'

At once he said, 'I would see Elizabeth and Norah naked in each other's arms, and they are laughing at me.' She had not expected anything like this. It was too much of a daylight truth. 'And what is behind your closed door?'

She said gratefully, knowing from a surge of emotion how much she would have liked to talk about her situation, 'There's a small girl stabbing a doll with scissors. The doll is bleeding.'

He went pale. Then, slowly, he nodded. 'And who is the doll?'

'Well . . . it could be my baby brother. But I don't really know.'

'Probably just as well.'

She did not speak again. Once he was actually brought to a standstill, as he walked, by some thought or memory. His whole body seemed to wince away from whatever it was. She set him in motion with a hand at his elbow.

They reached the gates, he to walk one way, she another. Unexpectedly he put his arms round her and kissed her. This was a chilled and chilling embrace. As he turned away she saw the mask take possession of his face, as if a hand—with the same action used for closing the eyes of a just-dead person, a downwards stroking movement that shuts out the light forever—had put weights on his lids and pulled down the corners of his mouth.

Sarah was in the office every day from nine in the morning till eight at night. She was doing not only her work but Mary's, Patrick's, and Sonia's. Patrick kept ringing to say he was ill—no, no, they mustn't think bad thoughts, he needed a rest. They knew he was lying. Sonia valiantly did not say what she knew, but they guessed. He felt guilty because of some plan or other for *Julie* they did not approve of. Well, they would deal with it. Mary was with Sonia at various provincial theatres to see if there was anything suitable for The Green Bird. In Birmingham they had run into Roger Stent. 'Ah, Barbarossa,' Sonia had said. 'Slumming?' It was *Oedipus Rex*. 'Bitch,' he had said. 'Quite so,' she had said.

'Presumably this is a courtship,' Mary had remarked on the telephone.

Sarah sat at one desk and Roy at another. They worked agreeably, as they had for years. They spent whole days together, bringing each other coffee, sharing quick meals at the café across the road. This undemanding friendship kept Sarah safe, and, she believed, it was doing the same for him. He was probably going to be divorced, but did not want a divorce. His wife had a lover. The child was unhappy.

She knew that this was what he often thought about while he worked there with her, just as her world of fevers and fantasy threatened to fill her head. It seemed to her she had become someone else. Not long ago she would have been ashamed to give room to such idiot dreams. The scenes she was being compelled to imagine were feeble, contemptible. Her lovers of long ago—or perhaps not really so long ago, but anything in the past was in another dimension— returned to say she had been the only woman in their life, the most remarkable, satisfying, and so on. These scenes always took place in the presence of others. Interesting that it was usually Bill: she would have been ashamed to inflict them on Henry. It was Bill who in these fantasies was struck into envy and desire by past charms that he could never enjoy. Or love scenes—memories she had not bothered to dust off for years. They presented themselves endowed with emotions of a trance-like intensity—emotions appropriate to the out-of-reach. These had not accompanied the actual event, and as each enhanced memory—where she was as romantic as in a very young man's fantasy, or in a sentimental novel—took possession of her, she forced herself to remember, in slow detail, what had really happened in this or that love, so that her memoirs *en rose* had to accept the stamp of truth. These exercises in correctives to false or flattering memory were exhausting and hard to achieve, because her present weakened state of mind kept returning her to adolescence, which cannot admit ordinariness.

And, too, she continued to marvel, with the histrionic part of her mind, that for years and years she had refused so much; yet in sane moments knew that it had been for the same reason she was refusing even to think of . . . *Guess who?* Single, extravagantly wrapped flowers kept arriving, roses, orchids, lilies, but having looked to see who they were not from (Henry), she forgot about them. Yet the state she was now in made past refusals seem like a wilful rejection of all-happiness. She had walked, a sexually desirable woman, through years of being courted and nearly always saying no. *Because there would have been no conviction in it.* One or two she had enjoyed. A good word, that, like *love*, meaning what you will or as you like it. But *enjoyment* does not carry with it that other dimension of . . . what? The word *enchantment* would have to do. A dimension where she had now become lost. Well, almost lost. Not entirely. Was she getting better? She noted that as the day approached when rehearsals would begin again—when Henry would arrive—the weight of grief lessened. Not much, though.

There is absolutely nothing like love for showing how many different people can live inside one skin. The woman (the girl, rather) who dreamed of past loves thought adult Sarah a fool for being content with so little. The ordinary and quotidian Sarah, with whom after all she would be living (she did so hope) for the rest of her life, would not have spent half an hour with that daydreaming girl. But the Sarah she was most often, sodden with grief, was not one who had much energy to care about the others, all subsidiary players. She simply felt, suffered, endured, in a hell of pain.

She wrote:

A season in hell. I don't think I can live through this.

She wrote:

A depth charge. What depths?

On the night before rehearsals began again, at the end of the first week in August, Henry walked into the office, and her misery went away, and she was at once in an atmosphere of charm, ease, comradeship. She was now entirely in love with Henry. She was in love with him because he was in love with her, and this enabled her to like herself.

When she entered the old church hall next morning and saw all the faces from Belle-Rivières among the new ones, it was as if she had taken a turn on a familiar road and found herself in a landscape where light fell like a blessing. The dark of her grief had quite gone. Yet they were again in the ugly hall, which seemed even worse after Belle-Rivières. The pillar of light they had joked about had withdrawn itself to a blurred rectangle of dirty yellow near a high window, reminding them how the earth had sped in its ellipse towards the equinox. By which time Julie would have been blown away, gone, and everyone here scattered across the world.

Outside, sunlight filled all London, all England, slowing people's movements and making them smile, and the company escaped at every possible moment to walk along the near canal, or sit by it eating sandwiches and drinking juices. Besides, these new rehearsals were a bit of a slog, because most of them knew the play by heart, and it was not only because of the heat that they all walked through their parts while Susan Craig and David Boles became Julie and Paul. The new Paul was nothing like as seductive a young lieutenant as Bill. He was a pleasant-looking, efficient actor, who, when he put on the uniform, would be convincing enough. Sally remarked, 'This one isn't going to keep us poor women awake at nights,' as she walked forward to speak her line as Julie's mother: 'Well, my girl, you must watch yourself if you do not mean to be a fool.'

Had Sally been ill? She was so much thinner and could be observed smiling much more than was natural. Richard Service had been replaced by another master printer. Why had Richard left? they were asking. Sarah had got this letter from him. 'I'm sorry, you must replace me. I am sure I don't have to spell out why. If it weren't for my three boys this would be a very different letter, I assure you. Best wishes for the success of *Julie* in England.'

Mature ladies are expected to put their troubles under their belts and get on with it.

As for the new Julie, she was a lithe, tawny-skinned girl with black eyes. She had not been at the first audition, otherwise she must surely have been chosen.

'This one's a bonus,' said Henry. 'She's a gift. And any minute now we're going to forget that Molly was pretty good.'

Stephen did not come until the end of the first week, with ten days to go before opening, and he sat beside Sarah, who asked, 'Well?' and he replied, 'Not very.'

The cast, knowing that here was their rich English patron, their host for the English run, put everything into the rehearsal. Susan and David, then Susan and Roy Strether (reading Andrew's lines because he hadn't yet arrived), then Susan and the new master printer, John Bridgman, a likeable middle-aged man who, when not acting, was a bomb disposal expert, all broke each other's hearts, according to script.

Sarah sat by Stephen and wondered how he would seem to Susan. A large, serious, self-contained man, he sat calmly in his chair, wearing a greenish linen suit which said discreetly that once, probably some time ago, it had been shockingly expensive, and shoes not made for hot pavements. The trouble was, Sarah had 'internalized' him. It was hard to see him as others must. When she did, she was impressed. He was a handsome fellow, this Stephen, sitting there with his arms folded, intelligently watching those fevered scenes.

She asked, 'And what do you think of Susan?'

He said, grimly, but with every consciousness of the absurdity, 'I think I lost my heart to Molly.'

She exclaimed, 'You're cured.'

'"If you are mad, then be mad all the way . . ." What song is that? It keeps ringing in my head. This psychological stuff I'm reading, I'm sure it isn't their intention, but it licenses you for folly. What I believe in—well, I certainly used to—is to keep a stiff upper lip, but after reading a few pages I begin to feel I'd be lacking in respect for the medical profession if I got over it without their help. If to understand it better is getting over it . . . I'm told that what I am experiencing is buried griefs surfacing, but, Sarah, I don't have any shut door and behind it a bleeding doll. What I have in my house—well, in my home, then—is visible all the time. What's buried about that?' His face was a few inches from hers, but he wasn't seeing her. 'I keep looking at the words—you know, they are pretty glib with words: grief, sorrow, pain, heartache—but I know one thing: *they* don't know what they are talking about. Anyone can write grief, pain, sorrow, et cetera, and so on. But the real thing is another matter. I never imagined anything like this existed . . . do you suppose it will come to an end some time? Every morning I wake—in hell.' At these melodramatic words he looked hastily around, but no one was noticing them. 'I found myself thinking this morning, What is to stop this going on for the rest of my life? You keep assuring me it won't. But what about all the old people? There's an old man on the estate. Elizabeth visits him—she's very good about that kind of thing. I went in her place once when she was off with Norah. He is depressed, she says. What a word! They are just bloody miserable, more like it. As far as I can make out, a lot of them just die of grief.'

The rehearsal was over. In front of them were Susan and Henry, facing each other. He was explaining something. They were alike, slim, lithe, beautiful creatures, with glossy black locks, dark expressive eyes, standing like dancers in a moment of rest. They will very likely fall in love: he's in the mood for love. (With an effort, she stopped the tune taking over her thoughts.) Just as I am. Chemical.

Henry went off and Susan stood prettily there, hands linked in front of her, apparently oblivious to the rest of the world. Slowly she relaxed out of her dancer's pose and began to stroll away. Sarah played her part. She called to her, introduced her to Stephen. Stephen looked down at the girl from his height. Every inch of him said, On guard! She gazed devotedly up at him.

Sally came past. So recently a large handsome black woman, she was positively thin, and her skin had lost its shine. Certainly not one of those who never notice what goes on, she took in everything about the man and the girl in one rapid glance, and her brief smile at Sarah paid homage with moderately good grace to human folly. Her face fell back into sadness, but she put on another smile, this time a patient one, because Henry had intercepted her in the act of taking sandwiches out of a bag. 'Sally, you've got to have a proper lunch. We can't have a thin Sylvie. I'm sorry, but go and eat pasta and cream pie.'

Mary, who had been deputed to do this, led Sally away.

'Love,' remarked Sally generally, as the two went off, 'is a many-splendoured thing.'

Stephen went too; he did not feel like lunch.

Sarah heard 'Sarah' breathed in her ear. Her heart at once melted, and then she and Henry were on the pavement outside. It was too hot to eat, they agreed, and strolled off down the canal path. They made jokes: it was their style. Henry was setting himself to entertain her. 'Very good at this,' he muttered, disparaging his talents, as he always had to do, and she laughed at him. They talked nonsense while the heat soaked London through and through, and people in bright clothes idled about, enjoying themselves. The hour of the lunch break disappeared. And I, too, have been in Arcadia, she said to herself, not caring how ridiculous it was. Perhaps one has to be past it to have earned the entrance ticket to Arcadia.

Henry was off to Berlin tomorrow morning. He was to do a production there next year, and it had to be discussed. They jested that she would go with him, and then there was a moment when it was not a joke. Why not? They both wanted it. But as it became a possibility, and then a plan, constraint entered, because arrangements had to be made and other people involved. Still, they parted after the rehearsal agreeing they would meet in the hotel in Berlin if it was too late to get onto the same flight. When she rang a travel agency, her elation subsided. For a woman of her age to share a room with a man of his would cause comment. Two rooms would be needed. When the agency rang back, it was to report that the two preferred hotels would not know until tomorrow if there would be rooms. They could always arrive in Berlin unbooked, take a taxi, and drive from hotel to hotel; but if they were not on the same flight, then . . . By now an irritable gloom had taken possession of her. All this was a million miles from Arcadia. She found it hard to ring Henry with all these problems and, when he was not in his room was both relieved and desolated. Instead of doing all the energetic things necessary to get herself to Berlin tomorrow, she decided to wait for his call from Berlin. She needed to hear his voice, his cry of 'Sarah!'—which, she knew, would make it possible for her to get to Berlin.

No sooner had she sat down to wait than the telephone rang. It was Anne. 'Sarah, I'm terribly sorry, but you have to come over.' 'I can't come now.' 'You must, Sarah. You have to.' And she rang off before Sarah could protest further.

It was a large family house in Holland Park. In the garden, still full of a weak sunlight, Joyce's sisters lolled almost naked in deck chairs. They looked like two pretty young greyhounds. Sarah's relations with Briony and Nell could best be described as formal: formalized around discussions about Joyce, rituals of presents, and invitations to the theatre. They had complained that their aunt believed she had only one niece. They were clever girls, who had done well, sometimes brilliantly, at school and then university. They were both in good jobs, one in a bank and the other as a chemist in a laboratory. Neither was ambitious, and they had refused chances of promotion which would have meant hard work. They were now in their mid-twenties and lived at home, saying frankly, and often, why should they leave home, where everything was done for them and where they could save money? They were both ignorant, being products of a particularly bad period in British education. Either girl was capable of saying with a giggle that she didn't know the Russians had been on our side in the last war, or that the Romans had been in Britain. Among things they had never heard of were the American Revolution, the Industrial Revolution, the French Revolution, the Mongols, the Norman Conquest of Britain, the wars with the Saracens, the First World War. This had turned into a game: if Sarah happened to mention, let's say, the Wars of the Roses, they would put on loopy smiles: 'Something *else* we don't know; oh dear.' They had read nothing and were curious about nothing except the markets in the cities they visited. To please Sarah, Briony had said, she had tried to read *Anna Karenina*, but it had made her cry. These two amiable barbarians scared Sarah, for she knew they were representative. Worse, an hour in their company had her thinking, Oh well, why should anyone know anything? Obviously they do perfectly well knowing only about clothes and having a good time. Enough money had been spent on their education to keep a village in Africa for several years.

Sarah went up to the top of the house, where Anne had a little sitting room. When she saw Sarah, she sighed, then smiled, stubbed out a cigarette, remembered that Sarah was not a patient, and lit another.

She came to the point at once. 'Are any of these yours?'

On a table was a magpie's litter. A large silver spoon. A silver picture frame. An amber necklace. Some old coins. A little Victorian gold mesh bag. An ornate belt that looked like gold. And so on.

Sarah indicated the necklace and the picture frame. 'Joyce?' she asked, and Anne nodded, expelling smoke into a room already swirling with it. 'We found this cache in her room. The police are coming in an hour to take away anything that isn't yours.'

'She's not going to get rich on that lot.'

'You mustn't leave anything lying around, Sarah. And your credit cards and your cheque books and anything like that.'

'Oh, surely she wouldn't . . .'

'She forged my signature last week on a cheque for three thousand pounds.'

'Three thousand . . .' Sarah sat down.

'Precisely. If it were thirty or even three hundred . . . And no, I don't think it is a cry for help or any of the things those stupid social workers say. She lives in such a dream world she probably thinks three thousand is the same as three hundred.' Her voice cracked and she coughed, then lit a new cigarette. She poured herself juice from a glass jug and waved her hand in an invitation that Sarah should do the same. But there was no second glass.

'So what happened?'

'We sorted it out with the police. They were wonderful. Then we lectured her. Only afterwards did it occur to us that what we were saying amounted to: Next time don't try for such a large sum—you know, if you're going to be a thief, then at least be an efficient one. Because if she's on drugs she's going to steal, isn't she?'

She laughed, not expecting Sarah to share it. Sarah thought her sister-in-law looked more than tired; she was possibly even ill. Pale hair fell about a gaunt face. That hair had been smooth and golden and shining. Like Joyce's.

'What are we going to do?'

'What can we do? Hal says I should give up my work and look after her. Well, I'm not going to. It's the only thing that keeps me sane.'

Sarah got up to go, taking the things that were hers.

Then Anne said in a low, intense, trembly voice, 'Don't think too badly of me. You simply don't know . . . you have no idea what it is being married to Hal. It's like being married to a sort of big soft black rubber ball. Nothing you do makes any impression on it. The funny thing is, I'd have left him long ago if it hadn't been for Joyce. Silly. I thought she'd get better. But she was a write-off from the start.'

Sarah kissed her goodbye. This was not exactly their style, but Anne was pleased. Tears filled her already inflamed eyes.

'How are your two?'

'Why—fine. I had letters this week from both of them. And George rang last night. He might bring them all over for Christmas.'

'Marvellous,' said Anne dreamily. 'That's how it should be. You just take it for granted—they are both fine and that's the end of it. You don't think of them all that much, do you?'

'Recently I've been so . . .'

'Quite so. Better things to think about. But I spend my time worrying. And I always feel guilty when I'm with you, because you took the brunt all those years. The *fact* is, I'd have had to stop working if you hadn't coped. The *fact* is, I've failed with Joyce.'

On her way out through the garden, Sarah saw the two deck chairs were empty. It occurred to her that the two healthy daughters had not been mentioned. Briony and Nell had taken to saying, 'Oh, don't bother about us, *please*. We're only the healthy ones. *We* are a success. *We* are viable.'

The musicians had arrived. Sarah and Henry sat side by side behind their trestle table, which was loaded with prompt books, scores, polystyrene cups stained with coffee, and the faxed messages from all over the world that show business cannot do without for half a day. She was determined to feel nothing at all when the music began, but a sweet shaft winged straight to Sarah's solar plexus, and she turned wet eyes to meet Henry's.

'Did you know there were philosophers who said music should be banned in a well-run society?' she asked.

'All music?'

'I think so.'

'I have spent the weekend with the headphones clamped on. Anaesthetic. Just in case I wasn't drunk enough . . . when I was a kid I learned to use it as an anaesthetic . . . listen.'

The flute held a long note while the counter-tenor chanted against it, 'bent' the note up half a tone, and held it while the voice followed.

'Do we really want to sit here crying like babies?' said Sarah, and he said, 'We have no alternative.' He jumped up, ran off to adjust the players' positions, ran back to his chair, moving it so it was nearer to Sarah's.

'This music-less utopia—suppose someone sings just for the hell of it?'

'Off with their heads, I suppose.'

'Logical.'

Suddenly Henry accused, 'You didn't telephone.'

'Yes I did. You were out.'

'I was waiting all weekend for you to turn up.'

'But I didn't know where you were.'

'I left the name of the hotel at the theatre.'

'I didn't know. And why didn't you ring me?'

'I did. You were out.'

'I was sitting waiting all weekend . . .' But there were the two hours or so with Anne. She said, 'I needed to be encouraged.'

'But you know that—'

'You really have no idea why I needed to be encouraged?'

'But perhaps *I* need to be encouraged.'

'*You* do.' Her laugh was only for herself. She loved him because he did not know what she meant. Or pretended he didn't.

Then he said, 'And I was relieved you weren't there, as well as being so . . . drunk.'

'I know. Me too.'

Then he said, unexpectedly, 'I am a very married man, Sarah.'

'So I gathered.'

'You did?' He mocked her and himself. 'And you actually do know that I have a little boy?' And laughed at himself again.

She laughed, while all the Atlantic swirled between them.

'Sarah, I tell you that nothing, nothing ever, has meant as much to me as my little boy.'

'Just what has that got to do with . . .'

'Everything,' he said miserably.

Across the hall, actors and musicians wrestled, hugged, and generally played the fool, as they must, to release tension.

Sarah bent forward and kissed Henry on the lips—a valedictory kiss, but he could not know this. It told them both what they had missed that weekend.

'My family will be coming to see *Julie*. In Queen's Gift.'

'I'm sure we will all have a lovely time,' she jested, but he said miserably, 'I don't think so.'

Then, on the same impulse, Sarah and Henry leaned back in their chairs, giving every indication of enjoying all that jolly horseplay. Their bare arms lay side by side, touching from wrist to shoulder.

In the afternoon, Susan came to Sarah to ask if Stephen ('you know, Mr Ellington-Smith?') was coming to rehearsals that week.

'I'll find out for you,' said Sarah, putting on her comfortable aunt manner.

'I do hope he comes,' murmured the girl, with a touch of spoiled-child petulance that went well with her general style, today emphasized by lively bunches of black curls tied on either side of a pale little face.

Sarah telephoned Stephen and said that Julie was missing him.

'Are you relaying a message?'

'I think so.'

'Does she fancy me?'

'Your instincts are supposed to be telling you that.'

'I'll come anyway. I miss you, Sarah.'

On Tuesday Andrew walked into the hall, straight from the airport. He flung down a suitcase, saluted Henry, and then came to Sarah. He sat by her, all focused energy. For six weeks he had been in the hills of southern California, where they were shooting a film about immigrant Mexicans, he being an American small-town cop. He could not look more alien than he did in this soft, shabby, amiable English scene.

'I suppose you are going to thank me nicely for the flowers?'

'I suppose I would have done, at some point.'

He put a sheet of paper in front of her. 'Hotel. Room number. Telephone number. I'm giving you this now because of course we won't be alone for five minutes. Ring me, Sarah?'

She smiled at him.

'Not that smile, please.' With a salute that he made rakish—it would have done well in Restoration comedy—he was off to join the others. This was the day Act Two would be put into shape.

Stephen came in on Wednesday for the run-through. On Thursday the company were all going up to Queen's Gift. There would be a dress rehearsal on Thursday night, then the traditional day of rest on Friday. The first night would be on Saturday.

The run-through went well, though to see *Julie* here, in this dull hall, after the colours and variety of the forest in France, was to diminish the piece so much that everyone was acknowledging it could never be anything but second-best away from Julie's own country. And this raised questions about a possible run in London. Every time the subject came up, all kinds of difficulties seemed insuperable, and soon they were already talking of how to improve the production next year in Belles Rivières.

Stephen and Sarah sat together. At the first opportunity Susan came to sit by him. She chattered about her part and sent him glances that were curious and troubled, for his face was not encouraging. Yet when she was being Julie, Stephen watched her closely. He was sitting, as usual, with his weight evenly distributed, every bit of him knowing its worth, while he gave full attention to each word and move. But it was a heavy attention, giving the effect of a concentration under threat. The girl—everyone thought—could not be more right for Julie. A little-girl quality, something winsome and self-flattering, disappeared the moment she became Julie. She came to Stephen to be approved, and he said she was a wonderful Julie, wonderful, but in a way that left her doubtful.

Then he and Sarah went out and stood on the canal bank in heavy sunlight. Some ducks were energetically propelling themselves out of the way of a passing pleasure boat, but the ripples rocked them about so that they looked like toy ducks in a child's bath. The ripples settled, and so did the ducks. They upended themselves, pink feet dabbling in air. 'Well, Sarah,' said he at last. 'I really don't know. I think I just give up. Really, that's about it.' And with a smile that was all ironic apology, he went off to find a cab to take him to Paddington.

Henry saw her standing alone on the canal bank and came to propose lunch.

'You don't understand about my little boy,' he said.

'Of course I understand. You are giving him everything you didn't get yourself.'

'And that's all it is?'

'All these terrible things we feel, they are usually . . . that's all it is.'

'Terrible? *Terrible?*'

'Terrible. What makes us dance.'

'Then at least let's have lunch.'

Bliss encompassed them, like breathing cool fresh air after stale. After lunch he went off, and as she walked to the bus stop she found Andrew beside her.

'You are not even moderately interested to know why I am pursuing you?'

'I suppose one might surmise.'

'One might surmise the aim, but not the reason.'

They had fallen into the pleasant sexual antagonism that goes with this kind of exchange. Sarah felt quite revitalized by it. She was even thinking, Well, why not? But it would have no conviction in it.

'The best experience I ever had was with my stepmother. And I am always trying to repeat it.'

'You being six and she being twenty-six?'

'I being fifteen and she forty.'

'Ah, I see.'

'No, you don't. It went on for ten years.'

'And then she was an old woman and you said thank you and left?'

'She died of cancer,' he said. His voice broke. The hard gaucho face was bleak as an orphan's.

She said, 'Oh, *don't* . . . ,' and her own voice was uneven.

'Well, Sarah Durham,' he said, exultant. 'Who'd believe it? Yes, do cry, do.'

The bus arrived. She shook her head, meaning she couldn't

speak because she would cry if she did, but he took it differently. The look on his face, as he stood there, disappointed, while the bus bore her away, was not one she could easily fit into her view of him, or wanted to.

If the erotic or romantic fantasies one has about a man can tell what he is like, then she had to conclude that with Henry it was the kind of love that, had she been in her thirties and not—well, better not think about that—would have led (to coin a phrase) to an ongoing committed relationship. For better or worse. She sat at her desk, her eyes on the two young men in Cézanne's picture, hardly knowing whether it was her daughter or Henry she saw in the thoughtful clown, and she steadily reviewed past relationships, ongoing or not. The fact is, there are not so many 'real' relationships in a life, few *love* affairs. That one was fit for a flirt, this for a week-end, another for—but she had not opened the door into perversity, she was glad to say—and yet another for a steamy eroticism. But *conviction*? Henry had conviction. (Would have had conviction?) Why did he? All one could know so early in the 'relationship' (which would never be one) was that there were no checks or knots, as there had been with Bill, reversals of feeling like cold water in her face or a bad taste in her mouth. The invisible weavers threw their shuttles, knitting memories and wants, match on match, strand on strand, colour to colour. A month or so ago, she had been 'in love' with Bill (she could not bring herself to leave off the quote marks, dishonest though that was). To the point of—well, yes, the whirlpool. But now she found that improbable and embarrassing, even if she was determined not to hate the poor young man and herself, as was prescribed. She would not find it shameful to have loved Henry when it was all over. A *smiling* memory? Hardly, with so much anguish in it, but then, the anguish, the grief, had nothing to do with Henry.

The real, the serious, the mature love. Rather, one of the inhabitants of this body, somewhat arbitrarily labelled Sarah Durham, was ready for kind love. She was in that state, had been for weeks, a girl is in when ready for marriage and falling in love with one man after another. But afterwards she first tones down and then forgets the men she has, as it were, sniffed at before the match was made.

Sarah imagined a couple, let's say in their thirties, early forties. They sit at a dinner table in . . . India—well, why not?—and it is the penultimate days of the Raj. Sarah was back, then, at least seventy years. Sarah had a photograph of her grandmother in a lacy formal dress, with ropes of crystals sloping over a full bosom. She set that woman as hostess at one end of a dinner table; at the other was a gentleman in uniform. Behind both stood uniformed Indian servants. One of the dinner guests, a woman, has just said, 'Oh, Mabs, you used to know Reggie, didn't you? I met him in Bognor Regis last week.'

The eyes of husband and wife meet in a hard look.

'Yes, I knew Reggie quite well,' says the wife. 'We played tennis together a lot in . . . let me see . . .'

'Nineteen twelve,' says her husband promptly. His tone is such that the guests exchange glances.

In the bedroom afterwards, the wife steps out of her trailing dove grey skirt and stands in her underclothes, knowing her husband is watching her. She turns to him with a smile. Sees his face. Stops smiling. Ten years before—no, it must be more than that; time does fly so—she imagined she was in love with Reggie, but something or other wasn't right, she could hardly remember what now, though it didn't matter, because she hadn't *really* loved Reggie, it wasn't the real thing, for that was proved by her being here with Jack.

For a long minute the eyes of husband and wife, neither conceding an inch, exchange memories of that summer when he proved himself more potent and persuasive—*convincing*—than the vanished Reggie. He is still fully dressed, she in her triple ninon pink camiknickers, her dark hair loosening over her half-naked breasts. Reggie actually lives there in that hot bedroom in Delhi, and then— pouf—he is gone. The husband takes her in his arms, and his embraces that night have a most satisfactory conviction. She forgets she was ever in that condition so ably described by Proust when he did not know which of the garland of seaside girls he was going to fall in love with. It might easily have been Andrée, but she turned out to be his friend and confidante, while a sequence of chance psychological events made it Albertine he was fated to suffer over so atrociously.

As for Sarah, that diabolical music had tumbled her into love with the dangerous boy, but her needs, her nature (the hidden agenda), had moved her on to Henry. And so it would be Henry she would remember as the 'real' one. And he was.

For her, Sarah, Henry was likely to be the last love. She did most sincerely hope so. Henry would remember an inexplicable passion for a woman in her sixties. That is, if he did not make a decision not to remember—which would be understandable. And Andrew? She did not believe the invisible weavers were up to anything much. There was something hard and what?—willed—about his— what?—certainly not a passion. (Here she allowed herself to ignore the look on his face as she was carried away from him by the bus.) The truth was, she could not keep her mind on Andrew.

She sat smiling at the thought of Henry. It was that smile put on a woman's face by delightful thoughts of *past* lovers. Let it stay for a while, she was praying—to her own inner psychological obscurities, presumably?—for when Henry was gone, a black pit was waiting for her; she could feel it there, waiting for the very moment that smile left her face.

And then there would be Stephen. That would remain. That was for life. But while she sat smiling, in his house at that very moment it was likely that an unhappy man sat at a window, thinking, I cannot endure this life, I cannot endure this desert. It was ten o'clock. Dinner would be over. Probably Elizabeth and Norah would have gone off somewhere, as they usually did.

She telephoned and got Elizabeth.

'Oh, it's you. I'm so glad you rang. I was just going to ring you. I do hope you approve of the arrangements. Of course, we can't put up the whole cast in the house. But the hotel is pretty comfortable. We thought that you and Henry and the new girl—Stephen says she's very good—and we have room for a couple more. Perhaps that young woman who can't keep her hands off her camera? How does it sound to you?'

'We are very lucky to be staying in your lovely house.'

'I don't know if we shall always be able to put people up. I mean, when we do real operas. But it is fun having you people around. And it will cheer up Stephen.' And now a pause, while Sarah waited for the real communication. 'Poor Stephen does seem most awfully glum.'

'Yes, I think he seems to be worried about something.'

'Yes.' Since Sarah did not seem inclined to offer anything more, Elizabeth said, 'It's probably his liver. Well, that's what I tell him.' And she gave her jolly laugh, which was like a notice saying Keep Out. Then, having behaved exactly according to expectation, type-cast as a no-nonsense sensible ex-schoolgirl, she rang off with 'See you tomorrow, Sarah. How nice. I do look forward to it all so much. And the garden is pretty good too, seeing that it's August.'

A woman of a certain age stands in front of her looking-glass naked, examining this or that part of her body. She has not done this for . . . twenty years? Thirty? Her left shoulder, which she pushes forward, to see it better—not bad at all. She always did have good shoulders. And a very good back, compared—long ago, of course—to the Rokeby Venus. (There are probably few young women of the educated classes whose backs have not been compared, by lovers blinded by love, with the Rokeby Venus.) Hard to see her back, though: it was not a big mirror. Her breasts? A good many young women would be pleased to have them. But wait . . . what had happened to them? A woman can have had breasts like Aphrodite's (after all, at least one woman must have done), and the last thing anyone thought of, looking at them, was nourishment, but they have become comfortable paps, and their owners wonder, What for? To cradle the heads of grandchildren? Surely the right time for these paps was when she was a mother. (*What* is Nature up to?) Legs. Well, they weren't too bad now, never mind what they were. In fact her body had been a pretty good one, and it held its shape (more or less) till she moved, when a subtle disintegration set in, and areas shapely enough were surfaced with the fine velvety wrinkles of an elderly peach. But all this was irrelevant. What she could not face (had to keep bringing herself face to face with) was that any girl at all, no matter how ill-favoured, had one thing she had not. And would never have again. It was the irrevocableness of it. There was nothing to be done. She had lived her way into this, and to say, 'Well, and so does everyone,' did not help. She had lived her way into it, full of philosophy, as one is supposed to do, and then the depth charge, and she was like one of those landscapes where subterranean upheavals had tumbled to the surface a dozen strata, each created in vastly different epochs and kept separate until now, revealing mountains made up of rocks red, olive green, turquoise, lemon, pink, and dark blue, all in a single range. She could sincerely say that one of the strata, or several, did not care about this ageing carcass, but there was another as vulnerable as the flesh of roses.

'I tore my body that its wine could cover Whatever could recall the lip of lover . . .' well, what else?

Yet Henry was in love with her. And Andrew. Bill had been, in his way. *What were they in love with?* And here she could not suppress the thought: In a group of chimps, the senior female is sexually very popular. Better look at it like that.

In the—fortunately—dimmish light into which she moved this

or that part of her anatomy, her body looked tender, comfortable, her arms of the kind that go easily round those in need of arms. Joyce, for instance. That poor little grub, before she had grown into a young woman, was ready at the hint of an invitation to curl up inside arms that were nearly always Sarah's. Where she at once put her thumb in her mouth. Even now, anyone with eyes had to see that invisible thumb forever in her mouth. The world is full of people, invisible to anyone but their own kind (it takes one to know one), who live with their thumbs in their mouths. Sarah knew what had knocked the thumb out of her own mouth: the need to bring up two young children with little money and no father for them.

Henry? A father if there ever was one. Perhaps to Henry she was the good mother. Everything about him proclaimed that what he had had to fight his way out of was something as focused as a demented female cat (driven mad, of course, by circumstances and therefore in no way to blame), who is capable of biting her kittens to death, or walking finally away from them, or killing them with kindness. Something obdurately hostile had set him in a trajectory away, until he had turned to face it at last, taking into his arms the child—himself—like a shield. . . thoughts of Henry shuttled in her head, mixing and matching likenesses, coincidences, memories, creating the invisible web that is love, visible—sometimes for years—only in glances like caresses or silences like hands touching.

Sarah looked in the mirror.

It was time for:

I think I heard the belle
We call the Armouress
Lamenting her lost youth,
This was her whore's language . . .

There are two phases in this illness. The first is when a woman looks, looks closer: yes, that shoulder; yes, that wrist; yes, that arm.

The second is when she makes herself stand in front of a truthful glass, to stare hard and cold at an ageing woman, makes herself return to the glass, again, again, because the person who is doing the looking feels herself to be exactly the same (when away from the glass) as she was at twenty, thirty, forty. She *is* exactly the same as the girl and the young woman who looked into the glass and counted her attractions. She has to insist that *this* is so, *this* is the truth: not what I remember—*this* is what I am seeing, this is what I am. This. This.

But the second stage was still some weeks away.

Sarah looked in the mirror, flattering what she saw, censoring out what could not be flattered, and she thought of Henry and allowed herself to melt with tenderness. But the tenderness was a tightrope, with gulfs under it. She might allow herself to dream of Henry's embraces, but at once her mind put her situation into words, and it was the stuff of farce and merited only a raucous laugh. A woman in her mid-sixties, in love with a man half her age . . . imagine how she would have described that aged twenty. Or even thirty. (She could see her own young face, derisive, cruel, arrogant.) No use to say, But he is in love with me. He wanted to be in bed with her, certainly, and if he did come into her bed it would be passion, most certainly, but—she faced this steadily, though it hurt quite horribly—with him there would be, too, curiosity. What is it like having sex with a woman twice my age? And was she going to say to this lover, 'I haven't slept with a man for not far off twenty years? A space of time which seems nothing at all to me (you will have heard, of course, how time accelerates with the years, and might even have experienced the beginnings of this process), but to you it will seem very long, almost two-thirds of your life.' Not even she—whose careless frankness in matters of love had more than once done her harm—would say that to a man. Yet she would be thinking it: It is twenty years since I held a man in my arms. For the first time in her life she would ask to have the light off, while knowing there would be that moment—this went with his character, which was impulsive, impetuous, and sensual—when he would switch on the light to see this body he wanted. And—who knew?—perhaps the ageing body would turn him on. (What turned people on was, obviously, not easily predicted.) But did she want that? Really? She, who had been (she now saw, with astonishment at what she had taken for granted) so confident that she had never felt a second's anxiety about what a man might see as he caressed, kissed, held . . . *where was her pride?* But the thought of his arms banished pride; she had only to think of the look in his eyes, the immediate sweetness of their intimacy . . . she wanted him, all right, everything she could imagine, even if the experience was bound to include the moment when the light went on and that quick—because tactful—and curious stare encompassed her body. And even now she could not prevent herself muttering: It's a damn sight better than most bodies you see around . . . these violent exchanges with herself were wearing her out. She kept almost dropping off to sleep from the excessive dragging fatigue of conflict, and yet she was as afraid of going to sleep as she had been in Belle-Rivières, because of what she would find in her sleep.

The company assembled in the theatre area to see the new amenities. Five hundred chairs crammed the space where people had stood or strolled or sat on grass. The great trees, the shrubs under them, the flowers massed around the stage, the grass, seemed surfeited with that summer's sun, and Julie's face and Molly's and Susan's, as Julie, appeared everywhere. The new building, just finished, could only dismay on a first viewing. Well-used buildings seemed inhabited: you enter welcoming or neutral rooms and spaces. While the exterior of this place seemed concerned to make as little of a statement as possible, was surrounded by screening shrubs, some newly planted, the interior was bleak, grey, echoing, and each room was a vacuum.

In two hours' time would be the dress rehearsal, and the company would have to act with confidence, though they had not performed in this setting before, but they assured each other the experience in Belle-Rivières would see them through and the new players would find themselves supported. And it was only a rehearsal, with an invited audience. At seven everyone went to the big house, where Elizabeth and Norah had a buffet supper for them. The two women stood behind tables in a room that could have given hospitality to players and musicians any time during the last four centuries. They were enjoying this role of theirs, serving the Muse, or Muses. They wore smart dresses under aprons, explaining the amenities of the house, playing both hostess and servant, while welcoming so many people and serving food adapted to this hot evening. They did not say why Stephen was absent. The host was not there.

Sarah was waiting for him. So was Susan, for while she stood chatting nicely over the plate she was eating from, her eyes sped continually to the big doors behind Norah and Elizabeth, which admitted girls bearing more dishes from the kitchens, or to the big door leading out to the garden. Not until the meal was nearly over did Stephen arrive. A small and unremarkable door to the interior of the house opened, and he stood there, an authoritative presence, though he had meant, it seemed, to appear unnoticed. Susan sped him a look over her plate and, when she was sure he had seen her, let her lids fall, with an effect of obedience. Stephen sent Sarah a glance like a wink, but then looked long and sombrely at Susan. He picked up a plate, was filling it with this and that, but absentmindedly, and then Susan was beside him.

Sarah stood across the room, a glass of wine in her hand, and watched the scene. She was so pretty, that girl . . . lovely . . . so young . . . just imagine she takes it all for granted. Just look at her: she intends to shoot arrows into every part of him, and yet at the same time she is full of uncertainty and forcing herself to stand her ground, looking up at him. If he addresses one rejecting word at her she'll melt away. Well, make the most of it, my dear one, Sarah addressed Susan, or Julie, in a wash of emotion that made her want to embrace Susan and Stephen together, as if they were all here to celebrate a marriage or sing an epithalamium . . . what nonsense that she was so afflicted by these disproportionate emotions. She turned from watching the pair and found Henry beside her. He had been watching her watch Stephen, for now he muttered, and there was no joke about it, 'I'm getting jealous of Stephen.' Her abasement before youth was such that she at once thought, He is in love with Susan, and daggers of ice splintered in her heart, but then she saw it was not so and could have wept with delight, because it was she, Sarah, he was jealous of. And so she laughed, far too much, and he said, put out, 'I don't see why it's so funny.'

'So you don't know why it is funny, no, you don't know why it is so funny,' she derided, her face six inches from his, as Susan's was from Stephen's. He grimaced, as if from a mouthful of unexpectedly sour food, and said 'Sarah,' reproachful and low. They stood beside each other, just touching. Bliss, well mixed with every kind of regret, was making itself available in unlimited quantities. At that moment Sarah was not envying the girl who stood admiring Stephen with looks that said, whether she knew it or not, 'Take me, take me.' Well, everyone had a bedroom on the same floor. It was inconceivable to Sarah that Henry would not come to hers that night, while she knew he would not, because his wife would soon be here.

Then it was time to go into the evening sunlight for the dress rehearsal. The cast disappeared into the new building, Henry with them.

Stephen and Sarah walked together towards the chairs, now filling with the audience.

He quoted, 'When a man is really in love he looks insufferably silly.'

She said: 'But: Love is the noblest frailty of the mind.'

'How kind you are, Sarah.'

'It has not occurred to you that since I am in love, and quite appallingly, I am trying to cheer myself up?'

'I've already told you that I am so much of an egoist I only care about your being in love because I have a companion in misfortune.'

'He that loveth is devoid of all reason. But: One hour of downright love is worth a lifetime of dully living on.'

'Do you believe that, Sarah? I don't think I do. The way I feel now I'd give a good deal to be dully living on.'

'Ah, but you're forgetting: the poet was talking about love. Not grief. After all, it is possible to be in love without wishing you were dead.'

'I suppose I was forgetting that.'

He went off to see the new building in use, and she sat down discreetly at the back, keeping an empty seat for whoever would choose to sit in it. Just behind her, a pink mallow spread branches where flowers perched like silk-paper butterflies. Beside it grew a yellow rose. All around spread the lively green of the lawn. It was all so charming, so balanced, so English, this setting for the new production. But Julie could never have prospered here in this sun, on this soil. And here they could not expect what no one had planned for in France: the hundreds crowding up through the pines, and the turkey oaks and the cedars and the olives and the untamed rocks, like spies or thieves—the effect that had given *Julie Vairon* in France its special charm.

It began. The four young officers in their glamorous uniforms (there were three extras now, justified and paid for by success) stepped up onto the stage, where the two women waited. But these were not the mother and daughter of a few weeks before. This Julie seemed to flash and flame. Sally had not put on the flesh she needed to be the stately matron. The scarlet dress had been taken in, and she had been padded out, but she was tall, quite slender, and this gave her admonitions and exhortations to her daughter an edge of rivalry, for it was impossible to believe the young officers did not find her as attractive as her daughter. Interesting, but not what had been intended.

Otherwise it all went on as before. Paul courted Julie to the accompaniment of the insipid ballad. Sylvie Vairon wept as her plans for her daughter were swept away by passion. The cicadas were absent, but a thrush sang from a hawthorn as the lovers fled. Then, the south of France, because the programme said it was. No, there was no doubt Julie did better on that warm red soil, in the southern forest. It was not that the tale became bathos, though these sad loves had to balance on that edge, rather that the English setting itself seemed a criticism of the girl. In the south of France, Martinique was only a thought or a sea's breath away, but here it was a tropical island, with associations of Captain Cook and South Sea hedonism (never mind that it was the wrong ocean), and Julie and her mother could only have the look of misplaced Victorians, just as the sentimental ballad at once earned appreciative laughter because of associations that had nothing to do with Julie. Who in this audience had not had grandparents or great-grandparents (remembered perhaps because of yellowing sheet music in a drawer or 78 records) attentive around a piano where some young lady played the 'Indian Love Lyrics' or 'The Road to Mandalay'? In Belles Rivières the girl was at odds with her society, certainly, but she was a not too distant cousin of Madame de Sévigné, Madame de Genlis, a daughter of George Sand; but here the passionate girl had to evoke comparisons with the Brontës, though their lives seemed for ever shrouded in grey rain. This audience was not lost in the tale like the other audience, crowding in the forests where the story had happened, the sounds of the river filling pauses in the music when the cicadas did not.

Henry slipped into the seat beside her and at once muttered, 'It's a flop.'

'Nonsense,' said reliable Sarah. 'It's different, that's all.'

'Oh yes, you can say that. My God, it's different.'

During the third act a calm northern twilight distanced the tale, the unearthly insinuations of Julie's late music filled the spaces between the trees. Somewhere close, blackbirds sang goodbye to the day. The moon, in its last quarter, rose up over the black trees on a high arc, a mildewed wafer with a decayed edge, but as they turned away from the sun, it was a golden moon, only a little asymmetrical, that shone conventionally on Julie's death. Then starlings swooped squealing about the house that held up its many chimneys dark into the sequined sky, and Henry said—but he was feeling better—that he was going to claim extra money for unforeseen stage effects. 'And danger money too,' he murmured, his lips at her ear, and for the space of a second they were in the place of sweet intimacy that knows nothing of grief. Then the applause began, enthusiastic but not wild, as in France.

Beyond the theatre, their house standing solidly behind them, and beside a yew carved into a griffin, were Stephen and Elizabeth, absolutely inside their roles as rich patrons of the arts. They accepted congratulations from innumerable people, friends and relations and friends of relations and their good humour had the slightest edge on it, because of the dicey nature of this enterprise of theirs, which could turn up failures as easily as it did successes. Against a dark hedge not far away, quite by herself, stood Susan, already in her own clothes, tight black trousers, black silk singlet, silver jewellery, black shoes described as 'medieval' and probably not far off what was worn centuries ago in this house. She watched the pair, host and hostess, and her eyes glistened with the sincerest tears. This girl had made her way up from a dingy little house on the edge of Birmingham, and for her the scene was an apotheosis of glamour.

There was to be a reception for the company in the town, arranged by a local society funding the arts. Stephen and Elizabeth had said the company must go. 'We don't have to go, but you do.

Sorry, but that's how it is,' said Elizabeth, with the jovial ruthlessness we all expect of the upper classes. 'We depend on goodwill. Without local goodwill we couldn't last a season.'

A coach stood waiting.

Sarah stood in the black shadow of a shrub, enjoying invisibility, but Henry came up and said in a low voice, 'Sarah, I'm going to get drunk.'

'I think that is a pity.'

'Another time, another place, Sarah.'

'Henry, this is the other time and place.'

The cry of 'Sarah!' he then let out was far from self-parody, but with the second 'Sarah' he was already mocking himself.

She had already turned away, noting that the legendary small voice, never more reliable than when giving bad news, was telling her: No, that's it, finally and for ever.

'Well, good night, then,' she said, her voice steady but only just, and walked past Susan, whose face shone with tears as she stood by herself in the moonlight. 'Isn't it *beautiful*?' she demanded wildly of Sarah. 'Isn't it all absolutely *beautiful*?'

And Sarah watched how Stephen went into the house by himself, for Elizabeth had separated herself from him to become half of that other couple, Elizabeth and Norah, who were walking away somewhere by themselves.

In the coach, Sarah sat by Mary Ford, who was going to take photographs at the reception. 'A pity,' mused Mary, 'that we couldn't have had Bill and Susan. Perfect casting.' Mary was not looking as well as she might: her mother was rapidly getting worse. The doctor said she should be in a home, but Mary was putting it off. 'One day it will be me,' she remarked.

'And me,' said Sarah.

At the reception Sarah behaved well, just like all the rest of the company, talking as long as she had to with anyone who wanted to talk to her, and she stood to be photographed with what seemed like infinite numbers of local people, all of them in love with the arts. Henry appeared, already tight but hiding it, sending her imploring but grieving looks, and only half histrionic, and then he disappeared with a smile that set fire to the air between them. Well, to hell with him. Susan was surrounded by men, as she was always bound to be, and had the look of a valuable thing conscious it might be stolen if she for one moment relaxed her guard.

Sarah was sitting in the coach, by herself, when Andrew came to lean over the seat in front of her and, with a smile that made no attempt to mask anger, said, 'You made sure I wasn't going to be in the house.'

'I had nothing to do with the sleeping arrangements.'

He did not believe her. Rightly, for if she had said to Elizabeth ... Still smiling, his arms folded on the back of the seat, those pale blue eyes of his hard, he said, 'Why not, Sarah Durham? Just tell me why not. You're a fool.' He gave that short laugh that is earned by wilful stupidity. Then he removed his folded arms from the seat, regarded her steadily, not smiling, and disappeared. She saw him walk past the window of the coach as it set off. He turned to give her a look that shortened her breath. Well, yes, she probably was crazy, at that.

Sarah never took sleeping pills, or sedatives, did not drink to achieve sleep or numbness. Tonight she wished she did. Stood at the window of her room knowing that Henry was three doors away and might, if he wished, come to her room. But he would not, because he had made sure he would be drunk. And if his wife had not announced she was arriving and bringing his child? An interesting question, which she did not feel equipped to answer. She stood by the window and watched the moonlight carve black shadows on the lawn. In the hollow of her shoulder, above her left breast, was centred an ache, an emptiness. A head was lying there, and she shut her eyes and put a hand over the place. Grey light was filling the bushes, and the birds had awakened, when at last she slept a little. Ghostly lips kissed hers. A ghost's arms held her. When she woke and went to the window it was still early, though sunlight lay everywhere. The astonishing summer was continuing, as if this were not England.

Two men appeared beyond a low hedge that interrupted, with a stile, a path leading to a field where horses stood absorbing the sun. They were large, slow-moving men, who stopped to admire or evaluate the horses. The scene could easily have a frame around it, to join others of the same kind hanging on the walls of this house. They went strolling around and among the horses, stopped to talk, strolled on, patted one horse, slapped the rump of another, went over to a hedge to look at something or other, came back. This went on for a good half hour, while the sunlight strengthened and the roses in the bed below Sarah's window glowed more confidently with every minute. Now the men were coming towards the house. They halted to examine the trunk of a beech, walked around it, advanced again, bent over a bush that, from the look of it, was growing in the wrong place, straightened, and stood facing each other, talking. This conversation too lasted for some minutes. Again they came on, towards the stile, and halted. Behind them a woman came out of the trees, carrying a saddle, going towards the horses. It was Elizabeth, her red head scarf like a tiny sail against all the green. Her voice rang out: 'Beauty, Beauty, Beauty . . .' A tall black mare raised its head, whinnied, and stepped towards her to take titbits from her hand. Her hand was gentling its ears. The men had swung round at the sound of her voice, and now turned around again, still talking. First one, then the other, stepped over the stile. They were walking with a steady assurance on this earth they owned, or ordered. One of the men was Stephen. They both wore earth-coloured clothes, and their trousers were pushed into their boots. They carried . . . what were they? Sticks? No, Stephen had a stick, the other man a riding switch. They stopped, conferred, and went off to one side, into a little apple orchard. There they walked about, studying the trees and at one point apparently disagreeing about one of them, for first Stephen doubtfully shook a branch, and then the other man pointed with his whip approving, or so it looked, at a satisfactory amount of apples. From the field behind them came Elizabeth's ringing voice: she was shouting endearments at her horse, which did not feel like being saddled. It was backing and even rearing, the black glossy mane flinging about like the fringe on a dancer's shawl.

Now Stephen's face was in focus. The men were about fifty yards away. He looked ordinary and even cheerful, certainly good-humoured. The other's face was large and red, emphasized with black brows. Not a face she wanted to be any closer to than she was. He had a lowering defensive stare and shot out gloomy looks to either side of him, as if enemies might be lurking among the trees.

The men stood facing each other again, on a gravel path. The voices rose and fell, but she could not hear the words. They gave an appearance of holding their ground against each other. Elizabeth had got on the horse and was cantering around the field, encouraging and calming the beast, and this sounded almost like a song, or a chant. 'There, there you are, there *Beauty*, now *Beauty*, there's my girl *Beauty*, there's a good girl, there's *Beauty*, now come on, calm down, gently there *Beauty*.'

The two men now took off fast into a wood and there walked around a very old oak that had a branch propped on a stick, stopped, and walked around the other way. They were disagreeing. A peaceable argument lasted for quite a time, and then they returned to the path. Now Sarah could see that the black-browed man's face was red because it was meshed with fine lines, his nose had the lumpy glare of a drinker's nose, and he seemed swollen with unhealthy blood. They stood talking. Nothing could seem more amiable than this long, leisurely chat. At last the riding whip lifted in a careless goodbye, the man nodded at Stephen, and he strode off back towards Elizabeth. At the hedge he stopped, bent to look at something on the sunny grass, and stamped once, twice, swivelling his heel on whatever it was, to make sure it was well and truly ground out of life. Then he went on, head lowered, riding crop at the ready. He vaulted heavily over the stile. Elizabeth was crooning at her horse and patting it to keep it patient. The man picked up a saddle from where he had left it in the grass to talk to Stephen, flung it on a brown horse, fastened it, climbed heavily on it, and then he and Elizabeth turned their horses' heads towards a far hedge. Stephen stood alone on the gravel path and gazed over the hedge at the scene of his wife and the neighbour talking as they rode slowly off together.

Stephen was now standing over a pile of lemon-coloured honeysuckle that was interweaved with a purple clematis. He poked his stick into the mass of bloom, and at once intense waves of scent rose to her window. He was fishing out a green rubber ball, which had a glossy look: it had not been lying there long. He threw the ball hard, for at least fifty yards, onto a lawn at the side of the house.

'Good throw,' she remarked to his head. He said, without looking up, 'I knew you were there, Sarah.' Then he did look up and gave her a warm and even tender smile. He waved a hand at her and went into the house.

She was feeling angry with herself—foolish. She had been watching this man, inside his own real life, for well over an hour. This was Stephen, this the reality of Stephen. Sarah told herself, repeated it, to make herself take it in, that Stephen the man of the theatre and Julie's besotted lover was only one aspect of Stephen. Suddenly Sarah was wondering about that black-browed red-faced man now cantering away with Elizabeth a long way off across the fields—what did he say, he and his sort, about Stephen and this hobby of his, the theatre? For after all, Stephen's visits to France, and attending rehearsals in London, and arranging the Entertainments, probably had not taken up so much time. His real life was here, on this estate.

About fifteen years ago, a conversation on these lines must have taken place in all the houses near this one:

'Elizabeth's done it. Queen's Gift will be all right.'

'Good for her. He's got money, then?'

'Yes, plenty. Stephen Ellington-Smith.'

'Gloucestershire? The Gloucestershire Ellington-Smiths aren't too well off.'

'No, Somerset. It's a branch of the Gloucestershire lot.'

'Oh, I know him, then. He was at school with my cousin.'

'Anyway, it's wonderful. Awful if she'd lost Queen's Gift.'

So they must all back Stephen, stand by him, even if they think him eccentric. But after all, the arts were fashionable, and Queen's Gift was not the only country house round about that went in for summer festivals. Was there anyone among the people he must call his friends with whom he talked about his secret miseries? Probably he wouldn't dare, for if his confidante (bound to be a woman) was indiscreet, then he would be seen as mad, barking, round the bend, loco. Well, he was. But it was easy for her now to turn that life of his around slightly, as one turns an object to catch a different light, and all she could see was the life of a country gentleman, and Julie just a little dark blot on a sunny scene of trees and fields safely enclosing this ancient house. Just as her own life, Sarah's, which she had seen for years as a competent progression, with proportion in all its parts, could be turned around to be seen as a stoic one, ending now in old age with an ache and a hunger for love—but that is not how it would look to her, she knew, quite soon. Within weeks, probably, her present state would seem like a temporary fever. And—but *this* was the point: her concern for Stephen was like a kind of illness. Anxiety invaded her at the thought of him. Just as it did when she considered Joyce. *What was the matter with her, Sarah?* Why did she seek burdens?

Meanwhile there was breakfast, in last night's supper room. Mary Ford was there. So was Roy. Two large, competent, healthy people placidly consuming sensible breakfasts. The other person there was Andrew. He had no right to be there at all. Had he spent the night somewhere in the grounds? Perhaps sitting on a bench somewhere, mooning—yes, Sarah actually *almost* used that word—at the house where his love—herself—was lodged. He was not eating. A cup of black coffee stood in front of him. His face was as pale as a face can be that is surfaced with a tan. He stared long and deliberately at Sarah, with enough irony to shrivel her. If he was hating her, with all the fury of a despised lover, then she watched in herself that primitive reaction (had she felt it since she was pubescent?), the outraged *amour propre* expressed by *How dare he?* How old is the girl who feels this mixture of indignation and contempt because of the impertinence of an old man (probably thirty years old) who dares to think himself good enough for her? Thirteen? She poured herself coffee, her back turned, trying to recover some sense of the appropriate, let alone some humour, and heard a door slam. When she turned he had gone. She looked deliberately at Mary and Roy to see if they wanted to comment, but neither looked at her.

Then Mary said, 'I think I'll go and see if I can get some pictures. The light is good now.' And Roy said, 'Sarah, I'm going to have to take some leave. I'm due two weeks. This divorce thing is doing me in.' With this, he left.

Sarah told herself that what this good friend of hers was going through was every bit as bad as anything she was feeling, but it was no good.

Henry arrived. He looked quite awful, which Sarah felt served him right. He scattered a dozen corn flakes into a bowl and sat opposite her. They sat looking at each other. There is a stage in love when the two stare in incredulity: how is it that this quite ordinary person is causing me so much suffering?

'All right,' said Henry, in reply to a thousand silent accusations from the rhetorics of love (which there is no need to list since no one has not used them), the first of which is always the incredulous: But if you love me, how can you be so unkind? 'All right, I got drunk and it didn't help. I clapped on those headphones you despise and put the music on so loud I couldn't think, and when I woke this morning it was blasting into my ears. Well, all right'—for she was laughing at him—'I did get through the night.'

'Are you expecting me to congratulate you?'

'You might as well.'

He even seemed to be waiting for her to do this, but she had to shut her eyes, for the lower half of her body had dissolved into a warm pond. He was asking, 'Are you coming to Stratford today? Did you know we are all going to Stratford?'

'No, I'm not coming with you to Stratford.'

'*Sarah,*' came the low reproach, for he was unable to prevent it, and then, already in parody, 'You aren't, you *aren't* coming with me to Stratford?'

'No; nor, it seems, anywhere else,' she said, while tears made the room and Henry's face swim in a watery kaleidoscope.

'*Sarah!*' He leaped up, as if to go to the sideboard, and actually did whirl around towards it, but turned back and stood behind his chair in a posture of wild accusation, but whether of her or himself she could not have said. Then he visibly took command of himself, actually got to the sideboard, poured coffee, which he drank there and then, a consoling or a narcotic draught, came back, sat down. All she could see was two wounded, accusing eyes. She blinked, and the shining white cloth, the silver, and Henry's face dissolved and reassembled.

'It's messy,' said Henry suddenly.

This was so absolutely in line with the culture clash that she began to laugh. It seemed to her so funny that she was thinking, Oh, God, if only I could share it with someone—who? Stephen? She said, 'You mean, I'm in one room dreaming of you—if I can put it like that—and you're in another room dreaming of me. But that's not messy?'

He laughed, but he didn't want to.

'Well,' she said, her voice back under control, 'if anyone had told

me when I was young that when I was—I'm *not* going to say old—
that I would be reasoning with a young man in love with me . . . I
suppose I may say you're in love with me without straining the truth?'

'I suppose you could, at that. And I'm not so young, Sarah. I'll
be middle-aged soon. I notice that the young girls these days, they
don't see me. It happened quite recently. I tell you, that was a bad
day for me, when I first realized.'

'Reasoning with him into sleeping with me, I think I would have
slit my throat. But to put it another way—it's amazing how often
this one comes in useful—"We know what we are but we know not
what we may be." And thank God we don't.'

'Shakespeare, I have no doubt.'

Susan appeared from the garden. 'The coach is here for
Stratford,' she said, obviously disappointed about something, which
could only be that Stephen wasn't there.

Henry got up, saying, 'This deprived American has never actually seen *Romeo and Juliet.*'

'A pity it isn't *A Midsummer Night's Dream,*' said Sarah.

'A quip that's wasted on me. I haven't seen that either.'

Susan was shocked by the anger in this exchange: she looked
from one to the other with the timid smile of a peacemaker who
doesn't much hope. 'Aren't you coming, Sarah?'

'No.'

'No, she isn't,' said Henry, and accused her with his eyes. 'Enjoy
yourself,' he said bitterly.

Sarah borrowed Mary's car and drove to the Cotswolds to see her
mother. This was an impulse. It had occurred to her that she sat for
hours brooding about the puppet strings and their manipulators, but
after all, there was nothing to stop her asking her mother. Why had
she not done this before? This is what she was asking herself as she
drove, for the idea had seized her with all the force and persuasiveness
of novelty. It was absurd she had not thought to ask. Now she would
say to her, Why am I like this? and her mother would say, Oh, I was

wondering when you'd ask. But as she contemplated the forthcoming scene, doubt had to set in. Her relations with her mother were good. Cool, but good. Affectionate? Well, yes. Sarah visited her three or four times a year and telephoned her sometimes to find out how she did. She did very well, being alert, active and independent. She had lived in the little village for as long as Sarah had in her flat. Briony and Nell liked her, and might drive up to visit her. The one person she wanted to see—Hal—did not visit her. It occurred to Sarah that she could not ask, 'Why is my brother, your son, such a deplorable human being?' Her mother still adored him. She boasted often about the famous Dr Millgreen, but made polite enquiries about Sarah's work.

When Sarah arrived, her mother was working in her garden. She was pleased enough to see her. Just as Sarah in her mid-sixties looked fifty on a good day, so did Kate Millgreen, over ninety, seem a lively seventy. They sat drinking tea in a room where every object spoke to Sarah about her childhood, but she could not attach memories to any of them, so thoroughly had she blocked it all off. Her mother believed Sarah had come to find out how she was holding out. Old people are afraid of their children, who will decide their fate for them, and so she was a little defensive, as she offered information about her neighbours and her garden, and said that luckily she suffered from nothing worse than mild rheumatism.

Now that Sarah was sitting there with this very old woman, who reminded her of the old woman on the bench that early morning in Belles Rivières, in her neat sprigged cotton dress and with her white hair in a bun, she was thinking, I want her to remember things that happened over sixty years ago.

She did attempt, 'Tell me, I was wondering what kind of a child I was,' but her mother was disconcerted. She sat there, holding her teacup and frowning and trying to remember. 'You were a good little girl,' she said at last. 'Yes, I'm sure of that.'

'And Hal?' And as she asked, she thought, Why do I never think of my father? After all, I did have one.

'He was ill a lot,' said the old woman at last.

'What was wrong with him?'

'Oh—everything. He got everything when he was a child. Well, it's such a long . . . I don't remember now. He was threatened with TB at one point. A patch on the lung. He was in bed for . . . I think it was a year. That's how they treated it then.'

'And my father?'

Again her mother was surprised. She did not like the question. Her eyes, which were blue and direct, not used to evading anything, reproached Sarah. But she did try, with 'Well, he did everything that was needed, you know.'

'Was he a good father?'

'Yes, I am sure he was.'

Sarah saw she was not going to get anywhere. When she left, she kissed her mother as usual and said, as she always did, that if things got too much for her, living by herself, she could always come and live with her in London, for there was plenty of room. And as usual, her mother said that she hoped she would drop dead before she needed to be looked after. Then she clearly felt this was too brusque, and added, 'But thank you, Sarah. You always were very kind.'

I was? thought Sarah. Is that a clue? It sounds a bit suspect to me.

As she parked the car, she saw Stephen and the three boys walking away from the house. They carried spades, crowbars, a jump-drill. Elizabeth stood in a large vegetable garden with a young man who was presumably a gardener. He wore jeans and a red singlet. She was still in her riding clothes—green shirt, olive green breeches—and the red scarf confined her hair. Her pink cheeks flamed. She held one edge of a plant catalogue and the young man another. Both were alive with enjoyment of their task. Elizabeth invited Sarah to admire the garden, and she did. Then Sarah saw Stephen and the boys a good way off near a cottage or small house that had no roof. Presumably its forlorn look was temporary, for as Sarah came up, she saw Stephen was standing over a deep hole, levering with a crowbar at a stone that obstructed the insertion of a new gatepost. The three boys stood watching their father. The stone came loose, Stephen stood back, the younger boys lifted the stone out. On an indication from Stephen, the three politely greeted her. Over their sunny blond heads Stephen gave her a smile that said he was pleased she was there.

A large squat post lay on the grass, obviously salvaged. It was oak, weathered like elephant's hide, and newly soaked in creosote. Now Stephen and the eldest boy, James, lifted it and slid it into the hole. All four gathered up the stones that had packed the bottom of the discarded post, which was splintering and rotten, and when the new post stood in a bed of stones, the boys took up spades and filled the hole and trampled the loose earth hard. The job was finished. James said to his father, 'Mother said we must be home by twelve. She says we must do our homework.'

'Off you go, then. Don't forget the tools. Put them away properly.'

The three boys put the heavy tools over their shoulders and marched towards the house, knowing they were being watched. Stephen put the discarded post over his shoulder, balanced it with one hand, and they too walked towards the house.

'I am making sure they have all the physical skills I have,' he said, as if she had criticized him.

'You mean, in case they have to earn their livings as workmen?'

'Who knows, these days?'

'Who was that man you were talking to this morning?'

'I was wondering what you'd made of him. Yes. Well. That's Joshua. He's our neighbour. He's leased some of our fields. We were discussing renewing the lease for next year.' A pause. 'He was the chap Elizabeth wanted to marry.' He gave her plenty of time to absorb the implications of this, and even shot her a glance or two, to watch her doing it. 'It's a pity. Elizabeth would have enjoyed being a marchioness. Lady Elizabeth. He's extremely rich. Much richer than I am. And his marriage is not too successful, so he would have done better to take Elizabeth. As it has turned out.'

'There's no accounting for tastes.'

'They have a lot in common. Race horses—that's his line. And Elizabeth is good at horses. But she took me. If she'd got Joshua, then she'd have been absolutely in the right place.' Now they were nearing the house. 'Poor Elizabeth. How can I grudge her Norah? It wouldn't be fair, she thinks, to have married me and then given short measure by taking on Joshua again. Though I'm sure he wouldn't say no. But Norah—that's within the limits of fair play.' He stopped and lowered the post so one end rested on the ground, the other supported in a large strong hand which could easily have been a workman's. His clothes were old and work-worn. He smelled of working sweat. He was looking judiciously at the house. 'A nice house,' he remarked.

'No one could disagree.'

'Do you think that girl sees me separately from the house?'

'Do you mean, does Susan love you for yourself alone? Of course not.'

'And you?'

'You forget I knew you long before I saw the house.'

They stood in a country silence. Birds. An insect or two. A jet droning far overhead. A tractor at work some fields away.

'Did you know Susan is thinking of marrying me? What do you have to say about that?'

'Oh—fantasies.'

'But suppose I am thinking about marrying her?' He hefted the post again, and they went to where wood was stacked, ready for the winter. He added the wormy old post to the pile and brushed his hands together. 'Anyway, it's ridiculous. I'm possessed by the ridiculous. At night I find myself waking up and laughing. Can you beat that, Sarah? Something's going on. . . .' He stood facing her, his eyes holding hers. 'Sarah, somewhere or other I'm burned out.' She did not know what to say. 'Finished,' he said, turning away.

Unfortunately, when apparitions from the places behind the closed doors, truthful moments, arrive in ordinary life, they seem so at odds with probability they tend to be ignored. Bad taste. Exaggeration. Melodrama. They are, quite simply, of a different texture and cannot be accommodated. Besides, today he seemed as full of vitality and health as Elizabeth.

She walked into the little town, along shady country roads. She lunched alone in a hotel and thought what a pleasure it could be to do this, reminding herself there would come a time when she would again enjoy doing things by herself, not feeling that a part of her had been ripped off because Henry was not there. She walked around streets that seemed as if they had no one in them, because there was no chance of bumping into Henry. She was back at the house about tea time, and there were Elizabeth and Norah under a chestnut, with a well-laden tea table between them. They waved at her to join them. She did so, knowing that competent Elizabeth would see this as an opportunity to gain useful information. The two women were usually far from alike, for Norah was appealing and devoted, like an affectionate dog, and even when she wore a linen coat-dress, as she did now, her clothes seemed soft and maternal, yet when they turned their faces towards her, sharpened by anticipation, they seemed like sisters being offered a nice treat. Sarah accepted cups of tea and chattered about Belles Rivières, particularly about the handsome and dramatic Jean-Pierre, so French and so clever, and about minor rivalries in Belles Rivières' town council over *Julie Vairon*. She described the three hotels, Les Collines Rouges, the house Julie had lived in, and the museum. She said that Cézanne had lived and worked not far away, and saw how the name pleased them, a signpost in unfamiliar territory. She talked about everything and everyone except Molly, though she knew Elizabeth was much too shrewd not to suspect something like Molly. She entertained them well, to their profit and to her own, because it was useful to have the emotional turmoil of Belles Rivières diminished to a few mostly humorous anecdotes.

Shadows had taken over the lawn when the three boys appeared in the trees, and Elizabeth clapped her hands and called, 'Go and get your baths and have your suppers. They are in the refrigerator.'

It was too pleasant sitting here to go inside, and they sat on under the big tree, drinking sherry in the twilight.

'You'll have supper with us, of course,' stated Elizabeth. Stephen was not mentioned, and again Sarah reminded herself that he had a complicated life with a thousand obligations and connections.

They ate at leisure in the little room next to the kitchen, and it was quite dark outside when the boys appeared. They wore short red dressing gowns and were brushed, and they smelled of soap. These fair creatures with their transparent skins, their clear blue eyes, their diffident charm, had even more the look of angels who had chosen to grace an earthly choir.

'Have you had your baths? Yes, I can see you have. Well done. Did you eat your suppers? Good. Well, it's going to be a big day tomorrow. This is the calm before the storm. Put yourselves to bed.' They came to her, one after another, and she planted efficient kisses on three offered cheeks. 'Off you go, then.'

And off they went, with decorum, to the door, where suddenly they became children, in a flurry of little squeaks and giggles. The door banged shut after them, and their crashing race up the stairs shook the walls.

Boys will be boys, said Elizabeth's smile, and she sighed with satisfaction. Norah's sigh echoed hers, a long expiring breath that was a confession of sorrow. Elizabeth glanced sharply at Norah, who bravely smiled, but with a small grimace. Childless Norah. Elizabeth patted her friend briskly on her shoulder and gave her a chin-up smile. Norah sat quiet for a moment, then got up and began clearing away plates.

The door opened and James stood there. He was looking at his mother.

'What is it?' demanded Elizabeth, and as he did not speak, but hesitated, holding on to the door handle, 'Well, what do you want?'

That he had come for something, that he wanted something, was plain, for those blue eyes were full of a question, but after a moment he said, 'Nothing.'

'Then run along,' she said, not unkindly.

Again the door shut behind him, but this time quietly. Almost at once he came back. He stood staring at his mother. 'What *is* it James?' she said. He did not go and he did not speak. There was something like a battle of wills between the two pairs of eyes. Then James seemed to shrink, but when he turned away he was stubbornly holding himself together.

Sarah made sure she was in her room when the coach returned, bringing the members of the company who had not been delivered to the hotels.

Under her door came an envelope. 'Sarah. *Why not?* You never look at me. You never see me. I could kill you for it. I'm drunk. Andrew.'

Having scarcely slept the night before she slept at once. Dreams need not go by contraries. Her dreams that night could not have been more to the point, scenes from a farce, men and women running in and out of doors, wrong rooms, right rooms, a joker changing numbers on doors, cries of indignation and laughter, a girl sitting on a bed noisily weeping, head flung back, black hair streaming, a finger pointed in accusation at . . .

Since the company had returned from Stratford so late, they were not in the breakfast room when Sarah got there. She left it as Henry came in and said 'Sarah . . . ,' but she went into the interior of the house, to escape him, not replying. There she saw Stephen climbing a small back staircase, again with the three boys, and they all carried an assortment of tools. He stopped on the landing and called down, 'We are about to have a lesson in basic plumbing.'

'It is the business of the wealthy man to give employment to the artisan,' she quoted. At this the three young heads turned quickly, from three different levels of the stair, looking down at her, each face wearing that delighted but half-scared smile children accustomed to authoritarian rule use to salute rebellion. She was being insubordinate, they felt, but this must define their schools, not their parents.

Stephen said, 'Nonsense. Everyone should know how the machinery of a house works. But there's quite a decent bench under some beeches if you follow the path we were on yesterday and then turn right.'

The two younger boys pounded up the stairs, giggling. James stopped on the landing and then lifted his head to gaze out of the window there. He did this in the way one uses to check up on something, or greet someone. At any rate, he was lost to the world for a long minute, and then Stephen came back, seemed to hesitate, then put his hand on his son's shoulder. 'Come along, old chap.'

James slowly came out of his contemplation, smiled, and went with his father up the stairs. Sarah quickly ran up to the landing, and saw out of the window an enormous ash, waving its arms in the morning sunlight.

Then she followed instructions and, a good way from the house, found a wooden bench under old beeches. She sat canopied by warm green. *A green thought in a green shade.* At least the weather continued good: not an observation to be made lightly on a day a play was to be presented in the open.

She contemplated the old house. Its bulk dwarfed the ash tree, James's familiar, which had a look of standing on guard. From here, nearly a mile away, the green masses merely stirred and trembled, drawing in or repelling black specks, presumably rooks. She had been there an hour or so when Stephen came. He sat down beside her and at once said, 'She came into my room last night.'

'Julie?'

'I wouldn't exactly say that.'

She nibbled a grass stem and waited.

'I couldn't have brought myself to go to her.'

'No.' When he did not go on, she enquired, 'Well?'

'You mean, how did I acquit myself?'

'No, I did not mean that.'

'I have to report that I surprised myself. And I gave her a pleasant surprise or two, I am sure. *A good time*—as they put it over there.' She said nothing, and now he turned a hard critical grin full on her. 'You mean that was not what you meant? But women wait for us to fall down—oh, forgive me.'

'Speaking for myself—no.'

'Perhaps I shall marry her. Yes, why not?' he mused.

'Oh, congratulations. Oh, brilliant.'

'Why not? She lisps about the wonderful life here.'

'Elizabeth doesn't seem to her an impediment?'

'I don't think she really sees Elizabeth. I suspect she thinks Elizabeth is not pretty enough to count.'

'I remember being the same. I was rather younger than Susan, though.'

'Yes. She's juvenile. Yes, I'd say that was the word for her. Anyway, Elizabeth wouldn't be an impediment, would she, if I decided to . . .' All this in the hard angry voice she did occasionally hear from him. 'Could Elizabeth really complain? She could marry Norah.' And then that personality left him, in a deep breath that let out, it seemed, all the anger. His voice lowered into incredulous, admiring, tender awe. 'It's the youth of her—that young body.'

Sarah could not speak. She had been thinking, far too often, I shall never again hold a young man's body in my arms. Never. And it had seemed to her the most terrible sentence Time could deal her.

'But, Sarah . . .' He saw her face averted, put his hand to it, and turned it towards him. He calmly regarded the tears spilling down her face. 'But, Sarah, the point is, it's a young body. Two a penny. Any time. She's not . . .' Here he let his hand slide away, making it a caress, consoling, tender, as you would for a child. He looked at the wet on his hand and frowned at it. 'All the same, if I married her, what bliss, for a time.'

'And then you'd have the pleasure of watching her fall in love with someone her age, while she was ever so kind to you.'

'Exactly. You put it so . . . But last night I was asking myself . . . she really is sweet, I'm not saying she isn't. But is it worth it? To hold Julie's hand is worth more than all of last night.'

Is.

She said, making her voice steady, 'Although Henry is in love with me—he really is—'

'I had noticed. Give me credit.'

'Although he knows I am crazy about him, he hasn't come to my room.'

'His wife, I suppose.' As she did not reply, 'You don't understand, Sarah. For a monogamous man to fall in love—it's terrible.'

'But, Stephen, it's only monogamous people who *can* fall in love—I mean, really.' She felt she was doing pretty well, with this conversation, though her voice was shaking. 'We romantics need obstacles. What could be a greater one?'

'Death?' said Stephen, surprising her.

'Or old age? You see, if I had been Susan's age, if I had been . . . then I don't think morality would have done so well. There would have been nights of bliss and then wallowing in apologies to his wife.'

Stephen put his arm around her. This was a pretty complex action. For one thing, it was an arm (like hers) that easily went around a friend in tears. Once it had comforted Elizabeth, weeping bitterly because Joshua had chosen someone else. It was an arm that went easily around his children. But the arm would rather not have gone around this particular person: it was her arm that should go around him. When he assumed this brotherly role, he relinquished reliable Sarah. Never had a supporting, a friendly arm so clearly conveyed: And now I am alone. But she knew she could expect words of kindness and consolation. A complicated kind of *noblesse oblige* would dictate them.

'There's just one little thing you are overlooking, Sarah. AIDS.'

The arrival of that word, like the arrival of the disease itself, has the power to jolt any conversation into a different key. In this case, laughter. While she was thinking that church bells warning of plague must often enough have tolled across these fields, and this was just another instalment of the story, she had to laugh, and said, 'Oh, that *is* a consolation. That makes everything all right. And anyway, it's ridiculous. *Me*—AIDS.'

'But, Sarah,' said he, enjoying, as she could see, her genuine indignation, 'we have been living in a dream world. The one thing I wasn't going to say to Susan was, But I couldn't possibly have AIDS because I've been chaste. For various reasons I don't propose to go into . . . because one doesn't say that to a woman . . .'

'No.'

'But imagine it. A beautiful young thing, all maidenly hesitation, the bashfulness of true love, appears in your bed, ready to flee away at a cross word, but the next thing, she is enquiring efficiently about condoms and one's attitudes towards oral sex. I did allow myself to say, But, Susan, you really don't have to worry about me, and she said, What makes you think you don't have to worry about me? I've been working in and around New York theatres for five years . . . it does take the romance out of the thing.' She was laughing. He was observing this, she could see, with relief. 'Do you realize how lucky we were, Sarah—us lot?'

'How kind of you to include me in your lot.'

'Pre-AIDS. Post-AIDS. That's the point. We were liberated from the old moralities. Guilt was never more than a mild flick of the whip.'

'We were still romantic. We talked about being in love, not having sex.'

'We didn't worry all that much about pregnancy . . . and I never knew anyone with VD. Did you?'

'No, I don't think so. I don't remember anyone saying, I think I've got syph.'

'There you are. Paradise. We lived in paradise and didn't know it. But these young things, they have more in common with our grandparents and great-grandparents than with us. Ridden with fear, poor things. Well, for my part, I wonder if it's worth it.'

'You're telling me that when Susan arrives in your bed tonight you're going to say, I don't think it's worth it, run along back to your bed little Susan, there's a good girl?'

'Well—no. But, Sarah, I know absolutely what *she* meant by There's no conviction in it.'

'But, Stephen, you won't be feeling like this for long. Just as I quite soon will return to being a severe elderly woman, and I'll say about other people's follies, Really, how tiresome.'

'So you keep saying.'

'Yes, I do. I have to.'

'Anyway, I was never much good at pain. I simply cannot put up with it.' As if he were talking about a fractured knee or a headache, and not a brutal fist slamming again and again into one's heart.

'There's only one thing we can all rely on. Thank God. What we feel one year won't be what we feel the next.'

They sat on in silence, knowing their thoughts ran on parallel lines.

At midday they walked to the house, passing a shady glade full of children, fifteen or so, Stephen's among them. Recent fiction has taught that a tribe of children may only be seen as potential savages capable of any barbarism, but it was hard to associate these with anything much more than the friendly waves and smiles they were offering the adults. Stephen sent his offspring and their friends a lofty wave of the arm, as to a distant shore. James's face, as he followed the two with his eyes, was thoughtful, brave, and stubborn too. So he had looked at his mother and, today, at the ash tree. The two were thinking, as adults do, with discomfort, it was just as well that between the mental landscapes those youngsters knew and their own lay such gulfs of experience that the children could have no notion of all the effort that would be demanded of them. Out of sight of the children, out of sight of the house, Stephen unexpectedly stopped and put brotherly arms around her. 'Sarah, I don't think you begin to know what you've meant to me. . . .' He let her go, without looking at her, as if any emotions he might find on her face were bound to be too much.

In the room where a buffet meal waited for them, Henry was already seated, with Susan. Henry at once got up and leaned over Sarah to demand in a rough voice that this time did not mock itself, 'Sarah, where have you been?'

Sarah was watching how Susan smiled at Stephen, whose returning smile held ingredients that she must find contradictory. For one thing, it was clear that Stephen was more 'in love'—but why the quotes?—than he let on. His whole body was flattered, was pleased, and seemed to be sending messages, of its own accord, to Susan's. But his face was full of ironies and was saying, Don't come too close. What he said aloud was, 'Slept well?' She giggled delightfully, blushed, but looked confused.

'Sarah,' Henry was saying, in the same voice, 'what are you going to do this afternoon?'

'I'm going into the town to the hairdresser.' She smiled, she hoped, nonchalantly at this man whom she loved—oh yes, she did, for the invisible weavers were doing their work well—and her heart was babbling, 'I love you,' as she offered him a plate of healthy country bread.

'The hairdresser!'

'And what are you going to do?' she enquired, though she had been determined not to ask.

'I'm doing a couple of hours with the musicians. They were a bit ragged last night. I'll be there from three till five.' He made it a question.

'If I've finished, I'll come.' She was thinking that nothing would induce her to be there and, with equal force, that nothing could keep her away.

Later, having done with the hairdresser, she took a taxi back and went straight to the theatre area. Henry was leaning moodily against the edge of the musicians' platform. He had his hands pushed deep into his pockets, and he seemed tired and discouraged. He was pale. He was ill. The musicians were coming from the shrubs that screened the new building. Henry had seen her, for now he remarked, 'Be still my heart'—not to her, but to the trees and the sky. He at once parodied himself, going into a pose like Romeo's under Juliet's balcony, on one knee with arms outstretched. On his feet again, he was unable to prevent himself sending her a long and wretched look, but parodied that too, by intensifying it to the point of ludicrousness. She had to laugh, even while dissolving into sweet nostalgia for long-lost shores.

When the music rehearsal was done, he came to her and had just said, 'Let's go and walk,' when she saw Benjamin coming purposefully towards them.

'Here's your admirer,' said Henry, surprising her, for she did not know he had noticed Benjamin's attentions, and plunging her into loss as he ran off, swiping at a shrub as he went, and jumping over another.

Sarah could not help being thrilled by Henry's jealousy, though he was off the mark. You may fall into liking, as you do into love, though it is a less common surrender. It is easy to confuse one with the other. Benjamin had fallen into liking with her, on first sight,

just as she and Stephen had done with each other at that first meeting in the restaurant. Could she say she had equally fallen into liking
with him? No; she had only to make the comparison. Which is not
to say she did not like him well enough.

He advanced towards her, seeming out of place in his formally
elegant white. His face had warmed as he looked at her, but almost
at once his eyes had moved on behind her to the great trees enclosing the circle of emerald lawn, where the musicians in their pale
floaty dresses were drifting towards shrubs that hid the rehearsal
rooms. Now his face was that of a young boy listening to a magic
tale. Benjamin had fallen in love with the theatre, with the arts.
Having determined to take advantage of casual theatre manners and
mores, he kissed her heartily on both cheeks, and seemed pleased
with himself for achieving this freedom. As for her she was envying
him his state of pleasurable intoxication. Yet such were the influences of recent experience, she was examining the handsome face
for signs of grief or even of anxiety. There were none. Was she sure
about that? No. Should she not at least be wondering why this man
ensconced in his so satisfactory and—surely?—satisfying life had
succumbed to the theatre and its intoxications? (O, for the life of a
Gypsy, O!) What lacks might there be in that life of his? She did not
know. How little we do know about what goes on inside our nearest
friends, let alone agreeable acquaintances—she was damned if she
was going to give the name *friend* to Benjamin and call Stephen a
friend. Roy Strether, her good friend, a friend of fifteen years, was
going through hell, and she knew it and he knew that she knew it,
but apart from Mary, who else in the company had any idea of what
went on inside that so friendly and competent fellow? Who of the
people in this house had any idea about Stephen? Certainly not his
wife. Sally would probably say later of this time that it had been one
of the worst in her life. She had hinted something of the kind, half
laughing, to Sarah. But of the people who had worked with her
every day for weeks, who gave Sally's loss much thought? Mary

looked terrible: much more than was due to worry over her mother.

They walked slowly to the house, while she told him about this new production here, and the new members of the cast. She listened, or tried to, for her thoughts would go straying off, while he told her about the Edinburgh Festival. Thus they reached the house, and it was time for the early buffet supper, for soon the play would begin.

The two young women from the town, Alison and Shirley, were there that evening, large, calm, blonde, with red cheeks, as healthy as apples, shedding pleased and maternal smiles on the hectic scene. First nights were not new to them. As for Elizabeth, she might as well have been saying aloud, This sort of thing is to be expected; it is the theatre after all . . . and she smiled at Susan while handing her a plate of summer pudding. 'You really are so good, Susan,' everyone heard her say. 'You're such a wonderful Julie.' This to remind her of what she was doing here, in this house—Elizabeth's house.

Benjamin left Sarah to talk to Stephen, and the two men stood side by side conversing, holding glasses of wine and waving away food. They were for that time inside their roles as patrons of the arts, for if they were not thinking this, were too modest, even feeling privileged to assist all these talented beings, then others, watching them, had to think: the money men—and we are all dependent on their decisions.

Henry came to Sarah and said in a low voice, 'Sarah, I've had a fax from Millicent. She is coming tomorrow. With Joseph. She'll see tomorrow night's performance, and then we'll both be off.'

'A change of plan?'

'Yes. Elizabeth very kindly invited her to stay a few days, and we said we would, but—well, we're leaving the day after tomorrow, and then we're going to drive around France for a couple of weeks.'

She said nothing and could not look at him.

'So that's how it is, Sarah,' he said, putting down an untouched plate of food. 'And now I'm going out to see how the audience is coming along.'

He went. Soon the players followed him.

Stephen, Sarah, and Benjamin stood on the steps to watch the audience leave their cars and wandered over the grass towards the theatre. It was a perfect evening. Wispy gold clouds floated high in the west, and quiet trees were outlined against them. Birds robustly quarrelled in the shrubs. With nearly an hour to go, the seats were already nearly full.

Sarah saw her brother Hal, Anne, Briony and Nell get out of their car. She had not expected them. He had come from work and wore the dark suit he used for his afternoons in Harley Street. His women wore floral dresses, their fair hair glittered with this evening's sun. For all of them an excursion into Sarah's life was a holiday: for the parents, from hard work; and the girls after all did spend a good part of their lives in an office and a laboratory. Where was Joyce?

Sarah waved at her brother, who granted her an allowance of his confident self in a measured palm-forward salute, like royalty, but because he didn't flutter his fingers he seemed to bestow blessings: light could easily be streaming from that palm towards the three on the steps. Through a gap in the hedge she watched him advance to the front row. She saw a large light black ball being borne shorewards on the frothy crest of a slow wave. He stepped lightly, his head level, his eyes staring straight ahead, and the look on his face was one Sarah had been studying all her life, though it was not a look, in fact, that repaid study: with his full cheeks, his slightly pouting mouth, his protuberant eyeballs, he was like a ship's figurehead. She had often thought he was like a drugged or a hypnotized man. It was his body that expressed absolute assurance, an impervious self-satisfaction. A mystery: he had always been a mystery to her. Where had he got it from, this self-assurance? Where in him was it located? Having reached the front row, he removed the Reserved signs on some chairs—he had not reserved seats—and sat down, assuming his women would arrange themselves. There he sat, the large soft black ball beached, while around him frothed the flowery wave.

In the front row, critics from London were taking their seats, some with a characteristic look of doing the occasion a favour by being there at all, others sliding furtively along the rows, in case they were observed and someone might come to talk to them, thus compromising their integrity. The audience softly chatted, admiring the sky, the gardens, the house.

Henry escorted Stephen, Sarah, and Benjamin to wish the players well. They took with them goodwill faxes from Bill in New York and from Molly in Oregon. 'Thinking of you all tonight.' 'I wish I was with you.' The new, raw building was crammed with people now and already filled with . . . it is a matter of opinion with what. But the place was no longer an echoing vacuum.

The four took their places, right at the back.

Experienced eyes assessed the critics. Only two of the first-rank ones were here. Elizabeth had been heard thanking them in ringing tones for being so very kind. The others were second-rank, or apprentices, among them Roger Stent, who, having looked cautiously for Sonia and found her, gave her a severe and unsmiling nod, like a judge before opening the day's case. She gave him an 'up yours' sign back, meant to be noticed. The critics were all one of two kinds: theatre critics, who would judge from that point of view, or music critics, here because Queen's Gift had a reputation for its music and its Entertainments, who knew nothing about stage production. None was equipped to judge this hybrid. The audience was another matter, for they at once showed they liked the piece and understood, and when the troubadour music began they applauded, to show they did not find it strange. For one thing, the programme devoted a full page to this kind of music: its history, its origins in the twelfth and thirteenth centuries, its Arab influences, its instruments, adapted from Arab originals, its unexpected emergence so many centuries later in the music of Julie Vairon, who—it was safe to assume—could never have heard it.

But that music was in the second act, and the two main theatre critics left after the first, because of driving back to London or catching their train. They both had the affronted put-upon look of critics who have wasted their time. Sarah joked that their pieces would certainly include the phrase 'an insipid piece,' and Mary added, "'Faux exotica,'" and Roy, "'Unfortunately an exotic background will not save this banal play from failure.'"

The rest of the theatre critics left at the end of the second act, so they would not know about the limpid other-worldly music of the third act, which transcended, even repudiated, the personal. 'Do you know what?' said Mary. 'I bet every one of their pieces will be headed: "She Was Poor but She Was Honest."' 'Or,' suggested Roy, "'I can't get away to marry you today—my wife won't let me.'" The music critics all stayed to the end.

But the audience stood to applaud, and for them, at least, *Julie Vairon* was a success, if not as much as it had been in France.

Meanwhile Sarah's attention was being distracted, because during the second act she saw Joyce with her friend Betty and an unknown youth standing near the gap in the hibiscus hedge which was the entrance to the theatre. They had the look of children listening outside a door to the grown-ups talking. Easy to reconstruct what must have happened. Joyce had been invited—no, begged—with the exasperated end-of-tether voices she did hear from her family, to accompany them on their jaunt to Aunt Sarah's play, had refused, but had told Betty, who had said they might as well go. The three had hitchhiked. Even now, when hitching was so risky, Joyce begged lifts, usually from lorry drivers accosted in the forecourts of petrol stations. Joyce had recounted tales of near-disaster, with the timid smile she did offer to adults, partly to find out what the world of authority thought. Sarah had not previously had more than a glimpse of Betty, but now here she was, in full view. The three young people made their way around the back of the seated crowd, Joyce on tiptoe, Betty with bravado, the young man expecting to be accosted and thrown out. Betty plumped herself down on a grassy slope, the two sat by her and Joyce sent frantic waves and smiles to her aunt.

Betty was a large girl, and she sat with fat blue-jeaned thighs spread in front of her, arms crossed on great unsupported breasts. On her face was a look of sour scepticism: you aren't going to put anything across me. The face was large and plain and coarse. Her black hair straggled greasily. Joyce seemed even more of a sad waif beside her, for it was at once evident that Betty mothered her. The young man, who sat apart from the women, was very thin, pallid, limp, with a long bony neck. His hands were thin enough to see through, and his face was covered in red blotches.

During the applause when the play ended, the three disappeared.

An informal party for the company and neighbours had been arranged on the side of the house away from the theatre. Long tables held wine and cakes. Behind these the two pretty blonde girls, Shirley and Alison, served while Elizabeth and Norah, with Stephen, welcomed guests. The audience streamed away to the cars and coaches that would take them to the town or to London, but about two hundred people stood about on the lawn. Hal appeared and went straight up to Stephen, introducing himself not as Sarah's brother but as Dr Millgreen. Stephen did not know who he was but behaved as if this was a great honour for him. Hal refused a glass of wine, saying he had to return to London because he must be at his hospital early, said in a kindly way to his sister, 'Very nice, Sarah,' and went off, not looking to see if Anne, Briony, and Nell followed, or if they might perhaps like a glass of wine. From the other side of the lawn he did look back, apparently to approve the house, for he was wearing his professional look of a generalized benevolence. Various people hastened up to him and to Anne. For a moment he stood in a group of colleagues, or patients, or friends, a figure of kindly authority. It occurred to Sarah that just as she had never

seen much more of Stephen than his Julie side (his dark and concealed side), so she saw nothing of the social life of her brother and
her sister-in-law. Formal parties were not in her line, and their
friends were not in her line either. But possibly there were a good
many people who knew this eminent Dr Millgreen, and his clever
doctor wife, Anne, and their two pretty daughters, as a likeable
family. They might perhaps remark if they remembered, 'A pity
about that girl of theirs. A bit of a handful apparently.'

Just as Sarah was thinking that she should ask Hal and Anne
about Joyce, the family got into their car and drove off. So she went
on talking, as it was her part to do, with anyone who wished to talk
to her. Yes, she had found it rewarding to work on this play—if you
could call it that—but there were two authors, and Stephen
Ellington-Smith, their host, would have a lot to say about it too.
This went on for an hour or so, and the dusk had settled in the trees
and shrubs when she heard a young man say with a laugh that he
had been accosted after the performance as he came out of the new
building by a couple of girls who were offering the male members of
the cast a blow-job for ten pounds a time. It was Sandy Grears, talking to George White. Sarah at once went up to them and said, 'I'm
afraid one of the girls was probably my niece. I suppose you don't
know where they went?' She was finding it hard to appear calm,
because the thought of Henry—who would have been in the new
building with the others—anywhere near a paid-for blow-job was
too painful almost to bear, like a grotesque sexual joke directed at
oneself. The two young men at once adjusted their manner, from
one appropriate to laughing at a couple of slags to one sympathiz-
ing with the relative of a problem child. George said he thought it
was likely the girls were in The Old Fox in the town, for it was the
only place open in the evenings. He offered to take Sarah there.
Sandy went off, and this enabled Sarah to ask if there had been a
young man with the girls. Yes, there had. George hesitated; he could
have said more, but Sarah decided not to ask. She found it hard to

believe that Sandy went in for blow-jobs offered by unhealthy youths, but one never knew. She was surprised she felt a genuine pang—an aesthetic one—that anyone who had enjoyed (for once an absolutely accurate word) the beautiful Bill Collins could even think of a blow-job with that poor derelict.

On the way to town she told George about Joyce, and he was suitably sympathetic. His own sister was a problem. She was anorexic, sometimes suicidal, and it had all been going on for years. Once again, here was the unwelcome shift of perspective when a colleague's private life (never more than the backdrop to the life you know them in, their working life, their real life, so you prefer to think) comes forward and you are made to know with what difficulty and how precariously this friend maintains independence from that matrix the family. George for a time had had this sister living with him and his wife, but then it all got too much when the children were born. Now, unfortunately, she was in and out of hospital. Sarah and George then exchanged the lines of that conversation which takes place more and more often, to the effect that for every whole, competent, earning person are every day more of the people who cannot cope with life and have to be supported, financially or emotionally. The two went on to wonder if there were really more, or perhaps it was only that they were more visible because of our (after all quite recently adopted) view that disadvantaged people are infinitely redeemable. And what about those people who are seen as whole, healthy, independent, 'viable', but in fact are dependent on others? Sarah of course was thinking here of her brother, for what would he be without that drained-of-blood person his wife?

The Old Fox called itself a wine bar, but it was a restaurant with a bar and loud music, and so full they could not see the other side of the room. Then, suddenly, there Joyce was. A group of young people squeezed themselves around a table, drinking. This was a far from disreputable place, and Joyce's group was the only doubtful element in it. Sarah, who was now faced with the necessity of doing some-thing, but not knowing what, was saved by Joyce, who was pushing her way through the crowd with cries of 'It's my Auntie Sarah.' She was holding a tumbler of whisky above her head for safety. Standing in front of her aunt and reeking of whisky, Joyce chattered about the lovely play. She did not look at George White. It had not been more than a mild twilight when the play ended, but perhaps she did not look, on principle, at possible customers.

'How are you going to get home?' asked Sarah.

'Oh, we'll manage. We got ourselves here, didn't we?'

The two adults stood listening while the poor child offered the smart phrases that were obligatory when she was near her friends. 'No dis, Auntie, but you're right out, we've nuff carn, we're safe.' Translated: No disrespect, but you're worrying about nothing, we've got lots of money, we're okay. Meanwhile her gaze moved continu-ally to the door as new people came in. Clearly she knew this place well. Her smile, as always, seemed fixed. Her eyes were all pupil. Drugs enlarge pupils. Like the dark. Or like love.

George caught sight of someone he knew. He moved off. After all, the company had been here for three days and this was the place for the youth of the town. At once he was surrounded: he was ami-able, good-looking, always popular.

'Joyce,' said Sarah, lowering her voice. 'Are you remembering all the things we tell you?'

Joyce's eyes moved about evasively, and she said brightly, 'Oh, Sarah, of course we do; you're right out.'

'What's this about your offering blow-jobs to all and sundry?'

At this the beautiful eyes swivelled desperately. 'Who told you? I didn't . . . I never . . . please, Auntie . . .' Then, recovering herself, she quoted (who—Betty?), 'But that's what men are like. That's all they care about; give them a good blow-job and they are satisfied.' And she looked proudly at Sarah to see how this bit of worldly wisdom was going down.

Sarah watched those pretty lips struggle to offer her a smile and said, 'Oh Joyce, do have some common sense.'

'Oh we do, I promise. But it's brass, you see. The trouble is, brass.' Then, unable to bear it another minute, she waved her thin and grubby hand not six inches from Sarah's face, saw she was misjudging distances, squinted, and retreated backwards, crying, 'Later on . . . later on . . .' Meaning goodbye, goodbye. She wriggled off into the crowd to rejoin her friends.

At the bar sat Andrew, on a stool, drinking. Feeling that he was being looked at, Andrew turned and stared at her. Then, deliberately, he turned back to the woman on the stool next to his—smart, middle-aged, flattered by him. Then he could not stand it and swung about, steadied himself, for he was tight, and came over to her. 'I don't have a car,' he said. 'If I borrowed one, would you . . . ?' George appeared. 'No, I see you wouldn't,' and Andrew stalked back to the bar.

'A pretty dramatic character, our Andrew,' commented George.

'Yes.'

'I wouldn't like him as an enemy.'

Men, if not women, saw Andrew as dangerous.

'Come on, I'll take you back.'

She sat silent in the car as it sped through moonlit lanes, thinking for the thousandth time that there must be something sensible they could do about Joyce.

'Are you thinking that there must be some solution if only you could think of it?'

'Yes.'

'I thought you were.'

He did not stop the engine when she got out. Off he went, back to the wine bar, leaving her outside the now dark house. It was twelve, late for these parts. On a bench by some shrubs sat a tense and watchful figure. She walked towards Henry. As Susan had seemed earlier with Stephen: Henry was reeling her in on a line. She sat by him. He at once moved over so they touched all the way from shoulders to feet.

'Where have you been?'

She heard herself sigh: it meant, How irrelevant.

'Benjamin was looking for you. He's gone to bed.'

Her mind was spinning out its rhetoric: How often are two people in love with each other at the same time? Hardly ever. Usually, one turns the cheek . . . What she did say aloud, quite evenly and creditably, though her heart was thudding so he must feel it, was, 'There is always that moment with Americans when one feels thoroughly decadent. You can know someone for years, and then there it is. Good wholesome ethical Americans, tricky and decadent Europeans. Just like a Henry James novel.'

'If I had ever read Henry James.'

'In your heart of hearts you think of me as immoral.'

'I don't want to know what you think of me.'

'Good. And now I'm going to bed.' She got up, and he grabbed her hand. Pulling her hand away from his hand tore out great slabs of her heart. So it felt. He leaped up. He held her, still did not kiss her mouth, but his lips touched her cheek, sending fire all through her (sending *what*?), and her lips were on his hair. Soft hair . . .

'Good night,' she said briskly, and went upstairs.

She sat at her window, utterly overthrown. The sky was full of moonlight, so she saw as her sight cleared. Words welled up in her. She found herself sitting (with her eyes shut, for the moonlight was too empty and heartless), feeling the sweet touch of his hair on her mouth, while she muttered, 'God, how I did love you, my little brother, how I did love you.' Astonishment pulled her eyes open. But it was not now she could attend to what the words were telling her. She lay on her bed and wept, most bitterly. Well, that was better than what lay in wait for her. Tears and even bitter tears are not the country of grief.

She woke late, was late at the breakfast table. Stephen had come in to look for his sons, for he wanted them to have a shooting lesson. Benjamin sat over coffee. He had been waiting for her. It was his turn to look ironical: he believed her to have been kept late in town by attractive temptations. Henry came in, just after she did, poured coffee, brought the cup and himself to the chair next to hers. He did not look at her. She did not look at him.

Benjamin said, 'I've got to leave at two, if I'm going to catch my plane.'

Stephen said, 'Then I suggest Sarah shows you around the place a bit.'

Benjamin said, 'If Sarah's got time.'

'Of course I've got time,' said Sarah, but it was after a pause, for she did not immediately hear him.

'And Henry, perhaps you and your wife would have dinner with us? It's not too bad at The Blue Boar. The show'll be over by ten, and we can be in town by half past.'

'We'd love to,' said Henry. 'It might be a bit late for Joseph, but he'll manage. He's used to late nights.'

Stephen had not thought the child would be at the dinner, and now he remarked, 'I'm sure Norah would keep an eye on him for you.'

'I don't think he'd let me go. He hasn't seen me for a month.'

'Just as you think best. I'll book. And Sarah—you too, of course.'

Here his boys appeared, and he said to them, 'Come on, then, there's good chaps. Run and get the target.'

The four went off.

Sarah found she could not drink her coffee. Her mouth was already bitter with loss. She said to Benjamin, 'Shall we go?' Benjamin stood up, and this tall and solid man, in his immaculate, impeccable, improbably perfect creamy linen, succeeded in making the delightful old room seem shabby. He enquired too politely of Henry, 'Do you want to join us?'

'I've got things to do,' said Henry.

Benjamin and Sarah set off to stroll around the estate. They took paths as they came to them, sat on benches to admire views, found a field with horses in it, a dozen or so lazing under a willow near a stream. The horses watched the two to see if they were bearing titbits, then lost interest. A field yellow with grain and so smooth it seemed to invite them to stroke it slanted to a sheet of blue sky. In an enormous shed, or workshop, a harvester like an infinitely magnified insect stood throbbing while two young men in smart blue overalls leaned over it with cans of oil.

This is the last day, the last day—beat through Sarah. Landscape, sky, horses, and harvester were all Henry, Henry. The shocking egotism of love had emptied her of anything but Henry. She told herself that Benjamin deserved at least politeness, and tried to chat suitably, but she knew that her words kept fading into inattention, and then silence.

Benjamin began to entertain her, remembering how successful this had been in Belles Rivières, with 'projects'.

'How does this grab you, Sarah? A Kashmiri lake, an exact replica, with houseboats, musicians, the boatmen imported from Kashmir. It'll be in Oregon. Plenty of water—we need the right kind of lake.'

'It certainly grabs me,' said Sarah, knowing she sounded indifferent.

'Good. And what about a development of a machine that emits negative ions? It hangs from a moveable stand so you can push it from room to room. Dust is attracted to it and falls into a flat tray under the machine. After an hour or so there is very little dust in the air.'

'That one certainly grabs me. No housework.'

'It was my wife's idea. She was working for a firm that makes ionizers. She's a physicist. She's developing the machine.'

'You can sell me one any time.'

'I'll get her to send you one.'

'Was the Kashmiri lake your wife's idea?'

'We had the idea together. We were in Kashmir three years ago—before all the fighting, that kind of thing. I put it to a hotel group we are interested in, and they liked it.'

'You sound as if you think it is a little frivolous.'

'Perhaps I did, at first. But my ideas about what is frivolous and what isn't seem to have changed.' Here he would have liked to exchange with her a look deeper than words, but she could not afford to let her eyes meet his. Swords seemed to stab into her eyes, which might easily dissolve and flow down her cheeks.

They walked towards a group of trees from where voices and an occasional gunshot emanated. They stood among trees and looked down into a glade. In the middle of this grassy space stood a thick wooden post, which, because of the times we live in, had to make them think of a man or woman with bandaged eyes, waiting to be shot. Rather old-fashioned? Did a post belong to an older and more formal, even more civilized, time? On the post was nailed a home-made target. Some yards away from it, below them but to the left, were Stephen, his three sons, two other boys, and two girls.

Against an oak tree leaned an assortment of guns. The scene was remarkable because of its combination of the casual and even amateur—the home-made target and Stephen's and the children's clothes—and the strict rituals of the shooting.

The children stood in a group a few paces behind a boy who was holding a gun: he had just finished his turn and was taking it back to the little armoury by the tree. They were restraining the two red setters who were excitedly moving about, their tails sweeping the grass. The child whose turn had come to shoot was being led by Stephen to the tree, where a weapon suitable for his age and degree of skill was carefully chosen. Every movement was monitored by Stephen: barrel tilted down, hold it like this, walk like this. When the boy was in place at the point they shot from, Stephen stood just behind him and a little to one side, issuing instructions, though what he said could not be heard from this distance. The boy carefully raised the rifle, aimed, shot. A black hole appeared on the target, slightly off centre of the bull's-eye. 'Well done' was probably said, for the boy joined the group, looking pleased.

Now a girl of about twelve went with Stephen to the tree. She chose a rifle, without guidance, strolled to the right place with Stephen, who was much less careful with her than with the boy, then aimed, then fired. Apparently it was a bull's-eye, for the target didn't change. The children emitted appreciative cries, and Stephen laid his hand briefly on her shoulder. The dogs barked and bounded. She rejoined the group, and another boy, Edward, Stephen's youngest, went to the tree with his father. What he was handed seemed to be an air gun. This time Stephen monitored every little movement: position of the forward hand, set of the left shoulder . . . of the right shoulder . . . position of the head . . . of the feet. Intense concentration. The shot appeared as a black hole on the edge of the white square with its concentric rings. The group was so hard at work no one noticed the two watchers, who moved on.

'I would like to think we took as much trouble teaching our children to shoot. I suppose it shows ignorance, but why do they need to know how to shoot in this green and peaceful land?'

'It's a social skill.'

'And the girls too?'

'One has to remember whom a girl might marry—I'm quoting.'

Benjamin duly smiled.

'You see, there would never have been any need for my daughter to learn to shoot.' As he seemed puzzled: 'We aren't aristocrats.'

'But surely it might come in useful? Didn't you say she lives in California?'

'Not this kind of shooting. Those children will never shoot at anything that isn't pheasant or grouse or deer. If there isn't a war, that is.'

'I have to confess there are times when this country seems an anachronism.'

'When I visit your Kashmiri lake in Oregon I'll remind you of that.'

He laughed. She was so far from laughing she could have fallen and lain weeping on the grass. They finished the tour and then he said he might as well be off. She accompanied him to his car. Guilt caused her to be effusive. She could hear herself making conversation, but she hardly knew what. He said he would be in England again in November. Off he roared in his powerful car. To the airport. Then to California. To the pleasurable work of financing attractive ideas and then watching them become realities. A modern magician.

Only Stephen and Sarah were having lunch. Henry had gone to meet his wife and son. Elizabeth and Norah were visiting friends. The company had hired a coach to take them around the Cotswold villages.

Their food remained untouched on their plates.

'Sarah, I know I'm a bore, but I must ask you . . . when your husband died, did you grieve for him—that sort of thing?'

'I've been asking myself that. I was unhappy, very. But how I wonder . . . What else have I not *really* grieved about? I mean, a proper allowance of grief. I see you are still consulting your textbooks?'

'Yes. But behind this line of thought is an assumption. If you don't feel the right emotion at the right time, it accumulates. Well, it seems pretty bogus to me.'

'But how does one know?'

'Why didn't you marry again?'

'You forget, I had two small children.'

'That wouldn't stop me if I wanted a woman.'

'But we didn't know each other then.'

He allowed this a smile, made an impatient movement with his hand, but then was overtaken by a laugh. 'A pity we haven't fallen in love with each other,' he said. Here the faintest cloud of reminiscent anxiety crossed his face, but she reassured him with a shake of the head. 'Because we are really so extraordinarily . . . compatible.'

'Ah, but that would be too sensible.' Then she faced him with 'But I've been remembering something. When I had love affairs, I never took him to my bedroom. The bed I shared with my husband. Always the spare room. Then one of them made a point of it. He said, "I'm sick of being the guest. You're still married, did you know that?" And that was it. He left.'

'You were very fortunate, Sarah. At first I think Elizabeth and I did pretty well, but never—'

'Would you say those two women are married?'

'Yes, I would. They certainly exclude everyone else.' His voice was full of hurt. A noisy wasp was investigating a puddle of mayonnaise on a plate. This gave him the excuse to put a knife blade under it and get up to shake it into the garden. He came back, having determined to go on, and went on. 'That includes the children.' A pause. 'Elizabeth was never a maternal woman. She never pretended to be. Why should women be? A lot aren't.' A pause. 'I try to make it up to the children.'

'I think Norah would like to be more of a mother to the children.'

His face showed this was not a new thought to him. 'Well, I'm not stopping her.' He pushed away his plate, chose a peach from a bowl, and methodically cut it up. 'Believe it or not, I'm sorry for her. Norah, I mean. She's a sort of cousin of Elizabeth's. She was down on her luck—her marriage went wrong.'

They let the subject go. There are people who seem to compel heartlessness or at least neglect. Everything, everybody, would always seem more important than Norah.

'When are you leaving, Sarah?'

'Tomorrow. Jean-Pierre's coming to tonight's performance. And we shall discuss everything in London.'

'I'm coming to London too.'

'You're going to leave . . . Susan? I wouldn't have the strength of mind.'

'Nothing to do with strength of mind.' He sprinkled sugar on the melting yellow pieces of peach, picked up his spoon, set it down, pushed the plate away. 'The one thing I didn't bargain for was that Julie would dwindle into a good fuck. You're a good fuck, she says. I can't say I'm not flattered.' Here he smiled at her, a real, affectionate smile, all of him there. 'She's a hard little thing. But she doesn't know it. She keeps saying that I'm sexist. With a coquettish giggle. I told her there was nothing new about her ideas. Women have always agreed that a man must be redeemed by the love of a good woman. She gave me a real curtain lecture, the full feminist blast. The trouble is, you see, she's pretty stupid.'

Another wasp, or the same one, came to the cut-up peach and began to drown in melted sugar. He left it to its fate.

'Sarah, my life doesn't add up to anything—no, listen. If I'd earned the money, it would be a different matter. My grandfather earned it all.'

She was too surprised to speak.

'I envy Benjamin. He uses money.'

'Don't you?'

'I keep things going, anyone could do it.' He got up. 'I told the boys I'd take them riding.'

'I saw you this morning teaching them to shoot.'

'If one only knew what sort of life they should be educated for. I wish I knew. They learn all the new things at school—computers. As well as the usual things. James can drive. He can use maps and a compass. They can shoot. They can ride. I'll make sure they won't be dependent on craftsmen to do their plumbing for them—that kind of thing. They aren't artistic at all, not musical. They do well at games at school. That's still important.'

'Do they know how to read?'

'A good question. But that's asking a lot these days. James has some books in his room. Norah still reads to the younger ones. But perhaps shooting will turn out to be the most useful thing in the end. Who knows?'

Mid-afternoon. Henry's car came to a crunchy stop on the gravel. He jumped out to open the door for his wife. Out stepped a small woman, almost invisible because of the large child in her arms. She set him down, and the little boy, about three years old, rushed into his father's arms with screams of delight. Now it could be seen that Millicent was pretty and blonde, if that was an adequate word for the casque or fleece of yellow hair which, like Alice's, fell almost to her waist. From it a little determined face smiled while Henry whirled his son around and then again, before setting him down, but Joseph refused to be put down. He clung to his father's legs until Henry picked him up again. Millicent stood looking about her. It was a competent but above all democratic inspection: she was refusing to be diminished by ancestral magnificence. She smilingly faced the big steps, where Stephen, Elizabeth, Norah, and Sarah were waiting. She had a philosophical look. They have a hard task, the wives, husbands, loved ones generally of the adventurous souls who so recklessly (and so often) immerse themselves in these heady brews and who have to be reclaimed for ordinary life: talked down, brought down, reintroduced to—reality is the word we use. Norah descended the steps to help carry up the innumerable cases, hold-alls, bags, of toys and clothes and comics necessary for a contemporary child's well-being. (Children, that is, of certain countries.) She and Millicent managed it all, because Henry's arms were full, and likely to remain so. His face and his son's were joyous.

Introductions were made, and the family went upstairs; Norah went with them to show the way. She came down in a few minutes, joining the others in the little sitting room, where tea was waiting for them. Her smile, as so often, was brave, this time because of the tender scene she had been observing. Elizabeth and Stephen were there, and Mary Ford had arrived, with apologies from Roy, who had departed to London. His wife had decided after all not to live with her new lover, and he hoped to talk her into returning to him, restoring the marriage. He was armed with arguments, and statistics too, one of which was that 58 percent of men and women in new marriages regretted their first marriages and wished they had never divorced at all. The company drinking tea wished poor Roy well: he had really been looking awful recently, they agreed. They wished him well for the space of about half a minute, and then Norah remarked, 'I'm afraid Millicent has put a veto on the restaurant. It seems the little boy is overwrought. I can't help feeling he would put up with me. I am supposed to be good with children.'

Mary said, 'I'm afraid we are up against that good old culture clash again. Well, I'm on their side. I love it when I'm in Italy and France and you see everyone from granny to the new baby out together having a meal.'

'Speaking for myself,' said Elizabeth, 'I think it's extraordinary they should take it for granted a three-year-old child would go out to dinner with adults.'

Stephen said, 'But they wouldn't see it as going out to dinner. It's normal for them to go out for meals in restaurants.'

'Since they're off tomorrow, I suppose that's it. I'll ring up the restaurant and cancel,' said Elizabeth. When she was doing something practical, her body filled with vitality, her haunches moved with a look of intense private satisfaction, her hands seemed ready to take hold of a situation and manage it. 'And the next excitement,' she said, coming back from the telephone, 'is your Frenchman. Do you think we should take him out to dinner?'

Sarah said, 'You don't seem to realize—just being in this house will be a thrill for him, as it is for all of us.'

'I suppose we do rather take it for granted. Damn. I wouldn't have minded going out to dinner. They'll just have to take pot luck.'

'Never mind, darling,' said Norah. 'I'll take you out to dinner when everyone has gone.' She spoke emotionally, and the darling had slipped out. She was embarrassed, and Elizabeth did not look at her.

Stephen said quickly, 'Too much cooking and catering these last few days. I did warn you that it might be too much of a good thing.'

'I've enjoyed it,' said Elizabeth, smiling at them all. Then she gave Norah a smile, just for her. The two women began talking about the people they had gone to lunch with, in a hearty social way, and this became a joking exchange of gossip about neighbours, Joshua among them. Stephen was listening to the women with that look one sees on the faces of husbands and wives—and lovers—not in the confidence of their partners, when they talk in their presence to other people. It was a strained eavesdropper's look. Elizabeth and Norah then said they had thought of taking a week's holiday when *Julie Vairon* was done. Stephen remarked that it was possible he would not be here. Elizabeth said, 'Well, never mind; the boys will be at school by then.'

The gravel announced an arrival. It was Jean-Pierre, who shook hands all round, kissed Elizabeth's hand, and then kissed Mary, one, two, three. For the space of seconds the two were in a time of their own. Again the grounds had to be shown, and soon, because Jean-Pierre would be off early tomorrow, with Sarah. They all strolled about in the late afternoon sunlight, and Jean-Pierre exclaimed in polite enthusiasm about everything he saw, as well he might. He was overwhelmed, he said, it was magnificent, he said, and so it went on till they showed him the theatre area, when he began to show doubt. They had expected him to.

The chairs had no numbers on them: did the audience not reserve seats?

It was not necessary; people sat where they could find a seat. And if they're late, too bad, they have to stand. We only reserve the front row.

The paths leading to the theatre were not marked. The posters were everywhere, so how did people know where to go?

'Don't worry, they work it out for themselves,' reassured Norah maternally.

And there was no definite place where refreshments were served. He supposed there were refreshments?

Stephen said all that kind of thing was very well organized by Elizabeth and her staff. Wine, ice cream, soft drinks, cakes, appeared on trays in the intervals, borne by volunteers from the town, who enjoyed this contact with the world of the theatre.

'Of course, sometimes they don't turn up,' said Elizabeth, who was enjoying teasing Jean-Pierre. 'But if they don't, then I and Norah and the children, if they're here, we fill in the gaps.'

Here Jean-Pierre dramatically shrugged his shoulders. He certainly did not approve of the owners of this imposing house working as servants. But there was more in the way of a style or even drama in this shrug. The French expect from the English a falling off from some paradigmatic excellence of which they are the natural custodians for the whole world, and this English indifference is not even from an innate inability to conform to the highest when they see it, but from choice. What can one expect? said the shrug.

The usual pre-performance supper, at seven, had people sitting around a table in the smaller room, not standing about for a buffet meal, because most of the players had telephoned to say they would eat in the town.

Stephen, Elizabeth, and Norah were at one end of the table, with Susan sitting opposite Stephen. Jean-Pierre was by Mary. Sarah saw she had put herself in the middle where she had empty chairs on either side, a statement of how she felt: to her such a dramatic, not to say self-pitying one that she hastily moved up to sit by

Joseph, who was near Millicent, who sat at the end opposite Elizabeth.

While Henry had been upstairs with Millicent, he had confessed his misdemeanour, as he was bound to do. A bizarre solution, but who does not know about Oedipus complexes, and a shock it could not be. Besides, for a young and pretty woman to accept that her husband has a crush on a woman old enough to be his mother, or hers, does not demand the maximum in the way of marital toler- ance. There was an attractively humorous little look on Millicent's face. At the same time, because Henry, an honest fellow, had not minimized the extent of his lapse (which he had been careful to make sure had included not so much as a kiss), Millicent was appraising Sarah with every intention of giving credit where it was due. Sarah was sure that the slight—slightest possible—indications of unease were due to, as the proverb has it, 'If one drop, then why not two?' But Millicent was an intelligent person, and her demeanour said: I understand it all. And I remain in control. Of my husband. Of my child. Of the situation. As for Henry, he had not abdicated his rights, such as they were. His eyes did not fail to inform Sarah that they would be parting tomorrow, and that he remembered it.

The 'pot luck' turned out to be braised pheasant, and its accom- paniments, which presented problems for Joseph. Susan and Mary offered him bits of this and that to make up for this unknown meat which he was refusing to eat. The child was wildly excited, out of control, enjoying being the centre of attention.

Millicent commanded her husband, 'Give him your potatoes.'

Henry at once put his two potatoes on his son's plate.

'But we aren't short of potatoes,' Elizabeth protested.

'Give him your water,' said Millicent to Henry. Henry put his glass of water before Joseph, but hastily swallowed some wine, mak- ing a point.

Taking the roll from Henry's side plate, Millicent buttered it, spread it with red-currant jelly from Henry's plate, and presented the roll to the child. Joseph held his hands around the pile of food on his plate and laughed and yelled, his face red, his eyes wild, wickedly full of enjoyment.

Elizabeth indicated with her eyes that Henry should help himself to more food, but Henry shook his head and pushed his plate away. There was pheasant on it, which Millicent ate, reaching across with her fork to take up mouthful after mouthful, though there was pheasant on her own plate. Then she calmly ate her way through her own food. Henry was again pale and dejected, but when he looked over at his son, his face went soft with love. He smiled at Sarah, his eyes full of tears.

Joseph stood on his chair and began running a small lorry over the cloth. Millicent said to Henry, 'You take him.'

Henry obediently walked around the end of the table behind his wife, lifted his son, but, instead of returning to his seat, sat down in the chair near Sarah. The child leaned over, patted her hair, and ran the lorry up and down her arm.

Stephen, Elizabeth, and Norah sat watching, and vibrated together gently in disapproval. It is safe to say that the three boys had never, ever, been indulged in this way. And where were they? Off in the fields somewhere, or upstairs, and when the performance began they would eat their supper in the kitchen with Alison and Shirley. There would be gales of giggles, all kinds of fun, and treats from the dishes filled with cakes and pastries for the audience. Perhaps they were in the kitchen already? Alison and Shirley came in to remove the plates, and they were flushed, with a look of suppressing laughter. They set puddings on the sideboard and went out. From the kitchen, as the door closed, 'Oh, you're naughty . . .' The guests were invited to help themselves. Millicent got up and served herself, her husband, and her son. She set two plates in front of Henry and Joseph. It was a light creamy pudding from a seventeenth-century recipe, a speciality of Norah's. While Jean-Pierre served himself and

Mary, demanding to be given the recipe to take to his wife, the child spooned up his pudding with cries of pleasure. When his own plate was empty he pulled his father's plate towards him, with a wicked look. Millicent, not looking at Henry, took away the child's empty plate and pushed Henry's in its place. Joseph ate up his father's pudding. Millicent ate her pudding. She did this thoughtfully and calmly, not looking at anyone.

Only just audible, as it were offstage, it was as if someone laughed—a wild, anarchic, derisive, sceptical laugh—and against such forces of disorder a young American woman humbly but firmly asserted the rights of civilization with 'Henry, take Joseph up to bed, see that he cleans his teeth, and say good night to him before you go to the performance.'

Outside, people were streaming into the theatre. Word had got around, and music lovers and theatre lovers alike were prepared, as in Belles Rivières, to stand several deep to watch. Afterwards they stood in lines to congratulate Elizabeth and Stephen.

Then it was proposed that they should all drive to where an inn served drinks on lawns sloping to a river. Millicent said she would like to go. Everyone waited to see if she would command Henry to stay with the child, who was too excited to sleep, but Henry walked with Joseph in his arms to the car, handed the child in to his wife, and they joined the procession of cars that were filled with the company, their friends, and—by now—the friends of friends.

On darkening grass slopes overwatched by ancient trees, they sat about drinking, while Jean-Pierre exclaimed about the gentle beauties of England. For he was from the south, had never lived further north than Lyons, and this was the first time he had been introduced to the subtle charms of a northern summer. At last Joseph fell asleep, and was wrapped in his father's jacket, safe in his father's arms. Sarah had put herself a long way from Henry, near to Stephen, who had Susan next to him. Susan had just heard that Stephen was leaving tomorrow, did not know when he would return. 'Probably not till the end of the run,' he remarked. Her eyes were red. Tears were filling them as often as tears filled Sarah's and Henry's and, so it had become evident, Mary's and Jean-Pierre's. But Henry had his face turned away and was staring over the riverside lawns through the thickening dusk. And then the night came down and they were enclosed in its mercies.

Back at the house, Sarah confirmed with Jean-Pierre that an early start would suit her. She said goodbye to everyone she would not be seeing in London. There were many hopeful cries of 'See you next year in Belles Rivières'—which pleased Jean-Pierre. 'Because the real *Julie Vairon* has to be in France. I must say it—it is not the same thing here.'

And he was absolutely right: everyone agreed.

Henry went upstairs with the child in his arms, looking neither to the right nor to the left.

Sarah hurried to her room to put an end to the goodbyes. She did not sleep. In the early morning she crept down the stairs, and there was Jean-Pierre waiting on the steps, watching thrushes and blackbirds busy on the lawns. They walked to the car park, while the leaden hand tightened around her heart. As they drove off she looked back and saw Henry on the steps, looking after her. He was alone. The last sight she would have of him was his white face, his bitter, burning black eyes.

They drove fast, but not so fast that, approaching a lay-by, Sarah did not see a group of youngsters standing around a shabby van that had on its side an amateur scrawl in red paint, *Tea and Snacks*. She asked Jean-Pierre to stop. She said, 'I won't be a minute,' and got out, slamming the car door to attract attention. Joyce, Betty, the unknown youth, who seemed even more pale and ill in this strong sunlight, and half a dozen others all turned to watch her approach. Sarah could not have felt more absurd, arriving in that sleek car from the world of interesting work, success, money. Joyce greeted her with her predictable hilarious smile, as if good news was her portion in life and her Auntie Sarah its reliable purveyor. Betty smelled sour even at several paces away and seemed hung over, with red eyes and a sick brave look. Sarah felt two strong conflicting impulses: one to take her in her arms, like a child; the other to shake her hard. The wretched youth stood blinking, his eyes too weak for this sunlight.

'Well, Joyce,' enquired Sarah briskly, 'are you all right?'

'Oh, lovely, thank you, how lovely to see you,' enthused Joyce.

'Do you want a lift back to town?'

'But there are lots of us.'

A bitter wouldn't-you-know-it smile appeared on Betty's face and on other faces too, as Sarah said, 'We weren't offering a lift to everyone; there wouldn't be room.'

'Oh no, Sarah, we'll stay together.'

'Then give me a ring,' said Sarah, but after she had gone a few paces, she returned to give Joyce money, thinking, What use is twenty pounds to a girl who tried to steal three thousand? Joyce stood there with the notes in her hand, until Betty took them from her, with a housewifely air.

'That one there with the pretty hair is my niece,' said Sarah as they roared off, thinking it was as well he did not know she had been offering lifts on his behalf.

'Sarah, I must say it is surprising to see you with such people.'

'I take it you have no disreputable relations?'

His half-shrug insisted that in France things were better ordered, but after a moment he said with a sigh that his younger brother, aged sixteen, was giving their poor mother problems.

'Drugs?'

'I think so. But so far not the very bad ones.'

'Well, good luck, then.'

'Good luck is what we all need,' said Jean-Pierre, acknowledging the times we live in.

She went straight to the theatre. In the office, she found the reviews from the dailies. Too soon for the weeklies. 'She Was Poor but She Was Honest'—as a heading—twice. 'An exotic setting does not conceal . . .' 'Martinique is obviously just the place for a package holiday.' 'As a feminist I must protest . . .'

In the afternoon there was the meeting to decide the future. They were all there. Mary Ford had come from Oxfordshire by train. Roy had interrupted his leave to come. He remarked that his wife said she had had enough of men to last her a lifetime, but on the whole he felt confident she would take him back, for the sake of the child. Patrick was there, and Sonia, and Jean-Pierre and, at the last minute, Stephen.

In the few weeks since the end of the run in France, Jean-Pierre had done a lot of work. He was presenting them with plans, not possibilities. *Julie Vairon* would be put on next year for the two main months of the tourist season, July and August, but there was talk of beginning earlier, in June. He had checked the availability of Henry, Bill, Molly, Susan, Andrew. Henry was the most important and would be free. Bill would not, a pity, since he was more right for the part than the new Paul. Both Molly and Susan would be available, and that left them with a difficult choice. If they wanted the same musicians, they must be engaged now. The singers must be approached at once: they were perhaps the most important element. Andrew was engaged for a film. A pity. It would be hard to find such a good Rémy.

And now he had to tell them something he was afraid they wouldn't like. The town authorities had already agreed that a large stadium, to hold two thousand people, would be built in the woods around Julie's old house. If that shell could be called a house. No, he must insist they listen to him: he knew it didn't sound well, but that was only because the idea was new to them. He himself had had difficulties to start with.

'You are going to cut down trees?' asked Mary.

'Only nine or ten trees need to be cut. They are not very beautiful trees.'

And now there was a silence, while Jean-Pierre, sure of himself and his plans, went to stand tactfully at the window, his back to them, while they looked at each other: that is, the Founding Four did. Patrick had an air of holding a good deal back. Sonia had not been to Belles Rivières. Stephen seemed to be reserving judgement.

In that silence a good many things were acknowledged. Jean-Pierre and the town authorities had every right to decide what to do with the town's chief asset. The English really had no right to say a word. Yes, they had had the original idea, but that was not something they could stake a claim on for long. Anyway, it was no one's fault—as usual. The gods of tourism were to blame.

Jean-Pierre turned around and said, 'We know it is a shock. It is not the most attractive thing that could happen—I am speaking for myself now. But put yourselves in our place. *Julie* will bring prosperity to the whole region.'

'It is surely not a region of France that lacks visitors,' said Sarah.

'No, that is true. But Belles Rivières is just a little town. It has nothing else, only *Julie*. There will be new hotels and restaurants—they are being planned already. And this will affect all the towns of the area.'

'You haven't said anything about the language,' said Stephen. Of all of them, he must be the most affected by the news of the destruction of the original *Julie Vairon*—but only Sarah could know that.

'Of course that was discussed. For a while we decided to go back to the French, but we changed our minds. This will sound absurd, but we thought it might even bring bad luck. Julie has been so lucky. To change her completely . . . but there was the other reason, and that is more important. Most of the tourists in our part of France in summer are English-speaking. And that decided it.'

He waited, but no one said anything.

'And now I must leave you all. I must catch my plane.'

'Next year in Belles Rivières,' said Roy, for this joke seemed likely to stay, and Mary and Jean-Pierre looked at each other, and

Sarah was reminded of Henry's wretched face that morning as she left.

'Oh no, we must discuss it all before that. I hope to see you all . . . Sarah . . . Stephen . . . and you, Mary . . .' He nodded at Patrick, and it occurred to them that since Patrick had scarcely been in Belle-Rivières, that nod, with a special smile, was carrying more meaning than they knew the reason for. And Patrick was in fact looking guilty. 'All of you, we will fix a meeting and we will go through everything. I shall telephone Benjamin when I get to my office. Stephen—it would be a sadness for us if you decided to withdraw.' That meant that if Stephen did, there would be other willing angels.

Jean-Pierre left an atmosphere of mourning. The audiences filling the new stadium next year and—presumably—succeeding years would be enjoying successful, fashionable theatre, but only those people who had been there the first year—still this year—would know how rare a bird *Julie* had been, a magically perfect event that had seemed at its beginnings no more promising than a hundred others, had gathered substance and shape in what it was easy to believe was a series of mere lucky chances, one after the other, blown together by the winds of heaven, and then . . . but there is only one thing to do at the vanishing away of a wonder: put a clamp on your heart.

And it was only the theatre, after all.

'It's only the theatre,' said Mary, ending their silence and sounding miserable.

Now, finally, they had to decide whether to put *Julie Vairon* on in London. But it seemed this decision had already been made, for they hardly discussed it.

'Now,' said Sarah to Patrick, 'let's have it.'

Patrick stood before them, grinning. Full of affection, yes, but fuller of a cheeky guiltiness.

'Sarah . . . guess what . . . you'll never guess . . . you'll have to shoot yourself . . . well, shoot me, then. . . . We can't have victim heroines any more—remember? Do you remember? Well . . .'. And here he hesitated on the brink, gave Sonia a look of comic despair, plunged on, 'How do you like the idea of a musical?'

'A musical!' protested Stephen.

'Oh, don't tell me,' said Roy, in a fury. 'There's this pathetic little half-caste from Martinique who falls in love with the handsome lieutenant. He ditches her. She earns her living doing the can-can in Cannes. There she is seen by the patrician Rémy—'

'Too complicated,' said Patrick airily.

'No Rémy?' said Stephen.

'No Rémy. She has a child by Paul. She puts her in a convent with the nuns. Julie earns her living as a singer. The master printer wants to make an honest woman of her—'

'But she commits suicide because of . . . ?' enquired Sarah.

'Because she knows the townspeople will never forgive her, or forgive him for marrying her. If he marries her she will ruin his life. There's a great scene where the citizens sing they will boycott his business and bring him to bankruptcy. They won't have that whore Julie. She leaves a suicide note: Remember my Minou! She flings herself under a train. Just like you know who. Last scene: the master printer and Minou, already a nubile nymph sought in marriage by a handsome young lieutenant.'

'You're joking,' said Stephen.

'He's not joking,' said Sonia, sounding huffy. From this it could be seen she was involved with this musical.

'I'm not joking,' said Patrick. 'The libretto is written.'

'You've written it?'

'I've written it.'

'Is she allowed any intelligence?' asked Roy.

'Of course not,' said Sarah.

'I expected you and Stephen to be much more cross than you are,' said Patrick, obviously disappointed.

'Well,' said Stephen, 'I'm off.'

'Well,' said Sarah, also getting up, 'when is this masterpiece going to be put on?'

'We have to get the music written,' said Sonia.

'Not Julie's?' asked Mary.

'We are thinking of using one of the troubadour songs as a theme song. Not the words, of course. You know. "If this song of mine is a sad one . . ." It's a torch song, really.'

'So what words?' enquired Sarah.

Mary said, 'I love you, I love you.'

'Very good,' said Patrick. 'Brilliant. All right. Sneer if you like. It's possible they'll première it in Belles Rivières the year after next.'

'The bad will drive out the good,' remarked Stephen. 'It always does.'

'Oh thanks, thanks a lot,' said Patrick.

'Let's wait and see,' said Mary. 'They aren't going to let our *Julie* go if it's successful next year.'

'Honestly,' said Sonia, 'I don't think you people should start panicking. It hasn't happened yet.'

'No, but it's going to,' said Patrick. 'And there's something else. My *Julie*'s going to be called *The Lucky Piece* . . . no, wait—I found it by chance. The lucky piece is early-nineteenth-century slang. It means the child of a mistress who has been left well set up by her boyfriends. Well, no one could say that Julie's mother wasn't living in clover.'

The meeting ended early, and a long sunlit evening lay ahead. Stephen and Sarah walked for a while in Regent's Park. Stephen said he was going to visit his brother in Shropshire. After that he might visit friends in Wales. She recognized his need to move. If it were not that she had so much to do in the theatre, she would be buying an aeroplane ticket to almost anywhere.

There was no way of putting off what faced her. She sat and thought how already the family would be speeding along French roads that were dusty and burned by this summer's sun. As soon as the car stopped, the little boy would be in his father's arms. In fact one could be sure that during the three weeks they were in France, whenever the car was not actually in motion, Joseph would be held by Henry. Meanwhile her body sent inconsistent messages. For instance, that sensation of need in the hollow of her left shoulder demanded that a head should lie there . . . was it Henry's head? Often it seemed to her it was an infant newly born, and naked, a soft hot nakedness, and her hand pressing it close protected a helpless-ness much greater than could be encompassed by this one small creature. An infinite vulnerability lay there: Sarah herself, who was both infant and what sheltered the infant. When a hot wanting woke Sarah from a dream she knew had been about Henry, the face that dazzled behind her lids was Joseph's, a bright cheeky greedy smile announcing that it would grab everything it could. And then, an intimate and loving smile—Henry's, and both of these wraiths disappeared as her hand went to the soft hollow, and she was filled with a wild and cherishing love.

In her diary, page after page was filled with entries like 'Emptiness.' 'Pain.' 'It is such a *weight*—I can't carry it.' 'Wild grief.' 'Storms of longing.' 'When will it end?' 'I can't stand this pain.' 'My heart hurts so much.' 'It *hurts*.'

To whom was she writing these messages like letters in bottles entrusted to the sea? No one would read them. And if someone did, the words would make sense only if this someone had experienced this pain, this grief. For as she herself looked at the words pain, grief, anguish, and so forth, they were words on a page and she had to fill them with the emotions they represented. Why then put them on a page at all? It occurred to her she was engaged in that occupa-tion common to (even diagnostic of?) our times: she was bearing witness.

She stopped writing 'I did not know this degree of misery could exist,' and her diary reverted to: 'Worked with Sonia and Patrick all day on the costumes.' 'Worked with Mary.' 'Mary says she saw Sonia and Roger Stent having dinner together in The Pelican. Sonia doesn't know we know.' 'Patrick has gone to visit Jean-Pierre about *The Lucky Piece.*' 'Sonia and I worked all day on . . .'

In fact she was doing half the work she usually did. She woke in the morning with a groan and often sank back into . . . if it was a landscape of grief, then at least it was not the same as the one she inhabited awake. If at home, she might sleep all afternoon, work a little, be asleep by ten. Sometimes she dragged herself out of bed in the morning and got back into it by mid-morning. Normally she slept lightly, with pleasure, her dreams an entertainment and often a source of information. Now she crawled into sleep which was both a refuge and a threat, to get rid of the pain—a physical anguish—in her heart.

She was also observing her symptoms with curiosity, none of them—surely?—necessarily a symptom of love.

Worst of all, she was bad-tempered, might snap and snarl suddenly, without warning, as if she only just managed an even keel, but the slightest demand, or even a too-loud voice, was enough to tip her over. She wanted to make unkind and sarcastic remarks. Normally not particularly critical, she was critical of everything.

Unpleasant characteristics she believed long outgrown came back. She spoke loudly in public places in a boastful way, for the benefit of strangers whose opinions did not matter to her.

She actually had to stop herself boasting of past loves to Mary, but had said enough to embarrass both: Mary, whose acute, quick look told Sarah that her condition was being understood. One day Mary remarked, apparently about Roy, who was having a difficult time with his wife and was bad-tempered and morose, 'What we forget is, people know much more about us than we like, and forgive us much more.' Was this a plea for herself?

Music still affected Sarah too strongly. She found herself switching off music on the radio, going out of the theatre when they were doing rehearsals and there was music, closing a window if music floated towards her down the street, because even a banal and silly tune could make her cry, or double up in pain. A workman reslating the roof of the house next to hers burst into the torch song from *Julie*, or, rather, *The Lucky Piece*—the song had taken wings because of a radio programme. He was sending it up, straddling the house ridge, arms extended, like an opera singer accepting applause, while his mate, leaning against a chimney, clapped—and Sarah's hands flew of their own accord to cover her ears. She felt the sounds were poisoning her.

From the moment she woke, daydreams had to be pushed away, dreams like drugs. Then, at last succumbing, she could spend hours in day-dreams, like an adolescent.

She was greedy for sweet things, wanted to eat, had to stop herself if she didn't want to buy a complete new wardrobe.

Words that had the remotest connection with love, romance, passion, she believed twisted the same nerve as that weakened by music, so that phrases or words or stories she normally would have found stupid brought tears to her eyes. When she was able to read at all—for it was hard to concentrate—she nervously watched for them, these places on the page, able to see them coming half a page before, and she skipped them, forcing her eyes to bypass or neutralize them.

She bought beauty products which a sense of the ridiculous forbade her to use. She even thought of having her face lifted—an idea that in her normal condition could only make her smile.

She began to make a blouse, of a kind she had not worn for years, but left it unfinished.

Sometimes a conversation, apparently without any intention by her, acquired sexual undertones, so that every word of an exchange could be interpreted obscenely.

But worst of all was her irritability; she knew if she could not outlive it, she was heading straight towards the paranoia, the rages, the bitterness, of disappointed old age.

Stephen cut short his visits and came to London to see Sarah. They walked about and around streets and parks and even went to the theatre. They left some comedy at the first interval, saying that normally they would have enjoyed it.

Susan had written to him. It was a love letter that offered everything. 'I shall never love anyone as I love you.'

'I swear it's that damned music,' said Sarah.

'I was hoping it was because of my intrinsic qualities. But I suppose it does make things easier to stick a label on them.'

This was the same need to snap and snarl that so often possessed Sarah.

'Sorry,' said Stephen, 'I simply don't recognize myself.'

A week later she telephoned him at his home and at first thought she had got the wrong number and had reached someone whom she had awakened. She could hear breathing, and then a mumbling or muttering which could be his voice, and she said, 'Stephen?' Silence, and more difficult breathing, and he said, or rather slurred, her name. 'Sarah . . . Sarah?' 'Stephen, are you ill? Shall I come?' He did not answer. She went on talking, even pleading, urging, for a long time, but while he did not put down the receiver, he did not answer. She was talking into silence, and her own voice was sounding ridiculous, because she was making the reassuring optimistic remarks that always need an interlocutor similarly cheerful to carry conviction. At last she felt he was not listening. Perhaps he had even gone to sleep, or walked away. Now she was full of panic, like a bird trapped in a room. She had the number of the telephone in the kitchen at Queen's Gift, used for domestic matters, but there was no reply. She sat for a while in indecision, feeling that she ought to go to him at once, but telling herself that if he had wanted her to come he would have said so. Besides, why did she always assume he had no one else to turn to? In the end she took a taxi to Paddington, then the first possible train, then a taxi to the house. She asked to be put down outside the gates, for her sudden uninvited appearance at the house itself would seem too dramatic. The great gates had been newly painted glossy black with gold touches, like the 'highlights' hairdressers use to enliven a hair-do. She went in through an unobtrusive little door in a brick arch at the side. This was like an allegory of something, but she could not think what. In her present condition, signs and symbols, portents and presages and omens, comparisons apt and silly, formed themselves out of a voice overheard in the street, a dog barking, a glass slipping out of her hand and smashing loudly on a hard surface. Her irritation at this unwanted and insipid commentary on everything she did contributed to her bad temper. Now her heart was racing, for she was possessed with the need to hurry, while she felt her trip here to be absurd. There seemed to be no one about. Posters for *Ariadne on Naxos* were everywhere, and Julie's face was nowhere. Of course: they were trying out this opera. A small cast and delicious music, Elizabeth said. Where was Elizabeth? Not in the vegetable garden, nor with the horses, nor anywhere near the house. And what would Sarah say when she did find her? 'Look, Elizabeth, I had to come, I was worried about Stephen.' (I am worried about your husband.) Elizabeth must at least have noticed that Stephen was—well, what was he at this moment? Worse: he was much worse. After wandering about for some minutes, feeling like a thief or at least an intruder, she saw Stephen sitting on a bench by himself, in full sunlight. He sat hunched, legs apart, hands loosely dangling and folded between them, like tools he had forgotten to put away. His head was lowered, and his face was dripping sweat. A hundred yards away stood the great ash tree, James's friend. Under it was a bench, in deep shade. She sat down by him and said, 'Stephen . . .' No response at all. Right, she thought, this is it: I know this one, I've seen it before. This is the real thing, the Big D (as its victims jocularly call it when not in its power), it is the authentic hallmarked one-hundred-percent depression: he's gone over the edge. 'Stephen, it's Sarah.' After a long time, at least a minute, he lifted his head, and she found herself the object of—no, not an inspection, or even a recognition. It was a defensive look. 'Stephen, I've come because I'm worried about you.' His eyes lowered themselves, and he sat staring at the ground. After another interval, he said, or mumbled, in a hurried swallowing way, 'No use, Sarah, no good.' He was occupied deep within himself, he was busy with an inner landscape, and did not have the energy for the outside world. She knew this because she sometimes underwent a much less total version of this condition. She was absent-minded, heard words long after they were spoken, felt them as an intrusion, had to force herself to pay attention, and then spoke hurriedly to get the irrelevance over with. At meetings at The Green Bird, in conversations with colleagues, she had to make herself come up out of depths of an inner preoccupation with pain actually to hear what they said, then frame words appropriate for an answer. But at least she could do it, and she was getting better. Stephen's state was worse by far than anything she herself had known, and the panic she felt deepened.

What should she do? As a beginning, get him into the shade. She said, 'Stephen, get up, you must get out of the sun.' He seemed surprised, but her hand at his elbow prompted him up and then, slowly, to the cool under the ash tree. His clothes were soaked with sweat.

What he needed was someone to sit by him all day and all night, bring him cups of this and that, cool drinks, tea, a sandwich of which he might perhaps eat one mouthful, while she—or someone—talked, saying anything to remind him he was in a world with other people in it, and these people did not all live in a world of suffering. No one performed this service for her, but then she was not and never had been anything like as ill as he was now. Her mind approached carefully, and in controlled terror, the thought that if the pain she felt was a minor thing compared to what he felt, then what he felt must be unendurable. For she had often thought she could not bear what she felt.

She went on sitting there beside him. She wiped the sweat off his face. She felt his hands to make sure he was not now chilled by the coolness under the tree. Sometimes she said, 'Stephen, it's Sarah.' She made casual and even random remarks, trying to keep his exterior landscape in place: 'Look, the horses are racing each other in that field.' 'That's going to be a pretty good crop of apples.' He did not look at her or respond. Not a hundred yards away was where she had seen him walking and talking with the neighbour Joshua. Now, that was Stephen, surely? That was what he was? A competent and serious man in command of his life? Again her emotions reversed, and she felt ridiculous being here at all.

After a couple of hours she said, 'Stephen, I'm going to get you a drink.' She went to the kitchen, directed there by women's voices. Shirley and Alison were making pastry tartlets for that evening's *Ariadne on Naxos.* They wore scarlet plastic aprons too small for their ample bodies. These two amiable, infinitely wholesome and reassuring women worked on either side of a table where heaps of flour, dishes full of eggs, and bowls of butter cubed into ice water made a scene of plenty, and they were giggling because Shirley had flour on her cheek, and Alison, trying to wipe it off, had brushed it onto Shirley's plump golden plait.

'Oh, sorry, Mrs Durham,' said Shirley. 'We're just being silly today.'

'I'd like to take Mr Ellington-Smith a drink,' said Sarah.

'All right. What? Orange juice? Apple juice? Pineapple juice? James likes that. Mango juice—I like that.' And Shirley broke again into giggles.

'Oh, Shirl,' said Alison, 'I'm going to lock you up if no one else does. Help yourself, Mrs Durham. It's all in the big fridge.'

Sarah chose orange juice, thinking vitamin C was good for depression.

'Do you know where Mrs Ellington-Smith is?'

'She and Norah were around not long ago. I think they went upstairs.'

As Sarah left she heard the two young women start up again: giggles and teasing. It occurred to Sarah she was thinking of them as if they were two new-laid free-range eggs; and that she didn't want to know if one was a single parent and the other looked after an invalid mother.

Stephen had not moved a muscle. She said to him, 'Stephen, please drink this. You've got to drink in this weather.' She set the glass down on the bench, but he did not take it; she held it to his lips, but he did not drink.

She said, 'I'm going off for a little, but I'll be back.' She had to find Elizabeth. If not her, then Norah. It was mid-afternoon. She went up the steps at the front of the house, where Henry had stood looking after her on that last morning, and into the hall, and then into the room where the company had had their buffet meals, and through the room where the family ate informal meals, and then into the back part of the house, not to the main staircase, but the one where she had seen Stephen's James stand to gaze out at the tree as if it were a friend. She went on up past that landing to a room that Elizabeth used as an office. She had to force herself to knock, because she was afraid of Elizabeth: not her anger, but her incomprehension. And what was she, Sarah, going to say? 'I'm worried about Stephen—you know, your husband.' And what would Elizabeth say? 'Thank you *so* much, Sarah. It *is* kind of you.'

No reply. She heard voices. Yes, they were Elizabeth's and Norah's voices. It occurred to her that not only Elizabeth's office but her sitting room and her and Norah's bedroom were up here. She had never been into these rooms. There was a wide corridor with rooms off it, a pleasant corridor with old-fashioned floral wallpaper.

It was dimly lit from a skylight and from the tall window halfway up, or down, the stairs. The scene was domestic, intimate.

She stopped halfway along the corridor. The strength was going from her legs. She leaned against the wall. Elizabeth and Norah were laughing. There was a silence, which Sarah was hearing as Stephen might, then more laughter, loud and conspiratorial, and the two voices were talking, and they went on in an intimate murmur, not from the office, or the sitting room, but from the bedroom. It was no use saying that Elizabeth and Norah often laughed, that women like laughing and make occasions and excuses to laugh, that often these two seemed like schoolgirls, enjoying babyish jokes. They laughed again. A small cold horror was invading Sarah, because she was hearing it through Stephen's ears. It sounded suggestive and ignorant and even cruel. But of course they were not laughing at Stephen. They were probably laughing at some small silly thing. They lay in each other's arms on the top of the covers, because of this hot afternoon, or side by side, and they laughed as the two women downstairs giggled at the flour on Shirley's hair. But the laughter hurt, squeezed her heart, as if it were her they mocked . . . if so, fair enough; she was a traditional figure of fun. Why did she take it for granted they did not ridicule Stephen? Perhaps they did. Stephen had said he avoided this part of the house when he knew Elizabeth and Norah were up here.

They must not, absolutely must not, find her here. She crept down the stairs. She stood on the back steps, making and discarding plans, such as that she would put Stephen into a taxi and take him back to London. She walked slowly through the heat towards the ash tree. When she turned a corner, a brick pillar tapestried with variegated ivy, she saw the empty bench and the untouched orange juice, where she had put it.

She called once—'Stephen'—in a low voice. Then she went fast, half running, along paths, past fields, looking for him, thinking, I'll see him now . . . I'll see him when I get to that tree. But the benches they had sat on were all empty, and the glade where the shooting lesson had gone on did not now have a post sticking up in the middle. It was only a sunny hollow patched with shade from old trees. It was much later than she had thought, getting on for five. Soon the evening's audience would start arriving. She thought she might write notes for Elizabeth and Norah and leave them with the girls in the kitchen. Like this?: Dear Elizabeth, I came down because I was worried about Stephen. Perhaps you should . . . Or: Dear Norah, please don't be surprised I am approaching you and not Elizabeth, but I cannot help feeling that she . . .

In the end she walked out through the big gates, then along the road, caught a bus and then a train home.

That night she rang Stephen. Never had she felt more ridiculous and she had to force herself to do it. It was because on the one hand there were all those acres, the house, his life, his wife; there were his brothers and friends everywhere, his children, their schools, where he had himself been . . . against this mesh, this web, this spread and proliferation of responsibilities and privileges, she had to offer only: let me bring you here and look after you. But this sensible offer did not get made, because when he answered his voice sounded normal. It was slow, certainly, but he did not mumble, or lapse into interminable silences. He understood what she was saying and assured her that he would look after himself. 'I know you were here today. Did you come to visit me? If I was rude, I am sorry.' She told herself, Perhaps I am exaggerating it all.

Two days later Norah rang to say she was telephoning for Elizabeth: Stephen had killed himself, making it seem an accident while shooting rabbits. 'The rabbits are very bad again, you know. They got into the new garden—the Elizabethan garden—and ate everything to the ground.'

Sarah went down for the funeral service, which was in the local church. Several hundred people crowded church and churchyard. It occurred to her that Stephen and she had never discussed what they did or did not believe, or what he felt about religion, but this scene was certainly in key with what he was: the old church—eleventh century, some of it—the Church of England funeral service, these country-living people, some of whose names were on the church walls and the gravestones.

She went back to the house for the usual drinks and sandwiches. Every room she went into was crammed, including the kitchen, where Shirley and Alison were at work, both tear-stained. She glimpsed the three boys—pale and sick-looking—across a room, with Norah, but otherwise did not see one face she knew. There was a heavy, gloomy, and even irritable atmosphere. Let's get this over with. Condemnation. These people had passed judgement on Stephen and found him guilty. Sarah was accusing them of letting him down. She did not like them, or what she saw of them today. These are people—that is, the English upper classes—at their best at balls, formal occasions, festivals, when dressed in ball gowns and tiaras, the men handsome in their uniforms and their rows of medals and orders. But funerals are not their talent. They wore clumsy dark clothes and were graceless and uncomfortable in them.

When the crowds began to thin, Elizabeth asked Sarah into a gloomy room that had a billiard table in it and, on the walls, every kind of weapon, from pikes and arquebuses to World War I revolvers. Elizabeth stood with her back to racks holding shotguns and rifles, with a glass of whisky in her hand. She looked heavy and commonplace in her black. She probably kept it at the back of a cupboard just for funerals.

She was blazing with anger, her cheeks scarlet, her swollen eyes glittering.

'Do sit down, Sarah,' she commanded, sitting down herself and at once getting up again. 'I really am sorry. You are such a cool and collected person. . . .' She did not say this as if she thought these were qualities to be admired.

'Well, actually I am not.'

'I'm not saying you're not upset about Stephen. I know you were fond of each other. Oh, don't think I mind. No, I don't mind about all that. I never did. What I mind is—it's the utter damnable irresponsibility of it.' Here she collapsed into a chair and energetically blew her nose, wiped her eyes and then her cheeks. But it was no good; the drops that scattered everywhere were distillations of pure rage. 'While the boys are young they'll believe it was an accident. But they are already wondering, I'm sure. It's very bad for children, this kind of thing.' Again she blew her nose. 'Oh, damn it.' She took out a comb, a compact, lipstick, from a black leather handbag as solid as a saddle and good for many funerals yet. She began to make up her face, but tears oozed again, and she gave up. 'We had an agreement. We made promises to each other. This place is a *partnership*.'

While it did not seem that Elizabeth needed more than a listener, Sarah attempted, 'But, Elizabeth, don't you see? He wasn't himself.'

'Of course I see it, but . . .' Here she sat silent, sighing, contemplating (for the first time in this commonsensical life of hers?) the possibility that people could be in states of mind where they were not themselves: it was not a mere figure of speech.

From outside came the sound of cars driving away, the slamming of car doors, the gravel crunching under feet, loud and cheerful voices. 'See you next week.' 'Will you be at Dolly's?'

'What am I going to do now? Oh yes, I know what you are thinking—that I have Norah. Yes, I do have Norah, and thank God for that. But I can't run this place all by myself, I can't.' And now, overtaken by what sounded like incredulity, she let out a yelp, and down flooded the tears. 'I'm not saying I am going to give up; *I* don't believe in reneging on responsibility. Oh bloody hell, I can't stop crying. I'm so angry, Sarah, I'm so angry I could . . .'

Sarah carefully asked, 'Have *you* never found it all too much of a good thing?' Meaning our old friend life, and so Elizabeth understood her.

'Of course I have. Who doesn't? Who doesn't think it's just a bloody farce sometimes? But you simply don't renege. And he did.' And with this, putting behind her the possibility—at least for this time—of understanding the country where pain is so much a cruel king that his subjects would do anything at all to escape, she jumped up, saying, 'This isn't doing any good. What I wanted to say is that I'll keep on all Stephen's commitments—financial, I mean. I am sure he liked your lot more than the other things we do. I'm not sure his preoccupation with Julie—you know, as a person—was always healthy. I don't know if you knew it, but he was really obsessed with the story. I believe that suicides should simply be ignored, not made a fuss of in operas and plays and all that kind of thing. They are a bad example to everyone. Most people are really very weak-minded. One should remember that.' Here she pulled a comb through her hair and then with both hands tried to push the lank—because soaked with tears—locks into place. She gave up and wiped her face with fresh tissues. This time the tears did not spring forth again. 'Sorry about all this, Sarah. I'll send you Stephen's Julie stuff when I've sorted everything out. I suppose that museum should have it. But you decide. And there's something he left for you. No, I haven't looked at it. I saw the first page and that was enough. I don't have much time for that morbid kind of thing.' She handed Sarah a red exercise book, of the kind children use, and strode purposefully out of the room.

The exercise book had stuck on it a white label, and on that was a pencil scribble: *This is for Sarah Durham.*

The first entry was the date of the first performance of Julie's music at Queen's Gift in June. Day after day there were entries of single comments, thus: 'I didn't know it was possible to feel like this.' 'This longing is like a poison.' 'I think I must be very ill.' 'My heart is so heavy I can hardly carry it around.' 'Surely the word *longing* isn't right for this degree of longing.' 'I understand what it means to be ill with love.' '*My heart hurts, it hurts.*'

The handwriting grew progressively worse. Some entries were nearly illegible. The last entries were scribbled in formless writing, the end of the words straight lines, like the graphs of brain waves, spiky and full of life, but then, as life runs out, a long line going on and on.

The cries from the country of grief are impersonal. I am lonely. I am so unhappy. I love you. I want you. I am sick with love. I am dying of a broken heart. *I can't endure this non-life. I can't endure this desert.*

They are like bird calls: this is a blackbird, a gull, a crow, a thrush. Or like the songs of Anon:

> *An Englishman once loved a girl,*
> *Oh woe, oh woe . . .*
> *(Or Ob-la-da, ob-la-di!)*
> *He heard her singing, lost his head,*
> *She was a French girl, wild and free,*
> *Oh ob-la-da, oh ob-la-di.*
> *They told him she was dead.*
> *Oh woe. Et cetera.*

In November, Benjamin came to London on business, making it clear that he was staying for longer than necessary, so as to see Sarah. This was when she hit the peak, or the gulfs, of grief and did not have much energy for anything but a struggle with an enemy so strong she was tempted to do as Stephen had done, simply because she couldn't stand the pain of it. 'I'm not good at pain,' he had said. Well, she wasn't good at it either. She didn't believe in it. What was it for? She read entries in his red exercise book again, those banal words, because her own diary was too dangerous, and asked, with him: What is it that aches? Why should one's physical heart ache? What is this burden I am carrying? It feels like a heavy stone on my heart. Why does it? Oh God.

The year continuing mild, they walked a good deal around London and the parks, often following paths she had known with Stephen. Sometimes she felt she was walking with two men, not one. Stephen certainly was not dead for her, because she seemed to feel his presence close to her—better be careful, look what it had led to with him: did she really want to be possessed by a ghost, in the same way he was? When Stephen was truly dead for her, would she then begin to grieve for him? Or was she grieving for him now? While preoccupied with these thoughts, she had agreeable if sometimes slow and absent-minded conversations with Benjamin. He was entertaining her still. Some of the 'projects' she was sure he invented there and then, though he presented them to her with an emphatic solemnity which was part of the joke.

'How about a van coming to your home full of materials or samples of materials? You know how they make you a suit in twenty-four hours in Hong Kong or Singapore? Well, you'd choose your material, give them something to copy, and you'd have it back in a day.'

'You'll make a fortune on that one, I promise you.'

'You're sure? Well, how about this. We are thinking about reviving Leamington Spa and Bath and Tunbridge Wells—we would add gyms and health clubs and health farms and this new cold water therapy. All it would need is for some VIP to make them fashionable again. The way your royal family did with the old spas.'

'That and a lot of money. You mean you can afford all that and your Kashmiri lake?'

'I must confess that we have decided the Kashmiri lake was a bit too much for us. Money is a bit tighter than it was.'

'But reviving all the spas in Britain—that's all right?'

'I believe in it,' he said. 'This is a downturn, that's all. I'm sure the markets'll pick up after Christmas.'

So the money men were talking in 1989, just before the new Slump, or, if you like, the Recession.

He told her, too, about his family. It was clear that between the two of them he and his wife made a good deal of money. His children, male and female, were in university and doing well. He showed photographs of them and of his house and of the Associated and Allied Banks of North California and South Oregon. He did this as if reminding himself, as well as her, of the value and worth of his life. Yet time had passed since he had observed her against the glamorous backdrops of Belles Rivières and Queen's Gift. So how did he see her now? As glamorous still, and her life here in London, which was humdrum and at the moment unbearably so, seemed to him as sophisticated and worldly as the life depicted in books of memoirs about the theatre. Which he said he was reading. Surely her flat must seem to him small, a poor thing compared to the big house he lived in? But her rooms were full of pictures, books, theatre memorabilia, photographs of people she knew as friends or acquaintances but whom he thought of as famous. How did he see her solitary and chaste way of living? He imagined a lover of many years' standing, and remarked that he envied him.

About Stephen's death he spoke angrily and disapprovingly. He could not understand why anyone who had so much could be willing to leave this world. She tried the word *depression* but saw that for him it was only a word, not more than when someone exclaims, 'Oh hell, I'm depressed today.' Suppose she told him, 'Stephen was living in despair for years' or 'He was in love with a dead woman'? These accurate statements would not leave her tongue. She could not say them to this sane, sensible, and serious man. Did that mean she did not see Stephen as sensible and serious? Yes, but sane, no. She contemplated the word *serious*. Whatever Benjamin was or was not, he was certainly serious. To be precise, humour, or the ambiguous, was not his gift. With him she was never on that frontier where attitudes can change themselves into their opposites, good and bad reversing themselves with a laugh. More than once she made the kind of joking remark she could share with Stephen, but had to say quickly, 'Sorry, I was only joking; no, I didn't mean it.'

Benjamin thought over—as was his way—what she had said about Stephen, and next day came back with 'But why did Stephen do that awful thing?'

Suddenly impatient, she said, 'Stephen died of a broken heart. There is such a thing, you know. Why it was broken in the first place—well, that is for the psychiatrists. But not everything is curable. The point is, he had been living with a broken heart and he couldn't stand it any longer.'

He could positively be heard thinking that broken hearts were not for serious people. 'I'm sorry, but I can't accept that.'

'That's only because you've never had a broken heart.' She knew he was hearing this as a flippant or frivolous remark.

After a while he said, stumbling over it, 'I believed that you and he . . . I think I told you I envied him.'

'No. We were friends.' She heard her voice shake. But went on, 'Believe me, that was all.'

All.

An acute look: he did not believe her. He thought it was a plucky lie. He put his arms around her. 'Poor Sarah,' he murmured into her hair. He laid his cheek against it and then kissed her cheek. She remembered another kiss and stood back, smiling. Smiling, he let her go. They were standing on a pavement. Early afternoon, but lights were coming on in the houses and talked directly to her heart of intimacy, of love. The trees in the square they stood in were wild and full of noisy wind, and underfoot was a thick layer of sycamore leaves, black-webbed and slippery, like cut-off ducks' feet. She thought, If I were to tell this man, even try to tell him, watering it down, making it less, what I've been feeling all the time since I first met him, he would walk quickly away from the lunatic.

They said goodbye, and she said, 'Next year in Belles Rivières.'

When he did not react, she asked, 'Did you ever see the film *Last Year at Marienbad*? It was about people who remembered different things about what happened the year before, and they were remembering possibilities, different parallel possibilities, too.'

He at once said, 'Believe me, Sarah, I shall never forget one single minute of anything that has happened when I've been with you—with you all.' He added, 'It's certainly an interesting idea. I'll get the video.'

'It's the same idea as the song "I remember it well."'

Here she was relieved when he laughed and said that he remembered it well.

It was about then that she got a letter from Andrew.

Dear Sarah,

I am in Arizona, making a film about a screwed-up cop but he has a heart of gold. What screwed him up? His childhood. I never told you about my childhood. It would be taking unfair advantage. Do I have a heart of gold? I have a heart.

I am living with my sister Sandra. She is my real sister from my real mother. She has left her husband, my good friend Hank. She says they have nothing in common. That's after twenty years. She is nearly fifty. She is starting life again. I like her kids. She's got three. We are in a house twelve miles from Tucson among all the sand and the cactuses. Coyotes howl at night. If the TV goes wrong a man arrives from Tucson to mend it within the hour. I did not think this strange until my girlfriend Helen from Wiltshire England said we take too much for granted. But she thinks it's cute. Rather, fascinating. When I said girlfriend, she's one of the women I lay. My sister wants me to marry one of them. Why is it people who were unhappily married are so keen on others doing it? I'd rather marry her. I say this and she laughs at the jest.

I do not think I will achieve marriage. It took me far too

long to understand that a man with a childhood screwed up as
badly as mine (see above) will not be able to achieve the neces-
sary suspension of disbelief.

I heard Stephen died. He was one hell of a good guy. Belles
Rivières and Queen's Gift seem a long long way off. In time.
But most of all in probability. Do you understand that? Yes
you do.

Here comes my date for the evening. Her name is Bella.
Have you ever wondered why if it's lust it's easy but if it's love,
then . . . something there is that does not love love, sweet love.
Are you surprised I said that, Sarah Durham? Yes, I thought
you would be. Which proves my point.

If you ever have a moment in your busy and responsible
life, I would value a letter.

Andrew

He enclosed two photographs. One was of your authentic
skinny little kid, freckles, crew cut, and a scowl. He held a ferocious-
looking gun, presumably a toy, since he was about six. The other
was of a man about twenty, lean, handsome, bow-legged, with his
arm around the shoulders of a rangy blonde, older than he by a
good bit. His stepmother? The hand on her shoulder was protective.
She had her arm around his waist and gripped his belt.

At Christmas, trouble with Joyce. Hal liked to take the family to
a certain famous hotel in Scotland for Christmas. They persuaded
Joyce to go with them. After two nights she ran away and hitched
south. 'It really is so unfair of her,' said Anne, as Hal's wife; but as
herself: 'Good for her. I loathe all that dressing up and having sherry
with so-called important people.'

Joyce turned up at Sarah's a week later. What had she been
doing in the meantime? Better not ask. She was bedraggled, smelled

bad, and her hair was actually muddy. She looked yellow. Jaundice? Hepatitis? If a test were to be done, would she be HIV positive? Pregnant? Sarah made efficient enquiries.

With her usual smiling casuistry, which is how Sarah experienced it, though Joyce would not know what she meant, Joyce assured Sarah that she could not be pregnant. 'I don't like sex,' she confided.

Should Sarah then say, 'Oh good'? Or, 'Never mind, you'll get the hang of it'? What she actually did was cry, wild tears that took her by surprise. They certainly took Joyce by surprise. 'Why, Sarah,' she murmured, and patted Sarah's heaving shoulders. 'What's the matter?' she enquired dolefully. Like Stephen, she did not like to see Sarah overthrown: one should know one's place on the psychological graph and stick to it.

'Can't you really see that we get worried about you?' howled Sarah, furious.

'Oh dear, oh dear,' said Joyce. She hung about while Sarah wept. Then, in order to do something to please her aunt, she had a bath. When she came back, her hair was washed, and she sat (for the hundredth time?) in Sarah's dressing gown, drying her hair with the hair dryer. Sarah was no longer crying. She watched that hair lose its heavy wetness and, as Joyce combed and combed, become soft sheaves of glittering gold. There sat Sarah, as so often these days, eye to eye with Nature. 'What for? Why? Why bother to give her that hair when you've done her in from the start?' A pretty basic question, really, an all-purpose multidirectional question. An ur-question.

Spring.
Sarah realized that instead of being in pain for every moment of her waking time, instead of coming out of sleep several times a night in tears, instead of the drudge of grief, she was experiencing

periods of pain, very bad in the late afternoon and early evening for two to three hours, less in the hours after waking, though they were bad enough. Twice a day, like a tide rolling in. She was actually taking aspirin for the physical pain of grief. In between were long grey flat times when she felt nothing at all. A dead, dry world. At least she was not in pain then, her heart did not feel so heavy that she had to keep moving, or shifting her position to ease the weight of it. In these bleak and empty times she behaved towards herself as people do who suffer from a disability or a disease that causes them sudden attacks of pain: she was wary of anything that might 'bring it on': lines of emotional verse, a glimpse of a black tree against a starry sky, a sentimental tune—she could not bear to listen to the theme song from *The Lucky Piece*—or, worst of all, turning unexpectedly into a street where she had been with Henry or with Stephen. When the yearning returned, it was impossible to believe that Henry would not walk into her room or telephone her, because he must be needing her as much as she did him. She no longer bothered to tell herself this was lunacy. Anyway, it was passing. Through attacks of pain she held on to that. In the flat calm times, it was not possible to imagine the intensity of grief she had just experienced and would feel again. She knew that quite soon she would not remember, except as a fact, how terrible a time it had been. The pains of childbirth cannot be imagined in between pangs, let alone an hour, a day, a year afterward. Once could see that there might be a reason for Nature not wanting the pains of childbirth to be remembered, but why grief pains? Why grief at all? What is it for?

She went back to visit her mother, in another attempt to get answers to questions, but failed. When her daughter—that is, Sarah's—telephoned from California, Sarah asked, 'Were you homesick as a child? When you went off for your summer holidays?' 'I don't remember. Yes, I think I was a bit.' 'Please try to remember.' 'Mother, it wasn't your fault you had to work, was it? Sometimes I did feel sorry for myself because I had a mother who worked. But now *I* work, don't I?'

In April, Sarah and Mary Ford flew to Montpellier, were met by Jean-Pierre and driven to Belle-Rivières. The weather was not good, that is, it was not good compared to the expectations we unreasonably have for the south of France, where in our imaginations Cézanne's and Van Gogh's suns forever pour down an incomparable light. The sky was a cool pale blue, and a wind flung random cold drops against their faces as they stepped from the car into the new town car park, which was large enough for several coaches and a thousand cars. The charming old market had been demolished to make room for the car park. They had a meal inside Les Collines Rouges, for it was too chilly to sit on the pavement, and drove slowly up through the woods on a new wide road that had been built for the lorries transporting wood for the stadium and would turn out useful for the new hotel to be built half-way up the road, with its car park. This hotel had been, was still, controversial. Jean-Pierre was nervous, with a morose tension gripping his forehead, and he had not been comfortable meeting their eyes since greeting them in the airport building. He had a headache, he said, and joked that everything to do with *Julie* was a headache now. The town authorities had created a committee to deal with these problems, and his—Jean-Pierre's—wishes seldom coincided with those of the majority. He thought the new big hotel—visible now only as a devastated place full of lorries, cranes, cement slabs, excavators, and the wreckage of oaks and olives and pines—was a mistake, and the car park was a mistake too, for it would be enormous, destined not only for the hotel's visitors. As for the stadium, they would see for themselves. They could already see it as a raw yellow–red wood structure towering enormously above the trees. They murmured that it would look better when it had weathered, but he did not reply, only led

them through a gap in the structure to the centre of the amphithe-
atre. Julie's house had gone, and there was a great round of dull red
concrete. No trees were visible over the top of the stadium. A cold
wind that made them wish they had on warmer clothes shook the
boughs outside.

'It is not what I wished,' said Jean-Pierre, almost in tears.
'Believe me, it is not.'

The path to the waterfall had a notice: JULIE—SON FLEUVE. The
three of them took the path. The river was running fast and furious
because of rain in the hills. The pool was so full of white water and
spray the rocks could hardly be seen. They stood by the railing that
guarded the drop where Sarah had stood with Henry and with
Stephen. Well, it was a place well suited to ghosts, or at least it was
today, so dismal and cold. Was it really ten months ago? No, that
was another region of time, seductive and deceiving, and if she
turned her head she would see Stephen sitting on the bench, see
Henry smiling and hear his low 'It's Sarah'. She cautiously turned
her head, assured herself the bench was empty, and walked back
past it, talking to Jean-Pierre about the musical. She had to raise the
subject, for he was too embarrassed. Yes, he said, the committee did
like the musical. Speaking for himself, he thought it was deplorable.
But he could assure them that this year at least the authentic *Julie*
would be played here for a full three months. Here he took Mary's
hand and kissed it. 'With your help.' The musical would be tried out
next year. He was confident everyone would see the musical was
inferior. Yes, Patrick had been clever, he had incorporated some of
Julie's musical ideas, but in a very ordinary and commonplace way.

But there was good news too, said Jean-Pierre. The Rostand
family wanted to take Sarah's and Stephen's version and put it on as
part of a fête they planned for the summer. In French, of course, but
they liked the shape of *Julie Vairon* and what Sarah had done. Would
Sarah mind? She assured him from the heart that she was delighted,
and any help that she could ... 'Perfect,' said Jean-Pierre. 'So this

summer will be interesting. There will be *Julie Vairon* in French, as she should be, and there will be *Julie Vairon* in English. For the tourists. No, we shall make sure that they will not overlap.'

Mary took pictures of Sarah and of Jean-Pierre, separately and together, while they stood in the middle of the stadium, then sitting on the lower tier of the seats, and then on the highest seats, where—if the camera was positioned just so—Jean-Pierre's and Sarah's heads would be seen against a flying scroll, a metal banner that stretched from one umbrella pine to another: JULIE VAIRON. 1865–1912. Jean-Pierre said it was a pity Stephen's face would not be with Sarah's near the banner, but Mary said it was no problem: she could blow up a picture of Stephen and superimpose his face beside Sarah's on the banner.

Then Sarah told the two she would walk down by herself to the town, for old times' sake, for she could see they wanted to be alone.

On the plane going home, Mary said, 'I thought I had come to terms with everything, but I hadn't, really. So I have to do it all over again.'

This was shorthand for: I thought I had accepted that I would not marry or have a serious lover to live with, because my mother is ill and is getting worse and anyway I am getting old, my hair is going grey, and I was very unhappy, but I came to terms with it, but now . . .

'I understand perfectly,' said Sarah.

Sometimes women remembering past follies can exchange Rabelaisian laughter, but it was too recent. Later, no doubt.

'And there's another thing,' said Mary. 'I don't care about Julie any more. They've done her in.'

'Yes, she's well and truly dead now, isn't she.'

And that was the moment, frequent in the theatre, when, after months or even years of total immersion in a story—an

Entertainment—the people who made it simply turn their backs and stroll away.

Sarah returned from France to find Joyce in her flat. This time it seemed she intended to stay. Again something had happened but Joyce was not going to talk about it. She had gone home, saying that she was going to stay there because 'they aren't nice people'—meaning Betty and the gang. Her father had heckled and shouted, and found himself confronted by Anne, who announced that if he was ever 'nasty' to Joyce again she would leave him. Hal said Anne was being silly. Anne began packing. Hal said, 'What are you doing?' Anne said, 'What do you think I'm doing?' She had seen a lawyer. At that, hell was let loose. Sarah heard all this from Briony and then Nell on the telephone. The two grabbed the receiver from each other in turn. They were full of the awe appropriate to reporting a major hurricane. 'But when Daddy stopped shouting, Mummy said, "Goodbye, Hal," and started to leave,' said Briony. 'Yes; she got to the door before he realized she meant it,' said Nell.

He made promises. He apologized. The trouble was, Hal had never believed he was anything less than adorable. Worse, he had probably never wondered what he was like. He did not know what his wife meant by 'behaving nicely', but his manners did change, for whatever he said to Briony or Nell or his wife came out as short incredulous exclamations: 'I suppose if I ask you to pass the butter you are going to threaten me with a lawyer?' 'If I get your meaning rightly you're going to the theatre without me.' 'I suppose you'll fly off into a rage if I ask you to take my suit to the cleaners.'

Joyce removed herself to Sarah's. Anne said she was absolutely fed up with him and was going to leave him anyway. 'But I'm going to retire soon,' said Hal. 'Do you expect me to spend my last years alone?'

He came to see Sarah. He did not telephone first. Standing in the middle of her living room, he asked, or announced, 'Sarah, have you thought of us spending our last years together?'

'No, Hal, I can't say I have.'

'You aren't getting any younger, are you? And it's time you stopped all this theatre nonsense. We could buy a place together in France or Italy.'

'No, Hal, we could not.'

There he stood, gazing somewhere in her direction with wide and affronted eyes, his palms held out towards her, his whole body making a statement about how badly he was being treated—he, who was entirely in the right, as always. This big babyish man, with his little tummy, his little double chin, his self-absorbed mouth, making a total demand for the rest of her life, was not seeing her even now. Sarah went close to him, stood about a yard away, so that those eyes that always had so much difficulty actually looking at someone must take her in. She said, 'No, Hal, no. Did you hear me? No. No. No. No. No. No, Hal—finally, no.'

His lips worked pitifully. Then he turned sleep-wise around and rolled slowly out of the room, with the cry, 'What have I done? Just tell me. If someone would just tell me what I've done?'

Anne took a flat, and Joyce went to live with her mother.

Briony and Nell were outraged and would not speak to Anne or to Joyce. They announced they intended to marry their boyfriends, but their father wept and begged them not to leave him. At last they understood how much their mother had shielded them from, how much they had not noticed. Pride did not allow them immediately to forgive Anne, who, they kept saying, must shortly come to her senses. Meanwhile Sarah was a transmitter of messages.

'What did Mummy *say* when we said we wouldn't ever speak to her again?'

'She said, "Oh dear, but when they get over it remind them they have my telephone number."'

Briony said angrily, 'But that's patronizing.'

'Do you want me to tell your mother so?'

'Sarah, whose side are you on?'

And Nell, a week or so later: 'What are they *doing* over there?'

'You mean, how are they spending their time? Well, your mother's working as usual. Joyce is cooking for both of them. And she's trying to learn Spanish.'

'Cooking! She's never cooked; she can't even boil an egg.'

'She's cooking now.'

'And I suppose she thinks she's going to get a job with Spanish?'

'I said she is trying to learn Spanish.'

Sarah did not tell them how happy their mother was. She realized she had never seen Anne anything but long-suffering, tired, exasperated. Anne and Joyce were like girls who had left home for the first time, sharing a flat. They made each other little treats, gave each other presents, and giggled.

Then Briony: 'Doesn't Joyce ever actually say anything? I mean, she must be awfully pleased with herself.'

'Well, yes: she says all her dreams have come true.'

'There you are, we knew it!'

'What's wrong with that?'

'All her dreams have come true. That's all she ever wanted, just to have mummy all to herself.'

'But, Briony, just a minute . . . surely you don't imagine . . .'

'*What?*' demanded Briony, already affronted by the new dose of unpleasant reality announced by her aunt's tone.

'Well—don't you see? She's not going to stay at home, is she?'

'What? Why not?'

'Well, she's going to get bored, isn't she?'

'Oh *no* . . .'

'She'll be off and back again, it'll all go on the same.'

'But it just isn't *fair*,' said Briony.

From Elizabeth came a letter and a package. The letter said that when his divorce came through, she was going to marry a neighbour, Joshua Broughton. Perhaps Stephen had mentioned him? She had known Joshua all her life. It would be nice to run the two farms together. She said that her commitment to the Queen's Gift Entertainments would continue, but perhaps not as much as when Stephen was there to help. She did not mention Norah.

The picture she enclosed had hung on the wall in Stephen's bedroom. There was also a photograph.

When Sarah saw what the picture was, she felt she had never known Stephen, even that their friendship had been an illusion. It was of a bold smiling young woman, dressed in a fashionable white dress with a pink sash. She held a straw hat on her knee and sat in a chair under a tree. The picture could have been by Gainsborough. It had been painted, at Stephen's request, by someone or other from the little photograph, now yellowing and faded, which was of Julie sitting on a rock in half-shade. She wore a white camisole and a white flounced petticoat. Her arms and neck were bare. Her feet were bare. Her dark hair was loose and blowing away from her face. She was offering herself to whoever had taken that photograph, in her posture, her smile, her passionate black eyes. The photograph had been tinted, and the crude boiled-sweet colours had faded. A tree behind the rock had hints of sickly green, and the rock had a rouged side. Around her neck—was that a necklace? Little blobs of red . . . no, a ribbon. Why had she tied on that ribbon? It was out of character, so much so it shocked. Perhaps the man who took the photograph—Paul? Rémy?—had said to her, 'Here is one of the new cameras. Yes, I know you were wondering what was in this great case, but no, it isn't a musical instrument, it's a camera.' She was sitting on the edge of her bed, in her camisole, about to slip it off, or having just slipped it on, saying, 'Oh no, you aren't going to take me naked.' Then he said, 'Come outside. I'll always think of you in your forest.' She tied that red ribbon off a chocolate box around her neck. The chocolate had been a present from a pupil or . . . could it have been the master printer? Boxes of chocolate were much more in his line than Rémy's, or Paul's. He probably sold them from his shop. What had she said, tying on that ribbon? Or Rémy had said, 'Wait, tie that ribbon around your neck. It makes you look . . .' No, that was not in Rémy's character. Or the person who had tinted the picture of the seductress (the studio which developed the photograph could not have been in Belles Rivières, more likely Marseilles or Avignon, for if anyone in Belles Rivières had caught sight of it then . . .)—had that person painted in the ribbon? Now, when you examined the thing carefully, and even with a magnifying glass (Sarah did this, switching on a strong light), you could not see if the ribbon had been painted in afterwards, the photograph was so dulled, the tinting had been so clumsy. Had Julie painted in the ribbon after being given the photograph? It was easier to imagine it had been done afterwards, because it was hard to connect the young woman dissolved in love sitting half dressed on the rock with the red ribbon that was a statement of such a different kind. Or was she identifying with the doll she had buried in the forest in Martinique, which had a red ribbon around its neck, as a memento of the guillotine? If so, the only word for that was *sick*.

Sarah was examining the photograph as if it were a clue in a mystery story, but presumably Stephen had been staring at it for years. It was the picture that he had hung on his wall, though. Where had he found the photograph? It should be in the museum. Stephen had stolen it, and now Sarah stole it. She tacked it beside the Cézanne picture of the haughty young Harlequin and the serious youth who had put on the clown's costume to accompany his friend to Mardi Gras. She put the portrait of the fashionable beauty into a drawer.

Andrew wrote:

Dear Sarah Durham,

Since I wrote I have been engaged to be married.

My sister said to me, Why do you always have to act your-self? This on an occasion I will leave you to imagine.

*I said to her: *****! XXXXX!. . . ????*

She said to me, Be your age.

I said to her, But that's the trouble.

So I proposed to Helen. Your compatriot. She said Americans are solemn and don't know how to have fun. Helen was working as a stable hand at the ranch near here. It is a ranch where people come to ride and eat and have sex. Helen does allow I am a good stud. She says I work at it. 'Why do Americans always have to work at everything?' she wants to know. I said, You can't buck the work ethic. So I proposed to Bella. She is a Texan like me. For three months Bella and my sister have been discussing the how-to's. House or apartment? In Tucson—Dallas—San Antonio? Natural childbirth? How many? and how many films shall I be permitted a year? How should I change my image? They say I am stereotyped. They never talk about happiness, and I would not dare to mention joy. Joy? Who she?

I've learned one thing. My image was right from the start. They got my size all right. So I lit out. As you see. It is lonely here.

Andrew.

Poste Restante, Córdoba, Argentina.

Sarah wrote to Córdoba, Argentina, intending a temperate correspondence, but by the time her letter reached Argentina he was in Peru. Her letter was forwarded there, but his letter in reply, a passionate love letter in which he several times called her Betty (his stepmother?), arrived when she was in Stockholm for the opening of *Julie Vairon*, and by the time she got round to answering, the problems seemed insuperable. Where was she to address the letter? Should she sign the letter, Much love, Betty?

By the end of the year, this was the situation in The Green Bird: Meetings were no longer held in the upstairs office but in a rehearsal room large enough to accommodate everyone, for now the theatre seemed full of talented and attractive young people, one of whom had been heard asking, 'Who is she?'—meaning Mary Ford. 'I think she was one of the people who started The Green Bird.'

Sonia dominated everything. She was incandescent with accomplishment, with the discovery of her own cleverness. Her impatient confident young voice and her bright bush of hair, now in an Afro (she wanted to identify with black people and their sufferings), seemed to be in every part of the theatre at once. Virginia, known as 'Sonia's shadow', was always near her. None of the Founding Four had been much in the theatre. Roy's wife had returned to him on condition that he 'worked on' their marriage, and this had meant a family holiday. She was pregnant. He was thinking of accepting a job in another theatre. He said it was bad enough being married to a militant feminist, without having to spend his working days with another. Mary had taken weeks off to spend time with her mother, who was, as a result, better again. If Mary spent all her time at home, the old lady would have a new lease on life. Mary could not afford to do this but might do part time at the theatre and find work to do at home. She was in fact adapting Meredith's *The Egoist* for the stage, which novel Sonia had read with approval, saying it was a useful addition to feminist propaganda. Sarah was travelling a good deal, to discuss *Julie Vairon* and, even more, *The Lucky Piece*, which out of Britain was called, simply, *Julie*. Already *Julie* was playing triumphantly in a dozen cities in Europe and—the demand for beauti-

ful but doomed or damaged girls being gluttonous and insatiable—
she would soon be in a dozen more and was about to conquer the
United States, as the advance bookings showed. *Julie Vairon* was certainly being appreciated, but by smaller and more discriminating
audiences and in fewer places. In short, Julie had become, like Miss
Saigon, the latest in the long list of gratifying female fatalities, and it
was easy for people hearing the two stories, Julie Vairon's and Julie's,
to believe that from Martinique had come two interesting and beautiful girls to try their chances in France. Sisters, perhaps?

Sarah was pleased she was kept on the move. She needed to
move, did not want to start yet on the new and better translation of
Julie's journals, for which she had a contract. The time was not yet,
it would be too dangerous, she must recover completely first.

Often she and Patrick travelled together, and this new phase of
their friendship was the pleasantest part of the new regime in The
Green Bird. Patrick was as full of newly acquired confidence as
Sonia. He was no longer an *enfant terrible* and had given up his out-
rageous and gallant clothes because of Sonia's criticisms. 'You are
middle-aged, for God's sake,' she had said. 'Grow up.' Sonia had furiously attacked Sarah, Mary, and Roy for babying him. 'Why did
you?' she accused. Patrick defended them, saying he had enjoyed
being babied, but Sonia wouldn't have it. Enjoyable conversations
had taken place between the Four, where Patrick had said his musical was his adolescent act of defiance, enabling him to grow up and
become emotionally independent of them, but these had gone on
behind Sonia's back. A good deal did go on behind her back and,
they agreed, probably always would. Unless her style—her character—changed, surely unlikely. She would never understand why. She
was the chief provider of gossip in The Green Bird, particularly her
war with Roger Stent. He had confessed he adored her. Would she
live with him? She had replied that while she quite fancied his body,
the problem was his mind. 'I couldn't face waking up beside you in
the mornings.' What could he do to change her opinion of him? he

asked, like a knight of old prepared to overcome obstacles for his lady. 'You could stop being a theatre critic for a start. You are as ignorant as a toad.' He confessed his dilemma to her. If he didn't write negative theatre criticism he would lose his job. That was why he had rubbished *Julie Vairon*. In fact he had enjoyed it. 'How do you know? You never even saw the third act.' She refused to see his difficulties: she had been immediately successful in the first job she had after leaving university. But though pure chance had made him one of the Young Turks, without them what would he be? Merely one of the hundreds of literary hopefuls in London. He was full of conflict. The raucous jeering tone of the Young Turks had now become how people recognized him, but in fact he was a good-natured young man who longed to be a serious critic. Should he write a novel? He was now well known enough to be sure the thing would be reviewed. But how could he write a novel when all his evenings were spent seeing plays? All Sonia said was, 'Oh, for Christ's sake, just get another job.' He asked if he could come and work at The Green Bird. What qualifications did he have? she demanded, and suggested a course in theatre history. His pride would not let him do this. Besides, it would certainly lose him his job. Sonia told him to grow up—as she had Patrick. Meanwhile everyone waited for the next instalment of the drama, confident that Virginia would keep them informed.

The Founding Four met sometimes in 'their' café, which had been taken over by 'the children'. Not that they would have dreamed of using this pet name to their faces. For one thing, they had to discuss why it was that *Julie Vairon*—or Julie—had put an end to the old Green Bird. 'Before Julie' and 'after Julie'—that was how they talked. But they could not come to a conclusion and at last agreed they had been fortunate to have had those years of wonderful comradeship; perhaps, while they were living through them, they had not sufficiently understood how wonderful they were. But now it was all over, and what better could they have done than relinquish the reins to Sonia? It was obvious to everyone else, though not to her, that she was destined to become that recurrent figure in the theatre a clever, competent woman, impatient of other people's slowness, abrasive, tactless, 'impossible', and as salutary as a thunderstorm. She would always have passionate friends and as passionate enemies.

By early summer Sarah's anguish had lessened to the point that she would say it had gone. That is to say, what remained was mild low spirits of a kind she could match easily with this or that bad patch in her life, but they were as far removed from the country of grief as they were distant from happiness. She stood in a landscape like that before the sun comes up, one suffused with a quiet, flat, truthful light where people, buildings, trees, stand about waiting to become defined by shadow and by sunlight. This is the landscape recommended for adults. Over the horizon, somewhere else, was a place, a world, of tenderness and trust, and she was removed from it not by distance but because it was in another dimension. This was right, was as things should be . . . but the parallel line continued, of feeling. For if she was removed from grief, she was removed too (her *emotions* insisted) from that intimacy which is like putting your hand into another hand, while currents of love flow between them.

A strange thing, that when in love or in lust the afflicted ones want most of all to be shut up together in some fastness or solitude, just me and you, only you and me, for at least a year or for twenty, but quite soon, or at any rate after a salutary dose of time, these once so terribly and exclusively desired ones are released into a landscape populated by loving friends and lovers, all bound to each other because they recognize the claims of invisible and secret affinities: if we have loved, or love, the same person, then we must love each other. This improbable state of affairs can only exist in a realm or region removed from ordinary life, like a dream or a legend, a land all smiles. One could almost believe that falling in love was ordained to introduce us to this loving land and its paradise kisses.

She could look now not only at Stephen's notes but at her own. They were words on paper, like Julie's *My heart is aching so badly I wish I could put it out of its misery the way you put an old dog to sleep. I simply cannot endure this pain.* Words on a page, that's all.

She was delivered, she was over the illness and would not go into danger again. She was not going to Belles Rivières for the rehearsals, or even the first night, but would try—she promised—to manage the last night. That is, when Henry was safely gone. Jean-Pierre thought she did not want to go because of missing Stephen. Perhaps he was right.

Before Julie and being turned inside out, she thought the country of love was so remote from her seasoned and well-balanced self that she could be likened to someone standing outside great iron gates behind which a dog flounced its hindquarters about, not unattractively, a foolish harmless dog no one could be afraid of. But now she knew that the gates separating her from that place were flimsy, no more than hastily tacked up pieces of thin wood, and behind them was a dog of the kind they breed now for murder. She could see the dog clearly. It was the size of a calf. It wore a muzzle. Or was it a mask?—the theatre mask that changes from a laugh to the grimace of grief, and back again.

It was mid-August, and some weeks had passed since the anguish that had so crushed her had taken itself off. As she had predicted, she could not remember its intensity, proving that Nature (or whatever) does not need its children to remember pain, unproductive for its purposes, whatever they are. She was finding herself in moments of quiet enjoyment, drawing vitality as she had all her life from small physical pleasures, like the feel of a naked sole on wood, the warmth of sunlight on bare skin, the smell of coffee or of earth, the faint scent of frost on a stone. She had returned to being a woman who never wept, though the idea of a good cry for the sake of it was certainly inviting: she had forgotten how to cry, it seemed. Other people's excesses of emotion tempted her to judge them as immature. She had actually caught on her face the smile that goes with, Really, how *silly*—on hearing of someone foolishly in love. (Did that mean then that she had learned nothing at all?) She monitored sadness which was steadily retreating, losing strength, and kept her attention on it as if it were a dangerous animal that might attack from an unexpected place. It might worsen, might drag her back: in old people's faces, in their eyes, she often saw the dry sorrow that now she understood. Oh no, she didn't want that, she refused it! And the way to keep it off, that vulture that fed on the heart, was never to relax vigilance.

She still could not listen to Julie's music, or to the old trouvère and troubadour music. Pain, to be 'sweet' must be mild. The anguish that threatened her at even a few notes from *Julie Vairon*, or even the vulgar torch song from *The Lucky Piece*, or *Julie*—no, absolutely not. Sounds could still seem too loud, too much, and there seemed no safe place anywhere for her. As for that sentimental shepherd boy from long ago, in his silent landscape these days a small wind blew, the dry whine that has set humankind's nerves on edge with apprehension for thousands of years, and the sound held almost audible voices, while the high scream of a hawk was the first note of Julie's third act music. Worse, one day some sheets of paper had blown up the hill towards the boy half asleep under his tree, and he stared at them, thinking he was dreaming, and the black signs on the paper, the words *grief, heart, pain*, seemed to him some kind of frightful magic-making, so that he woke up completely, but by then the wind had blown the sheets away down the hill and into the grass, and he believed he had imagined an apparition. And where was the silent haven she craved? Down in the oceans, fishes clicked and squeaked, and whales sang. Up in space, debris collided and meteors rumbled. At the bottom of mine shafts or deep caves? The silence of the grave? A likely story. There would be a roar of worms and of excavating roots.

Yet fear or, if you like, caution did not prevent that process familiar to everyone submerged in the *why* of something. Clues accumulate and fall into place. You pick up a book apparently at random, and it falls open on a page where what you are thinking about is explored. You overhear a conversation: they are talking about what preoccupies you. You switch on the radio—there it is. Sarah's dreams were full of information, and she felt as if she were on the verge of . . . *Know yourself*, says the old admonition, but it is not easy to decide what it is you ought to be trying to know at any given moment.

Sarah sat on a park bench, looking at an empty bench almost opposite hers, across a wide path that led out of the park.

Along a path from the gate came a young woman pushing a pram, holding one side of the handle, while a little girl pushed too, using both hands. When they reached the bench nearly opposite Sarah, the young woman hauled the pram onto the grass behind the bench, lifted out a baby of about ten months, and sat down on the bench. She held the baby on her knees. The little girl, who was about four, sat very close to her mother. She was a pretty little girl, and dressed in a crisp pink cotton frock, pink socks, pink shoes, and her straight thin black hair was held with a pink plastic barrette. All this pinkness did not suit her small thin anxious face, nor eyes that seemed too knowledgeable, like a sad woman's.

The mother was well turned out too. She had tight white trousers and a white singlet that showed carefully tanned shoulders and arms. Her hair was dyed bronze and stood out in a fashionable frizz. She was hugging and kissing the infant, who laughed and tried to grab her hair. Then he reached for her nose, while she laughed and flirtatiously averted her face. She began singing the nursery rhyme, 'Rock-a-bye Baby', and when she reached 'and down falls baby and cradle and all', she pretended to let the baby fall. He shrieked in delicious false terror: they had often played this game before. The child was trying to join in, singing 'Rock-a-bye Baby', but her voice was lost in the loud full singing of the mother and the baby's gurgles of pleasure.

The little girl was sitting right against her mother, and now she put up her hand to tug her elbow down, to get her attention.

'Oh, leave me alone,' snapped the mother, in a voice so irritable and full of dislike it was hard to believe this was the same voice she used to love the baby. And now she used this voice again, rich, full, and sexual, and she kissed the baby's neck with an open mouth. 'Darling, darling, darling,' murmured the mother. 'Little Ned, my darling, darling Ned.' And then, removing her mouth from the baby's neck for this purpose, she snapped at her daughter, 'I told you, stop it, stop bothering me, don't crowd me like that.' And she went on loving the baby as if the child did not exist.

The little girl wriggled a short way from her mother, and sat watching the love scene. When the woman began another rhyme, this time 'To market, to market, to buy a fat pig', she again tried to join in, but her mother smacked her hard and said, 'Oh, do shut up, Claudine.'

The child sat frozen, a few inches from her mother, looking sombrely in front of her—looking, in fact, at Sarah, at that dull old woman there on the bench. Unable to stand the loving going on that excluded her, she carefully turned to her mother, expecting a slap, and said, 'Mummy, Mummy, Mummy,' in a desperate voice.

'Now what is it?' snapped the young woman.

'I want my orange juice, I want my orange juice.'

'You've just had orange juice.'

'I want it again,' the child said, trying to smile, looking up at the woman's angry face, hoping to make her mother see her, see her misery.

But the mother did not look at her. She leaned her arm back over the bench into the pram, took out a carton of juice, and handed it carelessly to the child, who took it with the caution that governed every movement she made, even the smallest. She tried to get the straw off the side of the carton. The mother watched her fumbling over the top of the baby's head, which was lying on her breasts, or to be precise, in the hollow under her left shoulder, his cheek on her breast. She was watching with a practised irritation that waited for an excuse to pounce. 'There,' she snapped, as the straw fell to the tarmac of the path. 'Look what you've done. You'll have to drink it through the hole, that's all.' And she laid her cheek on her baby's head and crooned, 'Neddy is my darling, my darling, my darling,' and then, 'Baby is my darling . . .'

The little girl was not drinking her juice but sat with the carton in her hand staring at Sarah, who saw in those dark and most unchildlike eyes a desolation of unhappiness, a world of grief.

The mother: 'Why did you nag at me for orange juice if you didn't want it? Give it here—I'll put it in the bottle for Baby.'

She impatiently took the carton from her daughter, again reached over the bench back, fetched out the bottle, poured the orange juice in the bottle, and then, having taken a little swig herself, fed the juice to the baby.

The child gave a sob, and as if this was exactly what the mother had been waiting for, she screeched, '*Now* what is it?' and in a transport of dislike she slapped the little girl on the forearm. The child sat absolutely still, watching the ugly red come up on her skin. Then she let out a single loud hopeless wail and at once clamped her lips shut—she had been unable to prevent that cry.

'If you don't behave yourself,' said the mother to the child, in a voice full of hate, 'I'll . . .'

The child sat rigid, silent.

The mother reached back, took out cigarettes and matches, and tried to light a cigarette over the baby's head. 'Oh shit, you take him, then,' said she, depositing the baby on the little girl's lap. 'Now, you hold him nicely, don't jump about, just *sit*.'

On the child's face came a trembling smile. Tears stood in her eyes. She held the happy baby and clasped him tight to her body and kissed him. The little girl had her lips on the baby's head, on the soft hair just above the ear. Her eyes were shut. As she sat there in a bliss of love, her mother stared straight ahead, gasping lungfuls of smoke in and out.

The little girl was singing, 'Darling, darling, darling, I love you, I love you my Ned, my darling Ned,' eyes shut, thin arms squeezing the baby, who was suddenly woeful and might cry. And all at once, in a single movement, the mother flicked her cigarette on the path, stamped on it, and reached for the baby. 'Don't paw him like that, stop it, stop it at once.' And she lifted the baby onto her own lap. And now the baby sat with a trembling down-turned mouth, and it was touch and go whether he would let out a wail.

'It's your fault,' said the mother in the disliking voice she used for her daughter. And she hastily bounced the baby and sang and kissed him into good humour. Then, when the baby was happy, up got mother, who wanted to put him back in the pram, but he wasn't having that, he clung to her neck and laughed.

Her mouth tight and angry, the mother said to the child, 'You can push the pram.'

She went off cuddling the baby, not looking to see if the little girl was following with the heavy pram, which she had to manoeuvre off the grass and onto the path. When she had accomplished this task, the child stood for a moment, getting her breath back.

Sarah was silently telling the child, 'Hold on, hold on. Quite soon a door will slam shut inside you because what you are feeling is unendurable. The door will stand there shut all your life: if you are lucky it will never open, and you'll not ever know about the landscape you inhabited—for how long? But child time is not adult time. You are living in an eternity of loneliness and grief, and it is truly a hell, because the point of hell is that there is no hope. You don't know that the door will slam shut, you believe that this is what life is and must be: you will always be disliked, and you will have to watch her love that little creature you love so much because you think that if you love what she loves, she will love you. But one day you'll know it doesn't matter what you do and how hard you try, it is no use. And at that moment the door will slam and you will be free.'

She watched the child carefully set off, reaching up with both hands to the handle of the heavy pram, pushing it along the path after the mother. Over the woman's shoulder could be seen the baby's smiling face. The mother made no attempt to slow her pace, although the child was so far behind. At the gate she stopped and turned, and she shouted, 'Oh, do come *on*.' The child, trying hard, slipped and fell to her knees, and got up crying, and again pushed the pram. Then the baby was put into the pram and propped against cushions, and the three left the park as they had entered it, the mother with one hand on her side of the handle, the little girl reaching up with both hands.

Did Sarah believe that her mother, the admirable Mrs Milgreen, could ever have been like that young woman with her two little children? Certainly not; Sarah had been witnessing an extreme of unkindness. But wait—how could she, or anyone, know? The talk of old people can only be deciphered by contemporaries. A pause in the run of a reminiscence can stand for some monstrous quarrel. Half a dozen words as ordinary as 'We never got on, you know' mark implacable and decades-long hostilities. 'I'll always remember that summer' or 'We always did fancy each other' (and a laugh) remembers the most intense passion of a lifetime. An old man sighs, once, for a long season of mourning, an old woman stumbles over a word or a phrase, because she was on the verge of self-betrayal. That young woman on the bench: when she was old would there be anything left of her dislike for her little daughter? Perhaps only 'Boys are so much easier than girls.'

Much more likely, though—Sarah was remembering certain brisk and practical tones of her mother's voice—that the scene from last summer was more to the point, when the three boys had come to say good night to their mother in their short red dressing gowns, with their brushed fair hair, their washed faces, and then had rushed off up the stairs, but James had come back, twice, and stood at the door.

'What *is* it, James?'

'Nothing.'

'Then run along.'

As the boy turned to go out of the room his eyes had met Sarah's. No, it was not that bleak desolation, it was not grief, but rather . . . patience. Yes, it was stoicism. He was not four years old, or six years old; he was twelve. That door had slammed shut for him long ago, and he had forgotten it was there. With luck he would never know the door was there, never be forced to remember what lay behind it.

When Sarah's grandmother was dying in hospital—this was a good twenty years ago—Sarah sat with her through the afternoons and evenings of a dark autumn, sometimes with her mother, the dying woman's daughter. In the next bed was an old woman as small and light as a leaf, who called out hour after hour, 'Help, help, help,' in a soft little voice, like the call of a bird. Sometimes she called 'Help, Mother'—the word *Mother* on two notes: 'Help, Mo-ther?' the second note rising. 'Help'—while she waited and listened for a reply that never came. 'Help . . . Mo-ther?'

Sarah's grandmother did not seem to hear. She did not comment or complain. She lay conscious, eyes open, parts drugged, taking no notice of her surroundings or, much, of her daughter and granddaughter. The hours, then the days, went past, and Sarah sat on, noting with approval how stoically her grandmother died, but listening to the calls from behind the white curtains. 'Help . . . help, Mo-ther?'

When it was over, Sarah's mother said, 'I hope I do it as well as she did, when my time comes.'

Months have passed. Sarah is looking into her mirror, just as on the evening when we first saw her. At first glance she has not much changed, but a closer look says otherwise. She has aged by ten years. For one thing, her hair, which for so long remained like a smooth dulled metal, now has grey bands across the front. She has acquired that slow cautious look of the elderly, as if afraid of what they will see around the next corner. Sarah has changed, and so have the rooms she lives in. When her daughter telephoned to say she was bringing the children for Christmas, she saw her flat through the eyes of sunny and unproblematical California. What had seemed so difficult for years became easy. In came the painters, and soon her walls blazed white. She cleared out all the junk, and window sills stood clean and empty, and so did tables and the tops of book-shelves. She felt as if a weight had been lifted away out of her rooms, leaving her lighter and freer too. The Cézanne reproduction she did not discard, though if she had it would not have made any differ-ence, so much was it part of her emotional history. Nor did she dis-card the little photograph of Julie. These did not have pride of place near her desk but were part of a wall of photographs and posters in the spare room. There her grandchildren had lived for a couple of weeks. They scribbled a moustache on the touch-me-not young Harlequin and put spectacles on the thoughtful Pierrot.

She was still travelling a good deal for The Green Bird, because both *Julie Vairon* and *Julie* were doing well in various parts of the world. In between she was living at a slower pace than she had. She would sit for hours, looking into her past, trying to shine light into the dark places, even though the past had become a much less pro-ductive territory, because of her mother's death. The old woman had had her wish, for she had fallen dead one morning when she was out shopping. Was Sarah grieving for her? She believed not. She believed she had used up her allowance of grief for her lifetime. What troubled her was that she had not questioned her mother when she could have done, and at the right time, when she was much younger than when Sarah had reached the point of asking herself questions about her childhood. But perhaps Kate Millgreen would not have been able to answer. She had never been a woman much given to self-examination. Well, Sarah hadn't been either, until what she now privately thought of as The Calamity had overwhelmed her: but could anything be absolutely bad that had led to so much new understanding?

One day the thought had popped whole and fully fledged into her head, as if it had been waiting there for her to recognize it: Am I really to believe that the awful, crushing anguish, the longing so terrible it seems one's heart is being squeezed by cruel fingers—all that is only what a baby feels when it is hungry and wants its mother? Is a baby, even if not much larger than a cat, only an empty bag waiting to be filled with milk and then cuddles? That baby is wanting more: It is longing for something just out of its memory; it is longing for where it came from, and when need starts up in its stomach for milk, that need revives another, grander need, just as a small girl may pause in her play, look up, see a sky aflame with sunset and sadness, and find herself stretching up her arms to that lost magnificence and sobbing because she is so utterly exiled.

To fall in love is to remember one is an exile, and that is why the sufferer does not want to be cured, even while crying, 'I can't endure this non-life, I can't endure this desert.'

Another thought, perhaps of a more practical kind: When Cupid aims arrows (not flowers or kisses) at the elderly and old, and brings them to grief, is this one way of hustling people who are in danger of living too long off the stage, to make way for the new?

And whom did she share these thoughts with? With Stephen, though she knew that the sense of him, making him feel so close, like a presence, or another self, was only the projection of her need. And what she was remembering of him was the sweetness of their friendship, a lightness, even the gaiety, of those weeks before he had become hag-ridden, before the murderous black dog had landed with all its weight so finally on his shoulders.

She did not think about Bill, because she could not be bothered with the anger she felt at herself. Besides, that anguishing passion now seemed an irrelevance. A young man—much younger than his years, as unstable as an adolescent—had been magicked by Julie, just like all of them, and, like them all, had not been himself.

She thought of Henry, all right, but only in that realm behind or beyond ordinary life, full of smiles and ease, where—if they chanced to meet—they would at once go on with an interrupted conversation. Unlikely, though: she was taking good care this would not happen.

That place was where once had lived her little brother Hal, when loving him had seemed the only pledge there was or could be for the hope of love.

Her brother of now, however, was certainly not in any other place, for he had taken to turning up in the evenings, unannounced. 'But, Hal, couldn't you telephone first?'

'But you don't have anything much to do, do you?'

He sat himself plumply in the chair she thought of as her visitors' chair, and emanated a hot uncomprehending resentment against her and against everything.

If she said she was busy, he asked, 'What with?'

She might say—humorously, of course, for he had to be humoured—'I'm writing letters.' 'I'm reading.' 'I'm thinking out a theatre problem.' If she persisted: 'Then I won't disturb your important concerns,' and he rolled away again.

Sometimes, when he arrived and would not go, she might watch him, her little brother, sitting in his high chair, his little mouth moving wetly, his plump hands waving gently beside him, full of the confidence of the loved child.

'But, Sarah, why don't we go and live in France?'

'But, Hal, I like living in London.'

There was news from Briony and Nell, who were friends again with their mother and with Joyce—when she was at home. Anne had reported that Hal was 'seeing' the head of Physiotherapy at the hospital, and with a bit of luck she might take Hal on.

'It does look promising,' Nell told Sarah. 'He said he was going away for a week, and we think he's taking her.'

'*Please* don't be too nice to him,' Briony said to Sarah, 'or we'll never get him married again.'